TREVANION

Also by David Hillier

STORM WITHIN

TREVANION

David Hillier

WARNER BOOKS

A *Warner* Book

First published in Great Britain in 1994
by Warner Books
Reprinted 1994 (three times), 1995

A CIP catalogue record for this book
is available from the British Library.

ISBN 0 7515 0912 4

Phototypeset by Intype, London
Printed in England by Clays Ltd, St Ives plc

Warner Books
A Division of
Little, Brown and Company (UK)
Brettenham House
Lancaster Place
London WC2E 7EN

To my father

Prologue

JOHN TREVANION LAY ON HIS back in the middle of the stream. His cold grey eyes stared up at the sky. He had fallen from his horse only occasionally in his life, and his face bore an expression of mild surprise, perhaps even amusement, at his own carelessness. The water formed pools in the crooks of his arms and legs and, a short way off, his horse nibbled the grass which lined the valley floor. She had been feeding all morning, and her master had lain in the stream since the day before.

That was how Josaiah found him. At first light he had left the manor with the other men and retraced the squire's path over the hills towards Newlyn. And while the men searched, Emily Trevanion waited at home.

She already knew what they would find.

John had left the previous afternoon, but it had only been later, when midnight approached and she was alone in the house, that she could no longer deceive herself. Yet by then, her husband lay cold under the stars and all she could do was sit through the night, and then at sunrise send out the farmhands.

Two hours later Josaiah Penhale stepped down into the valley and sent up a cry which brought the others running.

PART ONE

Chapter One

So she still had not forgiven him.

Matthew Trevanion's large angular frame bent a little as he strode up the hill from his cottage. Although he lived only three miles from the manor, he had not heard the news until Josaiah came by late the previous day. It seemed that, even now his uncle was dead, she had not wanted to tell him.

Not that he needed her forgiveness. Or anyone else's, for that matter.

That night he had listened to his mother crying long after she had gone to bed and he thought of her now as his feet splashed through the puddles. By the time he reached the manorhouse the rain had matted his hair into thick, dark strands.

Although he had seen the house more often than he could remember, Matthew paused at the last rise and looked down to where it lay between the broad, flat hills of southern Penwith. It was an old settlement. Exactly how old, no one knew, but his uncle had said it was mentioned in Domesday. And for all those years, the Trevanions had lived there, or so his uncle claimed, so that their line stretched back into the distant past, unbroken, unchanging, like the grain running through a piece of wood.

He had thought of this place as home.

Matthew looked at the farm for a long time before he stirred himself and made his way down the lane.

5

When he got to the farmhouse, the yard was awash with soft churned mud. This mud was the only trace of the cart that had taken his uncle's body to the crypt. But Matthew did not know this at the time and went in without stopping to wipe his feet.

It took his eyes several seconds to adjust to the smoky gloom of the hallway and the parlour beyond. He had expected Emily, or maybe Lucy, to be there, and was almost relieved to see the room unoccupied. Then to his right, through the low doorway from the kitchen, Mary Vincent appeared. Mary was the manor cook.

'You've come! I said you'd come!' Mary smiled proudly and went as if to hug him, and then stopped. 'You heard?'

'Josey told me how they found him.'

'Yes. Josey reckons a hare or a bird must have startled him.' She came closer so he could see the lines on her broad, handsome face. 'Who'd have thought it?'

Who would have thought it indeed? John Trevanion had been fifty-five. He stood well over six feet tall and his chest was as thick as a tree. Now his neck was broken, snapped like a twig, and he was no more.

Matthew walked into the parlour. It was almost a year since he was last here. He considered the faded tapestries, the figures on the mantelpiece, the leather armchairs. Nothing had changed. Except his uncle was no longer alive. He turned back to Mary and made no attempt to hide his anger.

'So what about my aunt? How's she finding her *bereavement*?'

'If you'd been here yesterday you'd have seen for yourself. She didn't say or eat nothing all day – just sat staring into the fire.' Mary glanced at him. 'Don't be too hard on her, Matthew.'

He looked into the flames.

'Then where is she now?'

'Mrs Marshall came over last night and they've gone to see the parson.'

'I heard Lucy was back.' To his own ears, his voice sounded tense and brittle, but if Mary noticed anything she showed no sign.

'She's been in Truro this past week – Luke's fetching her. They'll be back tomorrow.'

Matthew breathed out, and the shadow of a smile appeared on his face. Soft, rueful perhaps.

'Then I'll wait.'

When Emily returned with Charlotte Marshall, night was falling. She came in quickly, a few steps ahead of Charlotte, then stopped in the parlour doorway.

'Good evening, Aunt.' Matthew was seated in his uncle's armchair. A glass of wine was cupped in his hand and glowed red in the firelight.

'Matthew.' She paused. 'I didn't expect you.'

'I know. I should be home with my mother. She was very upset.'

He took a mouthful of wine and his face puckered as if in distaste, but his eyes did not leave her.

'What have you come for, Matthew? John is no longer here. Reverend Morecombe took him to the crypt.'

'Perhaps I came to see you.' He got up and walked

towards her. 'Why wasn't I told? I only found out by chance!'

'After what you've done? You're no longer part of the family, Matthew.'

'He was still my uncle! He was like a—'

'What do you want?' Emily's voice was cold, yet there was something warm, something emotional buried there, which he could not read. Her cheeks were flushed. He considered her carefully.

'When will the funeral be?'

'On Friday, at ten o'clock.'

'And what happens next?'

'I don't know what you mean.'

'Emily, you may have been his wife, I won't deny that, but there was still a will.'

'Was there?' Emily raised her eyebrows.

'Of course there was!' Matthew took two steps towards her. She was breathing quickly but did not give ground. A faint, even triumphant, smile flickered across her lips.

'Not to my knowledge.'

'But John said—'

'Perhaps he was lying!'

Matthew stood poised, suddenly undecided what to do. The fire hissed and crackled in the hearth.

'Don't you think you should be going, Master Trevanion?' It was Mrs Marshall. He had forgotten she was there.

He took another step towards Emily then pushed past her and disappeared into the night.

His mother was waiting for him when he got home. Mary Trevanion was no longer young but she had been attractive, or at least fair, in her day: her high cheekbones and slender neck were testimony to this. But she looked particularly old and tired tonight, thought Matthew, and he regretted being gone so long. She rose from her place by the fire.

'I was worried something had happened to you.'

'It did. I had an argument with Emily.'

'Matthew! Why? What did you say?'

He went past her and stood warming himself by the fire.

'You know, she's always hated me. Right from the start.' He clapped his hands together. 'I don't know why I went over there today.'

'But you shouldn't argue with her, not *now*.' Mary paused. 'What about the will? Did you talk about the will?'

He kicked at the loose peats in the hearth.

'She says he didn't leave a will.'

'Oh. I had thought—'

'He lied, Mother! Or changed his mind. If there isn't a will she gets everything.'

Mary sat down.

'I can't believe he's gone,' she said at last. 'After your father went away, John was a dear friend.'

'That was before Emily arrived.' Matthew shrugged and began to unbutton his jacket. An evening chill had entered his bones on the walk back, and now he noticed it as if for the first time.

'You must be frozen. Let me help you.' She got up eagerly. At twenty-seven, he would have normally been embarrassed by her attentions but tonight he let her lose herself in helping him off with his wet shirt and bringing him a towel from the chest. It was strange, he thought, how little we appreciate the people near us. How easily we take them for granted.

He looked around at the small cramped cottage where he had lived all his life. The building consisted of one main room, twenty feet by twelve, which housed the broad fireplace and oven, the table, chairs, two chests and the desk which were the greater part of his worldly possessions. The room had no ceiling but opened straight into the rafters and thatching, which was just as well as it at least gave Matthew standing room. Off to one side Matthew had built a lean-to construction divided into two cubicles for himself and his mother, to his right, a separate room, which served as kitchen and store.

Matthew remembered the first time his mother had taken him to Trevanion. He must have been no more than two years old. He had been amazed at the size of the rooms – the slates on the roof – the huge oil paintings which stared down at him from the walls. He remembered his uncle staring down at him, his face as monstrous as a portrait, and then his great figure bending over him so that he felt his thick, hot breath on his cheeks. His uncle had seemed scarcely human then. He remembered when he was older his mother would send him to Trevanion when he had misbehaved and he remembered his uncle slowly unbuckling his belt. 'I'm doing this for your good,' he had said as if he meant it.

Much later when he was nearly full-grown, he remembered his uncle looking at him across the dining table and waving his hand theatrically. 'All this,' he had said, 'will be yours.' And Matthew had been sure he meant it – and why shouldn't he? – for his uncle had no one else to leave it to. For the first time in generations the squire of Trevanion had failed to produce an heir. Then he had married.

'The parson called for you today.' It was his mother who broke his thoughts.

'The Reverend Morecombe? What did he want?'

'He wouldn't say. He wants you to go and see him early tomorrow morning.'

'That's odd – I suppose it's to do with the funeral. You know, I don't think she was even going to tell us.'

Mary looked at him. 'Don't judge her too harshly, Matthew. I'm sure the poor woman's got enough to worry about.'

If he had guessed then even a little of what he came to know, Matthew would have agreed with her wholeheartedly, maybe even felt a twinge of remorse, or sympathy. But who, from this quiet beginning, this family misunderstanding, so to speak, could have foreseen the events which would so implacably unfold?

So Matthew said nothing. And his ordeal began.

Chapter Two

TIME HAD BEEN MERCIFUL TO Richard Morecombe. Nevertheless, there was no denying the fine crows' feet around his eyes and down the sides of his neck. With time, his already fine, hawkish, features had become accentuated, his cheeks more hollowed, his nose more aquiline, his complexion more pallid. In spite of this, a shock of jet black hair, that showed no trace of grey, still sprung from his crown in a manner most unusual for a parson. The same coarse black hair swarmed across the backs of his hands.

As soon as he arrived, Matthew was shown into the study. Richard Morecombe rose from behind his desk and gripped the younger man's hand. The desk was heaped with books, letters and sheaves of paper.

The parson came straight to the point.

'I'm afraid I didn't ask you here to offer condolences, Matthew. I have something to say to you, that is not easy. It concerns your uncle.'

Matthew grinned.

'My uncle was not always an easy man, Reverend. What is it?'

The parson smiled back but the shadow that hung over his face did not disappear. Then he suddenly tapped his fingers together and said: 'This has been troubling me for the past two days. And I am still not sure. All I might do is cause you and your family more distress. Yet . . .' He stared Matthew straight in the eye. 'Do you remember Pilate's words to our Lord on Good Friday, "What is truth?" '

'What of it?' Matthew was in no mood for this sort of conversation.

'I don't know if you're aware of this, but I was the first to be with your uncle's body after they brought it back to Trevanion. They laid it on the table in the dining room.' His face grew more sombre. He had known John well.

Matthew shifted in his seat.

'Yes. That is how it should be.'

'You are quite right, that *is* how it should be. There ought really to be nothing unusual.'

'And was there something unusual?'

Richard took a deep breath: 'Come and see for yourself.'

The parsonage stood next to the church. Richard led Matthew through the lychgate and into the graveyard. The door to the crypt lay down a flight of three steps running into the north side of the church so that it was half-above and half-below ground. The parson juggled briefly with a large bunch of keys, then the ancient door swung open. Matthew ducked beneath the lintel and entered. He breathed in cold, moist air, heavy with the scent of earth and stone. It was, with all its associations, an unpleasant odour. He stiffened involuntarily. Gradually his eyes grew accustomed to the dark and he suddenly realised he was looking at a large stone platform, maybe eight feet long and five feet wide. On this lay the body of

13

John Trevanion, naked save for the white winding-sheet draped over him.

'I thought it best to bring him here rather than leave him at Trevanion,' Richard whispered.

Matthew gave no reply. Stepping carefully forwards, he drew near the body and pulled back the sheet. The smell of the damp soil seemed to surround him. In the half-light the body appeared unreal, its features flabby and almost unrecognisable. Despite its great size, it was somehow smaller than life, smaller and less significant now it was no longer occupied by his uncle's mighty spirit.

'Would you care for a few minutes alone?' Richard asked.

Matthew shook his head.

'Maybe later. But for now, show me why you've brought me here.'

Richard looked at him, then reached over and gently picked up the body's left hand. Turning it sideways, he held it up to what little light entered from the doorway. There, looking almost black against the pale white skin, a dark stain spread across the knuckles.

'I saw this in the dining room,' he explained.

'What is it?'

'Dried blood. See for yourself.'

Matthew examined the hand. It felt cold and leathery. He looked at the stain. Even in this light it was certainly blood.

'So my uncle cut himself when he fell?'

'Hardly. Can you see any marks on him? He was fully dressed when they brought him in; there were no marks on his clothes or his body.'

Matthew felt a sudden reluctance to look for himself.

'But there must have been some blood when he fell?'

Richard walked to the top of the table so he stood directly behind John Trevanion's head. Taking it gently in his hands, he raised it slightly from the stone.

'Here,' he said, 'at the back of the head, there is a little blood. But look – ' he rolled the head from side to side – 'he must have died as soon as he hit the ground. His neck was snapped. See – he's hardly bled at all. Besides, even if he didn't die straight-away, if he was hit on the back of the head, he would use the palm of his hand, not his knuckles. Try it yourself.'

Awkwardly, Matthew followed his advice and raised his hand to his head. The parson was right. No one would touch a wound with his knuckles. He studied his uncle's hand again. Now he looked more closely, he could see it was not a large stain – merely a few drops which had dried dark. He felt the skin over the knuckles. It didn't appear to be broken. He looked up at Richard.

'So if it isn't my uncle's blood, whose is it?'

'I don't know. As far as everyone knows, John was alone that day. No one saw him when he was out.'

'So what are you saying – that my uncle was mur-dered?' The word sounded odd in the low stone crypt.

'I . . . I'm not sure – are you?' Richard answered quickly. 'It's not much to go on, is it, a bloodstain on the back of a hand?'

15

Matthew tried to think. Suddenly the stench of the crypt seemed to crowd in on him. He rushed outside, and stood there in the churchyard, gulping great lungfuls of air. The dull overcast day seemed almost dazzling. On all sides the memorials to Malaggan's dead stretched out before him. Two starlings were pecking and feeding among the gravestones.

'Are you all right?' Richard stood beside him.

'Have you told anyone else?'

'No one. As I said, I was not sure. Indeed I'm still not.'

'But the blood—'

'What is proof, Matthew? As I said to you earlier, think of Pilate. Yes, maybe it's proof of sorts, but to most people it's just a spot of blood on a dead man's hand.'

'But . . .' Matthew looked around him. The church-yard seemed empty. Even so he lowered his voice. 'My uncle might have been murdered!'

'That's why I wanted to talk to you. If I took this to Simon Trelawne, he's hardly going to thank me, is he?' Simon Trelawne had been elected parish con-stable that year. It was an office he filled only grudg-ingly. The parson continued: 'Besides, without any clear proof, and with no obvious culprit, who's he likely to suspect, if he suspects anyone?'

'What do you mean?' Matthew looked suddenly guilty.

'Just that he's got nothing to go on. Constables aren't paid to think. But just consider, Matthew: once we make accusations like this, there's no telling where they will lead.'

'And my aunt – what about my aunt?'

'She's got enough to worry her. If I were to talk to her, I wouldn't want to be responsible for how she might react.' That was not what Matthew had meant but he let it pass. The parson rested his hand on the tombstone next to them. 'That's why I came to you. You're his only kin, Matthew: if it's anyone's duty, it's yours.'

' "The voice of thy brother's blood crieth unto me from the ground",' said Matthew. He stared down at his feet and kicked at a clump of grass. 'So what are you saying I should do?'

'You may decide to do nothing. Perhaps it was just an accident. Perhaps we should let the dead rest in peace. As far as I'm concerned, it's my first duty to give your uncle a Christian burial on Friday. In the meantime, think things over. If you suspect the worst . . .' he paused '. . . then you must act, but only if you're certain. I don't want this affair to give rise to evils of a worse kind. Think things over – and pray. If a wrong has been committed, then it is a thing unsightly in the eyes of the Lord. Come and see me after the funeral.'

Matthew ran his finger along the top of a gravestone.

'I used to think I was close to my uncle,' he said. 'But now I wonder.'

'You were close enough, Matthew.' Richard looked back towards the open door of the crypt. 'Maybe you'd like those minutes alone now?'

Chapter Three

JOSAIAH PENHALE WAS POLISHING THE great leather saddle that had belonged to John Trevanion. He stooped over his work, a rag in one hand, a pot of grease in the other. As he worked, he whistled softly to himself and did not notice the man come into the stable behind him.

'Josey.'

At the sound of the voice, Josaiah spun round. A look of fright – fear almost – played across his face before dissolving into a smile.

'Master Trevanion! You shouldn't 'ave crept up on me like that!'

Matthew returned the smile.

'I'm sorry. Josey, I need a favour. It was you who found my uncle, wasn't it?'

Josey frowned: 'Yes. Up towards Sancreed, a couple of miles maybe.'

'Could you show me?'

Josey's frown deepened. Matthew could see him hesitate.

'It's very important to me,' he added. 'For my own peace of mind.'

'Does Mrs Trevanion know?'

Matthew knew Josey was not worried about Emily one way or the other. He seemed to be looking for an excuse not to go.

'This has nothing to do with her. It's just very important to me. Josey – please.'

Josiah put down the pot of grease resignedly.

'All right,' he said. 'But we'll have to be quick.'

The land leading up towards Sancreed was a patch-work of irregular fields and odd thickets of scrub, giving way to rough moorish downs. The two men walked quickly. They hardly spoke to each other, each lost in his own thoughts. Occasionally they would come upon a rabbit at feed, before it could dart off into the undergrowth, or a couple of birds, or they would see the figures of men in the distance working in the fields, but apart from that the land seemed empty and the air hung still. Matthew thought of his uncle riding over the same ground a few days before. Perhaps it had been one of those same rabbits which had startled his horse? His uncle was an experienced rider, yet out here, on the exposed hilltops, even the most mundane and harm-less things seemed invested with a strange presence.

He turned to Josey.

'Do you think a rabbit startled my uncle's horse?'

'What, old Jessie? It would be the first time.'

Josey carried on walking. After a minute or so, he stopped and looked at Matthew. 'Maybe it wasn't a rabbit but a hare.'

'How do you mean?'

Josey drew closer and lowered his voice. 'And maybe it wasn't no ordinary hare at that. Maybe it was no hare at all.'

'You can't be serious!' Matthew said dismissively,

but he knew what the other man meant. Josey read his thoughts.

'You know as well as I do. You were at the farm two winters ago when the Polzeaths' cow miscarried. We all saw the hare running out of the stall. And last summer when your uncle's pig cut herself in the sty and bled to death.' Matthew remembered seeing the pig's bloated belly, upturned and swollen in the mud. 'We saw the hare again, behind the sheds.'

The two men were alone in the middle of a great expanse of gorse. Matthew tried to look at Josiah calmly, but as the old man's features became more excited, so his own uneasiness grew. He remembered the long evenings he had spent around the fireplace at Trevanion, and how the storytellers would tell out the old tales – of Jan Tregagle and the devil's tricks, of the curse which befell Penzance and the Spanish invasion, of the demon mason of Lamorna. He had himself seen the ruins of the house the demon built in exchange for the owner's soul. Even though it was broad daylight, he had a sudden recollection of the black peat-smoke and the monstrous shadows flickering over the tapestries. And he remembered that of all the witches' familiars, by far the most potent was not the cat, or even the toad, but the hare. Matthew looked at Josiah, then, without saying anything, continued to walk.

It was not long before they reached the spot. The bare heath dipped into a low valley. A thin, brackish stream trickled over a bed of smooth round stones, each a foot or so in diameter.

'Here we are,' Josiah said simply.

A little to the right Matthew could see the mud had been churned and bootmarked. Uneven ruts several inches deep showed where they had lugged the body onto the bier. He could imagine the men struggling and cursing with his uncle's weight. He looked around him. It was a sad, desolate place, to be sure. Somehow he had expected to see something here, or capture some mood. All he felt was emptiness.

'Could you show me where you found him?'

'Right here.' Josey pointed to a patch of mud. Matthew noticed that one of the stones still bore a dark stain. He bent down then looked up at the heavens. So this was the last thing his uncle had seen. Nothing.

By the time they neared the manor it was almost dark. Matthew remained deep in thought. He had expected, quite irrationally, that going there would give him some sign of what he must do. Instead he'd found a bare patch of scrubland and a red stain on a rock. Yet for no conscious reason, he felt the parson was right: there was something wrong about his uncle's death. And then he realised.

It was the utter pointlessness of it all. Why on earth would his uncle ever go there? Let alone die there? And then, how had he died? The place was so devoid of shrub or bush, how could an animal of any description surprise Jessie? He thought briefly of Josey's demon hare, eyes like blazing coals, screaming through the night.

He turned to Josey. 'Tell me, what was my uncle doing before he left?'

Josiah thought for a while.

It appeared John had passed the day in a leisurely, desultory manner. After church he had strolled around the fields, throwing sticks for the dog, then spent the afternoon in the stables, inspecting the horses' tackle. Josey was repairing the cart and John came over several times. Had he said anything in particular? Josey shook his head.

'Nothing but idle talk.'

Matthew wondered. His uncle had never been idle in his life. Had he really had nothing to do – or had he been waiting for something?

Did John seem worried, he asked, or nervous?

Josey didn't think so. He regarded Matthew suspiciously.

But Matthew was insistent. Surely something must have happened?

They cleared the last hill, and could make out the low huddle of Trevanion in the dusk.

Josey scratched his head. Now you mention it, he said suddenly, there was something. Around mid-afternoon, Mrs Trevanion had called John in. He seemed annoyed, and was only gone for a short time before he stormed out and slammed the door. But what went on between man and wife behind doors, Josey added with a wink, he wouldn't like to say.

An hour or so later Luke had come back from Penzance with Joey and between them they had finished the cart. Shortly after that, John was shouting for Jessie, then he was gone.

'Matthew – I hadn't expected you.'

The voice caught him by surprise. They had come

up the field and were opening the gate into the yard. In the evening light of dark blues and mauves, her skin appeared almost luminous. Thick black curls – black in any light – fell over her face and cast it in shadow.

Matthew could not tell whether she was pleased to see him or not.

'I had . . . forgotten you'd be here.'

'Luke found me in Truro. I came straight back.'

He should have remembered, he thought angrily.

'Lucy, I'm sorry.'

'I can't believe how you upset my mother! It was so selfish of you. Selfish!'

'I was upset myself when I spoke – I shouldn't have said anything.'

'Being sorry's never good enough, Matthew. You know that.'

Matthew dropped his head and glanced at Josey.

'Well, I'd better be getting home,' Josey said. 'Evening, Miss Trevanion. Evening, Matthew.'

Matthew turned to him again. 'Good night, and thank you, Josey.'

They stood in silence, waiting for Josiah to leave.

'Lucy,' he said at last. 'This isn't the time.'

Her eyes flashed.

'Isn't it just? Your uncle's dead three days and all you want is your damned inheritance!'

Matthew winced.

'It's not like that!' he said in a whisper. 'She deliberately—' He stopped in mid-sentence, as if realising something for the first time. Lucy went to respond, but bit her lip. They stared at each other in the half-light. Then he spoke: 'I wish I'd been with you when Luke told you.'

'So do I.'

Her three words hung in the evening air, like ripe tender fruit, he thought. He lifted his hand to touch her shoulder.

'Matthew, don't!' Lucy took a step backwards. 'There is too much . . . unsaid between us. If my mother – I wouldn't – want—'

'I want us to be friends.'

'Maybe it's not possible. Not yet. You expect too much of me.' Her voice took on a new insistence. 'Go. Please.'

'Can I see you tomorrow?' He tried not to sound angry. 'I need to talk.'

She hesitated.

'I need to talk to you before the funeral.'

'I shall be taking a walk to Porthmedn tomorrow morning,' she said at last. 'You can join me if you like.'

'Yes, I will.'

'I'll call for you.'

'Good night, Lucy.'

Joey Polglaze was still polishing horsebrasses in the stable. The oil-lamp cast a poor, yellow light that left everything but his immediate work in shadow. Joey was ten or eleven years old and slightly short for his age. He looked up nervously when Matthew entered.

'Long day, Joey?'

'Yes, sir. I've got to get everything ready for the funeral. Can't sleep till it's done.'

'You've had a busy week – I heard you went to Penzance with Luke the other day.'

Joey carried on rubbing the brass in his hand. 'I often go in,' he said without looking up.

'Who did you go and see?'

Joey glanced up bashfully. 'Some lady-friend of Luke's.'

'What? Luke's going courting?'

'There's a girl who works in one of the sea captains' houses in Penzance. Every Sunday he goes to see her.'

'And he takes you with him?' Matthew sounded surprised.

'Sometimes, sir, so long as I don't get in the way. I like to look at the boats and talk to the fishermen. There's one that says he might take me as his boy next summer,' he added wistfully. Both Joey's parents had died in the typhoid epidemic of 1742. Since then he had a home of sorts at Josaiah's house, but he was fast growing up and soon he would have to fend for himself.

'So that's what you did all afternoon, watched the boats?'

The boy's face lit up. 'They'd got two schooners in. Carrying pilchards and cloth to the West Indies.'

'And what about Luke, did you see much of him?'

'He spent the afternoon with Miss Jenepher, sir.'

Matthew looked at him carefully. 'And you didn't talk to anyone at all?'

Joey hesitated for just a fraction of a second. 'No, sir.'

It was enough. Matthew reached over and seized the boy by the collar. With one movement, he jerked him bodily into the air and pinned him against the wall. Before he could utter a sound, Matthew had clamped a large hand over Joey's mouth. He stared into the child's face.

'Don't ever lie to me,' Matthew told him. 'I detest lies, understand? Now I'll ask you again – and if you lie to me this time – I'll snap your little neck like a stick, see?' Joey nodded. Cautiously, Matthew removed his hand from the boy's mouth. He could feel his small body shaking like a bird's.

'How did you know?'

'I know everything, Joey. And if you lie again, I'll know before the words are out of your lips.' He peered into Joey's face. The boy was wide-eyed with terror. Good. So this was how he would have to find the truth. 'Now, tell me who you met.'

'It was Mr Pascoe.'

'Joshua Pascoe, the lawyer?'

'That's right. I was sitting on the quay when I felt a hand on my shoulder, and there was Mr Pascoe looking down at me. I recognised him from the times he's been out to the farm. "You're Trevanion's boy, aren't you?" he asked. "Are you going back to Trevanion this afternoon?" I told him yes, we were. "In that case," he says, "give this to your master." And he pulls out a slip of paper all sealed with wax. "And here's a sixpence for your trouble," he says. I couldn't see anything wrong in it, besides, I thought, I'll be doing my master a service.'

'Did Luke know about this?'

Joey wavered. 'Well, no . . . not quite.'

'How do you mean? Did you tell him?'

'Mr Pascoe told me not to.'

Matthew thought on this for a moment. 'So what did my uncle do when you gave him the note?'

'He just took it and went off, that's all.'

'Are you sure? Didn't he thank you? Did he act surprised?'

Joey just shook his head.

'How long after that did he go out?'

'A few minutes, if that.'

'And you've no idea what was in the note?'

'No, sir, on my life.'

Matthew relaxed his grip a little. 'Why didn't you tell anyone about this, Joey?'

At this the boy's look of fear turned to puzzlement. 'Mrs Trevanion told me not to.'

'Emily knew?'

'Yes, sir!' Joey stared at him as if it was obvious. 'On Monday, after they brought the master's body back, she sent for me. She said she knew I'd brought him a note and did anyone else know? I said no, and she said the note was private, between Mr Pascoe and her husband and I mustn't tell a soul.'

'Did you ask why?'

'If Mrs Trevanion tells me to do something I just do it.'

'Hmmm.' Matthew suspected another sixpence had changed hands. Besides, perhaps Joey was too young to think anything of it.

Joey wriggled in his hands.

'Can I go now, sir?'

'Before you go I want you to remember our conversation this evening.' He drew Joey closer. 'At some point I may need you to repeat what you've just told me, do you understand? And you must do

27

it word for word, Mrs Trevanion or not. The truth is sacred. And if you don't . . .' Matthew paused. 'I hate lies, Joey, remember that.'

That night as he lay in bed, Matthew let his mind wander over the dark, formless waters of the Atlantic, and the endless winds moving over the face of the waters. He thought of the fishing boats floating over the vast depth of water, and how small and weak they were to the flexing of the ocean. He thought of the hunched and stunted bushes which clung to the tops of hedges, and the large wastes of gorse, gold in spring, bitter green the rest of the year.

Matthew let his imagination drift. His imagination floated over the hills around his home, lifting and plunging. His mind floated over the untidy village of Malaggan, and its small, granite church, with its stunted tower. Then his mind soared up to the great hills of central Penwith, the baldheaded tors, shrouded in mists and rain.

Matthew stared up into the blackness. All he could hear was the wind buffeting against the trees. He dreamed of a great darkness opening up around him, and in the middle of the darkness, the great figure of John Trevanion, laughing and bellowing, so that his voice took on the sound of the sea-wind and became one with it.

Chapter Four

MATTHEW AWOKE TOWARDS SUNRISE AND left the cottage without disturbing his mother. It was a mild, damp morning and the clouds appeared in the half-light as dull grey smudges only just above the tops of the hills. He made his way down the path towards the beach.

The cove of Porthmedn lies at the bottom of a valley. It is flanked on both sides by sheer, plunging cliffs and carpeted with a shingle of grey pebbles. These now slipped and crunched beneath Matthew's feet. The wind which had roamed wildly over the hills these last few days had sunk to the merest whisper overnight and the sea lay heavy and unruffled, a vast featureless pool. Small waves washed gently against the shore.

Matthew breathed the raw sea-air deep into his lungs and looked out over the waters. It was hard to imagine how their smooth, silky skin concealed such monstrous depths. Now the waters were at rest and gently rose and fell. Matthew felt his head clearing, and a sense of peace returned.

To the right of the cove, squatting against the base of the cliff, stood an old wooden shack. It was typical of the huts that dotted the coastline, used by fishermen for storing nets and tackle.

As he was looking, a figure emerged from the doorway. He waved and called over. Matthew returned the call and stepped across the beach towards him.

'George! Caught anything recently?'

George Trevose had a ruddy, unshaven, heavy-cheeked face and one of those rolling, barrel-chested figures sailors seem to have. He grinned broadly.

'Fishing's going well – we just brought back a haul from Roscoff. Good stuff and all.'

Although George Trevose looked like a fisherman, he made his living from the free import and export of goods across the Channel. To the communities along the coast, this trade was such a normal and essential part of everyday life, that they only had the vaguest notion of why the authorities called it smuggling. George called it venturing.

'I heard you had a bit of a run-in with a customs schooner.'

George Trevose spat expressively. 'Bastards were waiting for me in the Bay. I was putting into Marazion when they came round the Mount. I had to sow the crop and run for it.' Venturers carried their cargo slung over the sides of their boats, so if they were attacked they could drop it overboard and collect it later. This was called 'sowing the crop'.

'Picked it up yet?'

'It's drying out in my Cellar.'

George reached into his coat and extracted a clay pipe and a pouch of Virginian. He began to pack the bowl with a slow, methodical ease.

'Two days ago a gang of customs men rode into Mousehole and tried to search the warehouses. Threatened some of the boys, but they can't do nothing.' He cupped the pipe in his hands. A lucifer flared and he sucked on the stem until the blue smoke mushroomed from the corners of his lips.

'Sorry about your uncle.'

'Yes.' Matthew paused for a moment. 'So will you be needing a hand?'

'Don't know. I was expecting a load of tin this week, but this recent business has lost me the tide. I won't be off until next week at the earliest. I'll let you know.'

Although venturers made handsome profits on importing goods, in Cornwall much of the real business lay in exporting untaxed tin to France and the Netherlands. George Trevose ran a round trip, taking teas and spirits one way, white tin the other. For Matthew the shipments from Porthmedn provided a useful income.

'You don't think anyone informed on you?'

George shook his head. 'No. Or if someone did, it would be one of the casuals – but they don't know where the Cellar is. Here, did I tell you? Victor saw a ghost last night.' George winked. 'Or so he says. He was on his way to the Cellar and cut through the graveyard.'

'Are you serious, George?' Matthew's first reaction was that this was part of some elaborate joke.

'Dead serious. Victor says he was crossing the graveyard when he heard a loud scraping, like the sound of wood against stone. So he looked around and there, moving between the stones, was the figure of a man.'

'So what made him think it was a ghost?'

'That's what I asked. Apparently he thought it was a bit peculiar at that time of night, so he called out.

But the man didn't reply, and kept on walking, so Victor calls again. Still no response. "Right!" he thinks, and runs after him.' George sucked on his pipe. 'And this is where you believe him, or you don't. According to Victor, he was on the point of catching up with him, when the figure reached the hedge over by the Bell Field, and just ... disappeared. Into thin air, so Victor says.'

Matthew smiled to himself. This wouldn't be the first time he'd heard this tale. 'How much had he drunk, George?'

'What? Before or after? I reckon he ran all the way to the Cellar. He was shaking like a leaf. Did I tell you about the time I was travelling across Goss Moor ...' He trailed off, wondering whether Matthew would ask.

Matthew remained thoughtful. 'What made him so sure it was a man?'

'That's a good question. Knowing Victor, it was his wife come back to haunt him. She never approved of his drinking.' George kept his face straight but his eyes gleamed. 'You know,' he thought out loud, 'I always wondered why your uncle married so late in life. You'd have thought he valued his freedom at his age.'

'Yes – it's strange to think it was only four years ago.' Matthew still remembered the day the coach pulled up at Trevanion. Lucy was leaning out of the window. She must have been sixteen, certainly no more than seventeen.

'I mean it's not as if he married a young girl, is it?' continued George, pursuing his own line of speculation.

Matthew remembered Emily getting out of the coach. She had the same dark hair and full mouth as her daughter, and the same figure. But where Lucy was still soft-faced, her mother was not.

'You never know,' Matthew said. 'Perhaps it was love. Every man needs a helpmeet. Don't forget St Paul: "a man shall leave his parents and they two shall be one flesh, and this is a great mystery". Perhaps you'll get caught yourself one day.'

George Trevose gave a laugh which was not entirely spontaneous. 'A great mystery indeed.'

Lucy rode over several hours later. She had not been to Rosmear since coming back from Brittany and perhaps this showed in the lines on her face. She swung her horse into the clearing in front of Matthew's cottage and dismounted. The cottage seemed empty, so after calling out and checking the sheds, she set off on foot towards the beach. She had not gone more than a hundred yards when Matthew stepped out from behind the hedge. She stopped. There was something hard and cold in his expression, which she had not seen before, or maybe she had forgotten. He smiled and the look almost vanished.

'I'm glad you could come. It's going to be a beautiful day.' He was right. The dull greyness of the early morning had given way to bright blue skies and dazzling white clouds.

Lucy did not return the smile: 'It's been almost a year.'

'You've hardly changed.'

They stood looking at each other.

'Come on,' she said. 'Let's walk.'

As the path descended between the thick groves of sycamores the air grew cool and sweet with the scent of leaves. Overhead a woodpigeon called out. His call was taken up and thrown back across the valley. Far off they heard the sound of waves on the shingle.

She turned to him: 'Do you remember that day in March, when I came back from London? We walked here then.' She lowered her eyes demurely as if inviting him to take her hand, or come to her.

But Matthew's voice, when he replied, sounded as hard and cold as his expression had been. Only if she had really listened, would she have heard the emotion that lay behind his question:

'Why did you leave, Lucy?'

'I thought it was for the best. I heard about your fight with John. I'd never seen him like that. He was so *angry.*'

The path dipped into a tunnel of hawthorns. And now John was dead. Matthew spoke quietly: 'You shouldn't have listened to her. I don't understand.'

'I had no choice! Besides,' she rounded on him, 'you should be explaining yourself! That Poldeen woman – you didn't see what she was like. John was actually in tears.'

'So you ran away.'

'You don't realise how hurt I was, do you?' Lucy's words came in a rush. 'I thought it was for the best,' she repeated quietly.

'I never did those things! Don't you believe that?' She paused. 'George gave me your letter.'

'And?'

'Why do you think I came back?' She looked at him angrily, as if she were angry for believing him. 'I don't know, Matthew!' She carried on walking.

'Your mother lied!' he called out, then wished he hadn't. When she didn't slow down, he ran and caught her up.

Below them the beach opened out. A fresh wind had arisen and the waves fell against the shoreline with a rush. Matthew helped Lucy over the hedge and for a moment felt her body against his, then she was over and they walked across the shingle.

Matthew stared out to sea. On a day like this the sight was breathtaking. A sudden longing gripped him to be gone from this place, to go out there, in the simple expanse of water and air.

'Why did you take so long to write?' she asked, as if she were talking to the waves.

'I only found out where you were by chance. No one at the manor would tell me, then George ran into some fishermen from St Malo.'

'Your uncle talked to me last week, just after I got back,' she said suddenly. 'He told me your side of the story.'

'He did? Do you think he believed me, then?'

'I think so.'

Matthew bent down and picked up a stone from the beach. It glistened white in the sunlight.

'You know, he never said anything to me. Not since that day.'

'Perhaps he didn't want to take sides. But he was fond of you, Matthew.'

Matthew pulled back his arm and flung the stone

as far as he could. It described a fine arc over the sea then plunged behind a wave.

'Perhaps he hoped we'd make things up,' she went on.

'And you, do you hope so?'

Without thinking Matthew turned and put his arms around her. She came towards him and he kissed her. Then she relaxed against him and everything was momentarily forgotten. Then the kiss ended.

'It will take time, won't it?' he said.

'Maybe.' They held each other for a long time.

A thought struck him: 'Did my uncle say anything else – anything in particular – before he died?'

She looked puzzled. 'No. I'd gone to Truro. Why?'

Matthew hesitated for a moment. Were her return and his uncle's death just coincidence?

'No matter.' He took her hand.

She smiled and looked sad. 'Just promise me one thing, Matthew. At the funeral tomorrow, don't come up to us. I have to be there for my mother. I can't be there for you as well. Not yet.'

But those last two words gave him hope.

Chapter Five

B Y THE TIME MATTHEW AND his mother arrived, a
sizeable crowd had already gathered. They stood
against the north wall of the church, sheltering from
the brisk September wind which worried at the yews
and beeches hedging the graveyard. Matthew knew
most of them by sight if not by name.

Jonathan Hocking, John Trevanion's agent, stood
apart from the main group as if touched by especial
grief. As well as his interests in the estate, Mr Hocking traded in cloths and drapery. He wore a suit of
finest black wool, his wife a dress of grey brocaded
silk. Near them stood Mr and Mrs Marshall, both
formally attired, then Mary Vincent, with Rebecca
Penhale and Joey. Then came the people of the village: George Trevose and Jacob Vean, Simon Trelawne the constable, Ben Rhodda, Freddy Dunstan,
Victor Jago, and all the others: millers, wheelwrights,
hoopers, carters, labourers and craftsmen with their
wives, children and parents, who made up the com-
munity of Malaggan, each dressed in some form of
black or grey, huddled into the lee of the church.

The night before, the Reverend Morecombe had
removed the body from the crypt and placed it in
John Mitchell's timber store. Now it was borne down
the main street towards the church, carried under-
hand, as was the custom, by six of John Trevanion's
farmhands with Josiah and Luke at the front.

Behind them walked Emily and Lucy. They were accompanied by Joshua Pascoe. The lawyer was clad in a suit of purest black silk. His long white hair was pulled back in a queue and tied with a band, also of black. In front of them all strode the tall, aquiline figure of Richard Morecombe, dark, sombre, holding the *Book of Common Prayer*. The people in the churchyard fell silent. The cortège passed up the street, the coffin bobbing awkwardly in the middle. Somehow Matthew had expected it to look larger.

As he crossed the threshold of the porch, Richard Morecombe began to intone the words of the Service.

' "I am the resurrection and the life, saith the Lord: he that believeth in me, though he were dead, yet shall he live: and whosoever liveth and believeth in me shall never die." '

Now the only sounds that could be heard were the parson's strong, dry voice and the blustering of the wind over the trees.

' "We brought nothing into this world, and it is certain we can carry nothing out. The Lord gave, and the Lord hath taken away; blessed be the Name of the Lord. Amen." '

The parson passed inside the church. Quietly the people filed in behind. The coffin was laid in the centre of the aisle and Richard Morecombe ascended into the pulpit.

' "Behold, thou hast made my days as it were a span long: and mine age is even as nothing in respect of thee: and verily every man living is altogether vanity.

' "For man walketh in a vain shadow, and disquieteth himself in vain: he heapeth up riches, and cannot tell who shall gather them." '

The dense clouds outside cast a dull, grey light over the whitewashed interior of the church. The wind buffeted against the roof. At one point a flare of sunlight burst through the cloud and arced across the flagstones and the faces of the congregation before fading away. The words of the psalm moved over the congregation as sunlight may move over land, or water over the sea-bed. Matthew studied the rich, densely grained oak of the pew in front of him.

' "Thou turnest men to destruction; again thou sayest, Come again, ye children of men.

' "As soon as thou scatterest them, they are even as a sleep: and fade away suddenly like the grass.

' "In the morning it is green, and groweth up: but in the evening it is cut down, dried up, and withered.

' "For we consume away in thy displeasure: and are afraid at thy wrathful indignation." '

Matthew thought of John Trevanion. Vibrant, robust, his strong, thick shoulders, his sense of the profane and the comic, his rich, deep laugh, his implacable anger, now all were nothing. Yet he had the strangest feeling that there was something more to the man, something he could not explain. Time undoubtedly would tell.

' "Thou hast set our misdeeds before thee: and our secret sins in the light of thy countenance.

' "For when thou art angry all our days are gone: we bring our years to an end, as it were a tale that is told." '

The psalm drew to a close. The Reverend Morecombe paused, and then began again.

' "Now is Christ risen from the dead, and become the first-fruits of them that slept. For since by man came death, by man came also the resurrection of the dead." '

Matthew looked around him. The tired, drawn faces of the mourners stared up at the parson. Each one bore the marks of a life in which resources were always too scarce, security too flimsy a thing. Outside in the graveyard lay the bodies of the friends and relatives who had gone before them. The very hardness of their lives meant the parson's words carried a particular immediacy. Death sat daily at their table. He ate in their homes and slept in their beds. He walked with them when they went to plough and to reap.

' "Death is swallowed up in victory. O death, where is thy sting? O grave, where is thy victory? The sting of death is sin, and the strength of sin is the law. But thanks be to God, which giveth us the victory through our Lord Jesus Christ." '

Such was the funeral service of John Trevanion. Maybe his sins would be buried with him.

They followed the coffin out to the hole prepared on the south side of the graveyard. Matthew watched Emily follow the coffin down with her eyes. Joshua Pascoe stood across from her, ashen-faced. Lucy stood next to him; she was crying. Matthew wished he could go to Lucy and hold her, at that moment when the first clod of earth fell on the coffin. He put his arm round his mother and hugged her.

' "Man that is born of woman hath but a short

time to live, and is full of misery. He cometh up, and is cut down, like a flower; he fleeth as it were a shadow, and never continueth in one stay.

' "In the midst of life we are in death: of whom may we seek for succour, but of thee, O Lord, who for our sins art justly displeased?" '

The crowd began to break up and drift out of the churchyard in groups of two or three. Matthew looked back at Emily and Lucy. They had stayed by the graveside with Pascoe. He wondered what they were thinking. Mary pulled at his sleeve. The wind had cut her to the bone and she looked cold and frail.

'I'd better get you inside,' he said.

'Don't worry. I'll go to Mrs Mitchell's.'

Matthew looked back at the grave. Richard was leading them through the lychgate towards the parsonage.

'I trust we're not intruding, Master Trevanion?' It was Jonathan Hocking and his wife. Whereas he was big and bluff, Madeleine Hocking seemed an unhappy lady with a pale watery complexion.

Reluctantly Matthew introduced his mother and accepted Mr Hocking's outstretched hand.

'If we may offer our condolences,' the man continued. He paused: 'And also our congratulations. I hope I can look forward to our acquaintanceship developing?'

Matthew did not understand, and this must have been obvious, for the older man, still clasping his palm, leaned closer.

'The estate,' he whispered. 'Trevanion.'

Matthew withdrew his hand cautiously.

'The estate is none of my business, sir.'

Hocking coughed.

'You don't know, then? I assumed Pascoe would read the will straightaway. I was one of the witnesses,' he added, somewhat self-importantly.

'He left a will?'

Jonathan Hocking looked uncomfortable.

'Forgive me. I have evidently spoken out of turn. Perhaps you should talk to Mr Pascoe.' He made as if to leave.

'No, wait a minute.' Matthew rested his hand on Hocking's shoulder.

'I think I've already said more than I ought. Perhaps I was mistaken.' Mr Hocking tipped his hat towards Mary. 'Come, Madeleine.' His wife bobbed nervously. The street was almost empty now.

'Wait!' said Matthew. 'You must tell me. Please.'

Hocking hesitated.

'All I know is, about a year ago your uncle asked me to witness his testament. Of course, he could have changed it since . . .'

'And I was one of his heirs?'

'You were his only heir.'

Matthew stared at him.

'Everything – manor, estate, leases – they were all yours,' Hocking continued. 'Pardon me, but hence my congratulations.' He made to go, as if regretting his candour, and this time Matthew did not stop him.

'Can you trust him?' Mary said at last.

'I don't know if I dare.'

'But if it's true it's fantastic!'

'*If* it's true. Emily said there was no will. Perhaps

Hocking is wrong.' Matthew tried to sound level-headed, when inside he felt anything but. He knew how important it was to keep his thoughts to himself.

'You must see Mr Pascoe straightaway.'

'I'll go on Monday.' She was starting to shiver. 'Come on. Or you'll catch your death of cold.'

That night a storm rolled in from the Atlantic and after climbing over the hills which guard the north coast, swept down upon the unprotected farmlands with a vengeance. The black outlines of the trees pitched and swayed against the sky. As he made his way back to the village, Matthew pulled his coat tight about him.

Although he had been expecting him, Richard was forced to keep Matthew waiting. Mrs Odgers had taken ill after the funeral, and he had only just returned from seeing her. Matthew perused the pictures that lined the hallway. There were several ink sketches of churches: St George's, Bloomsbury, All Saints, Spitalfields. There was also a portrait of an elderly man with a bald head and a pinched nose, and underneath an inscription that read 'William Morecombe, Esquire, 1722'.

'Matthew! Mrs Dunstan shouldn't have left you in the hall!' Was there something else, not so innocent, in the parson's meaning? He came quickly down the stairs and gripped Matthew's shoulder.

'Sorry I couldn't come earlier. I waited until my mother went to sleep.'

'No matter. You look soaked to the skin, sit yourself by the fire.' In the parlour, logs spat and crackled on the hearth. 'Brandy?'

'Thanks.' Matthew held the rich tawny liquid up to the light. The cut glass sparkled and danced. The parson watched him and said as casually as he could:

'So, the matter we talked about, concerning your uncle?'

'Nothing.' Matthew leaned back in his chair and stretched with equal casualness. He was surprised to find he felt awkward deceiving a member of the church, but he knew there was nothing else for it. 'So far I've seen nothing to make me even remotely suspicious.'

'What about the blood on his hand?'

'Perhaps it got there when they picked him up, I don't know.'

The parson looked relieved. 'Then I was right not to call in the coroner.'

'It would have just caused Emily upset. You're quite close to her, aren't you?'

'I was one of the first people she met when she arrived.'

Matthew thought for a minute. 'It was strange to see him buried this morning.'

'Yes. May the Lord have mercy on him. And on all of us left behind.' The parson fell silent. The wind beat against the windows, the thick drapes stirred on their hangings. 'Are you really going back in this weather?'

'I don't want to leave my mother alone. Besides, I need to keep an eye on the farm.'

'What I really wanted to ask you about was Lucy.'

The parson's voice assumed a more confidential tone.

'Yes? What exactly?' Matthew replied warily.

'She came to see me before the funeral. She seemed upset, which was natural, but that wasn't all. I was sure something else was troubling her. Do you have any ideas?'

'I'm not sure it's anything to do with me.'

'I'm sorry, I thought you were betrothed once . . .'

'That was a long time ago. I haven't seen her since she came back from Brittany.'

'No matter,' said the parson quickly. 'I was just wondering. I'm concerned for both of them at the moment.'

'So am I, Reverend.'

Richard Morecombe reached over to the bottle of brandy on the side-table. Outside they could hear the rain falling across the glass in great drifts.

'Well,' he said, 'as you're here, we may as well continue that discussion on the Epistle to the Galatians.'

It was several hours later before the rain showed any sign of abating. Eventually Matthew decided he must leave no matter what. As the night wore on the conversation had become more involved. The parson had a wide-ranging mind and talked freely about the world. Several times, Matthew found himself wondering that the man had been content to confine himself to this small plot of earth on the extremity of England. Surely he would be more at home in the drawing rooms of Bath or Westminster?

On the doorstep the parson bade him good night.

Matthew was surprised he did not feel more chilled as the wind bit into his face. He realised dully he must have consumed the best part of a bottle of brandy and was probably quite drunk. No matter, he thought, I'll soon be home.

He cut across the lawn and opened the lychgate. The moon cast deep shadows across the graveyard. Matthew halted. Perhaps it was the burial that morning which made the tumbled gravestones and clumps of grass and the trees tossing in the wind seem strange and unearthly. He took a deep breath and closed the gate behind him.

Then out of the corner of his eye he saw a movement. Steadying himself against the jamb of the lychgate, he rubbed his eyes. At that moment the moon dipped behind a cloud and the graveyard lurched into impenetrable blackness. He stayed stock still and peered into the gloom. There was something moving. Then the moon blazed down from the other side of the cloud.

A tall, dark figure was moving away from him across the graveyard. He strained his eyes, trying to make it out in more detail. There was something oddly familiar about the figure and the way it moved, yet for some reason Matthew thought better than to call out. Where could it be going at this time of night? Keeping below the level of the gravestones, he began to follow it as best he could. His head spun and he stumbled over half-hidden markers and loose stones, but the rushing of the wind in the trees masked any noise. He looked up. The man – it must be a man from its height – was walking slowly, but always in a straight line, neither deviating to left nor right. He realised with a surprise it was heading towards his uncle's grave.

Matthew crept forwards. The man was now no more than thirty feet away. He had reached the graveside, where the fresh earth rose in a heap, and stood looking at the mound, with his back towards Matthew. Matthew watched him from behind a tombstone. Open ground lay between them. If he tried to cross it he was sure to be seen. The figure did nothing. Matthew waited. He was breathing heavily and his thoughts came in a confused jumble. Four, maybe five, minutes passed. Matthew leaned against the tombstone. Following the man through the graveyard had left him dizzy. He looked up. The figure had gone. Panic seized him. Leaping to his feet, Matthew covered the distance to the grave at a run. His head was pounding. When he got there the figure was nowhere to be seen. He spun around. The churchyard was empty. How could he have missed him? Then something black passed in front of white marble. Abandoning all thought of concealment, Matthew ran after him. The figure had crossed to the other side of the church. Even though he was running, the dark shadow appeared to be gliding away from him. Matthew fetched up against a stone. He felt sick and winded. 'STOP!' he shouted, his voice rising thin and reed-like over the roar of the wind. The figure appeared to hear. It paused for a fraction at the edge of the graveyard and turned towards him. Even in the moonlight his face was unmistakable. It was John Trevanion.

PART TWO

Chapter One

MATTHEW WOULD ALWAYS REMEMBER THE day four years before when Lucy stepped out of the carriage at Trevanion. When his uncle had returned from Bath, and announced he was going to marry a lady he had met, he had said nothing of her daughter. Lucy Marchant had just turned seventeen. She was tall, slim and vivacious. Her hair hung over her face in thick, dark curls, so dark they were almost blue, and her eyes were the deepest indigo. Matthew thought she was beautiful.

So while his uncle entertained his future bride, Matthew devoted himself to welcoming Emily Marchant's only daughter.

Every day, after tending the cattle, he would seek her out and she, for her part, appeared happy enough. Together they would explore the hills and valleys above the manor, or descend to the coast and gaze out to sea. It seemed to Matthew a perfect summer.

They talked as he had never talked to anyone. Lucy would question him about his thoughts and feelings, dreams and memories. He told her, and revealed the places haunted by his childhood. And she would tease him and laugh at him, and he, blushing and sheepish, laughed too. July turned to August and the wedding day approached. Yet no matter how easy their relationship became, they remained

51

separated by an *invisible* distance – invisible because neither would acknowledge it. So although Matthew could interpret her gestures how he liked, Lucy would never say or do anything which proved her feelings for him – only *implied*. In some ways, there was a pattern here. But he realised this only later, when too many had been killed.

At the time, his heart had no understanding that what he felt so passionately and surely, like the strong, hard pulse of a vein, might be to her nothing more than a source of entertainment.

'Don't assume too much,' his mother warned. 'She may like you, Matthew, but she'll want something better of life.'

'But Uncle John will leave—'

'Don't be stupid!' his mother snapped. She seemed angry. 'What right have you to expect that?'

'But he said . . .' He was aware his voice sounded thin and childlike and he was annoyed with himself.

'And now he's getting married what do you think will happen? Won't his wife have some say in this?'

Matthew had hardly noticed Emily Marchant. At first sight, there seemed little to notice: she was quiet, reserved, a widow in her thirties, somewhat severe and tight-lipped. Yet when the mood possessed her, Emily could strip this impression off like an old dress. She loved drinking and horse-riding with a passion, and would range over the moors with John or would drink and joke with John until the small hours. When she laughed Matthew could see something of Lucy in her. And then the mood would pass, and the demon of severity took her back. Emily

52

insisted on organising her wedding personally and she did this with the joyless efficiency of an executioner, and John was happy to acquiesce.

Perhaps there was something pathetic about her, thought Matthew, some aroma of melancholy which clung to her.

Then again, perhaps there was something pathetic about John Trevanion as he patted and preened himself clumsily in the mirror. Who would deny them both their chance of happiness?

Yet as the wedding day approached, Matthew found his own thoughts tinged with sadness. He and John had been strangely close, and he knew this closeness would pass away with his uncle's marriage. John dismissed his worries out of hand, but in this Matthew proved quite perceptive, when in other matters he was not.

Matthew could still remember the festivities at the manorhouse after the ceremony. Emily had spent her time well, he had to admit. The great table in the dining room was laden with a joyous abundance of foods and fancies: chipple pies and parsley pies, squab pie and stargazy pie, taddago, likkey, and conger pies, great sides of pork and lamb, geese broiled and garnished, chickens roasted and glazed, mackerel and pilchards, soused, salted or smoked, and then, after the savouries, the puddings and cakes: revel cake and figgy pudden, sago pudding, apple fuggan, fairings and scones, macaroons brought especially from St Ives. Salads and fruits gleaming in their baskets.

'Ladies and gentlemen!' John Trevanion's great

voice boomed theatrically above the assembled company. He stood at the head of the table, hands on hips, feet splayed apart. 'It is not often in a man's life he has just cause for celebration. But today, today is one of those times.' He glanced at Emily and winked.

'What about tonight?' someone shouted. Several of the guests had already been drinking and roared with laughter and jokes of their own.

John Trevanion took a deep breath. 'Eat, drink and be merry!'

The guests needed no further prompting, and the gathering dissolved into a riot as they fought and scrambled for food and drink, snatched at bowls and plates, elbowed and barged their way through. Squires, curates and venturers swarmed around the pitchers of muscatel and bordeaux and the huge vats of punch. Farmers from Towednack and Buryan, fishermen and seiners from Newlyn and Mousehole, mine captains from St Just and Wendron, and their wives, sons, daughters, cousins, uncles and aunts joined the fray, and above all the eating and drinking, laughing and shouting, rose the great and monstrous voice of the groom, like some spirit of Bacchus, urging his followers on. John Trevanion had been right: there were few opportunities in life to celebrate, so when one was offered, they seized it with a desperate joy.

As he looked back on the wedding in later years, Matthew often wondered if he could have then foreseen the way the future would unfurl. He recalled embracing his uncle and John wrapping his arms around him and kissing him on the forehead. He remembered congratulating Emily and calling her aunt for the first time. Emily's eyes glittered with drink and he remembered the peachy taste of her lips long after. He remembered fumbling to hold Lucy's hands and her pulling them away, a look of anger on her face.

Lucy left two weeks later. He only found out when he saw the carriage in the yard. He was too hurt to say anything more than goodbye. She smiled at him sweetly. Then she was gone.

He did not see her for the next two years. Emily told him, with only the faintest smile, that she had gone to stay with her cousins in Bedfordshire. He wondered what they were like. None of Emily's family had come to the wedding.

In the meantime John had settled into a magnificent and brooding state of matrimony – and had less time for his nephew. His former pursuits of hunting and carousing were usurped by a desire to win his wife's favour and he stubbornly dedicated himself to acquiring the airs and graces of a country gentleman.

The months passed and Matthew devoted himself to his farm. It was about this time that he began to work for George Trevose. Matthew had been well educated, and the venturer found him a useful and reliable administrator. At first he helped with loading and unloading, but it was not long before he was accompanying George to Roscoff or St Malo. In a way Matthew found in George a replacement for his uncle.

Occasionally he was invited to Trevanion for dinner, but the evenings passed with none of the easy familiarity of old. His uncle appeared happy in his marriage, and entertained the gentry with a gusto that became legendary, but to Matthew he seemed listless and ill at ease, as if some dark spirit troubled him. Matthew would catch him looking balefully at his food, or glaring into his glass of wine.

Once Matthew came back from the village to find his uncle's horse tied up outside his cottage at Rosmear. But after only a few minutes of broken talk, John made ready to leave. 'Don't tell Emily I came to see you,' he said, though what he was worried about was unclear.

In comparison, Emily blossomed. The lines around her mouth softened. She laughed more. At meal times, she lavished kisses on her husband's forehead and ran her fingers through his hair. John glowed with pleasure. Emily knew the best way to train a dog is to keep it hungry. Matthew saw she could switch with an almost graceful ease from indulging his uncle one moment to, for no appreciable reason, coldly rebuffing him the next. He wondered how much control she had over these capricious moods. As for his uncle, he seemed to enjoy the torment of trying to please her. Who was most pathetic now? wondered Matthew. He realised that in many ways Emily was similar to her daughter.

One evening in particular stood out in Matthew's mind. It was the night of his uncle's fifty-third birthday.

It was not often that a man became fifty-three, said John Trevanion, and in recognition of this, he staged a meal for his family and close acquaintances. Matthew had the impression that Emily was opposed to the idea, but John would not be swayed. In addition to Matthew and his mother, the other guests were Jonathan and Madeleine Hocking, the Reverend Morecombe, the Marshalls, and Joshua Pascoe. It was polite, amiable company, and the evening passed agreeably. A ship had just been wrecked in Mount's Bay and John was keen to show off two delicate porcelain figures that had come from it. Someone else – Matthew thought it had been Madeleine Hocking – asked if anyone had heard the news from Scotland. Would the Pretender be gone for good? Madeleine thought he might return in the spring. Scotland seemed too far away to interest anyone. 'Who cares for his birthright?' asked John Trevanion. 'What's his birthright anyway? Who cares if he's Scottish, French, or German – if he isn't Cornish?' The company agreed. But for the rest of his life, Matthew never forgot that comment. He wondered whether that was all John had meant.

The conversation returned to local matters and before long they were discussing the upturn in mining and the new shafts being sunk to the south of Redruth. John wanted to start prospecting on manor lands and picked up a debate he had been having earlier with Jonathan Hocking. There was a fortune to be made, of that John was certain. If only they could find the right site. You had merely to look at the Bassets of Tehidy to see how a family, not even half the age of the Trevanions, had become the richest in the county – all because of one seam of tin. Instead the Trevanions had lost much of what they had. Gregory Marshall was cautious. Speculation was not to his taste. But as the men talked, John

Trevanion grew even more bullish. Whole empires were conjured out of the smoky air, as he envisaged first one enterprise, then another, then the fortunes to be made shipping direct to the continent, then the advantages of the new equipment and how they could exploit the resources of the land in ways as yet undreamed.

After an hour or so, Matthew grew irritated. He pointed out that to date all of the successful mines were to the north, around St Just and Zennor, or farther to the east, at Redruth and Helston. 'I doubt if there's a ha'penny worth of tin to be had here,' he remarked. He meant it only as a point of view, no more than that, but they had invested too much in the conversation to be so easily dismissed. Besides, the wine had flown freely. Gregory Marshall was about to agree, when John Trevanion slammed his fist on the table. Matthew saw Emily wince.

'I can't understand you, Matthew! You of all people should be excited! You're still young,' his uncle continued, suddenly maudlin. 'You've got your whole life.'

'I don't see what good that will do me,' answered Matthew. 'I'll make my living from the farm, if at all. Rosmear is Trevanion land. Any tin you found wouldn't be mine in any case.'

'What do you mean, *Trevanion* land?' John looked around him. 'Who *is* a Trevanion if not you? And when I'm dead and buried, whose will it be, eh?' He leaned forward, his words running together with the wine: 'When I'm gone, all this is yours.'

The room had fallen silent. Matthew stared at his uncle. A thick patina of sweat was shining on the man's forehead. The guests looked embarrassed. Emily stared into her plate. Everyone was waiting for him to say something.

'I see,' he said at last. He forced a smile. 'I hadn't understood. Thank you, Uncle. Thank you.'

John Trevanion relaxed in his chair. He raised his glass to his lips.

'To the future!' he declared. Emily fidgeted with her knife.

Time moved on. The seasons changed. Since the night of the birthday party, Matthew saw even less of his uncle and whenever he called, Emily regarded him with unconcealed dislike. He for his part felt awkward and strangely guilty. John did not mention his inheritance again, yet his words haunted Matthew like a curse. Perhaps it was no more than a promise written in wine? He resented his uncle for it. Several times he tried to raise the matter, and his uncle would brush him aside or gruffly pretend not to understand.

But one Thursday when Emily had gone to Penzance, Matthew found his uncle alone in the study. He was poring over a large map of Cornwall and seemed deep in thought. Matthew recognised some of the names on the map, but others he did not. John Trevanion looked up and smiled.

'Just keeping an eye on the place,' he explained.

'What you said on your birthday, about the estate,' Matthew asked, 'did you mean it?'

The smile on his uncle's face faded. He looked serious, but not angry. 'How long have you known me, Matthew?'

'Ever since I was a boy.'

'And haven't I always said that when the time was right I would leave it to you?'

'Yes. It's just that—'

'Then be patient and trust me. I won't live for ever, you know.'

In December that year Josey saw the *bucca dhu*. He was coming round the side of the manor, by the workshed, when he saw it. It was a thin, dark shade which flitted quickly across the wall and was gone before he could shout. When Luke came running from the stable, he found Josey as white as a sheet, but of the *bucca dhu* there was not the slightest sign. That night one of the old women from the village painted a cross in holy water on the end of the wall. After that it was never seen again. Of course there were those who thought that all Josey had seen was his own shadow. But from then on Josey never went out after dark without wearing a little leather pouch round his neck. What was in the pouch, Matthew never knew.

It was early March. The sheep had lambed early, and the cows had given birth to five healthy calves. As he leaned against the gate, and looked out onto the fields, Matthew felt more at peace with himself than he had for a long time.

'Hello, Matthew.' He had not seen Lucy come down the lane and now she was standing right behind him. She smiled. 'Pleased to see me?'

He looked at her. Since she had said goodbye two years before, she had lost the last traces of her girlhood. Her features were fuller now, harder, more like her mother's. If anything, she was more attractive.

'Pleased? I didn't think I'd see you again.'

'Neither did I.' She looked thoughtful for a moment. 'I thought I was going for good.'

'What happened?'

'Later,' she said. 'I'll tell you later. Would you like to walk?'

So on a golden afternoon in March they picked their way down through the deserted fields to the beach at Porthmedn.

In two years a lot can change. Matthew had had a long time to regret his feelings. For months after she left, he imagined what he would say if she came back. But now she was here, he found he no longer needed to say anything. Instead they talked about small, unimportant things and it seemed like she had never been away. They had walked to the end of the beach and were turning to go back, when she stopped and caught his gaze.

'So, Matthew, are you betrothed to anyone else yet?'

'Didn't your mother tell you?'

'I didn't ask her.'

Without answering, he turned and set off back across the shingle. He could hear her feet crunching on the pebbles as she ran laughing to catch him up.

Over the next few weeks they fell back into each other's friendship. Often they would take their horses and go up into the hills – Amalveor or Carnaquidden Downs where you can see the two coasts, north and south, at the same time. Sometimes they would ride over to Market Jew and gallop across the flats of Mount's Bay. With Lucy's return, Matthew found himself brought back into the life of the manor. He was pleased to see more of his uncle, and he noticed Emily at least tolerated him, perhaps for Lucy's sake, he guessed, rather than her husband's. April blossomed into May. Yet in all that time Lucy said nothing more about why she had returned, and Matthew knew better than to ask. It would come when she was ready.

He remembered one evening after they had eaten at Trevanion. The days were long now and they had sat out in the orchard behind the kitchen. A light breeze rustled through the apple trees, and Lucy leaned back, letting the scents drift over her. She half opened her eyes and smiled.

'I'm glad I came back.' She laughed. 'Perhaps things will work out for the best.'

'They don't often.'

'I can remember the day I left,' she continued. 'It seems like a lifetime ago.'

'A lot has changed. The farm. Your mother and my uncle. You've changed, Lucy.'

'I know – do you prefer it?'

'Don't you?'

'I think so, but I didn't enjoy changing.'

'I thought you were someone special then, Lucy.'

'You were very young for your age.'

'Yes. You seemed very . . . sophisticated, I suppose, worldly-wise. But I feel now you weren't a real person. It's as if you were pretending to be someone.'

She laughed again. This time her laughter was brittle and silvery. 'I enjoyed it. Do you think some people go through their whole lives pretending?'

'What, you mean like the Young Pretender?'

'No – be serious, Matthew. You know what I mean.'

'Maybe.' He rolled onto one side so his face was only a few inches above hers. 'And how do I know you're telling the truth now?'

'You don't,' she said. 'But isn't that half the fun?'

It was not long after that she told him her story. They had ridden up to the hills overlooking Morvah and lay on the grass, staring up at the empty blue sky. It was as if they were in a huge vestibule of light, and they lay surrounded and suspended in light; brilliant clear light that ascended and descended around them.

'The truth about Lucy Marchant,' she said. 'Would you like to know that?'

He continued chewing on his stick of grass.

'You were quite right the other night,' she went on. 'I was pretending to be someone. But the funny thing was, I was pretending to be Lucy Marchant.' She smiled.

'You know when I left Trevanion I had no intention of coming back. None whatsoever. I wouldn't even have come for the wedding if my mother hadn't insisted. Hah! I had it all planned. I was going to stay with my cousins in Bedfordshire – my father's side of the family – and establish myself as a young and eligible lady. And do you know, I nearly succeeded? That autumn we went to all the balls.'

Such talk reminded him of the old Lucy. He turned away but the gesture was not lost on her.

'Anyway, I won't bore you with the details,' she

said quickly. 'Let's just say the next year went to plan. I cultivated my acquaintances, and after two seasons in London, and a certain amount of determination, I found myself betrothed.' She looked at him. 'Don't look so shocked! I'm surprised my mother didn't tell you. Piers Loxman was his name, the eldest son of the Loxmans of Hertfordshire. His father had made his fortune trading with the colonies – saddles, leather goods, that sort of thing. Oh, looking back on it, I know I didn't love him, but love didn't really come into it – and I was very happy. Piers was quite a catch. Of course his parents thought he was marrying beneath him, but for all they knew I was heiress to an estate in Cornwall. I still might be, I suppose.'

'So what happened?' he asked brusquely.

Lucy leaned back in the grass and stared out over the sea.

'All this happened in January. Then at the end of February I had a visit from a man by the name of Phinehas Smartt. It turned out he was an agent acting for Piers' father.

' "Two months ago you had the good fortune to become betrothed to my master's son," said Mr Smartt. "Consequently Mr Loxman commissioned my services to enquire after the virtue of your private life."

'Mr Smartt explained there was nothing unusual in this when so much was at stake, but I was furious! Wait till Piers hears about this, I said. Then he gave me a particularly gleeful look. "He already has," he said. "That's why I'm here." '

Lucy paused for breath.

'I won't mince my words, Matthew. Mr Smartt told me I am illegitimate. Worse than that, he couldn't even be sure who my father was. The man I had grown up calling papa – who was Uncle Geoffrey's brother and who died of dysentery – was not even my mother's husband. And as for my mother . . .'

She turned towards him.

'Surprised, Matthew? Who was the most deceived? You or me? But there you have it. A "love-child". But I prefer the word bastard.'

'But how—'

'Do you want me to spell it out? My mother worked the streets, Matthew! A whore! She went with men for money, and I'm her daughter . . . Do you know what that makes me?' There were tears in her eyes. 'Mr Smartt had done his work well. He had some contacts who knew a friend of my mother's, an old friend, and he'd found my name in the parish register. There was no doubting it.'

'So what happened?'

'In the circumstances the Loxmans were generous. They undertook not to tell my uncle if I left London for good. When I think of it, it must have been quite embarrassing for them.'

'And what about your fiancé?'

'Oh, him? I tried writing to Piers. Of course he refused to see me.'

'Have you talked to Emily about this?'

'She knew. As soon as I came home, she knew. There really wasn't much to say.'

'But surely—'

'She's still my mother, Matthew! All those things

Mr Smartt told me, they happened a long time ago. My father – the man I thought was my father – had taken good care of her. She was always a respectable lady in Bath.'

Matthew thought for a moment. Lucy was right, there really wasn't much he could say.

He leaned over and began to pull at the tufts of coarse grass next to him.

'So,' she said, 'are you going to be like Piers Loxman?'

He carried on tugging at the grass.

'Are you ashamed of me now? I've—'

'You've said enough for one day,' he said suddenly and took hold of her. There on the open hills above Morvah they made love for the first time. Hot, violent, as if both wished to drive and beat out their own private demons in the heat of their lovemaking. As he entered her, it was Matthew, not Lucy, who cried out in pain and a feeling of terrible tenderness came over him. He felt her soft body squirm against the ground and the hardness of the ground hurt and fought against them, and he wanted to protect her and cushion her, and at the same time thrust her harder against that ground until she was all he had. Her small hard hands were against his flesh. Her eyes were filled with the sky. She lost herself in her actions and fought him every inch of the way. All she could feel was the pounding of the hard hot sun against her flesh and the hardness of the sun upon her and within her and Matthew was suddenly afraid of the soft, indescribably soft, thing he felt inside himself.

Afterwards they lay very still while the sunlight

dried their bodies. This was the most blessed time. Somehow the madness seemed to have burned away and there was nothing but stillness, a great empty stillness, and the sound of each other's breathing. They rode back slowly as the sun cast their shadows into long and monstrous shapes over the hills.

This was their betrothal, both of them knew instinctively. They told John and Emily as soon as they got back. They would be married in the autumn.

They went to the Midsummer Fair together, John, Emily, Matthew and Lucy. It was a glorious, merry day. Matthew had gone to fairs and feasts for as long as he could remember, yet this one always stayed in his mind, even many years later, when he was old and had children, and grandchildren, of his own.

Malaggan Common was a flat piece of grassland about three and a half acres in size. By the time they got there, the field was already packed with fairgoers. Amusements and stalls, called stannings, stood at the front, while around the back were drawn up the stocks and pens for the cattle and dairy markets. Everyone from the parish was there, as well as many from the villages along Mount's Bay, all done up in their best clothes and dresses. There was spirited competition among the ladies to see who had the finest bonnet, and the men sported bright neckties of orange, scarlet, crimson and mauve. Everywhere there were children, boys and girls decked out in fine and gaudy ribbons and bows, running and screaming and shrieking. Many of the girls had picked posies to sell for pocket-money, and the wealthier ladies bought these whether they would wear them or not.

Arm in arm, the four of them walked round the stannings. Many sold sweetmeats and biscuits: almond and ginger fairings, macaroons from St Ives, cinnamon rock and treacle toffee. These were mainly for the children, but Lucy and Emily had a weakness for sweets, and indulged themselves shamelessly. One of the stalls was selling hard leather balls, made from goatskin, for the boys to throw at the girls. Matthew bought a whole bagful and pelted Lucy and Emily, and the two women ran laughing and shrieking through the fairground.

In the afternoon, a party of acrobats juggled fire and swords, and turned somersaults, and a balladeer wandered the grounds and sang for a penny. By that time many of the audience had drunk so much they were insensible and fell asleep in the shade of the beeches.

For Ben Rhodda it was the best day of the year. He had set out rows of benches along the bottom of the Common, but even so The White Lamb was packed to the gills. As well as the usual beers and spirits, he served shenagrum and punch, and roasted a side of mutton over a huge bonfire. Later, when the sun began to mellow, the fairgoers danced around the fire, accompanied by fiddlers and a man with a great wooden drum.

Matthew took turns with Lucy and Emily. He enjoyed dancing with Lucy. Her skin glowed in the soft evening sun, and she had never looked happier. As they danced he held her close, much closer than he need. Yet if dancing with Lucy was a joy, dancing with Emily was a revelation. As if for the first time, she let herself relax with him, and showed him a different, warmer side. She joked and teased him in a way that reminded him of Lucy, but her wit was sharper and tougher, and she was that much more sure of herself. When he replied to her jibes she would mockingly arch her eyebrows. Beneath the thin cotton of her dress he became aware of her body as she turned and twisted in time to the music.

'You seem to be getting on much better with mother,' remarked Lucy. Yes, he replied, he was, yet he found Emily's behaviour disconcerting. It was as if she was being too friendly, as if she was taunting him. He noticed it again on the next dance. The way she smiled at him, the way she put her lips next to his ear to whisper something, the way she let her body push against his as they danced. Or was he being seduced by his own imagination?

'Come on! Let's eat.' John Trevanion returned from the cattle market and led them to a stanning serving great slices of pie which they sat munching in the shade of the trees. 'This here is right and toothsome!'

'A glorious day!' exclaimed Lucy. 'Glorious!' The sun was sinking behind the hills and the sky was ablaze with red and ochre, mauve and cadmium. 'Who could want for anything finer?'

After they had finished eating John went to The Lamb to fetch drinks. Lucy offered to help and Matthew found himself alone with Emily. She stretched and gazed out onto the Common. The fair-goers were dispersing now. Only around the bonfire and the benches were there still crowds.

'So, will you make Lucy happy, Matthew?' she said suddenly without altering her gaze.

'If she lets me and God willing,' he replied.

'I would like to give you both my blessing, but I need to be sure I can trust you.'

'Of course you can. Why think otherwise?'

'She's my only child, Matthew. After I had her, the physician said I would never bear children again.

'I haven't regretted not having more,' she continued, 'but I am perhaps more protective than I should be. You're a good man, Matthew. Don't disappoint me.' Emily turned and rested her hand on his knee.

'I won't, Emily,' he said softly. 'I promise.'

'Good.' She smiled, keeping her hand there. 'And give me lots of grandchildren, Matthew Trevanion.' She lifted her hand and ran her fingers across his forearm.

Neither spoke. Just then John and Lucy appeared at the bottom of the Common carrying four large glasses of beer. Matthew waved. Emily gazed at the beautiful sunset.

As they drove back that night, Matthew felt Lucy's head nod against his shoulder. Gently he slid his arm around her. She felt soft and vulnerable like that, and he wished the journey would last for hours. When they got to the farm, John insisted on toasting the midsummer. He was very happy and his face glowed red in the firelight. Lucy wanted to go to bed, but he wouldn't hear of it.

'What do you think midsummer is for?' he bellowed and poured four glasses of rum. 'To the midsummer!'

'The midsummer!'

'And my beautiful wife!' John slammed his drink down his throat, and reached for a second one: 'Let's wet the other eye!'

Later in the evening Matthew had gone to the kitchen for a cup of water. It had been a long day and his head was thick and aching.

'Tired?' Emily was standing in the doorway.

'My head's hurting, that's all.'

'Here, let me.' Emily placed her hands on his temples and began to rub them gently, rhythmically. Matthew closed his eyes and leaned his head back. It felt good. After a couple of minutes the pressure beneath his skull had started to fade.

'Better now?'

'Thank you.'

'Good.' Emily stopped massaging his head and kissed him once on the brow, then before he could react she was gone.

'Are you all right?' It was Lucy. 'I thought I'd check on you.'

'Check? How do you mean check?' he answered irritably.

'Matthew!' Lucy looked hurt.

'I'm sorry,' he apologised, 'I've got a terrible headache. I didn't mean to lose my temper.' He was angry with himself. How could he spoil such a perfect day?

He hugged her.

'I love you,' he said.

'I love you, Matthew.'

Perhaps it would be as simple as that.

During the weeks that followed Matthew saw little

of Emily and John. He was kept busy at Rosmear and Lucy came there. In a few months they would be married. As they discussed the preparations, Matthew wondered how Lucy must feel, looking forward to her wedding for the second time, but if it bothered her she gave no indication, unless it was in her unwillingness for them to make love again. 'You can wait,' she insisted. 'It's not right. Not yet.' And he would silently curse. It wasn't as if she'd been a virgin, he thought grimly. Not like him. Still, they were good times, so good they later seemed unreal, perhaps untrue.

Then one afternoon when he was working in the fields, he saw a rider cutting across the grass towards him. It was Emily. She had on a sheer black riding jacket and britches.

'Lovely day, isn't it?' She smiled at him beautifully. 'I've come to ask a favour,' she explained. 'Something I don't want Lucy to know.' She looked nervous, Matthew decided, not her usual self.

'It's a small thing, really. Can we sit down?' She swung herself from the saddle and put herself next to him. 'There's a lady in Mousehole,' she went on, 'who's fallen on distressed times. A friend of mine told me. The poor woman's husband died and she has no money. If she isn't helped, I don't know what will become of her.' Emily sounded embarrassed and chose her words with great awkwardness. He was touched.

'You want me to help?'

'This woman needs to be brought money every week. Not a lot, but enough, until she can fend for herself. Could you take it for me?'

Matthew was puzzled. 'Certainly, but why can't you take it yourself?'

She looked flustered.

'I'd love to, but how can I say this?' She was momentarily at a loss. 'It's your uncle, Matthew, he's forbidden me to have anything to do with her. If he even found out I'd talked to you, he'd be furious.'

'But why? I don't—'

'There are some things about your uncle that are hard to understand,' she said quickly. 'Trust me, Matthew. I wouldn't be asking unless it was important.' She produced a small leather purse. 'Here, this is her first week's instalment. Oh, and there's a letter for her too.'

Matthew stuffed it into his pocket. 'All right, Emily, have it your way.'

'Thank you, Matthew. I knew I could rely on you.' She flashed a smile at him. 'Here, help me back up, will you?' He put his hands round her waist and she leaned against him while she got her grip on the saddle. Matthew watched as she cantered across the field and into the blue haze of the afternoon.

Matthew found the place on the third attempt. It was at the top of a flight of granite steps which ran up the outside of a sailmaker's store. He knocked on the door and a second later it swung open.

Marcy Towan was a lot younger than he had expected. She had a thick head of black hair, not unlike Lucy's, and broad handsome cheekbones. Matthew noticed she nursed a dull bluish bruise across one side of her face. Marcy knew who he was, for as soon as he mentioned Emily, she smiled and asked him in.

'I can see the family resemblance,' she said.

Her home consisted of a low dark room with a hearth in one wall and a window in the other. It was sparsely furnished with a table, two chairs, and a mattress slung underneath the window. An air of shabbiness hung in the room like a sour smell. Marcy wiped her nose on her sleeve and insisted on pouring them both a cup of wine from a large earthenware jug. He judged this would not be her first of the day. As they drank, she counted out the coins on the table in front of him, her face beaming like a child's. Matthew realised he had forgotten to give her the letter. She seemed even more delighted with this and read it greedily. 'I must write her a reply,' she said, and Matthew sipped at his wine while she scratched a few words on the back of the letter with a quill and ink. When she had finished she folded it, sealed it, and gave it to him.

'You've been very kind to me, sir. Please thank your aunt for me again.' Marcy seemed almost pathetically grateful and waved goodbye from the top of the steps. She caught the eye of a fisherman mending his nets.

'You've been busy today, Marcy!' he laughed. Matthew scowled.

'Shut your mouth, Jack, or I'll shut it for you!' Marcy shouted back and burst out laughing. She shot a glance at Matthew and disappeared inside.

When Emily called on him the next day she was delighted with the note. 'Excellent,' she said, 'I'll be round next week.' And so the routine started. Soon Matthew came to quite enjoy his trips to Mousehole. His meetings with Emily felt suitably clandestine and Marcy made him welcome with a cup of wine or beer. Each week she would count the money in front of him, and each week she would write to Emily on the back of the letter. August rolled into September, and Matthew began to reckon the days. In less than six weeks, he and Lucy would be man and wife.

One day late in August John took him for a ride towards Hayle. He had some business with a mining engineer and said he'd enjoy the company. For the first few miles they rode in amicable silence, but when they passed Penzance, John's horse became thirsty and they pulled up on the banks of the Trevaylor.

'So are you feeling nervous yet, boy?'

It was strange that after all these years his uncle still called him 'boy'.

'I suppose so. But I'll be glad to get it over and done.'

John gazed at Jessie's head as she bent down to drink. He smiled to himself. 'Who'd have thought it would turn out like this, eh?'

'Are you pleased, Uncle?'

'Pleased? I'm delighted! Just think, in six weeks time I won't be your uncle any more. I'll be your father.' John stared into the stream. 'I've been thinking – after you're married why not move into the manor?'

'What about Mother?'

'She can move in too. There's plenty of room.'

Matthew was not so sure his mother would agree, but he let that go. After all, it was the gesture that mattered.

Two days later, he went to see Marcy, but this time when he knocked on the door there was no reply. He looked round, then knocked again. Perhaps she had gone to the wells for water. He was just about to go there himself when he heard someone moving around inside.

'Marcy! Is that you? It's Matthew!'

It was quiet for a moment then he heard her voice, softer and weaker than usual.

'Matthew? Come in.'

Matthew opened the door. A blanket was hung over the window and it took a while for his eyes to adjust. Then he saw Marcy wrapped in a coat and lying on the bed. She looked at him through swollen eyes.

'Marcy! Are you all right?'

She shivered and sat up. 'I feel awful sick,' she said. 'I must have dozed off. Were you out there long?'

Matthew felt sorry for her. Her normally ruddy cheeks were sallow and dull, and her hair hung lank down the sides of her face. He felt her forehead; it was sticky and stale with sweat. He hoped his feelings of distaste were not obvious.

'You've got a fever. How long have you been like this?'

She thought.

'Three or four days.'

'Anyone seen you?'

Marcy shook her head. Matthew reached into his pocket.

'Here, take this to one of the women round here and get her to look at you.'

'Thank you, Matthew. Thank you very much.' She put the money in her coat. She smiled at him. 'Where am I, forgetting my manners like that? Won't you make yourself welcome?' She indicated the jug in the corner. Matthew knew it would be rude to refuse and poured himself a cup.

'Have you got a letter for me?'

'Yes. All in good time, Marcy.' He delved into his pocket and passed Emily's gifts over to her. Sick as she was, Marcy kept to the same ritual of counting out the coins. This week, however, something seemed wrong. After counting them once she shook her head and started all over again. Eventually she looked up.

'It's not all here!' she said, suddenly angry.

'Of course it's all there. It's just as she gave it to me.'

'It's not all here!' Marcy repeated stubbornly.

'Well, don't worry. I'm sure it's just an oversight. She'll make it up.'

'No,' said Marcy with some conviction. 'She won't! I know what's happened, you're cheating on me!'

Matthew would have been angry if her accusations were not so pathetic.

'Don't be ridiculous, Marcy!' He hoped he didn't sound too patronising, but he felt as if he were talking to a small child, not a woman his own age. 'No one's going to cheat you. Don't you think I've got better things to do than steal pennies off a poor woman like you?' But this angered her all the more.

'You're all the bloody same!' she shouted. 'I thought you were different, Matthew.' Marcy hurled the money across the room. She was almost hysterical.

'Calm down, Marcy! The whole street can hear you!' Matthew winced. How did he get himself into this? But she took no notice.

'Cheat me out of my money, would you?'

'Listen, Marcy, you've got it wrong.'

'Liar!'

'Tell me what's missing and I'll make it up to you. Just stop screaming!'

'Liar! You filthy—' She ran at him, tears streaming down her face.

'Shut up! Shut up!'

In panic, he seized her roughly by the shoulders and shook her hard. She screamed and struggled, but that made him only more determined not to let go.

'Shut up!'

Suddenly she stopped struggling and became weak and lifeless. She flopped against him. Matthew realised he was breathing heavily.

'Marcy? Are you all right?'

She made no sound.

I've killed her, he thought.

Then she began to sob. Thank God. Marcy wept uncontrollably, like a child. Matthew picked her up and placed her back on the bed. She lay there sobbing into the mattress.

'Marcy? I'm sorry.' Ignoring his own feelings, he

put his hand reassuringly on her back, but she made no response.

After a while, Marcy stopped crying but she stayed lying face down on the mattress. Matthew felt uncomfortable.

'Marcy – I've got to be getting back.' He moved towards the door.

'Wait.' Her voice came from the bed. 'I've got to write to Mrs Trevanion.'

Matthew looked at her. Marcy was smearing the tears across her face with the corner of her sleeve. She was clearly in no fit state.

'It's all right, Marcy. I'll tell her.'

'No.' Marcy sounded suddenly clear-headed. 'I must write to her. I promised.'

Matthew shifted uneasily. He just wanted to go.

'Look,' he said impatiently. 'Tell me what you want to say and I'll write it for you!'

This idea seemed to appeal to Marcy, and she sat up in bed and wiped her eyes again. Matthew wondered if she was often like this.

'All right,' she said.

He turned Emily's letter over and spread it on the table. 'What do you want me to write?' He dipped the quill into the pot of ink.

'Do you promise to write down exactly what I tell you?' she asked.

'Yes, Marcy.'

'Do you promise?'

'I promise.'

Marcy collected her thoughts. She closed her eyes and he watched her steady herself.

'My dear lady,' she began. 'May you accept my humble thanks for the great service . . .'

'Slowly, please.' He was having difficulty with the quill. It should have been thrown out weeks ago.

'And devotion you have shown me. Even though I must soon leave you . . .'

'Must soon . . . leave . . . you,' he repeated, making her slow down.

'I will never forget you and will remain . . .'

'Remain . . .'

'Your dearest and most loving friend.' Marcy sat back. 'There – that should be it. Let me sign it,' she added quickly.

Matthew finished writing. He passed her the paper and she read it word for word.

'Yes, that's it.' She pulled herself up to the table and signed with her initials, M.T., then she folded the letter and sealed it.

'Are you going away soon, Marcy?'

'In the next week or so. This might be the last time you see me, Matthew,' and with that she kissed him on the cheek.

'I must be going, Marcy.'

Matthew was relieved when he finally stood outside on the staircase. It was only when he breathed in the fresh sea-air that he realised how stuffy her room had been.

The next day Matthew was digging out a ditch in the Four Acre Field when he saw his uncle come riding down the lane. He was clearly in a hurry for he let the gate swing open behind him and kicked Jessie into a canter across the field. Matthew stood

up and leaned on his spade, he was glad of the
break. He saw the expression on his uncle's face too
late.

'You bastard!'

John's left boot caught him full in the chest,
knocked him to the ground.

'Bastard!'

Matthew doubled up. There was a terrible pain in
his chest. His lungs gasped for air. His head buzzed.
What? He willed himself to react, but John was
already down from the saddle and crossed the
ground between them. The first blow caught
Matthew on the left temple. Move! he screamed to
himself. Move! Then a fist hit him again and he lost
track of where he was. He spun his head round and
felt his uncle's boot as it passed his cheek. John
swore. Matthew tried to get on all-fours. If only his
head would clear. John was coming at him, snorting
and bellowing. This time Matthew got a hand to
his blow, but the brute weight of it punched him
backwards. Then John was on him. He's going to
kill me, Matthew realised, but his thoughts were
calm, as if from a long way away. John had him by
the throat with one hand.

'John! John!'

Mary was running from the cottage. John was distracted only for a second but it was enough. Matthew
jammed his fingers as hard as he could into his
uncle's neck. John gasped and released his grip.
Matthew fell to the ground, frantically clawing his
way backwards. But John was already on him and
they went over together, rolling and clawing in the
mud. The moist wet earth embraced them as they

wrestled, arms straining hard, biting, gouging, tearing blindly, grunting like animals. Then John got an arm round his neck. Matthew forced his hand upwards against his chin, but it was a poor substitute. His head swam. A hot pain burned in his temples. Somewhere his mother was shouting at them. In a moment it would be finished. With a last effort, he dragged his legs up under his body and heaved. John's arm was as hard as wood around his neck. He heaved again. There was a terrible buzzing in his ears. Slowly, at first very slowly, but then gradually gathering momentum, he felt himself shifting John backwards. Why was he so heavy? Blackness, all he saw was blackness. Someone was screaming. He heaved. With a grunt John toppled back and Matthew was free. The two men crouched where they were and eyed each other. They were both panting. Matthew tried to speak and found his lips were thick and useless.

'Stop it, both of you!' Mary was standing beside them. She looked frantic.

'Out of my way, Mary! This is between me and the boy.'

Matthew knew he couldn't take his gaze off him for an instant. His mother stepped forwards; she was in the way and he wondered whether John would come through her. He had never seen a look in his uncle's eyes like this. He would scarcely have recognised him.

'Get out of here, Mother!'

'He's right, Mary, this is not for you.' John backed away to where Jessie was standing. He pulled a thick wooden stick from the saddle. It was a good three feet long. He felt the weight of it against his palm. Mary screamed. Matthew could see she didn't know who to run to.

'Get out of here!' he shouted again.

His uncle came slowly towards him. Matthew poised himself, trying to guess when the attack would come. He wanted to say something, but in the end it came down to just one word.

'Why?'

'You know bloody well why!'

He tried to think.

'What? What do you mean?'

His uncle ignored him. He took a guess.

'Emily? Is it about Emily?'

John took a step closer. Mary came towards him.

'John, what's happened?'

He brushed her aside.

'Your bloody son! He's been fucking some whore in town! A filthy fucking whore!'

'What, Marcy Towan? Is that who you mean?'

'*Poldeen*, Matthew! Her name's Poldeen! She came crying out to the farm this morning!'

'She came to Trevanion?' Matthew tried to sound shocked. 'Wasn't Emily there? Didn't she see her?'

John snorted in disgust. 'We all saw her.'

'But I don't understand – if it's Marcy, Emily knows her.'

A monstrous expression passed over John's face. 'No!' Even though Matthew saw him coming, he only just moved aside. John was so quick. John lunged with the stick, then swung it sideways. Matthew jumped to the right; the tip of the club kissed his forearm. They circled each other. If only he could catch John off balance. Suddenly Mary threw herself on to John's back. He roared with anger and hit her hard with his elbow. Matthew watched his mother crumple to the ground. He sprang forwards and gripped the stick in the middle. His uncle's grasp was hard like a vice. They heaved and shoved at each other for the best part of a minute that seemed to last forever. Then John thrust forwards, and Matthew went with the motion. They went over again, but this time Matthew was on top. This was it. He got his knee on to the stick and pushed down hard. Before John knew what he was doing, he had worked the stick across his uncle's windpipe and began to squeeze downwards. It was all so easy. The harder he pushed, the weaker his uncle would become. The look of blind rage in John's eyes was now one of fear, dumb ignorant fear. It was the look of an animal, thought Matthew. He pushed down. He was a heavy man, only slightly less heavy than his uncle.

'Matthew! Stop it!' He ignored his mother. His head sang. He was laughing, laughing with relief, he was laughing because he saw the other man's fear. John's face was turning blue. Suddenly Matthew released his hold and jumped back. He stared down at his uncle. John was retching for breath. What was happening? His mother ran past him and lifted John's head in her hands.

Matthew stepped away. He let go of the stick. Mary gave him a frightened look.

'If you ever come to Trevanion again, I will kill you.' John's words came in hoarse pants. 'If ever you come near Lucy, I will kill you.'

Even now, he would attack me again, if he could, Matthew realised.

'You were like a son to me, Matthew! That woman's a whore! Whore!'

'But didn't Emily—'

'She's as disgusted as I am! How dare you!' John shook Mary off and struggled to his feet. 'Don't worry, Mary, I'll not waste my strength on him.' He limped over to Jessie and swung himself into the saddle.

Matthew watched him. Of course, he should have realised.

'Aren't you going to say anything?' asked his mother. 'You can't just let him ride off. What about Lucy?'

'No, Mother,' said Matthew. 'This is more complicated than you suspect.'

It was more complicated than any of them suspected.

John paused and spat on the ground. His spittle was thick and red. Then he pulled on Jessie's reins and made off over the fields.

Damn Emily! Matthew did not watch him go but was already heading back to the cottage as fast as he could. Now the heat of the fight had passed, he felt cold and his injuries were aching. Something was wet on his forehead, and putting his fingers to it, he discovered he was bleeding profusely. Damn! In the corner of the yard there stood a pail of water from the well. He kneeled and immersed his head. The water was cold but it cleared his thoughts. He looked round the yard as if trying to catch his bearings. The air was cold. He felt light-headed and steadied himself against the cottage, then the feeling passed and he was across the yard and into the stables. He had Saph bridled and saddled by the time his mother caught up with him.

'Matthew, stop! Where are you going?'

He made no reply, and only paused to check the girth strap was tight before hauling himself into the saddle.

'Wait! You can't go like that!' Mary tried to catch Saph's reins but he shook them out of her hands.

'I'll be back later!' He guided Saph into the yard.

'But, Matthew!'

Matthew turned in the saddle. Tears were streaming down Mary's face.

'If Lucy comes, tell her I've gone to sort things out. And tell her I love her.' He kicked Saph into a gallop and disappeared up the lane.

He took the steps to Marcy's room two at a time. The door kicked open. Empty. The bed, the table, the chairs were there, but Marcy's possessions were gone. He picked up the pitcher from its place in the corner of the room. It was half-full and the wine was fresh – she must have gone today. He threw the jug against the far wall and ran back outside. An old woman was looking up at him suspiciously.

'You!' he shouted. 'Have you seen the woman who lived here?' The old woman looked terrified. He realised his face was caked in blood. He clutched at the railings to steady himself. 'Please. It's very important.' By now a group of women were standing watching him.

'Here,' said one of them. 'I know you – you're that one been visiting her, aren't 'ee?'

'Where's she gone?'

'Don' know, must've been early – I've been doin' my washes all day, 'aven't seen her.'

'Didn't any of you see her? Surely one of you must have seen her!' He was desperate.

'You know, you're not the first to be asking,' piped up another woman.

'Who else was?'

'A lady – proper lady, mind. Came round about an hour ago.'

'This lady, what did she look like?'

The woman thought a bit. 'Dark hair, prettyish, dressed up all fancy. A proper lady.'

Emily, it had to be. He tried to think. He felt cold and stiff. 'What about the sailmaker, would he know where she's gone?'

'You'd 'ave to ask 'im.'

Matthew ran down the steps to the storeroom underneath. It was locked.

'Try 'im on the quay,' someone suggested. He ran to the quay. An hour later he found the sailmaker sitting in The Pelican and smoking. No, he didn't know where she'd gone. In fact, he said, scratching his chin, he was surprised she had gone. She'd paid him for another week only yesterday.

Matthew was leaving when a thought struck him. 'This girl, what was her surname?'

The sailmaker gave him an odd look.

'Why, Towan of course. Marcy Towan.'

By the time he got back to Saph, he felt exhausted. A sharp breeze was blowing and he regretted not taking a coat. He flicked the reins. For one wild moment he considered going straight to Trevanion and confronting them all, but the way he felt he wouldn't be a match for anyone. The bitch! I don't know how she's done it, but she's got us trussed like lambs for the slaughter.

It was almost night when Saph finally turned into the lane at Rosmear. Mary was at the door to meet him. She looked anxious.

'Don't worry,' he said. 'Nothing's happened.'

'Are you all right?'

'No, I don't think so.' He pushed past her and into the cottage. The fire was burning warmly and he slumped in front of it. He was so tired he could hardly move. Mary followed him in.

'Lucy, did she come?'

'No, there's been nothing.'

He looked up at her. 'I'm sorry,' he said.

Matthew woke after sunrise with a raging temperature and soaked in sweat. His skin felt as if it was crawling with a swarm of insects. He shivered. His arms and legs were shaking. When Mary found him, he was rambling wildly. He remained like that for the next three days. Mary nursed him as best she could, but when on the fourth day he showed no sign of any improvement, she grew concerned. Matthew was not normally sick, and he had never been ill like this. There were rare moments of lucidity, when he would talk quite sanely and ask her what was happening, once he asked if Lucy had come to see him, but apart from that he was wild and incoherent and full of madnesses.

Towards evening on the fourth day Mary sent Nancy for An Jenny Garrick.

An Jenny was an old woman who lived alone in a cottage above Boskenna. She made her living by selling charms and remedies and heal-alls. An Jenny was a witch.

Jack Pengilly claimed that when he was a boy he had once crept up to her window – she was old even then – and there she had been conversing with a huge, bloated toad sitting on a stool in front of the fire. As well as her fondness for toads, An Jenny kept an ugly beast of a cat called Tiff which hissed and spat like a spriggan. People said that on nights when the moon was full, Tiff became huge and monstrous and accompanied his mistress as she rode across the skies on a stick of ragwort.

Mary was waiting for her at the door. An Jenny went straight through to where Matthew lay in the lean-to. His fever had started to rise again and the small cramped space was heavy with stale sweat. An Jenny bent down and sniffed the body.

'How long's he been like this?' she whispered.

'Since Friday morning.'

An Jenny muttered something to herself and plucked at Matthew's face with a yellow claw-like hand. She prodded his neck and felt the temperature of his body. Finally she pulled open his mouth and peered at his teeth and gums.

'What is it? Do you know what it is?' asked Mary.

An Jenny scratched herself before answering. 'Tell me. Have you noticed anything strange recently?'

'Strange?'

'Did the milk curdle one morning – or the butter refuse to set?'

Mary tried to remember. She shook her head.

'How about the cows – has any of them stopped giving milk? Or have you seen any creatures keeping close to the cottage, like a hare or a toad?'

Mary was not sure how seriously she should take the old woman's questioning. She had expected a poultice or a compound of some kind, but seeing Matthew lying on the mattress, she felt more uneasy than she cared to admit.

'Why do you ask?'

An Jenny wetted her lips. 'I don't know. Maybe your boy's got an autumn chill. But I don't know. What was he doing before he fell sick?'

Mary told her.

'Yes,' she went on, 'he could have got a chill. But it's certainly no ordinary chill. Are you sure you've seen nothing unusual?'

'No, nothing at all. Surely you . . .'

But An Jenny was already ignoring her and crouched down over the mattress again. Months later Matthew could still recall the old woman's face looming over him and her dry foul breath against his flesh. She began to mumble something, some rhyme or form of words, in an odd, seesawing voice. Then she reached inside her shawl and produced a sprig of dried herbs that gave off a pungent, camphorous smell. With this sprig An Jenny proceeded to strike Matthew three times on the forehead.

'Hang this above his bed,' she instructed, then putting her hand inside her basket, she pulled out her prized possession. Mary had never seen a cat so big. 'Be off with you, Tiff!' She carefully placed the cat on the ground. 'If there's any little creatures about, Tiff is sure to catch them. Wicked nasty beasts!' she explained. Tiff sniffed the ground several times in a way that reminded Mary of his mistress, then darted off.

'In the meantime,' said An Jenny, 'boil a spoonful of this in a glass of water and give it to him three times a day – and nothing else mind.'

'Is that all?'

'If you want to be sure, use water you've drawn from St Levan's well.' And with that and her payment An Jenny left, though where her cat had gone Mary did not know.

The next morning Mary made the long walk to St Levan's well. For the next three days she nursed Matthew night and day, boiling the water and mixing it with the powder An Jenny had given her. 'Not that it may do you much good,' she thought, but she was too worried to be sceptical. Once, when she was chopping logs in the yard, she was startled to see a large dark hare sitting on its haunches and watching her. Mary reached for the axe but it had already gone. On the third day An Jenny came back and, seeing no improvement, spent a long time muttering and keening over his body. Then she gave Mary more of the bitter-tasting powder and went on her way. Again Mary made the walk to St Levan. She wished John was there to help – but that was out of the question.

Matthew remained sunk in fever. He had eaten nothing for the best part of a week and he was now starting to fail through lack of food. Mary began to doubt An Jenny's prescription. He seemed to be getting worse, not better. All Matthew could later remember of those days, was the never-ending sound of the sea, the sound of the waves as they pitched and rolled above him. Sometimes the room was filled with the roar and crash of the waves so he could hear nothing else, then he would feel he was drowning and would struggle for air. John Trevanion's arm was clamped around his windpipe and Emily swam out in the sea to embrace him. Where is Lucy? he heard himself crying. Why isn't she here?

Then just before sunset, on the seventh day after An Jenny first visited, Matthew woke from a light sleep and saw his mother watching him. The fever had lifted.

It took four days of food and rest before he could walk around the cottage, and another four days before he was strong enough to venture outside. During that time he pieced together what had happened before he fell ill – initially he could remember nothing. An Jenny came once more and seemed pleased by his progress. Before she left she insisted on burning the sprig of herbs and sprinkling him with the ashes.

The Reverend Morecombe also visited, though thankfully not on the same day. Matthew asked him about Lucy but the parson had not seen her.

As his strength returned, Matthew grew impatient. On the day he managed to chop a whole basket of logs he knew he was well enough and called Saph in from the paddock. He had no clear idea what he was going to say or do, except that the answer must lie with Lucy at Trevanion.

'Matthew!'

Matthew tried to analyse the tone in Emily's voice –

tenderness? hurt? resentment? mockery? – she could have felt all these things. She was standing in the porch, clutching a basket of flowers and watching him as he rode into the yard.

'Hello, Emily.' He sat hunched in the saddle – the ride had tired him more than he had expected.

'You won't find either of them here.'

'Then it's just you and me. I was hoping we could catch up.'

Emily blanched but did not look away.

'What is there to say, Matthew?'

'What about how you embroiled me with that girl in Mousehole, Marcy Towan, or is it Poldeen?'

'I asked you to do a simple, discreet—'

'Discreet? Don't make me laugh! You tricked me! There's no way you're—'

'Oh, I'm begging your pardon, Mrs Trevanion!' Mary Vincent appeared round the side of the building.

'I think you'd better come inside,' said Emily hastily.

'If you insist.' Matthew dismounted and followed her in.

'How dare you accuse me!' Emily continued as soon as the parlour door was closed. 'I trusted you with a delicate task, something I could not do myself, and before I know it, the girl's round here – of all places! – and pregnant to boot, and to cap it all she says it's your child! Can you really blame me—'

'What? She's pregnant?'

'So she said. How do you expect us to react?'

Pregnant! Matthew could hardly believe his ears.

'But this is all lies, Emily! As you damn well know.

I can't believe we're having this conversation – you tricked me! I thought I was doing you a favour. And then writing that note – I've worked it all out – how could I have been so stupid! You never wanted me to marry your precious little daughter, did you?'

'Don't be ridiculous!'

'Why do you hate me so much?' Matthew was shouting. He stepped towards her.

'If you lay a finger on me, Matthew—'

'Don't worry, Aunt, I'm not in your class, am I? You're used to men who can pay for the privilege.'

'How dare you!'

'You make me sick! Your sweet little Lucy can't marry into the right society because everyone knows you earned your money on your back – and then when she's reduced to the likes of me, you just can't let that be!'

Emily was white with anger and he thought she was going to slap him across the face. But she mastered her impulse and pulled herself back.

'Get out of here.' Emily did not even raise her voice.

'I pity you, Emily. I'm going to tell Lucy exactly what happened.'

'Lucy's gone.'

Matthew felt as if he had stepped out into empty space.

'What – where?'

'You don't honestly expect me to tell you? You're more stupid than I thought.' She arched her eyebrows. 'I didn't even have to persuade her. Your uncle insisted she left straightaway. You haven't got the faintest idea about Marcy Towan, have you? And you're fucking *her*! I never wanted you as my son-in-law. But I never realised you were such a vain, self-centred oaf.'

'What do you mean by—' Matthew felt suddenly uneasy. The conversation was not supposed to go like this.

'And don't play the puritan with me, Matthew. You can hardly say you loved Lucy – all you've ever wanted is John's estate!'

'That's not true!'

'Now who's lying?'

'You bitch!'

'Get out of here,' she repeated slowly. 'Or I'll scream. You've got no proof, have you? No one believes you, Matthew.'

It was only when she was sure he had gone and she was alone that Emily locked herself in her bedroom and broke down and cried.

Two weeks later they found Marcy's body. Her throat had been cut and her body wedged into a drainage adit just south of Zennor. A miner found her during a routine survey and as Mousehole was her last known place of residence, they buried her in the parish graveyard at Paul.

PART THREE

Chapter One

'I RECKON IT WAS A GHOST for sure.' George Trevose put down his glass firmly on the table. 'I told you Victor saw a ghost.'

They were sitting in The White Lamb in Malaggan.

Matthew stared sullenly into his beer. He shook his head. 'I'm telling you it was no ghost. He was as flesh and blood as you and I.'

'Don't be daft! We both saw him buried. You can go and see for yourself.' George gestured over his shoulder towards the churchyard.

'I'm telling you it was my uncle.'

'So what happened when you got to him?'

Matthew frowned. 'As I've said, I can't remember. He was no more than twenty feet away – thirty at most. He turned and then ... I must have passed out or lost my balance. The next thing, I was lying on the ground with my face full of earth.'

'And your uncle?'

'Gone. I couldn't tell how long I'd been there.'

George Trevose took another mouthful of beer. He wiped his lips with the back of his hand. 'It isn't right when the dead walk abroad. There's no telling where it will end.' He gave Matthew a queer look.

'It was no ghost!'

'So you keep saying,' said George patiently. 'What did he look like, then?'

'Just the same as he always did.'

'What – same clothes, same expression?'

'I don't know. It was very dark.'

'Have you heard about the time Danny and Amos met Captain Vincent on the road to Penzance?'

'What, Mary Vincent's husband?'

'That's the one. They met him walking up the hill from Mousehole. "Back all ready?" they asked, for he'd only set off that morning. "I must be going home, boys," he said in a strange sort of voice, as if his mouth were full of soil, and with that he walked right past them and on up the road.' George fumbled in his pocket for his pipe. 'It was only when they got home that night that they heard the Captain's ship had gone down off the Manacles. His body was washed up two weeks later.'

Matthew had heard the story told when he was a boy, but it was a different Captain, and a different death.

'What were you going to tell me the other day – about the time you went to Goss Moor?'

'Oh that. I still don't know whether that was anything or not.'

'What did you see?'

'See? Nothing at all. It was what I *heard*.' George leaned over the table towards him. 'It must have been four or five summers ago. I'd been up to Bodmin on business and was coming back over the moors when night fell. It's not a safe place, Goss Moor, after dark. There's a lot of venturing goes on up there and the locals don't take kindly to strangers. But I figured I knew most of the carriers, so I should be as safe as anyone. Anyway, I was riding along and all of a sudden I hear the sound of hooves galloping towards me. Coming on at a ferocious pace they were, so I pulled my horse off the path and down into a ditch. The last thing I wanted was to meet with someone riding like that. So I waited in the ditch and the hooves grew louder and louder and I could hear that the rider, whoever he was, had brought his dogs with him, for he was calling to them over the sound of the horse. "Hulloah! Hulloah!" he was shouting. Right, I thought, let's see who it is, for he sounded like he could be no more than a few feet away. So I looked out of the ditch.' George's voice had sunk to a whisper and he leaned across the table. 'There was no one there. The road was empty. But that horse sounded closer than ever. I could hear its breathing, and the shouting of the rider. But I couldn't see anything. Then the sound passed, and it was gone away into the distance.'

'Do you know what it was?'

'Not to this day.'

'Couldn't it have been a trick of the wind?'

George tapped his pipe on the table. 'Could be.'

'I don't know, George. That whole thing last night in the graveyard—'

'Are you sure you saw him, Matthew? You said you'd been drinking.'

'I've been thinking that myself.' Matthew regarded his glass of beer suspiciously. 'Of course there's one thing I could do,' he said finally. 'Dig up the grave.'

George looked at him as if he was mad.

'It's the obvious thing to do,' Matthew explained quickly.

'But for heaven's sake, man! He's been buried less than two days!'

'But has he?'

'You saw his body in the crypt, didn't you?'

George was right. Yet he had seen his uncle walking through the churchyard as alive as the day he was born.

'I went back there this morning to have a look around.'

'See anything?'

Matthew shook his head. 'Nothing. I thought there might be bootmarks or something.'

George drained his glass. 'You know,' he said, 'there is another explanation.'

'What's that?'

'Take a look at yourself, Matthey boy. You look exhausted! I'm not surprised you passed out in the churchyard. And it's not hard to know why. I felt the same when my father died. Don't you think you *wanted* to see your uncle in the graveyard?'

Matthew looked sceptical, but he knew George was probably right.

'If you go to the parson and say you've seen your uncle's ghost,' George went on, 'he won't be rushing around with the holy water. No, he'll be sitting you down and telling you to let the dead rest in peace.'

'Perhaps you're right,' Matthew conceded. 'I need to rest.'

Just then, Freddy Dunstan came in, and made his way over to them, and Matthew whispered to George: 'But not a word to anyone, about what I saw!'

So far, not even his mother knew what he had

seen that night. And that was the way he wanted to keep it.

The next day was a Sunday and after church Matthew went and stood in the graveyard for a few minutes. It seemed the same as it always had: quiet, peaceful, a little run-down. He went to John Trevanion's grave. The mason had not completed the stone yet, and it was still unmarked, except for a temporary wooden cross. On all sides, John was surrounded by his forefathers. This was how it should be. Matthew looked at the inscriptions.

'Joseph Trevanion, departed this life 5th December 1654, aged 47 years, may he rest in the Lord.'

'Delia Trevanion, gave up her soul this 14th day of March, 1671, aged 74.'

'Rose Trevanion, beloved daughter, sadly taken to the Lord in the first year of life, died March 13th 1699, born Sept 20th 1698.'

One of the engravings seemed larger and grander than the others. It read:

Here lies the body of
ROBERT TREVANION of Trevanion, Esquire
Who being born in the Year of our Lord 1657,
passed his life in the Service of his Estate and
Family.
Much troubled by the worries of this
World he departed this Life for a better one
the 2nd day of October 1705.

Here likewise be interred
his amiable and affectionate wife,

AMANDA,
only daughter of Richard Hamblyn
of Tredalston Manor, Gwennap.
She died March 3rd, 1703, aged 35 years,
leaving behind her two small children to lament
her passing.

Robert Trevanion, he must have been John's father
– my grandfather, thought Matthew. It was odd, but
he had never asked his uncle about his childhood.
George was right, it would be all too easy for me to
wish him back, he realised.

That afternoon he went riding with Lucy over the
hills to Morvah. The scenery reminded him of other
trips they had made together more than a year ago,
and he felt she had the same memories. They stood
overlooking the sea, boiling and foaming beneath
them, but they did not talk, and the memory faded.

Chapter Two

'MASTER TREVANION! TO WHAT DO I owe the pleasure?'

Matthew found himself shown into a large, disorganised office. Joshua Pascoe rose from his chair to greet him and extended his hand across a desk which must have been at least eight feet long and was littered with a vast profusion of papers, documents, and writing paraphernalia of every description. On the two walls facing him and to the left, bookcases stretched to the ceiling, crammed with series of leather-bound books and folders wrapped in scarlet ribbons. A poor grey light filtered in through two sash windows in the right-hand wall but was offset by the two writing lamps that glowed warmly on each corner of the desk. Matthew took the lawyer's hand and shook it firmly.

'It is on a professional matter, Mr Pascoe. One concerning my late uncle.'

'I see. Thank you, Edward, you can go now,' he said to the middle-aged, mouse-like clerk who had shown him in. The door closed behind him.

'Won't you take a seat?' The solicitor indicated a sturdy, leather-upholstered chair in front of his desk. Matthew sat down and studied the man opposite him.

Everyone in Penzance knew Joshua Pascoe, attorney and commissioner of oaths, by sight. Joshua

Pascoe had an unusually tall, wiry build like that of a youth, yet his hair was a brilliant grey and hung in an exceptionally long queue down the back of his neck. His face was also pale, and thin-lipped, and distinguished by a prominent hooked nose. Mr Pascoe accentuated these features by dressing in close-fitting suits of only the severest black or grey. It was his opinion these lent him the aura of probity and professionalism essential for his business.

Joshua Pascoe also sat down and made some show of carefully sorting his papers into orderly piles and squaring them off by tapping them on the desk. Matthew waited. Joshua Pascoe was in no hurry. At last he came to the final pile, looked up and smiled thinly.

'I hope you will indulge my fastidiousness, Mr Trevanion. It is an essential quality in my profession. Now, where were we? Ah, yes, your uncle. A very unfortunate affair. I knew your uncle for the best part of forty years. We'll miss him very much.'

Matthew shifted in his seat. He hated the ritual of condolences.

'You were my uncle's solicitor for most of that time.'

'Yes. And Mr Treloar, from whom I inherited the business, was the family solicitor before that.' Joshua Pascoe leaned back in his chair and putting his hands together as if in prayer rested his index fingers against his lips. 'What was it in particular you wanted to see me about?'

Matthew studied Pascoe's face. He wished he could ask out loud: 'What was in the note you sent my uncle on the day he died?' But he knew that this could be his only advantage, so instead he said: 'It was concerning my uncle's will.'

'Ah yes.' Pascoe slowly leaned forwards. 'Your uncle's will. Of course.' He looked seriously at Matthew. 'You were wondering what was its content, am I correct?'

Matthew nodded.

'Yes. I can remember that dinner party. Your uncle's fiftieth wasn't it?'

'Fifty-third.'

'Was it really? I remember him saying he might leave you something in his will.'

'And on other occasions as well.' Matthew tried not to sound too presumptuous.

'Yes. I always think it is very irresponsible of my clients to hint at the contents of their wills beforehand. It can lead to all sorts of problems.' Joshua Pascoe gave an embarrassed smile and fidgeted with a piece of sealing wax on his desk.

'Are you trying to tell me something, Mr Pascoe?'

'A moment please, Mr Trevanion.' Pascoe got up and crossed to an old oak cabinet standing against the wall. Reaching inside, he pulled out two glasses and a bottle of port. 'I apologise for not having talked to you sooner,' he explained. He poured out two glasses and handed one to Matthew.

'You were very much on your uncle's mind,' Pascoe went on. 'I am sorry the two of you were not closer.'

Matthew said nothing.

'Your uncle was very partial to a glass of port. He and I often shared a bottle. John said that if you came here I was to give you a glass and we could drink a toast to him. He'd have liked that.'

Matthew looked at him suspiciously. 'What about the will, Mr Pascoe?'

The solicitor sighed. 'I'm afraid that is more of a problem.' He looked across the room to Matthew. 'Your uncle has left you nothing at all.'

'How do you mean exactly?' Matthew tried to keep his voice level and was annoyed when he felt it crack a little.

' "Sit him down and give him a glass of my favourite port," your uncle said to me, "and tell him I wish him well. But when it comes to money, tell him the cost of a glass and my wishes are all I'm leaving him." Those were his exact words, as far as I can remember.' Pascoe looked apologetic. 'I'm afraid your uncle possessed an eccentric sense of occasion.'

Matthew flung his glass across the room. It smashed against the bookcase behind the desk. Port ran red down the books.

'But what about the will?'

'Mr Trevanion! If you do not apologise for your outlandish behaviour this instant, I shall have you thrown out!' Pascoe's voice was suddenly cold and hard.

Shamefaced, Matthew apologised.

'Very well, I accept your apology. But I must warn you any further misconduct, and our interview is at an end. Do I make myself clear?'

'I'm sorry. But Hocking said—'

'Damn! Hocking is a pompous oaf!' flashed Pascoe. 'He had no right!'

'But Hocking said he witnessed the will.'

Pascoe paced across the room. 'There was a will. You're quite right. And Jonathan Hocking was a witness.'

'So what happened to it?'

'If your uncle had died a year ago, you and I would be having quite a different conversation. You were his principal heir, you're right, if that's what you thought.' Pascoe sat down behind his desk. 'About three months ago your uncle asked to see his last will and testament. He said he no longer wished it to stand. He wanted me to annul it there and then. I thought this was somewhat irregular, but seeing he was not to be dissuaded, I complied. We burned it in the hearth.'

'So what happened next? Did he draw up a new will?'

'Unfortunately not. Your uncle was thinking it over.'

'So there is no second will?'

'There is not, I'm afraid, or else my work would be all the easier. Under the law, as your uncle died intestate, the estate has passed to his wife. However, from what your uncle said to me, I firmly believe he intended to make her his beneficiary in any case.'

'Can I ask you, Mr Pascoe, did my uncle say why he wanted to change his will?'

'He did not. But I was given to believe you had not been close for some time.'

'Does my aunt know of this?'

'I am currently drawing up details for her on the estate and its various entailments.'

Matthew looked at the solicitor for a moment, then

tapped his hands on his knees in a gesture of resignation.

'Then I can see no point in taking up any more of your time, Mr Pascoe.' He got up to leave.

'If I can be of any other assistance, please do not hesitate to call on me.' Pascoe shook his hand. 'I am sorry you did not enjoy your drink more.'

'I do not have much of a taste for port, I am afraid. I am surprised my uncle did not think of that.'

Pascoe gave him an odd glance. He put his own glass to his lips and let the rich juicy liquid roll over his tongue before he swallowed it.

Matthew left the solicitor sitting in his office and walked down the corridor to the entrance. By the door Edward Tonkin was sitting at his desk, scratching out a copy of a document with his quill.

'Good day, Master Trevanion,' he said. 'I take it your meeting did not go well?' He had an oily complexion and lank hair and gave Matthew a greasy smile.

'It all depends,' replied Matthew. He looked at the clerk distastefully. It amazed him that Pascoe who was, if nothing else, fastidious in every detail, should have chosen someone like this to be his pupil. A thought struck him. 'I suppose you copy most of Mr Pascoe's documents?'

'Almost all.'

'Did you ever make a copy of my uncle's will?'

The clerk hesitated, then smiled again. 'What you ask is more than my position is worth, Master Trevanion.'

'But did you?'

Tonkin fluttered his eyelids in embarrassment.

'Only Mr Pascoe is allowed to give out that sort of information.' As he said this, there came the sound of Pascoe's door opening and closing. Footsteps could be heard coming down the passageway.

'I think you'd better take your leave, sir. Mr Pascoe doesn't like to see me talking to the clients.'

In which case, thought Matthew, why did you start talking to me? He quickly moved to the other end of the room where his coat was hanging on a stand. The door into the corridor swung open behind him.

'Ah, Mr Trevanion! Still here?'

'Just putting on my coat. Good day, Mr Pascoe.' As he left he cast a pitying glance at Edward Tonkin. The latter carried on with his work without looking up. He must be at least thirty-five, thought Matthew, old for a clerk – and resigned to mediocrity. What sort of a man would work in a solicitor's office, he wondered, especially for such a one as Joshua Pascoe?

As he stepped outside, a fresh sea breeze met him, floating up from the harbour. After the dry, stuffy air of the office, it came as a welcome relief. He breathed in deeply. So Emily had been right all along. How stupid he'd been. The truth is rarely pleasant, and he had had as much as he wanted for one day.

For the next hour or so he wandered up and down the narrow alleys and walkways which led to and from the harbour front. He watched the pilchard-boats coming in, crowned with clouds of gulls, wheeling and crying for scraps. Women gathered at the water's edge, clutching their great wicker-baskets, and shouting across the water to their men.

He was making his way back up the hill when two fishermen suddenly came through a door and pushed past him into the street. He realised he was standing outside The Dolphin. Why not? he thought, and went inside.

The reek of stale beer and bodies, tobacco and log-fires greeted him. He stood on the threshold blinking – the small opaque windows allowed only a dull dirty light. After a while he made out the long tables and benches set in rows across the main room. They were full with men and women, drinking, smoking and talking. Matthew picked his way over to a small bench by the far wall and ordered a quart of ale. The beer was thin and watery, with a sour, smoky aftertaste, but it settled comfortably into his stomach.

So here he was, Matthew Trevanion, tenant of thirty acres of poor land on a three-life lease, alone in this world apart from his mother, and with no hope of anything better to come. As he drank he thought, and was struck by the shortage of his options. He ordered a second glass, and although it tasted worse than the first, it went down more quickly.

Someone was singing a ballad and the rough voice cut through the air. Several drinkers had stopped talking and were banging time on the tables. He looked at them, the men with their thick rough beards and sideburns, faces like huge leathery masks, the women, maybe pretty once, now old before their time, cheeks fat and blotched with broken veins.

'Yet is their strength then but labour and sorrow;

so soon it passeth away and we are gone,' he thought, recalling the liturgy of the funeral.

A profound sadness settled over him. Never a day goes by, he realised, but we are reminded of our mortality. And he found himself thinking of Lucy, at home at Trevanion, baking bread, or putting on the meat, a warm smell of hearth and food. A dull feeling of regret stirred in him. He would like to see her, talk to her. But for what good?

Matthew drained off his beer and ordered another. Perhaps he should go to Trevanion tonight. He remembered her lying in the orchard, stretching her neck back. Perhaps he had always loved her.

Soon the glass was empty. He called for a fourth. Emily be damned! A picture flashed through his mind of Pascoe and his uncle watching the parchment turn to ashes. Damn them all! He suddenly realised how little it all was worth. When his uncle had died, he had licked his lips like a greedy dog. And wasn't that what his uncle had wanted? Perhaps his uncle had never intended to leave him the land. It had been nothing but a monstrous hoax from the first.

He had got up to leave when he noticed the mood of the tavern had changed. The customers were quieter, and Matthew saw the barmaid was stocking the tables with beer. He caught her eye. 'It's Michael Pendarves, the drollteller,' she explained. 'He's just come in. He's over by the fire.' Matthew followed her gaze to where a small old man sat by the hearth, sipping a pint of beer. Matthew ordered another quart for himself and sat back. Michael Pendarves . . . Matthew had thought he was dead. He could remember the stories he told at Trevanion when he was a boy. He had seemed old as the hills then . . .

Michael Pendarves made his living from touring farmsteads and taverns and entertaining them with the tales of the ghosts, spriggans and giants who haunted these lands. The old man had lost the use of his left eye and had a twisted back, so that he walked with a queer, swinging stoop and would squint at you, when he chose, from sideways on. Matthew guessed some mining injury had befallen him in his youth – that was how most drolltellers came by their profession – but some claimed he was found like that as a baby on the moors above Penzance. Others said he'd been raised by the spriggans, the little people, for it was common knowledge that if you revealed their secrets you would go blind in one eye.

Michael Pendarves coughed and cleared his throat and the audience began to fall silent. Matthew took a deep draught of beer. It was a long time since he had heard a drollteller at his craft. Pendarves got up and eyed his audience with his odd sideways glance. A thin smile played across his lips and for a second he looked like one of the sprites or hobgoblins of his tales. Then, satisfied he had everyone's attention, he returned to his seat by the fire and began to talk.

Matthew remembered the voice even more than the man. It was a rich gravelly voice which had been worn dark in patches by usage, as if it were a belt or a shoe or some other leather object. The voice pronounced each word with a slow and deliberate care, as if he were a conjuror producing gold coins from the inside of his mouth, or a fisherman pulling up smooth, glistening fish from the deep. Yet over the strong pliant voice, resonant and sonorous, there hung a thin nasal tone – almost a hiss – which gave the voice a strange, eerie quality, and it was this quality more than any other that transfixed his audience.

'The tale I have to tell is about the love a mother has for her child. We all know this love, don't we, when we were babes ourselves and lay in mammy's arms.

'As I was walking by Trencrom one fine autumn day I met a young shepherd maid down by the brook. She was a pretty young thing, no more than twenty summers old with her hair in little brown curls. "What's wrong, my dear?" I said, for she was weeping bitterly into the stream.

' "Why, good sir," she answered, "I'm crying because my babe's been stolen away."

'Now I thought this was strange because there on the grass lay a young babe wrapped in swaddling, as pretty and beaming as ever.

' "That's not my babe," she said. "Oh, but I wish it were!" And with that she cried all the more.

'So I gave her my handkerchief to dry her eyes, and this is the tale she told.

'Jenny was her name and she was married to John Poldower from Nancledra. Now her babe must have been keen to get on in the world because within five months of them getting married, Jenny gave birth to a bouncing baby boy. "He's going to be a fast one!" she thought. "Just like his father!" ' There was general laughter at this. Michael Pendarves licked his lips.

115

'They named him Tobias after his father's father and all went well. The babe fed and slept, fed and slept, as babes do, and Jenny loved him dear – although she never left him alone, mind, not even to tend her sheep, but insisted on keeping him with her. Even at harvest-time it was the same: no matter how hard John was working, Jenny refused to budge but stuck at home with the babe. Of course, people talked, until, on the last night, John had had enough. "You can't miss Cutting the Neck," he said. "Leave Toby in the cottage and come – whether you want to or not." And no matter how hard she pleaded, John insisted, and that was that.

'So Jenny left her babe tucked in his cot and went to cut the neck. Oh, how she wept while she told me this! But, of course, once she was there, she soon forgot herself in the singing and dancing and drinking, until all of a sudden midnight struck. "What about my babe?" cried Jenny, and leaving her husband and the others, she ran off home. And when she opened the door, her worse fears came true! For there was the little boy's cot flung on its side and as empty as a glass on market day. He was gone!

'And then Jenny noticed another strange thing. When she had left, the fire had been burning merrily in the grate, but now the cinders were as cold as the grave. Jenny fell on her knees and searched the cottage high and low but Toby was nowhere to be seen.

'Jenny was frantic and ran to fetch her husband. At first John wouldn't believe her, but eventually she begged the others to come and when they got there, everything was just as she'd said. The cot was flung down, and Toby was gone. What could they do? Some of the men ran to the road, in case a traveller had stolen him. Others ran over the fields, then one of the women gave a cry. Here he was! Fast asleep in the woodpile at the back of the house. But how Toby had got there no one knew. Though some reckoned Jenny had put him there herself to spite her husband, or because the babe was crying so.

'Jenny should have been overjoyed, but as soon as she picked her baby up, she cried with fright. "This isn't my babe!" she cried. "This is nothing like my babe!"

'Now they all thought the worry had turned her poor mind, for the babe looked as bonny and beaming as ever. But Jenny was certain. She didn't want him.

' "It might look a bit like my boy," she said the next morning. "But if you look at his face, you'll see a little old man." Now she saw that Toby's eyes had a crafty, cunning glint which sent shivers down her spine.

'John wasn't having any of it, but then while they were arguing, the babe began to wail for milk, for he hadn't been fed since the previous day. Much as she hated it, Jenny couldn't let her child starve and went to feed him. And then she cried with horror! For instead of his soft little gums, her babe had grown a set of teeth, white and straight, and exactly the same size. Jenny was horrified! But what could she do? The babe was screaming with hunger and she had no choice but to suckle him. That was that, said her husband. You make sure you look after that child or when I come home tonight there'll be hell to pay!

'Poor Jenny! Toby had always been a hungry babe, but now he was never satisfied. As soon as he was put down, he was hollering for more. And how he would roar! A horrible unnatural sound, like a pig squealing, said Jenny. And if she refused him, he'd go bright red in the face and roar all the louder!

'Things went on like this for the next few weeks. It seemed the more she fed him the greedier he became. Yet no matter how much he drank, he never got any fatter. In fact he was wasting away, so her husband accused her of starving and ill treating him. By the end of the month poor little Toby was nothing but skin and bones, and his face all dry and wizened like an old man's, just as Jenny had predicted.

'What could she do? Then Jenny remembered there was an old lady in Zennor who was supposed to have the gift of charming. Martha Penmadden was her name. So the next morning she strapped her babe on to her back and, ignoring his hideous screams for food, set off for Zennor.

'As soon as she saw the child and heard him screeching, Martha was in no doubt.

' "Why," she said. "This isn't a human child at all. This is a changeling."

' "A changeling? What's that?" asked Jenny, hardly daring to ask.

' "This babe you found in the woodpile is not your Toby," explained Martha. "The spriggans have snatched him away and put this changeling in his place. On the outside he looks like your son, but on the inside he's a little devil, waiting to get out."

'Jenny was horrified. "My poor child!" she cried. "Carried off by devils!"

'But Martha told her not to worry unduly. She knew just what to do.

' "Take it up to Madron Well," she said, "and bathe it three times, passing it from left to right, against the sun, and after that you'll get your own babe back."

'So the next day Jenny straps the child on her back and trudges off to Madron Well. She was just coming down the hill from Boscreege, however, when from behind a pile of rocks she heard a high-pitched voice call out:

' "Tredrill! Tredrill!

' "Thy wife and children greet thee well!"

'Jenny almost jumped out of her skin, for she could see no one. Nor had she seen anyone for all her walk. And then the creature on her back sang back, in a most terrible voice, like that of a spiteful old man:

' "What care I for wife and child,

' "When I ride on Jenny's back to Madron Well

' "And have of pap my fill?"

'That was enough for Jenny. Shaking with terror, she hurled the wretched creature on to the ground and ran off home, leaving it shrieking and screaming, its spindly little legs flailing like a beetle. But Jenny had only gone halfway home when she got to thinking what would her husband and the villagers say when they found she had abandoned her babe in the middle of the moor? So, repelled though she was, Jenny went back and, summoning all her courage, she plucked the wretch up by its heel and ran off home with it as fast as her legs could carry her. But as soon as she neared the cottage, the babe laughed out loud and sang:

'"Ride away! Ride away! On a cock horse!

'"I'll ride my Jenny to Camborne church cross!"

'And it was clear from the way he was singing what sort of a ride the creature had in mind. It's no good, thought Jenny, and swinging him by his ankle, she threw him across the yard and on to the rubbish heap outside her cottage.

'"Martha! Martha! Come quick," she cried. "He's worse than before!" and the old woman came running to see the boy lying on the ground, laughing and singing and squawking, apparently none the worse for wear. The old lady was just working out what to do next, when who should come up the path but the husband! John was furious to find his son lying in a heap of dirt, the fire not lit and the table bare. He drove old Martha out of the yard and he beat poor Jenny until she promised to look after her son as she should. If there was any more of her foolishness, he would take the babe away and throw her out of his home! And that is how I found her, weeping her pretty eyes away by the side of the stream, with the little child lying next to her on the grass.

'"What am I to do?" she asked me and leaned her pretty head on my shoulder.

'Now I had a look at the babe myself, and I must say it seemed bonny and happy enough, but she was inconsolable, and when I looked in its mouth, there were the little teeth she had spoken of, all set in a row. And the creature gave me a wicked little grin, so that I could imagine the spriggan inside of him.

' "Now don't you worry, my dear," I said. "Leave this to Pendarves!" I told her to go home as if nothing had happened, and to wait for me at midnight when her husband had gone to sleep.

'The first thing I heard when I got to her cottage was the hideous mewling of the child. Poor Jenny had been too nervous to feed him and the creature was hungrier than ever. But that didn't matter. I know spriggans well. The one thing they can't resist is a bit of cream, and in my pocket I'd brought a great lump of butterfat off the top of the pan, and I popped it in his mouth and he fell quiet straightaway. I could see the look of relief on his mother's face. "Quick!" I whispered. "Before your husband wakes up!" And clutching the babe we ran off across the fields to Towednack, and placed it under the church-stile.

'No sooner had we put him down than the devil realised our plan and sent up the most piteous wailing I have ever heard. I could have sworn I heard him calling Mam! Mam! and him only a few months old! Jenny wanted to pick him up, but I held on tight: "No," I said. "You must leave him till first light, and if you're lucky when you go back your little Toby will be there in its place."

'So I made her promise and she went off home, more frightened of her husband, I think, than of what might happen to the babe.

'The next morning, as soon as first light, Jenny raced off to Towednack, scarcely daring to hope. But there, sure enough, lay her baby, tucked under the stile and sleeping like an angel. She picked him up and hugged him tight, and instead of the wretched, half-starved little brat she had left there, her child was as plump and chirpy as a fat little sparrow! And when she put her nose to the little lad's head, she could smell the scent of fresh ferns and heather. It was her own little Toby! Laughing, and kissing and cuddling him, Jenny ran back across the fields to the cottage.

'Of course, poor old John didn't know what had come over his wife. But she seemed happy enough with the child and he was just thankful for that.' Michael Pendarves paused for a moment. 'But that wasn't the end of it, no. A child can't spend so long with the fairies and not be touched. Even though Toby seemed happy and healthy enough, there was always something queer about him. Often he would point at an empty space as if he could see something his parents couldn't, or at night he would sing to himself strange lullabies, unlike any that Jenny had heard. As Toby got older, this strangeness grew more obvious. He would leave his parents for days on end and wander into the hills. When he became a man, Tobias forsook the company of humans altogether and lived on the moors with his sheep. People said he had a wonderful way with animals, and would send for him when any of their flock were sick or in labour. They called him a holy fool. I remember seeing him once myself. "I know you," he said. "You left me under Towednack stile when I was just a babe." And he gave me the queerest grin I ever did see.

'About a month or so after that, as I recall, some

farmhands were working in the fields when they noticed Toby's sheep were straying more than usual. When they came the next day, they saw the sheep were now scattered over all the hillside, so, fearing the worst, they went to investigate. They'd only been looking a few minutes, when they came to a valley. And there in the bottom of the stream, with his eyes wide open and his face in a sweet gentle smile, Tobias Poldower lay dead.'

Michael Pendarves stopped abruptly. He took a long drink from his glass. The room was hushed just for a second, and then, knowing the tale was ended, the audience broke into conversation again. More drinks were ordered and soon all thoughts the audience had of the Changeling of Nancledra were gone.

It was well into the night by the time Matthew started back. He let Saph set the pace. The moon was full and he caught glimpses of the hills over the tops of the hedges, cold and blue in the moonlight. A light breeze whispered in the trees, and helped his head to clear.

It was strange, but knowing that he now had no chance of inheriting the estate had given him a new sense of calm and control. It was as if he had been relieved of some great responsibility and was free again to lead his own life. He would see Lucy. That would be the best way.

The sound of hoofbeats jolted him from his thoughts. There was another horseman on the road, behind him, and riding fast. Instinctively, Matthew pulled Saph off the road and underneath a small group of sycamores which lay in a dip to the left. He dismounted quickly and held her head still. It was always best to avoid company on the roads at night. No sooner had he done this when the horse shot into view, a large black mare, galloping hard. The rider rode high in the stirrups and was bent over his horse's neck, his long white hair streaming behind him. Even with the full moon, it would have been difficult to make out the man's face, but the long white hair was unmistakable. It was Joshua Pascoe, and he was riding with a vigour and ease Matthew would scarcely have credited.

Where was he going at this time of night? Matthew's surprise gave way to suspicion. The solicitor did not look as if he was heading for a dinner engagement, or to meet a client. As soon as Pascoe had disappeared down the lane, Matthew led Saph out of the copse and swung himself back into the saddle. Kicking her sharply into a trot, he began to follow. This proved easier than he expected. The clatter of Pascoe's horse rang out across the deserted landscape, and Matthew found he could keep track without breaking into a gallop. Besides, he knew there could only be one or two places the solicitor was going. And one of them was Trevanion.

Sure enough, within a quarter of an hour, Matthew found himself at the head of the lane that ran down to his aunt's manor. The clatter of hooves were still distinct, though growing fainter. Matthew patted Saph on her neck and eased himself down. He would do the rest on foot.

By the time he reached the farm, the courtyard was empty. For a moment Matthew wondered if he had been wrong and Pascoe had continued on towards Sennen. Then he saw Josey coming out of the stables. Josey wouldn't be tending the manor's horses at this time of night. Pascoe must already be inside. Skirting the outhouses, Matthew crossed to the stable-door. Inside, the large black mare was still sweating from her ride. Matthew crept back across the yard. He felt a little foolish skulking around the farm, but he felt even more curious to know what urgent business had dragged Pascoe out so late in the evening.

From where he was crouched, Matthew could see one of the parlour shutters had not been closed properly and pale yellow light spilled on to the ground outside. Taking care, he crawled along the wall until he was directly underneath.

He was in luck. From where he lay, he could make out the sound of voices and of people moving around. A chair was pushed back. Someone walked quickly across the room. The fire popped and crackled in the hearth, and the familiar reek of burned oak crept through the shutters. For a moment the parlour was quiet. Then he heard a metal object – possibly a tray – being placed on a table, and Emily's voice saying, 'Thank you, that will be all,' and the sound of footsteps, presumably those of a servant, receding, followed by the click of the door. The room was quiet for a second then Emily spoke. This time her voice had none of the genteel restraint it had possessed only moments before. She was nervous, excited.

'Is it safe for you to come here?'

'That's why I waited till dark.' There was no mistaking the solicitor's crisp, reedy voice. 'Don't worry. I saw no one on the road.'

'But why risk coming at all? We agreed to wait at least a month.'

'Don't you want to see me?'

'You know I do, Joshua! It's just so soon, and we—'

'Spare me your reasons.' Pascoe sounded irritable. 'Matthew came to see me today.'

'Matthew? Whatever for?'

'Don't look like that! You know we've been expecting him. Hocking told him about the will. Hardly surprising. Hocking thought he'd curry favour.'

Emily made no reply immediately. Matthew wished he could look into the room. He found it difficult to gauge the significance of what was said by hearing alone.

'How did it go?' said Emily at last.

'Exactly as we expected. I told him John had destroyed his will and the estates automatically pass to you.'

'He went along with that?'

'Not happily – but what else could he do? Without a will he has no case.'

'And you're sure he suspects nothing?'

'My dear, I was his uncle's solicitor. My reputation is spotless. How could he possibly suspect anything about us?'

For a moment Matthew was tempted to jump up there and then and confront them both. What did Emily mean by *he suspects nothing*? There was something in his aunt's tone he could not recognise. If only he could see! He stretched himself. The cold ground had stiffened his limbs, but he forced himself into a crouching position and, by straining his neck, peered over the lip of the sill. He could hardly believe his eyes.

Emily was turning from the drinks table, holding two glasses of wine, one of which she offered to Pascoe. As she reached out her hand, the solicitor bent and took it, and tenderly planted a kiss on her wrist. Emily scarcely noticed this display of affection. She drained her glass in one and turned back to the bottle on the table. Her face was flushed, and her lips and chin were stained an ugly crimson. Only a few days later, Matthew would recall her appearance as he stood in the barn at St Levan.

'What's wrong, Emily?' Pascoe sounded unhappy. 'You seem tense.'

'Of course I am!' she retorted. 'I wasn't expecting any of this.'

Any of what? thought Matthew.

'Neither was I. Who'd ever have thought he'd be killed by a fall from a horse?'

Emily looked at him oddly.

'Let's not talk about it,' she said quickly. 'It makes me uneasy.'

Pascoe turned and walked to the other end of the parlour. Matthew lost sight of him. Emily went back to filling her glass. As she did so, her bottom lip appeared to tremble.

'So what happens now?' she asked after a couple of sips.

'Nothing. We bide our time, that's all, until your nephew has lost interest. A couple of months maybe. Perhaps you should think about appointing a new agent, but not just yet. We don't want to do anything too hastily after John's funeral.'

'Good,' agreed Emily. 'I've been thinking about what people—'

'What about Lucy?' interrupted Pascoe. 'What does she know?'

'Nothing as far as I know. She hardly spoke to John when she got back. There's no way she'd know what his intentions were.'

'No – not about John! About us!'

'Oh, I see.' Matthew could not mistake the reluctance in Emily's voice. Joshua must have heard it as well, for he crossed the room and came back into view. He walked straight up to Emily and seized her by the shoulders.

'Joshua—'

'What's wrong with you, Emily?'

'I tried to tell you. I've been thinking – what if people suspect the worst of me?'

'It's too late for second thoughts. Much too late.' Pascoe sounded imploring, yet also threatening.

'No,' she said quickly. 'I'm not having second thoughts. It's just I've been worrying what people will think.'

'I don't give a damn what they think, Emily! A bargain is a bargain! We said three months! I won't wait longer. Hocking can say what he likes!'

'I'm not worried about the will! Why won't you let me finish?' Emily pulled herself away. 'What if people suspect you of John's death?'

Her words sounded unnaturally loud and a look of intense fear played across her face. Pascoe hesitated for only an instant.

'What? People think I murdered John? That's ridiculous! Ridiculous!'

'Why not? You've been making love to his wife every time his back was turned!' Emily's fear broke into a flame of excitement. Her face flushed.

'I know,' replied Joshua, his mood suddenly softer, warmer. 'And I've loved every minute of it.' He came closer and tried to put his arm round her but she pushed him off. Matthew felt disgusted.

'Don't!' said Emily. 'Not now.'

But Pascoe was impatient. He grabbed her wrist and pulled her towards him.

'We agreed, Emily! Three months or you're finished – and your daughter with you.' Emily twisted away. Suddenly she walked straight to the window where Matthew was crouching. He dived to the ground.

'Careful how you talk, Joshua. This shutter's still ajar.' Matthew looked up to see her hand reach out and pull the leaf of the shutter to. He suspected Emily's sudden concern stemmed from a desire to avoid Pascoe's conversation, not from any real fear of being overheard. Still, it was a close shave. He spat out a mouthful of dirt and resumed his position. But now the shutters were closed, the voices were muffled and difficult to follow. Although the talking continued for some minutes, Matthew caught only odd words or phrases. The rhythm of their speech had changed, become disjointed, uneven. Pascoe's voice rose and fell. They seemed to be arguing, or contesting something, then their voices trailed off and the room went quiet. He wondered what they were doing.

The sound of a table – or a chair, maybe – scraping across the floor startled him. Then a new, terrible sound, loud and raw, the sound of a human voice, whimpering, gasping, though whether with humiliation or pleasure, he could not tell. Displaying her sins to the grim figures of the tapestries. Embracing or fighting . . . Matthew imagined Emily spread across the sofa or maybe bent over the table, her widow's dress hitched high round her waist, her arse bucking and heaving under her lover's onslaught. So Pascoe had got his way.

Strangely, he wished he could see the expression on her face.

Chapter Three

'MATTHEW! I HAD NOT EXPECTED to see you so soon!'

Emily appeared unruffled by his sudden entrance. He looked at her solemnly. Seated in the parlour in her black silk, he could scarcely believe what he had seen – and heard – the evening before. She looked so cold and pure. Like alabaster or marble.

Lucy sat next to her. She had lowered her gaze and was concentrating hard on her needlework. In the hall the grandfather clock chimed twice. It was two o'clock.

'Something important has happened, Emily. I need to talk to you, alone, if you don't mind.'

'I can't imagine what it could be that Lucy can't hear.'

'Oh, I can.' He looked at her steadily.

'Very well then.' Emily pressed her lips together severely. 'Would you mind, dear? I'm afraid Matthew insists on driving you out of your own parlour.'

Lucy made a great show of placing her sampler on her chair. She was clearly in no hurry, and Matthew strode to the other end of the parlour and glared at the tapestries. He was still standing there when he heard the door close, and realised they were alone.

Emily cleared her throat.

'Esau and Jacob,' he said rather loudly, without turning around. 'All this time and I've finally realised who they are.' On the hanging, two shadowy, muscular figures dressed in classical attire were caught in a vigorous clench. 'You know,' he went on, 'from this perspective you can't tell whether they are embracing or fighting.'

She said nothing, so he continued: 'I shall always regret the way we parted company, John and I. They were bad terms.'

'You've only yourself to blame,' she replied – then glanced nervously at the floor.

'But I haven't, have I? It wasn't my idea to go visiting that whore in Mousehole.'

'I trusted you, Matthew!'

'I trusted *you*!'

He paced angrily across the room. Emily kept her gaze rooted to the square of carpet at her feet, but he could see the skin was pulled taut over her cheeks: she reminded him of a child who is waiting for her father to shout at her.

'You know,' he said, 'in spite of all this, I realise I may have misjudged you.' He looked at her but she did not respond, so he continued. 'I never could understand why you hated me so much. Right from the moment you stepped off the coach you'd hated me.'

'And can you blame me?' she said with sudden emotion, and then almost immediately bit her lip. Lucy had the same habit, he realised.

'Blame you? No, not really,' he said. 'Because I understand you.'

Emily made a sudden movement as if she was

about to leave. He stepped quickly across the room and gently rested his hand on her shoulder.

'No,' he advised her softly. 'Don't get up. Look – I'll sit.' He leaned over her. She was trembling. Matthew kissed her lightly on the forehead. But before she could respond, he had backed away to the large armchair opposite and sat down. He rested his right foot on his left knee and smiled broadly.

'It wasn't your fault, was it, Emily? There you were in Bath: a pretty young daughter, her father dead – though he wasn't her father, was he – no visible means of support, what future could you hope for? It's not hard to imagine. Then along comes my big lovable, pig-ignorant uncle, and he falls for you.' An expression of disdain played across his face. 'I bet you couldn't believe your luck! I think all you ever wanted was security, didn't you? And here you were, the new mistress of Trevanion, and John older than you, with no children. Things couldn't have been better.

'Then you meet me. And John says when he dies, everything is mine. How long had he got, do you think? Five, ten years at most? And then you'd be out on the streets again, if I wanted. No wonder you hated me. Damn, you were no better than a tenant on a lease. My uncle's bit of pleasure until he died!'

'You bastard!'

'Maybe, but *my* legitimacy's not in question, is it?' Matthew retorted flippantly. He was to bitterly regret those words. 'What would have happened if John had found out about Lucy and how you used to earn a living?'

'And there you were, just waiting for him to die!

You're no better, Matthew. At least I made him feel loved. I—'

'Emily.' Matthew leaned towards her so that his elbows rested on his knees. His voice became quieter. In his hands he was fingering a small metal object that glinted in the amber firelight. She suddenly realised it was a buckle. 'I saw you with Pascoe last night.'

He could see she did not know how to react. Her lips parted as if to speak, but then she faltered and sank back in her chair. She felt his gaze bearing down on her, penetrating her. She knew he would like nothing better than to see her writhing helplessly in front of him. She stared into the fireplace.

Matthew held the buckle out towards her. 'I hope Pascoe didn't fall off his horse when he tried to mount it.'

'So it was you.'

'Careless of me, I know. But when I examined his saddle it came off in my hand.'

'How much did you see?' she asked sullenly.

'Everything, Emily. Everything.' He rolled the word slowly over his tongue. 'You put on a good performance. I was impressed. Maybe we shouldn't have sent Lucy away,' he went on. 'Does she know?'

'No. No one knows.'

'But why! My uncle is not yet cold in his grave and there you are, fucking that man like—'

'Quiet, Matthew!' she hissed nervously.

He sprang from his chair and crossed to the window.

'I will shout unless I get some very straight answers. Do you understand? My God!'

'Yes, yes, I understand. Now come away from the window!'

Matthew grinned. 'Good,' he said, and went up close behind her chair. 'Now, tell me why.'

Lucy was peeling carrots in the scullery. As Matthew entered, she was trying to wipe a strand of hair out of her eye with the back of her hand. Without speaking, and before she noticed him, he stepped forward and, catching the offending wisp in his fingers, slipped it back into place. She looked startled and turned quickly towards him, and he cupped her head in the palm of his hand.

'You frightened me!' she said. In the grey light of the scullery, his eyes seemed colder and darker than usual. 'Have you and Mother finished?'

'For now.' He reached down and plucked the knife and the carrot out of her hands and laid them on the bench. 'Let's go outside.'

She nodded and hung her pin-before on a hook beside the door.

As they turned out of the yard, they passed a pile of rubble on their right. A small lean-to workshed on the east wing of the house had been pulled down, presumably with a view to extending the parlour, or adding some extra rooms. The work seemed to have been abandoned since his uncle's death. Old timbers, slates, and lumps of stone and mortar lay in disorganised piles.

'Do you know what they're doing here?' he asked, more for something to say than anything else.

'Mother said John wanted a new study – a library he called it.'

'A library?' Matthew was incredulous. 'John was hardly a reading man!'

'I think it was for my mother.'

'Oh, I see.' Matthew walked over to the site. A starling was perched on top of a heap of old plaster and wattle, and took off with a flurry. He could remember playing in the shed as a boy. He noticed that where the shed had adjoined the house, some of the rendering and stonework had come away, exposing the inside of the wall. It would need to be replastered before the weather deteriorated, or the damp would seep in and break the wall apart from the inside. Matthew was tempted to see the rotting and broken wall, the abandoned workshed, as symbolic of Trevanion as a whole. Lucy sensed his disquiet.

'What is it, Matthew?'

'Oh, nothing. Someone ought to repair that wall before it gets any worse.'

'Perhaps Josey will do it.'

Matthew looked unconvinced and turned his gaze back to the wall. Something caught his eye.

'That's odd. There seem to be clay pipes set into the end wall.' He stepped over a mound of rubble and offered her a hand. She chose to ignore him and picked her own way over the debris. 'Here, look.' In between the stones and crumbling mortar, there could be seen the ends of half a dozen dull reddish pipes, each about five inches in diameter, set into the house wall about six foot up. They had obviously been covered by an earlier layer of plaster, but this had now fallen away with the demolition of the shed.

'Most odd,' observed Matthew. 'I wonder what they are there for?'

'Or why they were blocked off?' added Lucy. 'They look as old as the house.'

Matthew found that by standing on tiptoe he could just peer into the pipes. They went back about a foot or so into the wall, and apart from a few crumbs of plaster, were quite empty. A damp, sickly smell greeted his nostrils. He smiled.

'Dove-cots,' he announced and stepped down from the wall. Lucy stared at him blankly, so he went on: 'All the farms round here have them.'

'Then why did they close them?'

'When they built the shed, I imagine. That must be when they put up the cot behind the barn.'

'I see,' said Lucy, trying to sound interested.

The mystery resolved, they climbed back over the rubble and let the lane lead them up the hill and away from Trevanion.

They stopped by a gateway at the breast of the hill and looked out on the country falling southwards to the sea. From this perspective the land appeared in great flat rolls, bare and almost featureless, but for the black criss-crossings of the hedges and a few ragged trees. Across to their left lay the village of Malaggan and Matthew could just distinguish the stubby churchtower. A sudden squall of sunlight broke through the clouds and glittered on the roofslates of the larger buildings. He looked at Lucy. She was leaning against the gate next to him and was staring at some point in the mid-distance. He noticed she had begun to finger the beads of her bracelet, which she only did when she was deep in thought. The scene was very quiet. As he looked, the breeze quickened slightly and began to toy with her hair, blowing it back off her face. Her eyes narrowed. Suddenly she glanced up at him and said: 'It's beautiful, isn't it?'

'I went to Penzance on Monday,' he began, 'to see Joshua Pascoe. But that doesn't matter any more. While I was there I realised something more important.'

'Is that what you talked to Mother about?'

'In a manner of speaking.' He put his hand on her shoulder just as he had done to Emily. 'I love you.'

'Don't!' Lucy twisted away.

'This is ridiculous!' he snapped impatiently. 'After everything that's happened!'

'That's easy for you to say! I trusted you before . . .'

'I know. But it's changed now! We've got to face up to how we feel.'

'And what about the estate? I suppose that has nothing to do with it?'

He understood her now.

'Damn the estate! I've told your mother I don't want any part of it.'

'Have you really?' Lucy was genuinely surprised. 'It's all you ever wanted.'

'If I haven't got you, I don't want it.' His voice was tense, resentful. 'Listen to me!'

He grabbed her shoulders.

'No! Don't!'

'Why not?'

Lucy's eyes filled with tears. 'Because I want to believe you!'

*

Later, as he walked home across the fields, Matthew brooded on the events of the day. He had been more disturbed by Emily's confession than he cared to admit. But that was behind him now, and they had agreed terms. He had not really lied to Lucy, he decided. If he had her, and Emily's blessing, that was all that mattered.

That night Matthew saw himself settled with Lucy on his few acres by the sea. He imagined the years rolling by and with them all thoughts of vengeance or justice lying buried in the land. He imagined himself happy and at peace.

But that was not to be, at least not yet. We are time's fools and our futures rush upon us unseen and irresistible, whether we will them or not. And justice is a raw and elemental force without which the very stars and planets would lose their way and fall from the skies.

PART FOUR

Chapter One

NATHANIEL MORGAN HAD A PROBLEM. Nathaniel Morgan was the squire of St Levan and was standing outside his house looking at the magnificent black mare tied to the church porch opposite. From the mud splashed up her flanks, she had obviously been ridden hard over the fields that morning. He touched her coat. It was no longer damp – she must have been there for some time, and it was not yet seven o'clock. Nathaniel scratched the back of his neck irritably. What on earth was it doing here?

St Levan church lay at the top of a small valley on the most southerly tip of the Penwith peninsula. It was quite deserted, except for the manorhouse, from which Nathaniel had just emerged. So who, and where, was the rider?

He patted the mare on the shoulder and entered the small churchyard. Everything seemed quiet, but then, no one ever came here. He had just rounded the west end of the church when he stopped in his tracks

So there was someone after all! Just above the doorway, where the ground rose to his right, a woman was bent over a stone in the graveyard. She was clad in a rich burgundy cloak and seemed to be praying.

'I'm sorry. I didn't mean to disturb you,' he said

loudly. But when this didn't startle her, he chose to take it as an invitation to approach.

As he got nearer, he could see the lady had bent so low that her head was actually resting on the side of the St Levan Stone. Her fine black hair fluttered in the breeze. She could not possibly be praying, he decided, for she had huddled her body into her cloak as if sheltering from the wind. Perhaps she had fallen asleep like that. Nathaniel reached down a large hand and gently shook her shoulder. The figure seemed to stir and then, under the impetus of his hand, rolled over, its head to one side. She was a beautiful woman, he saw that immediately, or had been three or four years before. As it was, her strong, handsome cheekbones and strong eyebrows were still striking, and her skin was pale, delicate and unblemished. He breathed in quickly.

Then he saw it. Beneath the pale white skin of the lady's cheek and the lace ruff of her collar, a dull red smudge. Stooping down, he put a hand under her side and turned her over. Her head swung back – too quickly, he thought – and revealed a throat that had been cut from one side to the other. Not just cut, but hacked, as if with a blunt knife, so that the two sides of the wound gaped open like jagged lips, crimson and bloody. Previously concealed by her cloak, the front of her riding jacket was stained deep red, almost brown. In places the blood had formed into little clots and crusts, but was still sleek and oily on the grass where she had lain. At first Nathaniel simply stared at the body in disbelief, as if it were some unreal phantasy, then he realised he was staring into the remains of the lady's windpipe and with that he emptied his stomach on to the grass next to her.

'And you still don't know who she is?'

They were seated in Nathaniel's dining-room: Sir Anthony Bevis, Justice of the Peace, the Reverend William Boynton, and Doctor Philip Younger, who had performed the post-mortem in the barn that afternoon. Nathaniel ground his food between his jaws. The mockery in Sir Anthony's question was unmistakable. Why was he expected to know? Damn this murder! He put his knife down slowly.

'No, sir. No one knows who she is or when she arrived.'

'It's an outrage!' continued Sir Anthony without listening. 'What will these fiends do next?'

Nathaniel knew 'these fiends' were the smugglers and venturers that were, by all accounts, Sir Anthony's burning obsession. He tapped his fingers on his stomach in a gesture of reassurance.

'This isn't smugglers, sir. There's none this side of Malaggan. I won't stand for them.'

'Hmmm.' Sir Anthony looked sceptical and took another mouthful of port. 'What do you think, Doctor?'

Mr Younger wiped a piece of fat from his lips. His thin elegant hands were now scrubbed meticulously clean of all traces of blood.

'Whoever committed this crime was driven by a . . . barbaric frenzy. The poor head. There was no need to inflict . . . such wounds.'

Nathaniel sliced deeply and firmly into the mutton on his plate. Over them all hung the memory of the handsome corpse lying in the barn, cold and delicate, a lily crushed by a stone.

'Frenzy, be damned!' snorted Sir Anthony. 'I'm telling you, wives of the gentry do not get murdered by some accidental frenzy, whoever they might be.' At this he cast a penetrating glance at Nathaniel. 'I haven't been a Justice for twenty-odd years to know there's a reason behind this. Eventually it will come to light as sure as the sea gives up her dead.'

'Reason?' asked Nathaniel suspiciously. 'What did you have in mind?'

'I'd wager the poor woman saw something she shouldn't have.'

Damn this murder! Nathaniel scowled into his glass of port. Reason, indeed! He wondered what Sir Anthony would say if he knew that the port, like the brandy in his cellar and the tobacco in his pouch, had all been landed at the cove the week before. This couldn't have happened at a worst time. He turned to the JP.

'Sir, I take it as a personal insult that this innocent blood has been spilled on my land. I will find your murderer. Leave it to me. I insist.'

'Quite. Quite. I would expect nothing less from a gentleman.' Sir Anthony nodded sympathetically. 'But I will hold you to your word, Morgan. People must see Justice done.'

Nathaniel smiled and raised his glass.

'Oh, they will, Sir Anthony. I'll make sure of that.'

News of the murder came to Trevanion the next morning. Almost a week had passed since Matthew's talk with Emily. The day before, he and Lucy had walked down to Lamorna then around Carn-du to Mousehole. Although it was cloudy, the air was clear and from the cliffs they could look far across the bay to the Lizard. Below them and still some way out, a large fleet of fishing boats were pulling to, and their black silhouettes bobbed and shimmered in the midday waters. A flurry of seagulls, greedy for scraps, hung over the boats and followed them like a black cloud.

Later that afternoon they came running up the path towards Rosmear and collapsed in the field below. Lucy lay gazing up at the sky and listened to the sound of Matthew's breathing as it slowed and became quiet. The rich autumn sun made her giddy and her skin tingled with the sense of her own well-being. She reached down to where Matthew lay and began to caress the top of his head, forcing her fingers into his hair. She had never felt so full and sweet with life. They devoured each other in the thick sweating grass.

Lucy did not go home that night but, as she was with Matthew, no one at the manor thought it unusual. Besides, Emily had herself gone riding, so who was there to worry?

Then when Mary was laying the fire, Martin Kelly rode over from Boskenna saying had they heard a lady had been found murdered at St Levan? And no one knew who the poor woman was. Mary ran to tell Emily and it was only then she realised Emily was not there.

She was still looking for her when Lucy came sauntering down the lane from Rosmear.

Matthew rode to St Levan with her. The journey

took a good half hour and for all that time neither spoke.

Nathaniel heard their horses in the yard outside, and knew his mystery was resolved as soon as he saw them stiffly dismounting. What he did not anticipate was Lucy's expression when he opened the door. In a way, the cruel, brilliant sunshine accentuated the tension in her face and made her seem older and more handsome. But that did not strike Nathaniel at first.

It was as if he were gazing into the face of the woman laid in his barn.

He did not need to speak. Lucy understood the look in his eyes. She broke into tears. And Matthew simply hugged her close.

'I'm sorry,' said the squire awkwardly. His cheeks were puffy and sullen.

'Is there somewhere we could be alone?' asked Matthew.

Morgan nodded. Lucy let herself be led, still sobbing, into the squire's withdrawing room. It was darker in here and the grey light which filtered through the shutters soothed her. It reminded her of her bedroom in Bath when she was a child. Matthew held her gently and waited for the grief to wear itself out against his shoulder. The grey light moved slowly across the floor. Outside Matthew could hear Nathaniel talking quietly with a woman. Footsteps crunched on the gravel path, and somewhere a dog barked. After a while, a long while, her tears eased and he felt her stirring, as if she were waking from a deep sleep.

'How do you feel?'

'Scared. Empty and scared. What happens now?'

'I don't know. I'm sorry, Lucy. Would you like me to see the body?'

She took a deep breath and pulled away from him. 'No. I'm all right. I'll go. I want to. Oh, Matthew! Who could have done such a thing?'

He frowned, unsure how to answer her. 'I don't know. Let's not think about that yet, let's get the first things over.' But he was thinking about it already.

They found the squire waiting in the hall. He coughed and clumsily extended his hand to Lucy. She took it and managed a weak smile as he introduced himself fully – they only realised now they did not even know his name. Nathaniel knew of the Trevanions and seemed delighted to offer Lucy what help he could.

'How do you feel, my lady? Cook will bring you something. Meg! A glass of brandy, please!'

The sound of footsteps came from next door.

'We'd like to see the body, if we may,' Matthew told him.

Nathaniel seemed to notice Matthew for the first time. 'Yes. Of course. But please let me attend to Miss Trevanion first. I'm sorry, I do not know your Christian name?'

'Lucy. Lucy Anna.'

'Lucy Anna.' The squire savoured the sound of their syllables. He had thick, slightly sensual lips. 'Please come this way.' He showed her into the parlour.

Matthew followed at a distance. Although he had

only known him a few minutes, Matthew decided he did not like Nathaniel Morgan: there was something unctuous about the man, like a fruit that is overripe or a cake that tastes too sweet. He resented the squire's intrusion into their grief and waited in stony silence until Lucy had finished her brandy.

The barn door was made from thin slats of wood nailed on to two cross-pieces. As it opened it scraped against the dirt floor. They looked in. The inside of the barn was unlit except for a single shaft of light which spilled in through a gap in the roof. As they stepped into the darkness, Matthew remembered entering the crypt at Malaggan church. He shook himself involuntarily. From out of the gloom, they could make out a low bier, constructed from a series of planks laid between two barrels.

On this lay Emily Trevanion, clothed in a smooth white sheet. Her face seemed serene, beautiful, wiped clean now of worry and passion, and glowing white in the darkness. Matthew remembered her appearance in Trevanion that day, like a thing of alabaster, or marble. She would be like that forever.

Lucy did not cry. Somehow being in the presence of her mother's body comforted and stilled her and left her with a kind of awe. She felt afraid to approach any closer. Out of respect, Nathaniel Morgan turned away. Matthew placed his arm around her. Neither spoke but their thoughts were the same: it was less than three weeks since John had died.

'I want to go back to the house,' said Lucy after a

while and Nathaniel was glad to leave Matthew and escort her.

Matthew waited until he heard their footsteps receding. Now that Lucy was gone, he had no compunctions about approaching the body. He reached down, clutched the sheet firmly and pulled it back.

He was not prepared for what he saw. During his examination Doctor Younger had cut back her white cotton shirt and her high ruffed collar and beneath the sheet Emily was naked as a flower. There was no hiding the extent of her injuries.

Emily's throat had not merely been slit. Her head had almost been severed. Matthew could see that the wound stretched round from behind one ear to behind the other, so that the two ends of the gash were only kept from joining by the inch of flesh directly behind her spine.

He gently took hold of her jaw in his right hand. It was strange to be so close to her now, after all this time. And yet as he handled her, he became aware there was something in the feel of the jaw, or the angle of the nose, that reminded him of Lucy, and this awareness unsettled him.

The head moved from side to side with a sickening ease. The flesh had been torn or ripped apart and its two lips formed a lurching grin. He doubted they would fit neatly together. Great gouges had been made in the soft flesh, as if with a stabbing instrument, like a great spike or a man's finger. He let his fingers run over her nose and lips. Try as he might, he felt his eyes irresistibly drawn to her exposed white breasts. They had not lost the grace and form of their youth, but lay there, white and unsullied like two lilies. They felt cool to his touch.

There in the half-light, he cast his mind back to their conversation in the parlour at Trevanion only a week before.

He could remember every detail.

'Good, now tell me why,' he had said, and placed his hand on her shoulder.

Emily replied quietly, 'Go on. Despise me. If that's what you want. Do you think I care? Yet in spite of everything, I do care. I do. I think we could have been friends once, Matthew. If not for this. But I don't want your pity!' Her face became hard, proud, nervous. 'So, I was unfaithful to my husband, was I? Well, I won't deny it. While he tended his fields and went hunting and drinking and visited his friends, I played the whore. Is that what you think?'

She got up quickly and walked across the room. Her hands fingered the beads around her neck.

'Is that what you think?'

Matthew realised she wanted an answer, and suddenly felt caught off balance.

'You've just said so yourself,' he replied lamely.

'No,' she snapped. 'I've said what you wanted to hear! You see, we've got a choice. I either tell you what is convenient, or I tell you the truth. Which do you prefer?'

'The truth, obviously,' he said without thinking.

'Obviously? I tell you, there is nothing obvious about the truth, not with this family.'

It was only later, when he thought back on events,

that he realised Emily seemed to check herself at this point before continuing.

'Your uncle was a great man, Matthew. The life and soul of the party, a famous huntsman, a real local character. He was a monster!' She looked at him intently. 'You ask why I've never liked you, and that's not really true: there's something in you I do find attractive, but it's that same element that reminds me of your uncle. I don't want Lucy to end up the same way.'

'What are you saying? That my uncle did not treat you well?'

'No. No. I did love your uncle, Matthew. I did love him. I still do.' She stared down at her hands.

'Then why . . .'

'Matthew, there are some things you will never know! Do you have any idea what it is like to be a woman? Can you imagine what it is like to be brought down from Bath, from the royal spa, to this place?' She looked around at the low ceilings and the faded tapestries. 'I did not expect this.'

'So you were unfaithful to him.'

'No! I did not expect it, but I could have lived with it. It was not that.'

Matthew felt suddenly angry. He did not want to sympathise with her.

'Save me the detail, Aunt. I don't want to know.'

She almost smiled to herself.

'You said you wanted the truth, Matthew.'

'The truth is you were unfaithful to my uncle! That's all I need to know.' He glared at her. 'But why Pascoe?'

Emily smiled. 'Do you think he's so odd a choice?'

'He's so . . . old.'

'Not as old as you think, Matthew. No, he's young enough. Or maybe old age is a seductive quality in a man?' She seemed amused by the look on Matthew's face. 'No, age had nothing to do with it. Pascoe treated me as an equal, and perhaps he reminded me of better times. We met while riding.'

Emily's words left a rancid taste in his mouth.

'I don't want to know what you see in him, Emily. But I credited you with some taste!'

'Taste? Is that why I chose your uncle? At least Joshua cared for me, far more than John.'

'Is that why you killed him?' His words slapped her across the face. Suddenly she looked confused and scared.

'*Killed* him?'

'Save me the looks, Emily. The night John died Pascoe sent him a note. You know perfectly well what I mean.' This was the crux of the issue. He studied her face intently. He was tempted to say more, but he realised that anything he said would only sap the tension which hummed in the air between them. He had counted to thirty before she spoke.

'You've seen the note?'

'In a manner of speaking, yes.'

'How?'

'Pascoe asked John to meet him that evening, didn't he? Joey brought him the note. And you paid him to keep quiet. You can't deny it, Emily.'

'I know. I don't.'

'You amaze me, woman!' Suddenly his anger

boiled over. 'You stand there and tell me calmly how you connived in your husband's murder!'

'No! Believe me, Matthew, I had no idea.'

'Liar!'

'No! Please, believe me!' There was something in Emily's voice that made him, against his will, soften.

'Explain yourself.'

'I was having an affair with Joshua, but nothing more. I was content to play the wife when John would let me. God knows I stood by him. But I never wished to see him dead – you must know that.'

'So what are you saying?'

'Joshua killed him without my knowledge.'

There was silence, then Matthew said very slowly: 'Joshua killed my uncle. By himself?'

'I think so. Yes.'

'What do you mean, "think so"?'

'I don't know! I *think* so, because I saw the note, like you. But I . . . asked Joshua, and he denied it.'

'What did you expect him to say? He won't want to swing, will he?'

'No, maybe you're right. But I don't know, Matthew.' Suddenly something inside Emily seemed to snap. 'Matthew, I'm scared! If he killed John, what am I to do?'

'If you're really that concerned, go and tell Trelawne.'

Emily snorted in derision.

'Or what about Richard?' he suggested.

'Maybe. But then I'll have to explain why I suppressed the note to start with.'

'And why did you, if you're so innocent?'

'Because I loved him, Matthew. It was my first reaction.'

'Then could you betray him now?' His voice hardened. 'And why are you planning to marry him in three months time? My God! The grave's barely cold, Emily!' He walked towards her and for a moment he thought he was going to hit her. Then he realised that even if he did, she would not flinch.

'You don't understand, Matthew. I have to.'

'That'll be the day!'

'No, I have no choice. If I don't, he has . . . papers.'

'What papers?'

Emily gave him such a look of fear and indecision. She reminded him of a cornered fox, judging whether to try and jump to freedom over the heads of the dogs. Or stay and have its throat ripped out.

'I've never seen anything like it, have you?' The voice of Nathaniel Morgan jolted him from his thoughts. He looked down at the bloodstained mess in front of him and hastily lifted his hand.

'No. Nothing like it,' he said quietly.

Nathaniel walked into the barn. 'I'm sorry. Were you close?'

'Not particularly. But she has always been . . . important to me.'

'I heard her husband died recently. I knew John Trevanion, but only vaguely. It's supposed to be a fine estate. Unencumbered by debts, good pasturage. Better than this place at any rate, eh?'

Matthew found the conversation distasteful. He pulled the sheet back over Emily brusquely.

'I do not wish to discuss family affairs at this time.'

'I'm sorry, I meant no offence. Are you and the lady close?'

Matthew felt an almost uncontrollable desire to hit him. But instead all he said was: 'John Trevanion was my uncle.' He walked past the squire and out into the daylight. He wanted to be gone from this place. He found Lucy in the kitchen. She was sipping from a glass and her eyes were puffy and swollen. She smiled weakly and he suddenly thought how bruised and delicate she looked. It was as if someone had taken pink flower petals, and smudged them over her face.

'It's time we left,' he said.

She looked at him questioningly.

'I want to get back to Trevanion with your mother before nightfall,' he explained, then, almost as an afterthought: 'How are you feeling?'

'All right,' she replied, none too convincingly. 'I can't believe it's happened.' She stopped. 'It has happened, hasn't it?'

'Yes.'

Lucy put down her glass on the table, straightened her dress and went out through the open door. He followed her, up around the side of the manor and across the yard and through the graveyard until they stood looking at a patch of red, slimy grass, flattened by the feet of the curious. The wind buffeted against them.

> 'When with panniers astride,
> A pack horse can ride,
> Through St Levan's Stone,
> The world will be done.'

Matthew was startled out of his thoughts by the sound of Lucy's voice. He turned and looked at her. Her face was very pale, and her arms were wrapped tightly round her body. She looked very thin.

'Have you never heard that said before?' she asked him. 'Here am I, a stranger to this land, yet I'd swear I know more about its history than you do.'

Lucy looked down at the stone against which her mother had been propped. It was a large, flattish stone, about three feet across. A clean, straight crack ran through the middle, dividing it into two almost equal halves, about five inches apart. Judging by the wear of the stone, this separation had occurred some time ago.

'Legend has it,' said Lucy, 'that St Levan himself split this stone with his staff, and it has stayed here ever since. Some say it will stay here until the world ends.'

'Or until a packhorse rides through it,' Matthew observed. 'Then if the world doesn't end, they'll have no more use for it. Who taught you this?'

'Mary Vincent.'

'I might have known!' He bent down and felt the dull granite stone. 'Mary will tell you that every raven is a lost soul, and every hare's a witch's familiar.'

'I wonder why she came here?' Lucy said flatly.

Matthew reached for her hand: 'Maybe we'll never know.'

'But why, Matthew? Why?' Her voice mingled with the scream of the wind running up from the sea, and stayed with him long afterwards.

Why indeed? Matthew was angry with himself.

He had promised Emily to let things be. But maybe that promise had cost Emily her life. But why should Pascoe kill her? He was expecting to marry her! Jealousy? Rage? Or perhaps Pascoe had discovered their plan. Matthew jabbed his foot into the soft earth.

Chapter Two

MATTHEW HAD NOT BEEN LOOKING forward to this meeting but there was no denying the parson's summons. Richard Morecombe was waiting for him in his study, as usual. On his desk, a Bible lay open at a chapter from Job, and a copy of Cruden's *Concordance* at a page beginning with the word 'joyfully'. Presumably the parson was working on his sermon. His face seemed older and greyer since they had last met and he came straight to the point:

'What in God's name is happening, Matthew? John – and now Emily! Two weeks ago you told me—'

'I know! If I had any idea—'

'Don't lie to me, Matthew! The truth, remember! I can see it in your eyes.'

'If I had any idea she would be killed,' Matthew continued stubbornly, 'I would never have agreed to it.'

The parson caught the significance of the word. 'You *knew*?'

'In a manner of speaking. I talked to Emily last week. She told me everything. I should have foreseen this. It was Joshua Pascoe.'

Richard blinked at him in amazement.

'You can't be serious!'

'Of course I'm serious!'

'Then why haven't you done anything?'

'Because Emily was his mistress!'

Richard stayed stock still for a moment. Then he reached into the cabinet behind him and extracted two glasses and a bottle of port. His hand was shaking.

'Tell me,' he said. 'Everything.'

'So Pascoe killed John to marry Emily. Then why kill Emily?' Richard tapped his glass on the desk. He looked unhappy.

Matthew shrugged. 'Perhaps he found out about our agreement.'

'So what exactly did you agree?'

'Pascoe had a hold over Emily. Some papers, or evidence – I never found out what. She couldn't refuse him if he insisted, she said. I offered her a way out.' He leaned forwards. He had wondered whether he should reveal this now Emily was gone. 'Emily agreed to draw up a covenant entailing the estate to Lucy. This meant that no matter what happened, the estate couldn't be alienated, or sold, or tampered with in any way. So even if Pascoe did marry her, he could gain nothing.'

'I see, so you hoped he'd lose interest.' Richard drummed his fingers on his glass. 'You haven't said where you come into this?'

'In return for my . . . support, Emily agreed to my marrying Lucy.'

'So when she died, you'd get the estate.'

'Look, Emily could have lived for twenty years,' Matthew replied, defensively. 'I didn't want the estate. I wanted Lucy.'

'Does Lucy know about this . . . *agreement*?'

'We didn't want her to. After all, she could have said no,' he added.

Richard breathed out heavily. He looked no happier than he had five minutes before.

'And you really expect me to believe this?'

'It's the truth, Richard!'

The parson considered him for a moment: 'So what happens now with Emily dead?'

'The land passes straight to Lucy, entail or no entail.'

'And will you marry her?'

'Maybe. I don't know.'

'And what of Pascoe? If what you say is true, the man's a monster!'

'His time will come, Reverend.' Matthew leaned across the desk to where the Bible lay open and read: ' "For wrath bringeth the punishments of the sword, that ye may know there is a judgment." '

Chapter Three

WHEN HE GOT TO TREVANION, Matthew was surprised to see two horses he did not recognise tethered to the barn door. Josey was rubbing them down vigorously.

'I see we've got visitors, Josey?'

'Yes. Mr Nathaniel Morgan and his constable, Mary says.'

Matthew scowled. I wonder what they want, he thought.

' . . . Wheal Lizzy, they've hit a lode only five fathoms down.'

Matthew heard Nathaniel's voice from the hallway. He entered without wiping his feet.

The squire was clothed in a black riding-coat and waistcoat embroidered energetically in reds and golds. He was standing by the mantelpiece drinking canary and talking to Lucy. Lucy was dressed entirely in black, and her face and hands seemed paler in contrast. Another man, older and heavier, leaned against the far casement. He stood up as soon as Matthew entered.

'Mr Trevanion!' There was something forced and unnatural in Nathaniel's tone.

'Mr Morgan. What brings you here?' Matthew made little attempt to sound affable.

'Business, I'm afraid.' Nathaniel glanced towards Lucy. 'Business connected with your mother's death, that is. Is there anywhere I could talk to Mr Trevanion in private?'

'In *private*?' Lucy looked at Matthew uncertainly.

'There are certain matters,' explained Nathaniel. 'I would rather be . . . discreet.'

'Well, naturally, Nathaniel, but I don't understand why you cannot do that here. After all, it is my house.' Matthew noticed there was a new emphasis, slight but discernible, on the word 'my'.

'Quite.' Nathaniel gave her an embarrassed smile. 'Quite.'

'What's going on, Morgan?' Matthew asked irritably. 'You seem to have something on your mind.'

'All in good time. Please, Lucy – can I have a word?'

Lucy looked sceptical, but let the squire usher her into the hallway. Matthew could hear their muffled conversation. He and the other man eyed each other distrustfully.

After a few minutes Nathaniel returned alone and closed the door softly behind him. He looked very serious now, his cheeks fleshy and sullen.

'This is Michael Roskilly, Matthew. Michael is our parish constable.' Nathaniel nodded towards the other man. 'We are here because of a serious accusation.'

Matthew tried to keep his voice level. 'Why? Has something happened?'

Nathaniel Morgan enunciated each word slowly and carefully: 'I need you to accompany me to Penzance. On suspicion of your aunt's murder.'

Chapter Four

SIR ANTHONY BEVIS RESIDED IN A LARGE well-proportioned manor in the contemporary style, set back a little from the main street. Matthew was shown into a dining-room containing a long oak table surrounded by high-backed chairs, ornately carved and lavishly tasselled. Large portraits stared down from the walls, their faces pink, swollen and waxen, imprisoned in expressions of interminable worthiness. Roskilly pointed to a seat, then went out. Matthew was left alone with his thoughts and the empty tick of the grandfather clock.

He had lost count of the clockbeats when the door behind him swung open and in walked Nathaniel Morgan, followed by Roskilly and a short, blunt-faced man, with a grey wig and the same waxen complexion as the portraits. Behind them all, in a black frock coat, a scribe carried a sheaf of papers and some quills, ink, and other implements.

Sir Anthony Bevis was a man of some importance. He made 'good money', as he said, from smelting and shipping tin to the manufactories of Middlesex and Bristol. He had by far the largest share of the legal shipments from Penzance and hated smuggling with the self-righteous passion only the privileged can achieve. To this end, he had recently been appointed one of the stannary's coinage officers and devoted himself zealously to policing its regulations. He studied Matthew intently.

'So, Mr Trevanion, you are by all accounts an educated man, I assume you understand the nature of the deposition made against you?' Sir Anthony's tone was brisk and uninterested.

'No, sir, I do not!' Matthew stood up abruptly. 'I've been taken at gunpoint, arrested – on the basis of an "accusation"!'

'All in good time, Mr Trevanion.' Sir Anthony looked at Nathaniel. 'Mr Morgan, could you read the deposition?'

Nathaniel flourished a piece of paper. It looked slightly crumpled and worn, and must have been written several hours previously. Matthew wondered how the squire had known to make the deposition before he left home that morning.

'The deposition is as follows, your lordship:

' "Whereas Matthew Trevanion, tenant of Lower Rosmear, in the village of Malaggan, is accused of the murder of Emily Trevanion of the manor of Trevanion, that this murder was committed on the morning of Tuesday, twenty-third of September, 1749, in the churchyard of St Levan, I, Nathaniel Robert Morgan, squire of St Levan, and Michael Roskilly, constable of the same, do solemnly attest, in the presence of Sir Anthony Bevis, Justice of the King's Peace, this twenty-sixth day instant, 1749." '

The scribe's quill scratched furiously on his paper to record the deposition. It occurred to Matthew that whoever had written Nathaniel's accusation was quite fluent in the language of the Bench. He looked at them with growing frustration.

'But, my lord, what is the evidence against me? Surely for a deposition to be made you have to be convinced of my guilt?'

'Or the possibility of guilt,' the JP corrected him. 'Don't forget, it is the judge and jury who decide on that.'

'But surely I have a right to—'

'Quiet, man! Wait for his lordship to question you!' Nathaniel was clearly incensed by Matthew's obstinacy. Sir Anthony scowled.

'It is my duty to take a full and accurate record of the evidence against you,' he announced, 'together with your plea. However, you have no rights as such: it is at my discretion how we proceed, and it is in your self-interest, that most powerful of arguments, to comply, do you understand? Now, Mr Morgan, can you make known the evidence?'

Nathaniel wiped his mouth. 'I think we are all familiar with the accused's violent temperament and his passionate dislike for the victim. I can produce several witnesses to this effect, among whom Mrs Marshall of Buryan may be known to you?'

'Charlotte? Yes.' Sir Anthony smiled to himself.

'Likewise the accused has sufficient motive, with the possibility of laying some claim to the estate or simply to revenge himself on the woman who, in his eyes, usurped his position?'

'The rule of *cui bono*,' agreed the JP approvingly.

The scribe scribbled furiously. Matthew waited, so far there was nothing he had not guessed.

'Now we come to the specific evidence.' Nathaniel looked deferentially towards Sir Anthony: 'A letter has come into my possession attesting that the accused was not at home on Monday night, nor in the early hours of Tuesday morning, when the murder was committed.'

'A letter? From whom?' Matthew asked.

'Be quiet, Mr Trevanion!' announced Sir Anthony, then to Nathaniel: 'Who was the letter from, Morgan?'

Nathaniel looked uneasy.

'Well, Morgan?'

'My lord, the witness has asked that their name be not divulged at this moment, for fear of their life,' he added pointedly.

'Even so, I need to know!' Sir Anthony was clearly irritated by this nicety.

'What if I were to name this person in private?'

'Surely I have a right to know?' Matthew demanded.

'Trevanion, will you be quiet!' Sir Anthony beckoned Nathaniel over to the far end of the room. Matthew watched the squire bend his neck and whisper something in Sir Anthony's ear. The older man nodded, asked a question, nodded again, and the two of them returned.

'Good. Mr Morgan has convinced me of the need for his informant's privacy. That person's name will be revealed at the assizes, and not before.'

'But—'

'No buts! I will not tolerate any buts, Mr Trevanion. This is a due process of law. Do you understand?'

Matthew fell silent. Nevertheless, Nathaniel's very reluctance to name his informant had given him a clue to his – or her – identity.

'Now,' the JP continued, 'where were you on the night of Emily Trevanion's murder?'

Matthew glowered. It was true he had not been at home. They had been loading George's ship ready for Roscoff. But, of course, there was no way he could admit this to Sir Anthony Bevis.

'You do not answer, Mr Trevanion?'

'Who claimed I was not in? I don't recall having any visitors.'

Sir Anthony made a tutting sound: 'Does that amount to a confession of guilt, Mr Trevanion?'

'My mother was at home with me, she can vouch for that.'

'I must warn you that your mother may risk perjury, sir.'

Matthew said nothing further.

'Now we come to our second piece of evidence.' Nathaniel placed a rough calico sack on the dining-table. With the tips of his fingers he lifted its two bottom corners so that the contents spilled out. It was a white linen shirt. The cloth was blotched with dark red stains, almost brown.

'When we visited Mr Trevanion's cottage this morning, I found this stuffed inside a chest. It appears to be soaked in blood. I believe Mrs Trevanion will be prepared to vouch for us in court as well.'

Matthew stared at the shirt. It could be his, but he had no idea how it came to be bloodstained. Everyone was looking at him.

'Well, Trevanion?'

At that moment a loud knocking came from outside, and the indistinct sound of a man calling.

'What in God's name?' demanded Sir Anthony just as the door of the dining-room burst open and in strode Richard Morecombe, saying as he did:

'I beg your lordship's pardon. I came as soon as I heard.'

'You have no right—' started Nathaniel Morgan.

'My lord, I have every right if I believe an injustice is taking place, do I not?'

Sir Anthony was somewhat taken aback. 'Am I to believe you have fresh evidence for our consideration, Reverend?'

'Will you count the word of a man of God as evidence?'

'That all depends,' Sir Anthony answered cautiously. 'What exactly do you have to say?'

'Simply that I have known Matthew for longer than anyone else here, and I would judge him incapable of committing a murder like this. He is an upright man!'

'Incapable?' queried Sir Anthony. 'Surely the church teaches that even in Eden all men are capable of sin?'

'Of sin, certainly. Of murder, no. We are all sons of Adam, but not all of us are sons of Cain.'

'Yes, well.' Sir Anthony stared at his feet.

'Furthermore,' continued Richard, 'I can swear that only this morning Matthew told me how he'd resolved his differences with Emily.'

'But what else would he say?' interrupted Nathaniel. 'Do you have any proof, Reverend? Were there witnesses?'

'Matthew?' Richard looked at him enquiringly.

Matthew shook his head.

'See!' said the squire triumphantly. 'That is hardly proof!'

'Mister Morgan!' Sir Anthony felt he was rapidly losing control of the proceedings. He turned to the parson: 'While I have the greatest respect for your office, Reverend, I must ask you to respect mine. What you say, while no doubt of interest, is of a purely personal nature, and can have no bearing on this deposition. Do you have anything further to add?'

'No, my lord.'

'Good, then please be still. You may stay if you wish. Perhaps we will have need of you. Now, Mr Morgan, where were we?'

Nathaniel pointed to the shirt which lay on the table.

'The accused has still not explained this.'

'I was going to tell you when Reverend More-combe entered,' answered Matthew. 'That may be my shirt, though it is hard to tell. But that's not my aunt's blood. Last week I helped Josey Penhale kill one of the pigs. I didn't do a good job, I'm afraid.'

'So what are you saying – this is pig's blood?' asked Sir Anthony.

'Yes, sir, I am.'

'Morgan, what do you make of this?'

'The accusation still stands, my lord. We only have his word it's pig's blood.'

'But surely the proof is at best circumstantial?' interrupted Richard.

'That is for the jury. I must ask you to be quiet!'

'And what of me, am I not allowed to plead my own case?' demanded Matthew.

Nathaniel cut him off: 'But who else is there?'

It was not a strong argument but it seemed to carry some weight with the JP. Sir Anthony stroked his chin.

'Because of this crime, the whole county is in uproar,' he announced. 'Why, I am told that women refuse to leave their homes for fear of their lives. This is terrible! Terrible. If we cannot provide the people with some measure of protection and assurance, then the whole machinery of the Law, the sacred mechanism of Justice itself, will fall into disrespect. And without respect, without holy fear, Justice is an empty bag. Do I shock you? But, believe me, sirs, I speak the truth. Fear and implacable punishment – these are the two wheels on which our carriage of state must run, and only when it soundly rests on fear and fearful punishment, can it cosset the populace with mercy. Yes, Reverend, for me to be merciful, I must first be merciless, even when it is against my will. Unless Justice enforces order on every member of society, so that each man, woman and child lives in fear of the Law, and can consequently sleep in bed at night, chaos and civil strife will multiply beyond belief!

'My office is that of Justice of the Peace. How else am I to keep the peace unless I administer justice in a case like this? And if I do not, what will happen? You have seen and heard the evidence, as have I. Some of you see an innocent man wrongfully accused, maybe, and maybe he is. I for one see a man whom the people have already condemned. I see before me the means whereby I can maintain the peace of my office. That is Justice. Let the assizes say whether he is guilty or not. Clerk, make out the order. The deposition stands.'

'Your honour!' Richard went to speak.

'No! The decision has been made! Mr Morgan will convey the prisoner to Launceston tomorrow.'

'This is a charade!' Matthew shouted. 'I'm innocent! You virtually said as much!'

'I said no such thing!' Sir Anthony corrected. 'I merely said it was not my concern. Mr Roskilly, if you please.'

The constable laid a hand on Matthew's shoulder.

'But this is madness!' he protested.

'No, Mr Trevanion, it is the King's Law.'

'Surely there is something we can do?' interceded the parson. 'The assizes are almost six months away. If you consign him to Launceston, he will probably not even survive to stand trial.'

'Then Justice will be in the Lord's hands, Reverend,' replied the magistrate.

Roskilly dragged Matthew roughly off the chair.

'Wait! Do you want the law to look an ass, because that's what will happen!'

This at least struck a chord with Sir Anthony because he called for the constable to halt.

'What will the people think,' Matthew continued, 'if you imprison me and someone else is killed?'

Sir Anthony walked up and looked him in the eye.

'Are you saying you know who the murderer is?'

Matthew cursed. Damn! Now was not the time. Not like this. He wondered whether he should say anything.

'Yes, I do.'

'Who, then?'

'Joshua Pascoe.'

There was a momentary pause. Matthew could see the Justice briefly consider his two words, and then discard them.

'Mr Pascoe is beyond suspicion. Take him away.'

'But won't you hear him out?' Richard broke in.

He was still arguing with the JP as Matthew was led outside. It was night, and too late to transfer Matthew to the town gaol. However, Sir Anthony took his responsibilities seriously: in a shed behind his house, a thick iron bar had been sunk through the wall, from which there hung a chain about a yard in length. To this Matthew's hands, tied behind his back, were secured.

He sat in the half-light. From the house there came the faint sounds of doors opening and closing, of crockery, and servants' voices, that told him dinner was being served. Outside an owl called. He wondered who its victim would be that night. It was a long time before he fell asleep.

He was awakened by someone shaking him violently. It was bitterly cold.

'Matthew, wake up! It's me!'

It was Richard Morecombe.

'Here, let's get this rope off you, man.' The parson pushed him onto his side and began to cut the rope with a knife.

'What are you doing?' Matthew shook his head painfully.

'Setting you free, come on, I want to get going.' Richard winked at him. 'I persuaded Sir Anthony to grant you a recognizance.'

'A recognizance? But how?'

Richard smiled as the last strands of the rope gave way.

'Now be careful: you're bound to be stiff.'

Gingerly, Matthew stretched his arms and shoulders. He felt terrible.

'What's happened?'

'Time for that later, just keep quiet, and thank God I've got you out of here.' He gripped Matthew's right arm and helped him to his feet. 'The sooner we're gone the better.'

In a daze, Matthew was led back into the house. Sir Anthony scowled at him. He was clad in a rich silk dressing-gown and would clearly prefer to be asleep. The grandfather clock chimed six.

'Listen, Trevanion, against my better judgement your parson has persuaded me to bind you over instead of sending you to Launceston. I am only doing so because I believe the case against you is not certain, and of the time involved. Nevertheless, the deposition still stands, and you will be indicted for murder at the spring assizes, do you understand?'

Matthew nodded.

'Furthermore, I have only granted this recognizance on the risk of one hundred pounds, this sum being guaranteed by the parson.'

'One hundred pounds?'

'I quite agree – it is far too much for the likes of you. I only hope the Reverend is a better judge of character than I am, or else he has lost his money for sure. Now, the conditions of this recognizance are as follows: that you will continue to reside at your home, and will not go afield except on essential business. Furthermore, as I understand Miss Trevanion may be considered at some risk, and as you are still the primary suspect, I must instruct you under no circumstances to approach or have communication with her, nor also,' he added, 'with Joshua Pascoe, do you understand?'

Matthew considered the conditions with reluctance. 'Yes,' he said.

'Good.' Sir Anthony gave a sort of grudging smile. 'Now let me make you quite certain of this. If I hear of you performing any action of a suspicious or unlawful nature, or have any reason to believe your liberty might be harmful to any member of the public, I will immediately revoke this recognizance and have you conveyed to Launceston at once. Is that clear?'

'Yes, it is.'

'Do you swear by almighty God to abide by these terms and conditions, and to present yourself willingly and obediently at the Launceston assizes in the spring, and do you solemnly undertake to keep the peace to the best of your ability, so help you God?' Matthew was aware of a thick leather-bound Bible being pressed into his hand.

'Yes, I swear.'

'Then you are free to go. Get out of here. I pray to God I won't regret this, Reverend.'

Richard shepherded Matthew, still blinking, out of the front door and down the path to where two horses were waiting.

'Are you all right to ride?'

'Yes, but—'

'Then come on. We can talk about that on the way back – Morgan's going to be furious.'

It turned out that after Matthew was led away, Richard had stayed arguing his case with Sir Anthony and the others. When pressed, Sir Anthony had conceded that the deposition against Matthew was at best circumstantial, and in these instances it would not be customary to confine the defendant to gaol before trial, especially when the defendant was of some standing. It was Nathaniel Morgan who had raised the strongest objections and it had taken several hours before any progress was made. Eventually Sir Anthony agreed to grant Matthew recognizance, but for a sum he clearly regarded as beyond his means. Unless the parson could make over the sum in full before they set off for Launceston, there was nothing more he would do.

'Which is why I'm here at this unearthly hour,' the clergyman concluded.

'But one hundred pounds?' asked Matthew. Parsons did not normally have that sort of loose change in their collection boxes.

'I wonder,' mused the parson out loud, 'whether Sir Anthony would appreciate the public service George Trevose has performed by standing you bail? It is probably the closest he will ever come to seizing George's assets.'

Matthew breakfasted at the parsonage on bacon and eggs. They had never tasted so good and it was some hours before Richard saw him off.

'Take care,' he urged. 'And hurry home. Your mother will be worried sick.'

'I know, but how am I going to get hold of Pascoe?'

'Sir Anthony ordered you to stay away from him.'

'Which makes me all the more convinced he's the one who sent the letter.' Matthew slapped the parson on the arm. 'He also sent John that note before he died. If I can find that I may yet have a chance.'

Matthew had gone about halfway to Rosmear when abruptly he turned off to the right and cut through a small thicket of scruboak. He walked quickly and it did not take him long to reach Trevanion. He was just about to pass through the gate when he saw the horses. They were the same as the ones he had seen yesterday. So Morgan and Roskilly had not simply headed for home.

Matthew pulled back into the lane. If they saw him, he could be accused of breaking his bail before he had even started it. He wondered what Nathaniel was saying to Lucy. Then, taking care no one was looking, he climbed over the hedge facing the yard and settled down to wait.

It must have been at least an hour before he heard the heavy sound of the main door, and the voices of Morgan and Roskilly bidding goodbye. Nathaniel sounded bluff and hearty. Then he heard Lucy. For what seemed like an interminable length of time, they made polite, to-and-fro conversation on the front steps. They seemed to be enjoying themselves. Matthew could imagine the scene vividly, and he was suddenly overcome with a feeling of such intensity, that he could not define it further. At long last he heard Lucy calling to Luke for the horses. Nathaniel Morgan shouted his goodbyes once more. Then the two men rode up out of the courtyard. They passed within four feet of where he was crouched and were gone.

Matthew waited until he could no longer hear the sound of their hooves, then swung himself down into the lane.

Lucy was still standing on the steps, looking out into the yard, when she saw him. A strange expression passed across her face.

'Lucy. What's wrong? Aren't you pleased to see me?'

She smiled, but the lines remained on her forehead.

'They told me you'd been released – but what about your bail? They said—'

'Yes, I know, I saw them leave.'

He came closer and put his arms round her. Through her black cotton dress he felt her body stiffen. She glanced at him awkwardly. 'You'd better come inside – you look dreadful.'

In the parlour the same homely smells and odours greeted him.

'Nathaniel said you murdered her.'

Lucy's tone was flat and expressionless.

Matthew stared at her. 'And you, what do you think?'

'I don't know,' she answered, but too quickly.

Matthew gazed into the hearth. He was angry.

'What has Morgan been saying to you?'

'Nothing,' she replied but she knew it was a lie. 'Nothing at all.'

'For God's sake, Lucy, don't you know me better than that?' He spun to face her.

'There's always been something strange in your relationship with my mother.' Lucy's voice trailed off.

'What are you accusing me of? I told you, I made my peace with her.'

'And Trevanion had nothing to do with it? Nathaniel—'

'Damn Morgan! Damn him! I love you, Lucy!'

She tried to step back but he caught her and held her.

'Don't, Matthew! It's not right.'

He forced himself to ignore her, willing her to respond, but he could feel her growing more resentful by the minute. He pushed himself away and stood staring helplessly at her.

'Lucy!'

'Get away from me!' He remembered the look on Emily's face. He remembered Emily in St Levan, at the churchyard.

'I'm sorry,' his voice was brusque, aggressive. 'I wanted to hold you. I need you.'

Something in her eyes softened, almost against her will, then before she knew what she was saying, she blurted out: 'I'm so scared, Matthew!'

For the first time he realised how alone she must feel. Cautiously he put his arms around her and gradually, by degrees, she gave herself up to him.

'Nathaniel brought a note with him,' she told him much later. 'From Joshua Pascoe.'

'Pascoe? What did he want?'

'He said he wished to visit me tomorrow morning, and was it convenient.'

'Did he say why?'

'No.' Lucy propped herself up on one elbow and leaned against him. They were lying in her bed and her body was soft and warm. Gently he pulled her face over his. She tasted warm and sweet and tender.

Eventually Lucy teased herself away. She ran a fingernail down across his chest. He seemed so gentle now, and she felt a sudden thrill of triumph at how she had tamed him, tamed and exhausted him, so that he lay there, meek and spent like a child. She kissed him again and felt him stir lustfully but impotently, no longer able to respond.

'I've beaten you,' she whispered.

'Not for long.'

But it was victory nonetheless. She kneeled up on the bed and stretched herself lazily, feeling her skin tingle in the late afternoon air.

'I wonder what Mary Vincent thinks about my behaviour,' she said out loud.

'She's probably jealous,' he said smugly.

'And what about you,' she teased him. 'I do believe you were quite jealous of Nathaniel Morgan.'

His mood changed immediately, like a storm rushing in over the sea.

'That man is a bastard!'

'Matthew! I was only joking.' Lucy felt scared.

'Well don't! Because of him, I'm standing trial.'

'He really does believe he's doing what's right.'

'That's rubbish, Lucy! The man's after one thing.'

'And you're not, is that it?' She was angry and

amused at the same time. He glowered at her, and she fell upon him and hugged him close to her, so that their bodies rubbed together and she felt him grind himself against her, slowly and grudgingly to start with, and then more enthusiastically and desperately, as if his lust was driven harder by his anger. She smiled and tugged herself away.

'No. Not now.' She held him at arm's length. 'Will you be here tomorrow when Pascoe comes?'

'You know I can't go near him.'

'You're not supposed to have any intercourse with me, either,' she pointed out straight-faced. 'You can listen from the bedroom.'

'All right.' He thought for a minute. 'I need to look through your mother's letters.'

'Why?'

'Evidence. There may be something there.'

'Do you think so?' Lucy's poise vanished. 'What did happen, Matthew? Between the two of you?'

Matthew pulled himself upright and wrapped a blanket round her shoulders.

'There's something you've got to know,' he said. 'It's about Pascoe and your mother.'

'What about them?'

She doesn't suspect a thing, he thought. He wished he didn't have to tell her.

'They were lovers, Lucy.'

Chapter Five

THERE IS SOMETHING DISTURBING IN searching
through the belongings of someone who has
died. Both Lucy and Matthew felt it the next day,
although both left the thought unspoken. Perhaps
most unsettling is the added significance that each
object, no matter how trivial, now possesses. In fact,
the more trivial the possession, the more poignant it
becomes: a comb on the dresser, the brooch she wore
to dinner, a prayerbook on the bed with a page
turned down. Clothes. Some clean and neatly folded,
others crumpled and lived in. These are the most
upsetting. If you hold them to your nose you will
catch the unmistakable scent of that person as if she
were there in the room, next to you.

They worked quickly and in silence.

The most obvious place to start was the desk. It
was a fine piece of carpentry – elm, with an inlay of
maple and padouk, depicting birds peeping from
posies of flowers. Emily had brought it down from
Bath and now it stood in the alcove fronting the
window. The lid to the desk was, as they had
expected, locked. There had been no key on her body,
so Emily must have kept it at the house, presumably
in her room.

They began by rifling through the drawers of the
commode: they contained nothing of interest save
for dress-jewellery, cosmetics and ointments. Next

they tried the chest of shifts and petticoats beneath the bed. Nothing.

'It must be here somewhere,' said Lucy at last. 'Where on earth could she have put it?'

'What about the wardrobe?'

A large oak clothes-press stood against the wall. They worked their way through the assortment of dresses, jackets and bodices, feeling the pockets and the linings for telltale lumps. Again, nothing. Lucy slammed the door in frustration. Then Matthew had an idea. He stretched up and ran his fingers over the top of the wardrobe. This was slightly obscured by a wooden lip that stood proud of the edge. His fingers grazed against something cold. He grinned at Lucy and snatched down a small iron key. But when they tried it in the desk it would not fit. Lucy could scarcely believe it. Why else could the key be there?

Matthew muttered something to himself. Without waiting for Lucy, he bent down and inserted the tip of his pocket knife between the lid and the desk and with a snap of his wrist the lid was open.

He whistled softly through his teeth. Inside was a chaos of papers and documents, some in scrolls, others folded flat and bound with red or scarlet ribbon or sealed with wax, others just as single sheets of paper, or thicker, yellow sheets of parchment, and still other notes, and letters, jottings and chits, bills and slips of paper, some jumbled, some screwed into balls, others stacked neatly into little piles. Lucy pressed in close to him. From their size and bindings, Matthew recognised several as legal documents – deeds or covenants maybe. It looked as if Emily had been sorting them out, or perhaps she had been hunting for something.

It occurred to Matthew that as well as Pascoe's note to his uncle there might be much else of interest. The same thought must have crossed Lucy's mind, for she placed her hand on the lid of the desk and went to close it.

'I said we would look for Pascoe's note,' she told him. 'That's all.'

'But what about the other papers?'

'No. Not now. I want to look at them first myself.' She sounded sharper than she meant.

Even now, she doesn't trust me.

Lucy met the look in his eyes.

'Just leave it,' she said. 'It's more than I want to go into right now.'

Carefully she sorted the contents into two piles. The pile containing all of the larger documents, obviously of a legal nature, she placed back in the desk.

'I wish you hadn't broken the lock.'

Matthew ignored her. He was already poring over the second pile consisting of all the other sheaves and pieces of paper. It was going to take a long time to work their way through them, so moving Emily's prayerbook to one side, he settled down on her four-poster and spread them out on the counterpane. Lucy joined him.

The first sheets of paper appeared to be a series of notes in what Matthew recognised as his uncle's hand – large, bold strokes with little attention to detail. Lower Vean, Upper Vean, Long Meadow, Trevour, Plenangarry . . . it was a list of the fields that made up the old Trevanion estate. Some of the

names were crossed out. Others were marked with
a little dash or a tick. Matthew scratched his head,
but could not identify any particular pattern in the
markings.

Next came a letter to Emily from her relatives in
Bedfordshire. The tone was remote, formal, polite. It
talked of a cousin's ball, an aunt's illness, a neigh-
bour's election to parliament. Matthew passed it
quickly to Lucy.

Then a sheaf of tradesmen's bills. Kurgenven's of
Penzance for six yards of silk damask. Walkers
of Truro, for three hats and a dozen buttons. Nanse-
gollan the blacksmith for a bucket of nails. And so
on. Some were paid, most were not. Occasionally
John had put a broad ink stroke through the bill, or
had crossed out the original sum and daubed in his
own. Bundled with these papers were several letters,
some quite severe, from the aforementioned
tradesmen.

Then a note in Emily's hand, a lighter, more unpredictable style, with long sharp downstrokes: 'A. Holroyd, 35 Coinagehall Street', then 'William Cusgarn,
2 dozen'.

After this three more letters, from the Veryans in
Bodmin, and a short letter enquiring after John's
health, signed 'L. M., Kingston, Sept '48'.

On a larger sheet of foolscap were the traces of
John Trevanion's attempts at bookkeeping: out-
goings, incomings, debtors and creditors. But many
of the figures were missing or erased, and the
attempt seemed to have been abandoned before anything had been achieved.

While Matthew was trying to make sense of this,

Lucy had started on a thick wad of notes in her mother's handwriting. They seemed to be jottings of things to do, household chores and the like: 'floor rushes', '4 dozen eggs, 8 1/2d', '3 ankers pilchards, 6th Sept'. Lucy could remember the pilchards arriving from Newlyn, and her mother haggling over the price with Victor Jago. These scraps of paper had captured a moment of Emily's life. She had a sudden sense of the transience of all things.

It was now that Lucy came across a piece written in an altogether different hand – meticulous, poised, and cut across the page with a steely precision. She waved the note in front of Matthew. It read:

'Tuesday, towards 4 by the Maidens, love J.'

In their excitement they rummaged through the rest of the bundle, but found nothing. If my uncle had come across this note, thought Matthew grimly. Or maybe he had . . . At all events, these few words proved he hadn't been lying about Emily and Pascoe. But still, this would seem to have no connection with St Levan, or her death.

Putting it to one side, they continued their search. The next few papers proved disappointing. A letter addressed 'My dearest Emily' turned out to be from an aunt in Gloucester, and was followed by further lists of purchases and costs. Then came a rough sketch of the manorhouse and surrounding fields. Someone – perhaps John – had shaded in two of the fields, Little End and Trevour, which backed down to the coast. Matthew knew the fields well. There was nothing particularly special about them. Judging from the number of bills, however, he wondered if his uncle had intended selling them. But if so, to whom?

Then there was a document signed 'Jonathan Hocking, June 1749'. It was a simple audit of the Trevanion herd, together with a breakdown of Hocking's expenses, and his commission on the sale of six heifers. Underneath this Matthew was amused to find an epistle from Sir Anthony Bevis himself, instructing his uncle of the corrupting influence of smuggling on the social fabric of Cornwall, and urging him to act against 'these wicked malefactors'. He wondered what his uncle had made of it.

Then a letter in Pascoe's precise script: but this time it was addressed to John, advising him of a Mr Henry Waters' interest in acquiring the southern parts of his estate and setting out his uncle's options. Pascoe appeared to be encouraging his uncle to proceed with the transaction. This was dated 12th May 1749. As far as Matthew knew, no sale had taken place.

In another pile they found a list of debtors and creditors, this time compiled by Emily. She seemed to have achieved a more thorough mastery of the estate's finances. One of the entries read: 'To Mr Mitchell, for the construction of coffin &c. £1, 2sh.' Folded inside this was a note on thick white paper. It read:

Mrs Trevanion

I wld wish to acqnt y with certn truths pert. to yr late hsbnd & manner of hs death OF A MOST PERSONAL NATURE. i wld be oblgd if

y cud meet me plse @ St Levan churchyd Tus
morning sunrise. Psalm 27,10.
   A Friend.

The note was written in thick black ink with bold
rounded strokes.
   'I hadn't dared hope we'd find this,' he said. Lucy
smiled nervously and looked sad. He knew what
she was thinking. This note was perhaps the cause
of her mother's death. He held it up to the window.
   'There's a problem with this. It's signed "A
Friend", and whoever wrote it, it certainly isn't Pascoe's handwriting. Where's that note you found from
him?' He placed them side by side. There was no
comparison. 'Or maybe he got someone to write it
for him. When I think of it, there was no way your
mother would agree to meet Pascoe at St Levan.
She'd be suspicious.'
   'Are you so sure? You say she was planning to
marry him.' Lucy was still coming to terms with
what Matthew had told her. He wondered if she
resented him for it. 'And, anyway, who was his
accomplice? Don't be absurd!'
   'Maybe he disguised his writing,' he maintained,
although not with much conviction.
   Lucy pursed her lips.
   'But what if someone else did write it, someone
quite separate from Pascoe?'
   Her suggestion threw open a startling possibility.
   'You mean someone knows about my uncle's
death – and he was going to tell your mother, maybe
did tell her? Why didn't he just come to the farm?'
   'To protect his identity? I don't know. What do

you think happened? My mother goes to meet this man, Pascoe finds out, and . . .' Her voice trailed off. 'But there's another possibility altogether,' she said suddenly. 'What if the person who wrote this note killed her?'

'Then what about Pascoe? Lucy, it has to be him!'

'But just supposing it isn't him – who else could it be?'

Matthew could not tell whether Lucy was serious or not. He frowned. 'I don't know. Who else is there? *Cui bono*? as Sir Anthony would say.'

There was the clatter of horses coming into the yard. Lucy stepped quickly to the window. Four horsemen had pulled up.

'It's Pascoe, with some friends by the look of it.'

Matthew peered over her shoulder: 'Speak of the devil! What's Sir Anthony doing here?'

Lucy welcomed them into the parlour. After he had made her acquaintance with Sir Anthony, Joshua introduced the two others by saying: 'It is a sad testimony to the times when I cannot venture abroad without their company.'

Lucy looked at him questioningly, but he did not elaborate and the two men took up places at the far end of the room. Lucy showed Sir Anthony and Pascoe to seats in front of the fire. As he moved across the room, Lucy felt a strange and repellent fascination for the solicitor and she had a sudden image of his slim grey body copulating with her mother.

'Is anything wrong, my dear?' asked Sir Anthony in an avuncular manner. 'I hope our presence does not distress you unduly?' He smiled and looked pompous.

Lucy affected a laugh of surprise. It sounded shrill and false.

'Nonsense! I am afraid I have forgotten my new responsibilities! Won't you take a glass of canary with me?'

'That would be most pleasant,' Pascoe said, and rubbed his hands together.

Lucy looked quickly away and called for Mary.

They made smalltalk while the drink was served. As soon as Mary had withdrawn, Pascoe took a long sip and cleared his throat.

'A most delightful canary,' he remarked. 'A credit to your late father.' He glanced at her oddly. 'Now I expect you are wondering the reason for my visit so soon after your mother's terrible death.' A suitable expression of commiseration appeared on his lips. 'As you know, in due process I would normally consult with you to explain the nature of the estate and its entitlements et cetera, and would offer you whatever advice was appropriate. Is that not right, Sir Anthony?'

The JP nodded.

'I am pleased to hear that you are so attentive.' Lucy forced herself to be polite. 'But you used the word "normally"?'

The solicitor licked his lips.

'You are quite astute, Miss Trevanion. Quite astute.'

He leaned back in his chair and placed his hands together, fingertip to fingertip, in an attitude of prayer or profound contemplation. Lucy felt strangely perplexed. Sir Anthony smiled as if to reassure her, but achieved precisely the opposite effect. Then Joshua Pascoe began to speak. His voice quivered with a rare and sublime sensitivity, remarkable even for him.

'In the days following your uncle's accident, I had the pleasure of . . . assisting your mother. They were difficult times for her. Aah, if we had but known what we know now. Life is so delicate a thing, Miss Trevanion.' His face was momentarily hooded in grief. 'As you know, I have been your family's legal curator for many years, ever since John came of age. Consequently I have acquired an . . . appreciation of the estate which few others could claim.'

'I am sure my mother was very grateful for your attentions,' said Lucy icily.

'It is my hope also.' His voice was a model of humility.

Lucy frowned. Presumably the solicitor was trying to make some sort of point, but she could not tell what.

Pascoe must have detected this, for he paused significantly and then continued: 'However, we must put this past behind us, yes? "The dark backward and abysm of time" – how true those words. It is all around us! It was one of your mother's greatest fears that she too might perish and leave you alone in this world, Lucy. She told me she had nightmares, visions – that she felt herself watched by someone, or some *thing*, but who or what, she couldn't say. Naturally I thought her worries groundless, the effect of sudden loss, though with hindsight – ever wise – how I have condemned myself! She was a Cassandra.'

'You must not blame yourself,' urged Sir Anthony. He looked at his friend with concern.

'But I should have known, sir! The lady trusted me. That man visited me the week before – I should have known!'

'If you are referring to Matthew, I must tell you I believe him innocent,' interrupted Lucy. There was an awkward pause as the two men looked at each other.

'As I was saying,' continued the solicitor at last. 'As I was saying. Fear, death ... I did not believe, but your mother, rest her soul, insisted, and had me draw up various documents in the event of anything – anything, mind! – befalling her.'

'Documents? You mean a will?' asked Lucy.

'Not exactly,' corrected the solicitor. 'Your mother did not formalise a true will, any more than your father, but she was, as I said, devoted to your welfare. You were, after all, her only child.'

'So these documents, what are they, then?' she asked testily.

'These documents safeguard your wealth and well-being until you may enjoy them to the full,' Pascoe announced. 'Your mother asked me if I would offer you the same advice and guidance as I had given her. It was an honour.'

'I'm sorry, Mr Pascoe: I do not understand.'

'Miss Trevanion – Lucy – I am now your guardian. Your mother asked me before she died.' Leaning forward, Pascoe rested a hand on her knee. 'I am here to help you.'

'Guardian?' Lucy could feel her voice become taut and shrill.

'Do not look so alarmed, my dear, Mr Pascoe will explain,' Sir Anthony reassured her.

'But this is my property, my house! What do I need a guardian for?' Lucy tried to sound reasonable.

'My child, please understand: the situation is as delicate for me as it is for you,' explained Pascoe. 'Had I ever expected ... I would have perhaps declined, but an oath is an oath, and we both have our duties to perform. That is why Sir Anthony is here. He will act as your adviser. Sir Anthony?'

'Mr Pascoe is quite right, my dear. Your mother's testament quite clearly names Mr Pascoe as your guardian. Consequently, all of the estate falls under his trust until, of course, you marry or Mr Pascoe himself dies.'

'And what if I do not choose—'

'There is no choice for either you or Mr Pascoe. If you refuse, you will forfeit your inheritance. Your mother had the highest regard for Mr Pascoe, Lucy.'

'I appreciate this must be something of a surprise.' Joshua smiled at her. 'But I promise to make your situation as ... pleasurable as possible. The best care of you, Lucy. It's what Emily wanted.'

'You mentioned marriage, Sir Anthony?'

'That's right.'

'What if I married Matthew? Tomorrow?'

'My dear, I hardly think that would be prudent,' said Sir Anthony.

'That would be for me to decide,' answered Lucy.

'No, I don't think I could countenance that.' Pascoe spoke quietly. 'As your guardian I could not in all conscience give my consent to the man who killed your mother.'

'That's not true!'

'My dear, why do you think your mother was so afraid?' Pascoe talked as if Lucy were a naive and recalcitrant child.

'So I can only marry someone you approve of.'

'Yes, but I can assure you that, wherever possible, I shall respect your wishes.' Lucy slumped back in her chair. 'Is that not reasonable, Sir Anthony?'

'It is.'

Lucy clutched the arms of her chair. She felt sick. Above all, I must retain my composure, she told herself. To lose that would be the final humiliation.

'So, Mr Pascoe,' she said breezily, 'it seems I would be well advised to accept your tutelage.'

'Tutelage.' Pascoe rolled it over on his tongue. 'A most apposite word.' He stood up abruptly and offered Lucy his hand. 'I think you and I will understand each other exceedingly well. Now—' he gestured towards his companion— 'Sir Anthony is my witness, here is your mother's testament. It is exactly as I have said.' He produced a piece of folded parchment. Lucy tried to study it. Although she was unfamiliar with the terminology employed, its gist was plain enough.

'Of course,' the solicitor proceeded. 'You are a very fortunate lady, Lucy. Trevanion is a large and valuable inheritance by anyone's standards. Even with its present debts – which are not large – it will, with careful husbanding, prove quite bountiful.'

'Yes.'

'I promise I will not fail you, not once.' He looked at her intently.

'You? But I had not—'

'I would be a poor guardian if I shirked my duties, would I not? Your mother's testament specifically instructs me to husband the estate, until a suitable match can be found for you. It has not been an easy decision, but Sir Anthony agrees with me: I will have to take up residence here.'

Lucy gaped at him.

'You surely cannot be serious, Mr Pascoe! You have your own home, a fine home.'

'I gave my word to your mother.'

Lucy hardly knew what to say. She fingered the lace on her cuffs.

'But Trevanion is my home,' she said simply.

'And so it shall remain, my dear.' Joshua looked at her kindly.

Sir Anthony assumed a judicial air: 'My dear child, you are still overwrought with your mother's death. Do not worry. Mr Pascoe has no intention of moving here today, but really he is quite right. I advised him so myself.'

There seemed little point in debating the matter further. All Lucy could hope was to achieve defeat on honourable terms.

'You are correct, of course,' she conceded. 'When I think of it now, I reach the same conclusion. Besides, Mr Pascoe will be welcome company for me, yes!' She managed a smile. 'But please allow me the dignity of mourning in private.'

'Naturally.'

'Thank you,' she answered quickly. 'I think a

month will be sufficient.' She took Pascoe's hand before he could disagree. Sir Anthony got up from his chair. The two men at the end of the room rose sullenly from theirs.

'Splendid! Thank you for entertaining us, my child, I am sure you'll be very happy.'

'I hope so, Sir Anthony.'

'You should be grateful to your mother. She was, so Joshua tells me, a remarkable woman.' Lucy found Sir Anthony remarkably insensitive.

'Yes,' she agreed. 'Thank you.'

Joshua Pascoe extended his hand to Lucy.

'I'm sure we will both find our new lives quite rewarding, my dear. I was very fond of your mother.' He squeezed her hand. 'Emily never thought you took after her, but I can see quite a likeness.'

Lucy watched them leave from the parlour. What would she do now? The world seemed suddenly strange and dreamlike and unsafe. There was a sound behind her.

'You startled me.'

Matthew did not reply but stayed in the doorway, his face cast in shadow. Why were the others so suspicious of him? she wondered. As he emerged from the shadow, she realised why: no matter what the expression of his face his eyes were always the same cold black. She thought for a moment it was an expression of indifference, but she knew Matthew was never indifferent. Suddenly Lucy realised he was capable of killing her mother. A strange sensation ran through her.

'You heard?'

'Everything.' He looked into her eyes and she ran and clung to him.

'What are we going to do?'

He wrapped his arms around her. His fingers began to massage the small of her back, so that she began to wonder if he had heard her question. Then he laughed humourlessly:

'He has raised the stakes, hasn't he? Damn, I underestimated him!'

She looked up into his face.

'Don't you see? With that testament, your mother was suddenly expendable.'

He let go of her and crossed to the fire. A log had rolled on to its back and was smoking feebly. Kneeling down, he seized the tongs and levered it on to its belly. He wiped a smut of soot from his eyebrow and glanced up at her. He was smiling.

Lucy turned away. 'Why did she sign it?' she said quietly. 'She must have known . . .'

But Matthew had already got up and was walking to the door.

Lucy caught up with him in the hallway. She felt like crying.

'Where is Josey working today?' he asked her, and then added excitedly: 'I think I've just understood! Emily said she would entail the estate to you. If the entail was in the form of a testament, it would automatically cancel Pascoe's guardianship.'

'So why are we going to see Josey?'

Matthew looked as if the answer was obvious: 'To find out where Emily went the day before she died. I'm guessing she went to see a solicitor.'

They found Josey in the Seven Acre field digging

a ditch. Unfortunately he could only confirm that Emily had left first thing in the morning and returned long after dark. Who she had visited, he did not know.

Chapter Six

THE NEXT DAY WAS SUNDAY, and a fresh wind from the east rolled back the mass of cloud, exposing the great vault of heaven, pale blue and brilliant white. The bronze bell rang crisp and sharp over the fields. On a clear, fine day like today, Malaggan's bell could be heard in the neighbouring parish of Paul, and even Madron. Around the lip of the bell were inscribed the words:

Domine exclamo tuum verbum
Domine canto tuas laudes.

By the time Matthew arrived Lucy was already seated in the boxpew at the front where the Trevanions had always sat. Matthew could see the nape of her neck, shrouded in a black lace bonnet, as her head dipped in prayer.

In turn he closed his eyes and slipped to his knees. Next to him, he sensed his mother also kneeling. Oh dear Lord. He tried to empty his mind of thoughts. Ugly black thoughts which came crowding in from all sides. Oh Lord, please have mercy on my soul. Mercy . . . The scent of oak, polished by centuries of worshippers, a whiff of dampness rising from the flagstones. Forgive me for I have sinned. Peace. The subdued shuffling of feet, the crumple of skirts, a baby crying – a scalding cry – and a mother scolding it. Peace. He let his mind drift free, floating into the blackness. He pictured Trevanion in his mind's eye, but he was high above it, soaring like a gull. The house seemed tiny now, the fields mere patches of green and olive. Dear Lord, please have mercy on me, and show me guidance. He kept his eyes closed on the darkness, but gradually, almost imperceptibly, he became aware of a gentle lightening, a light, soft and even, that he realised afterwards may have been no more than the filtering of the sunlight through his lidded eyes. Then the sound of the church, momentarily hushed, came flooding back, muttering, coughing, scraping, but the sensation, the certainty of peace, remained.

' "I acknowledge my transgressions and my sin is ever before me.

' "I will arise, and go to my Father, and will say unto him, Father, I have sinned against heaven, and before thee, and am no more worthy to be called Thy son." ' The voice of Richard Morecombe called the congregation to attention. His face was stern and grey, and his voice fell against the cold stones of the church.

'Dearly beloved brethren, the Scripture moveth us in sundry places to acknowledge and confess our manifold sins and wickedness; and that we should not dissemble or cloak them before the face of Almighty God . . .'

The morning service commenced, and gradually Matthew and the rest of the congregation were absorbed into the great ritual of the prayer, timeless and endless, so that they became one people.

' "Then Jesus sent the multitude away, and his

disciples came unto him, saying, Declare unto us the parable of the tares of the field.

' "He answered and said unto them, He that soweth the good seed is the Son of man;

' "The field is the world; the good seed are the children of the kingdom; but the tares are the children of the wicked one;

' "The enemy that sowed them is the devil; the harvest is the end of the world; the reapers are the angels.

' "As therefore the tares are gathered and burned in the fire; so shall it be in the end of the world.

' "Then shall the righteous shine forth as the sun in the kingdom of their Father. Who hath ears to hear let him hear." '

Who hath ears to hear. Matthew looked around at the heads of the congregation, planted in rows like crops to be harvested. The devil has sown his weeds among the seed of this world. Who can tell where they might take root? Here in Malaggan, in a wet autumn? The very land itself bred spriggans and changelings.

Matthew called his attention back to the sermon as it was drawing to a close:

' . . . Wherefore, each one of us must hold a candle to our hearts, and if we espy a tare, some evil weed –' the parson's eyes flashed – 'we must tear it out and cast it on the fire. If we cannot do this, how can we claim to be the servants of that man we love above all others, our dear Lord himself?'

It was an hour or so after the service when Matthew

entered the church again. The building was empty and quiet. The candles had been snuffed, and their light replaced by the grey illumination of the aisle windows. Matthew closed the door quietly and crossed the nave to the northern aisle. Here it was, just as he remembered. He peered at a plaque mounted on the wall above a window depicting Abraham finding the ram in the thicket. He could just make out the wording:

This stone was raised in memory of Capt. Edward Marchant, born of this parish, who departed this life at Montego Bay, Jamaica, the 17th day of July, 1714; and was interred by the east wing of Kingston church in the forty-second year of his life.

Psalm XXVII. One thing have I desired of the LORD, that will I seek after; that I may dwell in the house of the LORD all the days of my life.

This man, although borne by winds of enterprise, and exalted by the fame of glorious action, never forgot the land of his fathers. He hath given eighty pounds towards the restoration of this church, and a further three hundred pounds for the relief of the poor of this parish. He left a widow and three children to mourn his untimely passing.

When my father and my mother forsake me, then the LORD will take me up.

' "As the hart panteth after the water brooks, so panteth my soul after thee, O God." '

The voice of the Reverend Morecombe echoed

down the empty nave. Matthew turned suddenly. At first he saw nothing, but when he stepped round the pillar, he made out a dark figure hunched in prayer at the foot of the sanctuary.

' "My soul waits on the LORD. May the LORD be merciful to me." '

As he spoke, the soft light from the east window, spangled with the red, yellow and indigo of the glass, played over the parson like some gentle kaleidoscope.

'A church is for prayer, Matthew,' Richard announced without looking up. 'What do you seek?'

'Guidance,' Matthew replied feeling suddenly ashamed.

'So does every man.' The parson got to his feet and dusted his knees.

'How long have you known I was here?'

'Ever since you walked in the door. I was expecting you.' Richard glanced at him. 'I wouldn't be much of a minister if I couldn't tell when one of my flock is troubled. I bury Emily tomorrow,' he stated, as if there were some connection.

'Yes.'

Richard walked up and rested a hand on Matthew's shoulder. Matthew saw with a surprise that he was bleeding across the knuckles.

'At the funeral, I don't think your presence would be wise.'

'Whyever not?'

'Be sensible, Matthew: you may be innocent, but there will be those who believe the accusations. I don't want there to be a scene.'

'But Emily was my aunt. And Lucy—'

'Lucy is very vulnerable, Matthew. Be gentle with her. The best way you can help her tomorrow is to stay at home.'

Matthew could see that Richard would not be swayed.

'I understand.'

He looked at the parson's face. It may have been the light, but Richard looked older and more strained than usual. It was as if a fine mesh had been pulled across his skin, leaving a lattice of fresh crow's feet over his cheeks.

'You look troubled as well,' Matthew said.

Richard rubbed a hand over his face and shook his head. Matthew was reminded of a dog shaking water out of his fur.

'I have been disturbed of late by strange dreams,' he said.

Matthew waited but the clergyman did not elaborate.

'Is there anything I can do to help?' he enquired eventually.

'No, thank you. I will feel better once Emily is at rest. It is a detestable business, Matthew.'

'Yes. And the man who did it is set to take over the manor. Have you heard—'

'About Emily's testament? Yes. I worry how it will end. And yourself, Matthew. There are still the assizes. Nathaniel Morgan came to see me the other day. He wanted to pay his respects, he said, but he was obviously angry at the assistance I'd given you.'

'I'm sorry if it caused you any embarrassment.'

'Not at all. Blessed are they which do hunger and thirst after righteousness – it is my pleasure, after all. But he is convinced of your guilt, Matthew. Convinced. How goes the case against Pascoe?'

Matthew paced across the front of the aisle. 'Did Emily ever mention a solicitor to you – apart from Pascoe, I mean?'

Richard looked puzzled. 'No – should she?'

'No matter.' Matthew gazed around the church. 'No matter.' He crossed to the lectern below the pulpit. The lectern was carved from a single piece of wood into the shape of an eagle, and Matthew's eyes fell on the huge Bible which lay open on the bird's outstretched wings.

'Did I tell you I thought I saw my uncle's ghost in the graveyard?' he said almost casually, without looking up.

'Often our grief can play strange tricks on us,' the parson advised gently.

'Even so, he was as real as the day.'

'He received a good Christian burial. He is at peace now.'

'But what if—'

'There are no ifs,' the parson said quickly. 'Only certainties. Of course I heard the rumours, do you think they are anything new? I remember when old captain Vincent drowned off the Lizard.'

' "Then shall the righteous shine forth as the sun in the kingdom of their Father." ' Matthew read out the words from the book in front of him.

'In God's time,' Richard responded. 'God's time.'

Matthew's eyes scanned over the ancient scripture. After that day's lesson the gospel continued:

'Again, the kingdom of heaven is like unto treasure hid in a field; the which when a man hath found, he hideth, and for joy thereof goeth and selleth all that he hath, and buyeth that field.'

He stared at the text and as he did so, an idea took root in his mind.

'Matthew, what is it? What's wrong?'

'Nothing, nothing.' Matthew brought himself back to his senses. 'Is there anything else you wanted to see me about?'

'See you about? I don't think so, though I was going to ask you to luncheon, or a glass of port at least.'

'What? Luncheon? That's very kind, but I must be getting back.' Matthew shook Richard by the hand. 'Thanks for the advice. I'll stay away tomorrow.'

'That's all right.'

Before the parson could say any more, the church door had swung to, and Matthew was gone.

Matthew cut through the village towards Rosmear, but as soon as he had rounded the first bend of the lane, he climbed over the hedge and made off across the fields northwards. As it was Sunday the fields were almost deserted and he was able to come down the Trevaylor valley and arrive at Jonathan Hocking's house unnoticed. Hocking and his family were at luncheon, and he was shown into the drawing-room.

It was a moderately proportioned room, fifteen foot by twenty, and furnished in a comfortable but not ostentatious manner. The walls were painted a light almond yellow and were graced with water-colours of Mount's Bay and the Falmouth estuary.

Matthew was standing studying these when Jonathan Hocking entered.

'Master Trevanion! A pleasant surprise, eh?' he said in a voice which suggested it was anything but.

'I'm sorry for disturbing you. I will be gone shortly, I promise.'

Hocking's fleshy features seemed to relax. 'Won't you at least have a glass of port? It's cold out.'

While his host poured him a draught, Matthew explained:

'I won't be at the funeral tomorrow.'

'You won't?' Hocking straightened up and gave him an odd look.

'No. You've heard the accusations against me?'

'Yes, by God.' Hocking coughed self-consciously and handed him the glass. 'So how can I help you?'

'Do you remember my uncle's fifty-third birthday? You were there with the Marshalls and the Reverend Morecombe.'

'Fifty-third birthday? That's an odd one, to be sure.' Hocking screwed up his face in an effort to remember something he knew he could not.

'Let me help you. I had an argument with my uncle. Over mining. Don't you remember – I said they'd never find anything on Trevanion land.'

Hocking paused for a moment. Then his eyes lit up.

'Yes, now you mention it. A good evening!'

'You and my uncle talked of prospecting for tin or copper. I need to know: did anything ever come of it?'

'What makes you ask?' Hocking sat down heavily in the chair facing Matthew.

'So he did find something!' Matthew told him. *Like unto treasure hid in a field.*

Hocking wiped a hand the size of a spade over his face. He appeared to be balancing his natural inclination for bluntness against his sense of professional discretion.

'Pascoe told me your uncle cancelled his will,' he said.

'So he said.'

'I'm not sure I can help you, not without permission.'

'Please – I wouldn't ask if it wasn't important.'

Hocking seemed to make up his mind.

'All right, but there's little enough to tell. It was the summer before this one. John was talking about it again, and I could see he wouldn't be put off. Anyway, he called in some prospectors, a captain and a tributer from Dolcoath – you know Dolcoath? – and asked them to survey the land from the manor down to the sea.'

'Did they find anything?'

'Not a thing. The land is passably good for grazing, they said, but for tin or copper it's all wrong.'

'Is that it?'

'No. You know what your uncle was like. As stubborn as a mule when he wanted. Wouldn't give up. There's money in that land, he used to say to me. Reckoned he could feel it in his bones.'

'So what happened?'

'More prospectors, this time from Ding Dong and Wheal Owles. Surveyed the rest of the estate. Nothing again.' Hocking smiled at him knowingly.

'I still don't know whether your uncle believed them. Called them all a pack of liars.'

'When was this?'

'Just this spring.'

Matthew took a mouthful of the port.

'It's strange he never mentioned it to me.'

Hocking shook his head: 'Not really. Maybe he knew he was being foolish. His indulgence, he said. He wouldn't be the first person to keep things hid. Often you only find out what a person was like after they've died.'

Matthew was thinking. 'Who else knew about this prospecting?'

'Apart from myself and Mrs Trevanion? No one, except for a couple of the men and Pascoe, of course.'

'Pascoe?'

'John had him look at the deeds to check on his mineral rights.'

'Was there any doubt?'

'You can never be sure, especially in Cornwall. When people sell property they hang on to the mineral rights if they can. But John needn't have worried: his family had owned every inch of that land since records began. Not that it did him any good.'

Matthew's face remained expressionless. He got up.

'Thank you. I won't keep you any longer. Oh, one final thing. If I wanted a solicitor, but no one in Penzance, someone to advise me on testaments and entails and that sort of thing, where could I go?'

Hocking thought for a moment.

'I don't know. There's any number of good lawyers

over in Helston, near the coinage hall. That's where they do most of their business.'

'Helston? Thank you.' Hocking showed him to the door. 'Are you still the agent for Trevanion?'

'As things have turned out, yes. Pascoe just wrote to me. He's a safe pair of hands, didn't think Emily would have thought of it, but there you go. Safe pair of hands.'

Matthew returned by way of Trevanion. Lucy would be alone today and it would do her no good to brood. He walked briskly. He had been so sure the verse he had read in the Bible was a clue: that there was something of great value in the land which his uncle had discovered, and Pascoe had found out about it. No, not even of great value, but of exceptional value, so valuable that Pascoe counted no risk, no crime, too great to secure it. 'For joy thereof he goeth and selleth all that he hath, and buyeth that field.' It would have all made sense. But it was not to be.

As he was turning into the farm, he saw Josey coming out of the stable.

'Working on the Sabbath, Josey?'

'No, as the Lord's my witness,' answered Josey. 'But Miss Lucy had that Nathan'el Morgan over this morning, and someone had to tend to his horse. You've only just missed him.'

That's a shame, thought Matthew.

He found Lucy kneading dough in the kitchen. As soon as she saw him she came to him and wrapped her arms round his neck.

'Pleased to see me?' he asked.

She kissed him on the lips.

'Where have you been?' she asked after a while. He told her.

'Do you think John was right? What if there were a seam of copper? It would solve everything.' She looked flushed and excited.

'Not while I'm still accused of murder and Pascoe's waiting to move in. How about you, what have you done today?'

She kissed him again and looked into his eyes.

'Nothing,' she said. 'Just waited for you.'

Chapter Seven

On Monday they buried Emily Trevanion.

That afternoon Matthew heard a horse on the track outside his cottage. Thinking it was Lucy, he came out to meet it.

It was Nathaniel Morgan. The squire was clad in black from head to foot.

'Just thought I'd pay my respects, Trevanion.'

'What do you want, Morgan? You're on my land.'

'I can come here as often as I like. As your prosecutor it's my duty to ensure you keep to the terms of your recognizance. Or I'll have you inside Launceston before you know what's hit you.'

'Try it.' Matthew stared at him.

Morgan managed a strong, falsetto laugh.

'Well, in the meantime I'm off to Trevanion. Lucy has invited me to dine with her this afternoon.' He kicked his horse's belly and it moved into a walk.

Matthew watched him leave.

The next morning he woke early and was at Trevanion with the sunrise. Before entering he checked the stables. They were empty. Mary Vincent was already up, scouring the pans and dishes from the day before.

'Is she upstairs?' he asked, and had passed through before Mary could answer.

There was no one in Lucy's room. He was at a

loss for a moment, then he crossed to Emily's old room and eased the door open. He could tell by the soft sound of breathing that she was still asleep, and pulling back the curtain of her bed, he saw her nestled between the stiff linen sheets. He bent and kissed her on the cheek. She stirred and murmured something but did not wake. She seemed innocent and tender like that and he felt a sudden desire to hold her and cherish her and keep her safe. He let the curtain fall back gently, and went to the desk. The lid swung quietly on its hinges. The loose sheets and notes were there, but the other documents, the ones she had not wanted him to see, were gone. He wondered where she had put them. He took out the papers that were left and began to sort them into separate piles as if he were dealing a deck of cards. The task absorbed him and he soon forgot himself.

'What do you think you're doing?' Lucy startled him. She was leaning out of the bed. 'You've got no right—'

'You were asleep.' He dropped the papers he was shuffling. 'I kissed you but you didn't wake.' He went to give her a demonstration but she snapped her head to one side.

'I'm not in the mood!'

Matthew sat down resignedly on the edge of the bed: 'I'm sorry, I didn't think you'd mind.'

'You don't own me, Matthew. Remember that. No one does. Get me my dressing-gown.'

'Yes, my lady.' Matthew smiled as he passed it to her, and she angrily wrapped it round herself. He stroked her arm.

'Don't you want to know what I've been doing?'

She looked sullen. 'All right.'

'I had a thought yesterday,' he explained. 'I was thinking about these bits of paper and I realised we were looking at the pieces to several different puzzles at once, all mixed up together. No wonder we couldn't make sense of it. Do you see?'

'I suppose so,' she conceded.

'So I thought I'd sort them into separate groups first.'

'What sort of groups?'

'Well, there's obviously one group for the estate, then there's one for general housekeeping, then two more for personal affairs, for Emily and John.'

'And this is what you've done?'

'Almost. This is the group for your mother's personal affairs.' He showed her the small collection and she began to sift through it. It contained:

Letter to Emily from her relatives in Bedfordshire.
Note to Emily from Joshua Pascoe.
Letter to Emily from aunt in Gloucester.
Invitation to a ball in Penzance.
Invitation to a whist evening from Mrs Marshall.
Letter from 'A Friend' requesting a meeting at St Levan.

Lucy passed them back.

'I don't see anything I didn't see the first time.'

'Don't be too hasty,' he replied and read the notes again. But Lucy was right. Nothing new at all. He lingered on the note from 'A Friend'.

'What is it?' asked Lucy.

'Nothing, it's just I can't help but feel this note is

the key to the whole mystery.' He placed it carefully on the bed.

'Wait a minute!' Lucy picked up a slip of paper. 'Isn't this in the wrong pile?' She showed it to him. It read: A. Holroyd, 35 Coinagehall Street, William Cusgarn, 2 dozen.

'That? That's just general business,' said Matthew. 'Cusgarn's that milliners in Redruth.' But there was something at the back of his mind.

'But what about—'

'I'm trying to remember something!'

'A. Holroyd,' Lucy ignored him. 'Who's A. Holroyd?'

'Of course, Coinagehall Street!' Matthew jumped off the bed, and snatched the note out of her hand.

'Holroyd, Coinagehall Street!' he told her excitedly. 'Hocking said the best solicitors were in Helston near the coinage hall. What do you think?'

He handed her the note. She read it again.

'There's only one way to find out,' she said at last. 'You go to Helston.'

'Why me?'

'We can't both go. Besides, I'm still in mourning. If you leave now you can get there by midday. I'll write a letter of introduction.'

After so many weeks of inactivity, Matthew welcomed the ride to Helston. Calling for Josey, he had Jessie saddled up and was gone within the hour. Sunlight streamed down over the hills, and he cut north towards Sancreed, then across the valleys to Madron, before climbing towards Tredinnick. Jessie had spent too long boxed in the stable and responded eagerly. After so much rain the moorland turf was soft and springy. Rainwater still lay in shallow drifts in the corners of fields and some places had degenerated into mire. Even so, they made good progress, and apart from a group of labourers enjoying a crust of bread and cream, met no one.

North Penwith is built around a series of granite outcrops bunched like the knuckles of a clenched fist. Boswarva, Mulfra, Trendrine, Trink Hill. Bald, unforgiving skulls of stone, some topped with quoits or carns, others bare save for the marram grass. And dropping away from the hills, the downs – Boswens, Bartinney, Carnaquidden, Beagletodn – bare and sparse and blessed with a bleak merciless beauty. It was over these that Matthew picked his route, following wherever he could the mulepaths of the traders, tinners and smugglers that criss-crossed the moorland.

Once he reached Carnaquidden, Matthew let Jessie lead him down into the valleys and around the base of the hills until he arrived at Ludgvan. Here there were tin smelting works and the clear October sky was smudged with reeking smoke as it was belched from the furnaces. Out of curiosity, he edged Jessie over the hill and looked down.

Ludgvan smelting house was a large industrial unit, its main building at least one hundred feet long and forty feet high. From inside there arose the sound of men's voices, loud, calling above the roar of the five great reverbatory furnaces and the clang and the din of the coal and the ore being shovelled. Even while he watched, a train of packhorses, laden with baskets of black tin, came down from

Nancledra, while, trailing up from Market-Jew, a similar caravan conveyed its cargo of coal. After the pure desolation of the downs, the impression of infernal, man-made production, of the grinding and groaning of man, beast and mineral in some hot, fiery pit, was all the more striking. He sniffed the air and tasted the bitter scent of burned coal and metal.

Matthew shook the reins and passed down towards Mount's Bay, until he found the Helston road near Goldsithney. From here it was only eight miles to Helston, and the going became easier. Rosudgeon, Germoe, Breage, then over Sithney Downs, to the final hill from where he could see Helston perched – almost sliding, he thought – on its slope above the Loe Valley.

By the time he reached Coinagehall Street, he was ravenous, for he had not eaten all day, but tethering Jessie outside The Anchor, he went straight up the street on foot. Number 35 was a granite-fronted townhouse with well-proportioned windows and a small portico. Next to the door was a small brass plaque which read:

A. HOLROYD, SOLICITOR AND COMMISSIONER FOR
OATHS.

Matthew knocked and was greeted by a servant and ushered into one of the front rooms which had been designated as the reception. He gave the man Lucy's letter and settled down to wait.

It was only five minutes before the servant returned and led him along the corridor to a bare white room, empty save for a few pieces of simple furniture. A man faced him from behind a desk. He wore a black woollen frockcoat without trimmings and a white cotton shirt with a plain collar.

'Mr Holroyd?'

'Adam. My Christian name is Adam.' The solicitor reached out a small neat hand towards him. 'Please take a seat.'

Matthew introduced himself and sat down. He guessed from his dress and manner that Adam Holroyd was a dissenter, possibly a Quaker.

'Any relation, Mr Trevanion?'

'By marriage only.'

'Yet you come on family business?' The solicitor eyed him shrewdly.

'Mr Holroyd, I believe my aunt, Emily Trevanion, visited you on Monday last.'

'She did indeed.' Adam Holroyd consulted a diary on his desk. 'At 12:30 post meridiem, to be precise.'

Matthew's face broke into a smile which he realised was totally inappropriate.

'Can I ask what it was regarding?'

Adam Holroyd thought for a moment before replying.

'Your aunt wished me to draw up a new will.'

'Was there anything unusual in her directions – an entail, for instance?' Matthew wondered if he appeared as nervous as he felt.

Adam Holroyd looked amused: 'A shrewd guess. Yes, there was an entail. Your aunt requested me to entail the estate in its entirety to her daughter Lucy.'

'And did you?'

'Here it is.' Holroyd pulled a large manila folder

from a drawer and slid it across to Matthew. Inside was a new sheet of parchment which read:

Whereas I, Emily Trevanion, formerly Marchant, of the manor of Trevanion, being perfect of mind and body by the grace of God, do hereby declare that all of my rightful estate, comprising the manor and land of Trevanion, consisting of the fields and pasturage hereunder named ... [at this point there followed a lengthy list of fields] ... together with the house, all barns, tenements and all other buildings, goods and possessions on the said land, together with the seisin of the bartons of Trewidden, Boskedgean and Rosmear, and all of their buildings, land, chattels, and rights, each according to their own several tenures, together with all other rights, privileges and dues deriving from the said properties,

Shall henceforth be irrevocably and irredeemably entailed to my daughter Lucy Anna Trevanion, also of Trevanion, and to her children after her, and may neither be sold, mortgaged or disposed of in any way, manner or means, or wagered or put at risk, in any way which would alter the condition of their entail, and the right of herself and her heirs to enjoy them in perpetuity.

And all such property and belongings which comprise this entail shall pass to her immediately and irrevocably on the event of my death without any restriction save as exist in the original seisins and tenures of the estate, and in the conditions of this entail.

If, however, God wills that she pass before me without issue, then all of the aforesaid shall pass to my nephew, Matthew Trevanion, of Lower Rosmear.

I, Emily Martha Trevanion, do solemnly create this entail and do confess the above to be a true and accurate expression of my last will and testament, this year 1749 of our Lord, on the 22nd day of the 9th month.

Matthew looked up.
'She didn't sign it.'
'No.'

Matthew considered Holroyd's account all the way back from Helston.

On the Saturday before Emily had died, the solicitor received a letter from her requesting an appointment that Monday at midday or as soon after as was convenient. Although he was somewhat taken aback, it so happened he had a free hour from half past noon and decided to make himself available.

The rest could be deduced from the final document. When Emily arrived, she had instructed him to draw up a complete will and testament immediately, together with the entail described. Looking back on the meeting, the solicitor would have said Emily appeared impatient, even nervous: her one stipulation was that her document be completed that very day.

In this, however, Holroyd could not oblige: his clerk had needed to transcribe the testament to parchment and had been out on business until the morrow.

Emily had offered to double his fees but when she could see his protestations were genuine, she desisted. She would return on Wednesday to sign and collect the document. That was the last he saw of her.

Matthew hurried Jessie along. The autumn sun was already low over Penwith and he wanted to be home as soon after dark as possible. A chill wind had arisen from the west and he suddenly realised he hadn't eaten all day and was famished. By the time he reached Market-Jew the fishing boats had pulled in for the night and the fishermen were wandering up from the shore in groups of two or three. Their wives sat waiting on the slipways, wrapped in shawls and sucking on their pipes and talking. Drinking houses lined the street and Matthew was tempted to stop, but judging them too busy, passed on into the open country. He had gone about a mile when he spotted a tavern he had seen on the way over.

It was a small place, quiet for the time of day, and Matthew had no trouble getting a table in an alcove where he could watch the other customers without being seen. The serving girl seemed friendly – about eighteen, he guessed, with strong hips and a broad ruddy mouth – and he ordered a piece of squab pie and a quart of ale. The pie was delicious and when it had gone he was still hungry so he ordered another, and sat sipping his beer until it came.

He felt tired and more deflated than he cared to admit. If only Emily had signed – she should have insisted. Instead it caused her death, he could see that now. He touched the stiff fold of parchment in his jacket. At least it proved he had nothing to gain from killing her before she signed it. And to think, after everything, she had named him as an heir. A feeling of great tenderness welled up inside him, so strong that he thought for a moment he might cry.

'Your pie, sir?'

The pie seemed less delicious the second time around and he chewed methodically, his mind elsewhere. He was staring blankly at his plate when he suddenly realised someone had carved their initials into the table top. The initials were ET. They were Emily's.

'Do you remember a lady sitting here – it would have been a week ago last Monday?' he asked the barmaid.

'Las' Monday?' The girl looked surprised and then suspicious. 'Don' know what I was doin' las' Monday.'

'She's a friend of mine – recommended I came here.' Matthew pushed a shilling across the table. 'A gentlewoman, handsome, dark hair, high cheekbones – she'd have been by herself.'

The girl looked at the coin.

'Take it,' he told her. 'I won't tell your father.'

She slipped a finger over the shilling. 'You know, there *was* a lady 'ere – a proper lady, mind – I remember saying to Da' we don' see many like 'er. Gettin' old, I'd 'ave said, at leas' thirty-five. But she weren't sittin' 'ere.'

Matthew felt the skin prickle on the back of his neck.

'Are you sure she wasn't sitting here? After all, it was a week ago.'

The girl knitted her eyebrows.

'Maybe you're right. Can't honestly say.' She scooped the coin into her apron pocket. 'Is she a good friend of yours?'

He ran a finger over the carving. It was still rough. 'Yes, a very good friend.' He blinked and seemed to rub a speck out of the corner of his eye. 'Can you remember anything else – did she talk to anyone?'

The girl shook her head and looked bored. 'Not that I recall. Will you be 'aving another, sir?'

'No, it's all right. And thank you.'

'Always 'appy to oblige a gen'leman.' She bent over him to take his mug and let him sense the soft warmth of her body through her shirt. He looked the other way.

He could imagine Emily, bored and nervous, scratching the table with the tip of her knife. He found himself thinking of the day they had spent at Malaggan Fair. Happier times. Though perhaps they only seemed happier. Perhaps the seed was already planted. Perhaps she was seeing Pascoe even then?

Matthew put his money on the table and left quickly. He had stayed longer than he had intended. It would soon be dark. He kicked Jessie into a fast walk as the sun died behind the hills.

As Matthew pushed on into the valleys beyond Carnaquidden, the darkness seemed to seep out of the earth like a dye and the colour of the shrubs and bushes was drained away. Stars shimmered and the moon blazed over the bowl of night. The wind had grown steadily and now it cut into his hands and face so that he sank deeper into his coat. Whenever he looked up, he could see the dark silhouettes of the hills stretching out on either side, rising, falling, featureless except for the occasional oak or rocky outcrop, and above them all, the dizzy height of the heavens, dazzlingly black and speckled with the hard silver points of the stars.

After an hour or so, he saw Sancreed church tower, low and squat, over to the west, and cut down towards Toldavas, taking an old market track which ran beside the fields. Jessie snorted softly in the night air.

Suddenly he realised he was not alone.

His ears, lulled by the steady rhythm of the hooves, caught the sound of breathing, heavy, regular, to his left. The breathing was so loud, like a monstrous bellows, that Matthew thought of the great furnaces of Ludgvan. He twisted in the saddle. He could see nothing. He pulled up Jessie short. The breathing stopped. Matthew looked again. Still nothing.

Ahead of him the path ran down into a small copse, skirted on both sides by low granite walls. An impenetrable blackness hung under the shadow of the trees. He waited, listening to the sound of his own breathing and that of Jessie. Perhaps it was nothing. There was a sudden rustle and with a great flapping, a crow, or a raven, launched into the air in front of him. Then silence again. Matthew strained to pick up the tiniest spark of noise, but the place was now unnaturally quiet. He listened. The sweat on his forehead felt cold in the breeze. Then there was a sudden squelching of mud and the sound of a large body shifting its weight.

He sighed with relief. Cows. Of course. He couldn't believe he'd mistaken their breathing for anything else. Stretching up in the saddle and peering over the wall to his left, he could make out the forms of half a dozen heifers. One of them snorted heavily. The two hedges must somehow have amplified the sound beyond all recognition. Relieved, but trembling a little, he flicked at his reins and moved on. He must be feeling on edge tonight. Half an hour more and he would be home with Lucy. He passed into the smoky darkness underneath the trees.

He had not gone more than a hundred yards when a twig snapped. A loud, heavy snap, behind him. He froze. It was just a breaking twig, one of the cows had stepped on a twig. He tried to shake off a feeling of fear, but found to his surprise he could not. Bright blue light streamed down through the trees. He looked around, cursing himself. Nothing, the same as before.

Up to his right lay the village of Sancreed, a slightly blacker shape on the hillside. Behind him, from where the sound had come, the path wandered back down into the copse. Sticks often snap. Often. Emily – riding in the moonlight to St Levan, a red necklace round her throat. The thought came to him from nowhere. He thought of Captain Vincent, his mouth full of soil. 'Where are you going, to lie with your women, and dandle your babes on your knees?' Or was that a different tale?

Matthew suddenly realised that where he had been staring into the trees, he could make out a large shape, darker than the surrounding terrain, in the shadow underneath a large beech. He willed himself to look harder. The shape emerged, then dissolved again into the gloom.

'Hello!' he called out. 'Who's there?' His voice sounded frighteningly loud. 'Hello!'

The shape, if there was one, made no response. Jessie snorted and stamped her foot. She seemed ill at ease.

Tensing his arms, Matthew jabbed his heels into her belly and urged her back into the copse. She wouldn't budge. When he tried again, she shied away. A gust of wind buffeted him and the cold cut him to the quick.

He swung down from the horse.

'Who's there?'

A low rushing noise, like the wind in the trees, but heavier, like the shifting of shingle on the beach.

Without thinking, Matthew threw himself to one side as a large dark shape passed over where he had been standing. The air shifted around him. It must have been at least eight feet tall, and of a huge, monumental weight. The thing landed with a dull thud about ten feet away. It drew itself up and he could feel it watching him. It was breathing. Low, gravelly, hissing – the sound he had heard earlier.

'Hold!'

Matthew called out, though more to hear the sound of his own voice, than from any other reason. The thing must be a devil. His hands scrabbled in the dirt for a weapon. Jessie was neighing wildly and her screams tore through the night sky.

'In the name of God, hold!'

If he found a stick or a stone, what good would it be? Or would one touch from that thing tear him down to the pit?

He remembered facing his uncle in the field above Rosmear. He sucked the fresh sea-air deep into his lungs.

Suddenly the creature pounced.

He tensed himself. It was incredibly fast, faster than it should be. Matthew dived to one side. A heavy arm or limb, encased in some coarse fabric or flesh, struck him on the side of the skull and sent him down. A foul bitter smell invaded his nostrils. His head spun. He felt like vomiting. The ground was cold and damp and he could feel his strength flowing away from him into the damp earth. He was a child again, lying in his bed asleep, unable to run as the nameless terror pursued him. Move! Damn you, move! He willed himself up.

He did so just in time. A massive blow shattered the stone where his head had rested. Matthew slewed to one side, heaving himself onto all fours. Something hit him full in the face. For a second he felt no pain, only a huge swollen numbness. His mouth was full of a thick sweet liquid. He realised later it was his blood. His tongue found the shattered stump of a tooth.

The figure was no more than four feet away. It towered above him, blotting out a third of the sky. 'And his tail drew the third part of the stars of heaven and did cast them to the earth', a voice said somewhere inside him. In another second the enemy would be upon him.

'Who are you?' He mumbled through his lips, slurring his words like a drunk. 'What do you want?'

Then a voice as cold as freshly turned earth. The first sound of a first word. Then before the sound could coalesce into syllables, another voice, a human voice, not more than thirty feet away.

'Ho! Who's there!'

A great dizziness came over him. He could feel the world tumbling away from him.

'Here!' his mouth cried. 'Help!'

Any second now and the thing would be on him. With one final effort he flung himself backwards.

'Help!' he cried.

And then nothing.

PART FIVE

Chapter One

'WHO ARE YOU?' THE VOICE called to him. He was in a dark grey room. A feeling of intense insecurity engulfed him. He could smell oak burning. Who was he? 'Where are you going?' The voice called again, more insistent this time. It sounded like the wind over the downs. 'Where are you going?'

Then another, closer, female voice. Something next to his skin. 'Matthew.' He awoke. Lucy was standing over him, the tresses of her hair were falling on his face. He felt a sudden irritation and went to brush them away but found to his surprise that his hand did not respond.

'Matthew.' She smiled reassuringly. His head felt as if it had been stuffed with a bale of cotton. A terrible ache ran down from his crown to his shoulders. He went to talk to her and the ache grew teeth and bit savagely into his skull. He winced.

'Don't worry.' She patted the sheets over his chest. 'You'll be fine in a couple of days. Here. Drink this.' A cold earthenware cup was forced between his lips and a hot liquid, tasting of cloves, was poured into his mouth. He felt some of it splash uselessly down his chin and on to his neck. He tried again to speak and choked on the liquid still in his mouth. It was some time before the coughing stopped and then he tasted the same warm sweet liquid in his mouth.

'It's all right,' she told him. 'Sleep. You'll feel better later.'

Greyness embraced him. Where is An Jenny? he thought. He had just ridden back from Mousehole and Emily had betrayed him. He had been in a fight with John Trevanion. . . .

When next he woke, he could tell by the cool grey light on the far wall that it was approaching dusk. He was in Trevanion, he realised. He must have been dreaming. Lucy was dressed in black and sat at the foot of the bed, a sampler in her hand. She looked very pretty, so pretty. In the grate a warm, orange fire hissed and crackled. He slept again.

People were talking, not too close, maybe in the next room. It was morning. A seagull cried out just above his window. He opened his eyes, slowly, reluctantly, and was pleasantly surprised that the sharp-fanged dog, which had spent the last two days gnawing on his skull, seemed to have gone.

Cautiously, he felt out the sensations of his arms and legs, flexing his muscles, letting the nerves tingle under his skin. They felt good. He stretched – his body ached but, he guessed, more through stiffness than real injury. Gingerly he shifted his head. Good.

There were still voices in the adjoining room. He could pick up the odd word or phrase. Lucy was there, but talking quietly, and at least two men. He ought to recognise them.

Matthew rolled onto his side and swung his feet onto the rough Turkish carpet. So far, so good. His head and chest ached, but he ignored them. Another heave and he was standing. He gripped the back of the chair. Why did he feel so light-headed? Over the fireplace hung a mirror. He looked at himself.

A monster stared back at him.

His left eye had obviously been severely damaged. Although he could now use it, it must have been closed the day before and was surrounded by a mass of red angry flesh the size of an egg. He touched it and winced. As if this was a trigger, pain leaped across his face and on to his shoulders. Damn. His nose was so bruised he guessed it had been broken, an ugly weal ran from its bridge almost to his right ear, and his lips were puffy and cut. He opened his mouth and saw he had lost two bottom teeth. He touched the shattered enamel with his tongue. It hurt like the devil.

Matthew rubbed his hand over his face. He felt strangely fascinated, as if he were staring into someone else's face. But the monster was real enough.

He realised dimly that whoever had done this had not expected him to survive. He examined his left ear: it had been either cut by the force of the blow, or torn in some way. Its top whorl was crusted with recent blood and stuck out from his head like a jibsail. He plied the soft cartilage with his fingers. A pain was stabbing at his right shoulder. He suddenly noticed that his chest and shoulder were firmly bandaged.

'You're up!' Lucy stood framed in the doorway. He turned stiffly towards her and tried a smile. She seemed concerned and tense.

'Lie down before you fall down,' she told him.

'What's wrong? I'm all right.'

'I know,' she said, and he realised she wasn't worried about him. 'Now lie down. Reverend Morecombe is here to see you.'

Reluctantly he let her nurse him back to bed. As soon as he was settled, she leaned over him and kissed him quickly on the forehead.

'I love you,' she told him.

He reached up and tried to pull her closer, but she stepped back and put a finger to her lips.

'What happened to me?'

She glanced back at him from the door: 'I'll tell you later.'

He lay there thinking about her until he heard a tap at the door. It was Richard Morecombe.

'Lucy tells me you're on the mend!' Richard smiled stiffly at him.

'What happened, Richard? I was riding back from Helston . . .'

'Josiah Penhale found you. He and Luke were coming back from Newlyn and they heard your horse neighing.' Richard sat down heavily in the chair. 'You were lucky they did, or you wouldn't be here today.'

'Who attacked me?'

'You don't remember?' The parson looked at him intently.

Matthew shook his head: 'All I remember is . . . I don't know . . . a figure in black, a man in black, I think.'

'You *think*?'

'I don't know, Richard. It was very dark. Whoever – *whatever* – did this was no ordinary man.' Sunlight had been streaming in through the east window. A cloud must have moved over its face, for suddenly the light failed and died, and the room grew cold. Richard stared into his face. Then the cloud passed and the room leaped with oranges and yellows.

'Matthew,' he said gravely. 'There's something I have to tell you. Something else.'

Matthew waited.

'The night before last, when you were attacked, your cottage was also broken into.'

Matthew sat bolt upright in bed. His head buzzed angrily.

'Unfortunately, your mother—'

'What do you mean? Is she all right?'

The parson leaned forward: 'She was badly beaten, Matthew. Very badly. Luke rode over to tell her about you and found her. But she'll be fine, God willing. Mrs Dunstan's looking after her at the parsonage.'

'Why didn't anyone tell me?'

'You were in no fit state yesterday. We thought you wouldn't understand, or if you did, it might make you worse.'

'Who did this?'

'We don't know. When Luke got there, the whole place was a shambles.' A look passed across his face. 'Luke found her by the fireside. She'd been burned, Matthew. She's scarcely spoken.'

Matthew pushed himself forwards as if to get up. Richard held him, gently but firmly.

'Don't! You're still sick!'

'Get off me!'

'There's nothing you can do!'

Matthew cursed himself for his weakness and sank back into the pillows.

'Who do *you* think did this?' he asked at length.

Morecombe frowned: 'Who would gain?'

'Pascoe. Pascoe for sure.'

'Was it Pascoe who attacked you?'

'No. Someone else. Someone bigger, more powerful.' Matthew looked into the parson's face. 'I'm not even sure he was human.'

Richard looked at him sceptically.

'You've been through an ordeal,' he said at last, somehow without patronising. 'Rest some more. Things will make more sense then.' He stood up.

'But things don't make sense, do they?'

'Do they ever, Matthew? Why should they start doing so now? We are born in pain and ignorance, and will die in the same. There is no sense in this world, only in the next, and for us to pretend otherwise is just folly. Folly and pride. Rest. Find your peace. In the meantime I will tend your mother.'

'But what of Pascoe?'

'What of him? You have no evidence. None at all. Now rest. I'll see you soon.' He put a hand on Matthew's shoulder and turned to leave: 'The Lord be with you.'

'And with thy spirit,' Matthew said after him.

The day passed slowly, and the next. Matthew was forced to stay in bed, feeling his body mend, and the steep valleys of his wounds heal over. He had fractured at least one rib, and it would hurt for some time to come. Lucy brought food and drink and remained with him, talking and reading while he brooded on events.

'I don't want you putting yourself in any more

danger,' she told him. 'It isn't worth it.' She paused, then added nervously: 'I thought I'd lost you.'

She kissed him softly and tasted like ripe peaches, and cradled his head in her arms. But Matthew had already made up his mind.

On Sunday, the fourth day, she let him get up. This time when he looked in the mirror, the monster had gone. Although his cheek would be permanently scarred, the angry swelling around his eye had faded and his shoulder, although stiff, was no longer a tender pulp of nerves and ligaments. Lucy allowed him to sit downstairs and watch the fire. Matthew agreed, but he soon bored of this and when she came back early from church, she found him getting dressed in her room. She wanted to ask what he was doing.

'Don't worry,' he winked at her. 'You can still have me for dinner tonight.'

'What makes you think I'd want to?'

'Wait and see.' He laughed and was gone.

Josey and Luke had not seen him since the night of the attack. They were delighted.

'We thought you were a dead man,' said Josey. 'Luke found you, all crumpled up, you were.' He folded his hand into a fist expressively.

Luke agreed. 'You were a proper ugly sight.'

'Did either of you see anything?' he asked. 'Or anyone?'

The men shook their heads.

That night they dined on roast lamb. The flesh was fatty and succulent and fell easily off the bone. The wine was a rich bordeaux which tasted of oak and cherries. They ate in silence. Tomorrow he would be well enough to see his mother. And what then? Matthew would admit nothing but Lucy knew him too well and picked and worried at her food until she could stand it no longer. She dropped her knife into her plate. 'Come on,' she said. 'Let's go to bed.'

It was the first time they had slept together since the attack and for a while they sat watching each other on the edge of the bed. Then Matthew reached out and stroked the side of her face.

'What is it? What's wrong?'

'I don't know.' She glanced at him guiltily. 'I feel afraid.' She was trembling.

Not knowing what else to do, he continued to stroke her, but she stayed staring at the fireplace. 'Lucy.'

Suddenly she twisted towards him. She made a soft noise and pressed herself against him. Her tongue licked at his mouth. He kissed back, this time eagerly, and felt her body soften and relax. They clung to each other like that for several minutes, then Lucy abruptly pulled away and pushed him on to his back.

'Don't move. You're not well,' she instructed. He was about to protest, when she placed a finger to his mouth. 'Just be patient, there's a good boy.'

Lucy ran her hands over him and then, carefully, tenderly, peeled off his clothes. She allowed him to flex his back or lift his legs while she teased off a garment, but no more, until he lay on the bed, naked save for the thick swathe of bandages across his chest and shoulders. Lucy looked at the marks on his body, some still red, others blue and grey. She traced her fingernails over them and smiled when he flinched.

'I like you tender,' she whispered, and dipping her head, moved herself over him, grazing his flesh with her lips, until she felt him stiffen in pain. She stepped back and made him watch her while she undressed, quickly and neatly. The light from the fire danced and flickered on her stomach and breasts. Then she came to him.

He felt his mouth go dry. Her skin was soft, peachy, warm, supple. When she ran her hands over him, she felt the knots of muscle shift and tense beneath the surface, and the hard lumps and gouges of his injuries, rough, angry. Resting her palm on his chest, she balanced herself over him. Her eyes sparkled, then she reached behind her and seized him and lowered herself on to him. She was soft, very soft.

'Hurt me,' she told him, and with that she drove her fingernails deep into the inflamed skin over his ribs.

He roared with pain and rammed himself into her. She could feel him stabbing up inside her and pushed down against him. She bit her lips. Suddenly she wanted to taste blood, hot and sweet.

'You'll have to do better than that, boy,' she gasped and pulled at his chest.

Matthew snatched up at her, but she dodged his hand and rubbed herself hard against the length of him; he bucked and twisted with pleasure. 'You bitch!' he said, then he began to mouth obscenities, using names which had lurked in the dark recesses of his imagination, for how long, he did not know. Lucy squirmed.

'That's better! Better!'

He reached for her again and this time didn't miss but yanked her forward so that her hair enveloped him. He strained up, and bit her shoulder, in sharp, wet bites. She bit him back, hard, on the wound which ran across his neck, and the skin broke like a ripe plum. She moaned and thrust her rear up, exposing herself to the air. He gripped her buttocks and, still inside her, forced her cheeks even wider apart, so that he could feel himself slipping in and out of her. I want you. I want you. He began to finger her savagely, jamming his fingers deeply into her. Her eyes opened wide in surprise, and she pushed herself down against him, down against him, again and again. His body was hot, aching.

'I hate you! I hate you!' Lucy was screaming at him and then he came.

'There's something I need you to do for me,' he told her later.

'What, love?' She smiled at him. The hatred, the passion, were gone now.

'I need a copy of your mother's signature.'

The smile left her.

'Why?'

'I've been thinking. We know Emily never signed the testament, but Pascoe doesn't. What if it had been lying signed and forgotten in that lawyer's vaults?'

'So we should forge her signature? That would never stand up in court.'

'It doesn't have to. I'm not planning to take it anywhere near court.'

She looked at him blankly. There was a faint smudge of blood on her lips.

Chapter Two

THE NEXT MORNING HE RODE to Rosmear. From the outside the cottage looked the same as it always had. Inside it looked as if the devil had run amock. Everything – table, chairs, chests, wardrobe – had been smashed and hurled across the room. The fire had been kicked out from the hearth and the pans thrown down. He put his hands to the walls: deep scars had been slashed across the plaster. He thought of Emily. Under his feet the contents of his chests and wardrobe had been ground into the earth. He bent down, and picked up the first thing that came to hand. It was one of his mother's white cotton blouses, the kind she wore to church. The material had been torn and bloodied. It bore the impress of a large muddy boot.

He went into the kitchen. Here the damage was less severe. Shelves had been torn down and pots and pans lay scattered where they had fallen, but they could soon be picked up. He stepped on crockery, and heard it snap. A fine tin-glazed plate, which his mother had cherished, broken in two. He looked at the design. Two figures, both naked, embracing.

He walked back into the living-room. The lid had been wrenched off his small desk, but here he noticed the attacker had been more careful: although the papers had been dropped on to the ground, they appeared to have been individually sifted, for no two sheets lay on top of each other. The back of the desk had been bludgeoned open in case of a false panel.

He sat down. It would be a long task, but with patience he could work out if anything had been taken. But he had no sooner started than he realised what was missing.

He searched the room again. The deeds were written on yellow parchment and would be instantly recognisable, but they were not there. He cursed and kicked the shattered pieces of his desk. In themselves, the deeds were not particularly important – everyone knew John Trevanion had granted Lower Rosmear to his father on a three-life lease. Even so, the knowledge that his enemy possessed them worried him, and made him feel vulnerable. What could Pascoe be planning?

Footsteps outside startled him. Matthew reached for a shard of broken wood. The footsteps came to the door, then entered. It was Joseph Poole.

'Matthew! I saw your horse outside.' Joseph was the tenant of Upper Rosmear. He was in his forties with round blunt features and thinning hair.

'Thanks for looking after the cows.'

'No trouble. How's your mother?' Joseph wrinkled his face in concern.

'I'm just going to see her.'

"E's a good man, that pa'ssun.'

Matthew kicked a copper pot across the room.

'Joseph, could you look after the cows a while longer? You can keep the milk for yourself.' Joseph looked surprised, so he explained: 'I've got some business to attend to – important business – don't know how long I'll be away.'

When Joseph had gone, Matthew went through into the room where he slept. The mattress had been slit with a knife and the stuffing hacked out. Matthew lugged the bedding to one side then began to work at the rough stone flooring with his knife. The intruder had not found this place after all. The blade dug into a chink between two stones and he levered them out.

Underneath lay a bundle of oiled calico. Matthew rested it gently on the floor and turned back the cloth.

The metal gleamed dully. He picked up the pistol and balanced it in the palm of his hand. The grease had preserved it well. In an hour it would be clean.

Chapter Three

WHEN HE ARRIVED AT THE PARSONAGE HIS mother was asleep. He sat by her bed and watched the blankets gently lift and fall with her breathing.

She looked old and frail. Her skin had acquired that delicate translucence which is the sign of advancing years, becoming diaphanous in places, like the finest bone china, around the brows and cheeks and over the bones of her arms and fingers. Her forehead was wrapped in bandages. Red crescents and thumbprints had crushed and torn her face like paper crushed and torn over red, juicy plums. Her cheeks were a mass of broken veins.

Matthew sat with her for maybe twenty minutes. After that time, perhaps sensing his presence, she opened her eyes. He was not sure whether she saw him immediately, for she lay for a long time unmoving and unblinking.

He touched her hand and quietly called her name. A thin smile worked its way across her face. After a while she closed her eyes again. Matthew squeezed her fingers, then called her name again. This time she looked straight at him.

'Mother, it's me, Matthew. Who did this to you?'

She made no response. He asked her again.

A look of distaste passed over her face, then he saw her lips move, slightly. They uttered just one syllable, scarcely more than a breath. He did not trust his hearing, and bending down put his ear next to her mouth. This time the sound was quite audible. Just one syllable:

'John.'

'John did this to you? What John?'

'John . . . came to me.'

'John is dead, Mother, don't you remember? So is Emily.'

'I saw him.' She looked up at him. Her pupils sparkled and flamed. He kissed her on the cheek. Her skin was burning.

Richard was waiting for him in the hallway.

'I didn't realise she was that ill.' Matthew looked subdued. He was no longer angry, just saddened at the pain and weakness of everything. 'She's sick with fever.'

'I didn't want to worry you, but her condition is still . . . uncertain. Mrs Dunstan is with her all the time. Pray the fever breaks.'

'My mother said she saw John – Trevanion.'

'She has said many things these last few days.'

'But why John?' Matthew remembered the figure turning towards him in the graveyard.

'I pray for her, Matthew,' the parson replied simply.

'Then pray for me also.' Matthew swung his great-coat over his arm and headed out into the damp afternoon air.

Chapter Four

NIGHT HAD FALLEN ACROSS THE harbour, bringing with it a soft, chill wind. Listening carefully, Matthew could hear the boats gently tug and sway at their moorings, and the tinkle of their rigging across the waters.

Joshua Pascoe was working late.

It must be gone six o'clock, he thought, and pulled the greatcoat around him. He had been in two minds whether to approach Pascoe at work or at home. At home the lawyer would be more vulnerable, but the documents would be at work. Patience. He looked down the street. Golden chinks of light glimmered at windows and somewhere close by he could smell bacon frying. A fisherman walked past him, feet unsteady with drink. He stopped at the next house along and knocked out his pipe on the step.

Matthew kept his eyes on Pascoe's office. Edward Tonkin had left early but the last client, a gentlewoman in her mid-forties, had gone in about an hour ago, and was still inside. Perhaps he is looking for someone to take Emily's place, Matthew thought grimly. He remembered Emily's cold tender breast, naked in death and Joshua Pascoe licking his thin lips, and rubbing his fingers over his chin.

Suddenly the door opened. The gentlewoman stepped down into the street, and Pascoe bent after her to bid her good night. Their voices were clear and crisp. Matthew stirred himself. A pang of apprehension flashed through his chest, then was gone.

Pascoe went back inside and closed the door behind him. Earlier, after Tonkin had left, Matthew had managed to reconnoitre the reception. There had been someone else there, one of the thick-set men who accompanied Pascoe to Trevanion, sitting in the far corner, sucking his pipe and looking bored.

Looking right and left, he crossed the street. He had thought about the bodyguard for the last two hours. He tested the doorknob. It turned. Would the guard notice? He listened. Not a sound. He turned it again until he felt the door give a slight click.

The guard had obviously not noticed, for when Matthew leaped into the room, he was still sitting with his feet on the stool opposite and his arms crossed comfortably over his waistcoat. He gave a short cry and tried to heave himself forward, but by then Matthew had jammed his pistol against his adam's-apple and held him. He leaned forward until the man could feel his breath on his face.

'Be very quiet and you won't die,' he whispered.

All the while he was listening for sounds from the corridor leading to Pascoe's office. Nothing.

'Down on the floor, on your belly.'

The man obeyed, Matthew's pistol still pressed tightly, too tightly, against his windpipe. Matthew kneeled on him, letting the man feel his weight, then produced several lengths of fresh cord from inside his coat. He bound the man's hands and feet, working quickly, with no regard for the man's comfort. Time was everything. Once the cords were in place, Matthew felt in his pocket, and pulled out a lemon. The *Maria* from Rotterdam had been wrecked the week before and her cargo of lemons and oranges were for sale in all the markets. Matthew prised open the man's jaw and crammed the lemon into his mouth. The man blinked up at him, but could not speak. Matthew bent close to his ear:

'Remember, don't move, keep quiet, and you'll live. I only want a few words with your master.'

Matthew crossed quickly back to the front door, locked it, bolted it and pocketed the key. He had been keeping a weather-eye on the door which opened on to the corridor. Pascoe surely must have heard something – what was he doing?

Switching his pistol to his left hand, Matthew drew his sword and tugged the door open. He preferred to use a sword. There was less noise, less chance of killing Pascoe by accident. It swung open. The corridor was a good ten feet long and unlit. He stepped forward softly. His foot creaked on an uneven floorboard. He was at the end of the corridor. He regarded the door suspiciously. Rachel Morgan's brother had been stabbed through a pine door two years before and he had no intention of going the same way. He leaned back and gave the door a hard kick. The timber around the doorframe must have been soft, for the bolt came away from its bed and the door flew open with a crash. He dived forward and ducked.

It was well that he did. For a man who spent his life pretending to be old, Joshua Pascoe moved with surprising speed. Matthew glimpsed the blade slash through the air where his head should have been. He pitched himself headlong and followed it in.

Pascoe was standing about three feet back, legs apart, and Matthew hoped to get close before he could react. He was disappointed. Neatly side-stepping, Pascoe lunged forward and drove his rapier at Matthew's body. Matthew swerved to the right, countering blindly. Pascoe's blade glanced off his ribcage. The blow was so fast Matthew would not have felt it, had it not struck where his ribs were already fractured. Pain shot across his chest. He wheezed, and flung his weight to the left, against the solicitor, before Pascoe could pull his blade out. This time he caught him off balance. In an effort to compensate, Pascoe sprang backwards and as he did Matthew clipped the side of his skull with his hilt. Pascoe stumbled and Matthew kicked him down. Pascoe swore. Matthew planted his left boot firmly on his sword arm. His own blade caressed the soft flesh beneath the solicitor's jaw.

Matthew held it there. He was breathing heavily and there was a pain buzzing in his chest. Pascoe wriggled, and Matthew stamped on his arm until he let go of his sword.

'Good.' He could not resist a smile. 'Now listen. I will slit you open like a pig if you don't co-operate, do you understand?' He jabbed the tip of his blade into the side of the man's neck. Pascoe squealed and a red shiny berry slowly appeared on his skin. 'Don't worry, you'll not die just yet. Now, get up. Slowly. Or I'll stick you.'

Matthew kicked Pascoe's sword into the corner, then carefully stepped back.

'Go to your chair.' Pascoe got slowly to his feet. His face was tense and white, his eyes blazed.

'You can't do this.' His voice was hoarse like a whisper.

'I already have. Look what you've done to my family.' Matthew gestured with his sword towards the solicitor's chair. 'Come on. No. Not like that – keep your face to me.'

Pascoe stumbled backwards until he got to his chair. Matthew put his pistol on the desk and ran his free hand over Pascoe's chest and abdomen. He appeared satisfied, and Pascoe went to sit down.

'Wait a minute.' Matthew tugged the desk drawers open and, never taking his eyes off the solicitor, rummaged through them. 'I thought so.' In the top drawer lay a woman's pistolet. Matthew pocketed it quickly and picked up his own. It was only when he was certain the desk offered Pascoe no further means of assault that he withdrew.

'All right, sit down, and put your feet up on the desk as if you're having a lazy afternoon.'

Pascoe did as he was told.

Now Matthew picked up the chair which Pascoe's clients used and dragged it against the far wall so he could keep both the door and the solicitor in full view at once. He sat down.

After his initial outburst, Pascoe had not said a word. He sat, hands resting together, finger to finger, sharp flinty eyes staring furiously ahead, thin lips clenched tightly together.

'Very good.' Matthew's scar leered, an ugly crescent, in the lamplight. 'Now, if you want to stay alive, we talk. But don't lie to me like last time. I'll not stand for it. Do you understand?'

Pascoe stayed quiet, his eyes fixed straight ahead.

Matthew put his pistol gently down and quickly getting up, crossed to Pascoe. He pressed the flat of his sword against the solicitor's top lip, forcing it back until it bared his teeth in a snarl.

'Don't make me,' he warned, and with a slow easy motion he wiped the sword across the lip. The blade bit cleanly into the soft flesh. A thick bloody syrup welled up and dribbled down his chin. Pascoe swore and went to put his hand to his mouth. Matthew slammed the haft of his sword down on to the man's fingers and held them fast to the desk. Tears of pain started in the solicitor's eyes but he did not cry out. With his left hand, Matthew grabbed the man's collar and twisted his neckpiece round, half lifting him from his seat. This time Pascoe gave a strangled cry but did not dare resist. He gazed wretchedly up while his face, previously deathly pale, began to turn the colour of fresh roses.

'All I want is the truth, Pascoe, and I'll let you be. Do you understand?'

'Yes! Yes!' Pascoe's voice was thin and reedy. There was a look of panic in his eyes. Matthew considered hitting him again, just once, to prove his point, but decided against it.

Matthew slackened his grip and pushed him back in his chair. Pascoe bent over in agony, trying to staunch the flow of blood from his lip with his handkerchief.

'Good.' Matthew settled back in his chair and cradled his pistol in his hand. 'Now tell me about your guardianship.'

The solicitor looked disquieted.

'What do you want to know?'

'When did Emily sign?'

'The week after John's death. It'll do you no good – it was properly witnessed. Sir Anthony Bevis has—'

'I don't give a damn what Sir Anthony's done! As you may know, the day before she died, Emily saw another solicitor, and had him draw up a full will and testament. Your guardianship isn't worth the paper it's written on.'

Pascoe sucked on his lip.

Matthew reached into his jacket and flipped Holroyd's document on to the desk.

'See for yourself.'

Warily, Pascoe lowered his gaze. Matthew could see his eyes dart over the fine black characters. He turned quickly to the tailpiece and the thin, spidery signature that cut across the page. Lucy had done her job well.

'You will see she signed and dated it Monday before last. Twelve hours later you killed her at St Levan.'

'*I* killed her? Don't be ridiculous! You killed her, Trevanion. Everyone knows that.'

Matthew got up and struck him in the face.

'How dare you!'

Pascoe cried out in pain.

'You're mad, Trevanion, mad!'

'I warned you, no games! I'm taking this testament to Sir Anthony and having your guardianship revoked. It's all over, Pascoe. Now – start at the beginning before I lose my patience.' He went to hit him but the threat was enough and the solicitor began to talk:

'All right! Don't hit me again,' he answered irritably.

'How long were you having your affair with Emily? I need to know.'

'A year and a half.'

'Why, Pascoe, why?'

'Why do you think, Trevanion? She was wasted on him.' There was more emotion in his voice than Matthew had expected, but all he said was:

'I'm not convinced. There was something about her, I'll grant you, but you wouldn't start tupping your most important client's wife just for that, would you?'

Pascoe looked at him sullenly.

'Did she perform good tricks, Pascoe? I saw you together – she tried hard, I'd say.'

'Damn you, Trevanion!'

'So what's the real reason? Or do you want to hear more? No, let me tell you. It's the Trevanion land, isn't it? That's all the Trevanions have ever had. So you worked your way into Emily's bed and then you killed my uncle.'

'I did not! It was an accident!'

'Don't lie, Pascoe! Maybe we can never prove you did it, but you can't deny the note you sent him.'

Pascoe said nothing. He nursed his cut lip.

'But then Emily wouldn't go along with you, would she? I talked to her, the week before she died, and she was scared, Pascoe, scared of you. That's why she entailed the estate to Lucy and you killed her in St Levan.'

'You lie.'

'No. I do not. Then you sent a letter to Nathaniel

Morgan, telling him I hadn't been home that night, and explaining why I wanted her dead. You see, I remembered Edward Tonkin's got a cousin, Peter Jennings, who helped us unload: that's how you knew. Am I right? Am I?'

'Yes, you're right.' Pascoe spat out the words as if they were poison.

'Good.' Matthew smiled to himself. 'But then, when I wasn't carted off to Launceston, you panicked. I found Emily's testament. I talked to Hocking about the prospecting John had done.'

Was it Matthew's imagination, or did Pascoe tense at this?

'I swear I didn't kill her!'

'But you can't deny the mining, can you? You see, Hocking told me you were investigating my uncle's mineral rights. Now I'd wager my uncle knew his rights on his own land – Trevanions have owned it since the flood – but he wasn't sure about the land he leased to tenants – at Trewidden, Boskedgean and Rosmear. I checked with Hocking today, before I came here.' This was not quite true, but it was a good guess. 'He said you had the prospectors' reports. Show them to me.'

'I cannot, they are confidential,' Pascoe replied with considerable sang-froid. 'Beat it out of me, Trevanion.' He looked at Matthew calmly. Matthew laughed.

'Later. But I think you've just answered my question. So there's tin there – or copper, maybe – so much the better. I knew there was more to it, there had to be. No one murders two people just to inherit a crumbling estate.'

'What makes you so sure?' Pascoe interrupted him. 'What if a man is driven by motives other than greed?'

Matthew looked at him coldly: 'What would you have done . . . sell the land to some third party? Such as a Mr Henry Waters, maybe, or some other fraud, like Marcy Poldeen?'

'So are you going to kill me now, Trevanion? You may as well, because I'll confess to nothing. And what about Tremaine? Will you kill him as well?'

'No – he's my witness. I want him alive. But thanks for reminding me.' Matthew stepped quickly to the door leading to reception. At the far end of the corridor one of Tremaine's boots poked out. He seemed not to have moved.

'Now.' He returned to Pascoe. 'The final piece of this jigsaw. My beautiful aunt. We both know why you wanted Trevanion, but why did she want you?'

'Your aunt had an affection for me, that was all.'

'No she didn't! Maybe once, long ago, but not at the end. I heard you threaten her and she opened her legs for you. She hated you!'

'You have a lot to learn.'

'No. I know Emily. Emily knew you could ruin her. And now I know why.'

'You do?'

'Yes. You see, while I was recuperating I explored Emily's papers at my leisure.' Matthew smiled to himself. He remembered Lucy surprising him in her bedroom. She hadn't suspected, but he had found where she had hidden the documents. 'Among them was a draft of my uncle's will, dated July 1749.' He continued: 'My uncle never withdrew his will, did he? He'd only just issued a new one. And I know who the heir was – as it always has been – me. Now, shall I hit you again, or do you agree?'

Pascoe slumped in his chair.

'Yes, I agree. Your uncle never withdrew his will. You are the heir.'

'Then let me see it.'

'It's in my safe.'

'Open it.'

'The keys are in my desk.' Pascoe reached inside the top drawer.

'No. I'll do it.' Keeping both eyes on Pascoe, Matthew transferred his pistol to his left hand and felt in the drawer with his right. The keys were not there. He felt for them again.

Pascoe kicked Matthew in the groin. Instinctively Matthew squeezed the trigger but his left hand was unsteady and Pascoe knocked the gun aside before it fired. Matthew folded up in agony, and Pascoe's knee caught him under the chin, snapping his head back. He was falling through space. There was blood in his eyes. He lashed out with his arm. Pascoe dodged easily. Something glinted. A knife! Pascoe had a knife! Matthew jerked his head to one side, and the blade kissed his cheek. The solicitor swung again, but this time he was wide, and Matthew ducked underneath. He sprang upwards, and felt his head punch into the man's midriff. Normally Pascoe should have been no match for him, but Matthew's injuries had left him weak – and slow. He felt a sharp knock to his right side, and he realised dimly that Pascoe had stabbed him. He wondered if it was a flesh wound. Shouting with rage, he smashed his right arm upwards and caught Pascoe in the face.

The solicitor's face was a mask of blood. We're equal, he thought. Then he realised Pascoe was running for his sword. It was in the corner of the room, and he had his hand to it before Matthew could react. Pascoe paused for a minute and fingered the blade. Matthew glanced behind him. His own sword lay by his chair. It was too far.

'So,' said Pascoe. 'I'll slice you.'

Pascoe ran at him. Matthew swerved, too slowly, he thought. Then he remembered the pistolet. His hand went to his pocket. Pascoe lunged at him and he tripped and fell backwards. There it was, smooth and hard, and he was fumbling with the trigger. Pascoe was standing over him now. He lifted the sword up. It had to be now. There was a sudden muffled explosion. Pascoe, his eyes wide with surprise, lurched sideways. A bright red rosette had appeared, as if by magic, on his breast. Matthew watched intently as he crumpled to the floor. Matthew got to his feet and squatted on his haunches, nursing his pain. He put a hand to the knife wound. It seemed all right. He looked over to the solicitor.

'You've shot me.' Pascoe seemed in a state of shock.

'I'll dare say you'll live, if I get you help. But I'll need convincing. The keys – where are they?'

'Inside the cabinet. Help me, please.'

'Ah yes, the drinks cabinet. Would you care for a glass of port, perhaps?' An evil tone entered Matthew's voice.

'For pity's sake, what more do you want?'

Ignoring him, Matthew went to the cabinet and

plucked the keys off their hook. The safe opened first try. 'The will – which one is it?'

Pascoe told him. Matthew pulled out a crisp beige folder. So here it was. After all this time. He opened the folder hastily.

Whereas I, John Trevanion, squire of the manor of Trevanion, being of sound mind and still enjoying the life which I was given, do this day humbly and thankfully bequeath my soul to Him from whom it was given, my one true redeemer, my Lord Jesus Christ. My worldly belongings I bequeath as follows.

To Matthew Trevanion, my nephew, on the provision that he be flesh of my flesh, blood of my blood, I give all of the estate of Trevanion, its lands, chattels, tenures, and rights, together with all of the bartons attached to it, together with their rights, livings and chattels, to have as his own with no encumbrance or entail, save only this, that in the event of my beloved wife Emily surviving me, he will allow her to reside in the manor for the remainder of her days, and shall afford her an income of not less than seventy pounds a year, on the condition that she do not marry again, in which case his duty to her shall cease, and to my daughter Lucy, I bequeath a living of forty pounds a year . . .

He looked down at Pascoe, hunched on the floor. 'I win.'

To his surprise, the solicitor broke into a dry, painful laugh.

'Have you not read the will?'

'Yes, of course.'

'Were you not struck by any peculiarity of phrase? Where it says, let me see, flesh of my flesh, blood of my blood?'

'It's a trifle odd, but what of it, I am his nephew.'

'And what if I told you you were not your father's son?'

'I'd say you were lying.'

'But what if I had a sworn statement made by your father?' For a man who might be dying, Pascoe seemed remarkably confident.

Matthew hesitated: 'You're lying!'

'See for yourself. It's in the folder with the will.'

There was a thin piece of notepaper on which was written:

I, Henry Trevanion, of Lower Rosmear, declare before witnesses and almighty God, that whereas that person Matthew Trevanion has been given the name and title of my son, he is son in name only. He is not, nor ever has been, my son by blood. I hereby disown him. This declaration signed before witnesses, this 17th day of September 1727, Hen. Trevanion.

Matthew read it again. His father had made this a week before he died. He looked at the solicitor:

'How did you come by this?'

'In the course of my profession, both Trevanion brothers were my clients.' Pascoe coughed, short, breathless coughs.

Matthew went over to him and pulled back the

cloth over the bullet wound. He peered at it and prodded with his finger.

'Ahh!' Pascoe cried out. 'What are you doing?'

'Checking your wound. I don't want you dying on me just yet.' The bullet seemed to have passed into the bank of pectoral muscle beneath the solicitor's left shoulder. It couldn't do much damage there. Matthew looked him in the eye: 'Is it true, this note?'

'Of course it's true. Why else would your father bring shame on himself like that?' Pascoe grinned. 'A cuckoo, that's what your father called you. Why, you're nothing but a changeling! You've got less right to Trevanion than I have.'

Matthew bent over him.

'What's to stop me destroying this now?'

'I have a copy elsewhere, under lock and key. Besides, I know you: even if you could destroy it, that wouldn't be the point, would it? You'd be living a lie.'

Matthew carefully folded up the documents and replaced them in the envelope.

'My father lied, whatever you say. Trevanion is mine, and I'll prove—' He stopped in mid-sentence, as the implication of what he was saying struck him. 'Of course! So that's why you attacked my mother! She knows the truth.'

'Truth? Don't flatter yourself. You'll find out.' In the lamplight, Pascoe's face gleamed red. 'I'll tell you what you'll inherit.' He spat out a mouthful of red phlegm. 'The past, boy. The past. Other people's lives.'

Chapter Five

MATTHEW STAYED AT ROSMEAR THAT night. He made a bed from the remains of his gutted mattress and wrapped a blanket round himself. He slept little. His dreams were a series of violent images, of red and black, which trembled and shook. Joshua Pascoe's gloating face leered up at him. He remembered hitting him and looked again and found himself staring at his father. His father loved him, he knew that. He was sitting by the hearth and his father was telling him a story about the *bucca dhu*. His father had his arm round him and he was squeezing him. Then he would wake and lie in the darkness, listening for the sound of a twig breaking and the crushing sound of breathing on the path near Sancreed.

Before it was light he rose and ignoring the pain in his back went out to call in the cattle.

He was just helping Nancy finish the milking when he heard the sound of horses approaching. He looked up and saw four riders making their way down the path.

He recognised Simon Trelawne but not the others.

'Morning, Simon, what can I do for you?'

Simon Trelawne looked grim-faced and awkward.

'Matthew, these are Sir Anthony Bevis's men from Penzance. I've come to arrest you.'

'Arrest me, what for?'

'The murder of Joshua Pascoe and Robert Tremaine last night.'

Matthew tried to keep his voice as natural as possible. 'I don't know what you're talking about.' Behind
him the cows lowed and sighed.

'As you know, you're on bail already, Matthew.
You've got no rights in the matter. I hope you'll come
easy.'

Faced with four men on horseback, Matthew had
little choice. He shrugged.

'Let me get my jacket.'

Simon looked at the others. One, a slightly older
man sucking on a thin-stemmed pipe, nodded.

'All right, but don't try anything funny.'

'In fact, while we're here, we'll search your home,'
added the older man. 'A number of documents were
stolen from Pascoe's office last night. You wait here.
Watch him, Trelawne.'

Matthew watched them dismount and go inside.

'It looks like a pigsty in here,' one of them called
out. 'Is this how you live, Trevanion?'

Matthew did not answer. Five minutes later the
three men emerged. They had not found his pistol
and the will. He had put them back in the hiding-
place last night. But he cursed when one of them
came out brandishing the pistolet. Left in his jacket
pocket, he had forgotten it.

'Is this yours?' asked the man. 'It has some initials
engraved on the stock: J.P. Very pretty. That wouldn't
be Joshua Pascoe, would it?'

They rode back to Penzance in silence. Matthew's
head was aching savagely. He needed time to think.
The older man, called Carter, turned out to be a

bailiff to the county sheriff. He insisted on strapping Matthew's hands behind his back. Matthew thought of Tremaine, trussed like a goose. When Carter pulled the ligature too tight, he did not bother to complain. He tried to clear his thoughts. So Pascoe was dead. He remembered the man clutching at the bullet-wound. And Tremaine as well.

This time he was taken straight to Penzance gaol. It was a small stone building that had originally been used for storing nets. Now it billeted suspects on their way to Launceston, or housed drunks and vagrants for the night. Carter – he seemed to be the leader – showed him into a small cell and left him.

The room was unfurnished except for a simple wooden bench hung on chains from the wall. What had prompted this one amenity, Matthew could not tell. In all other respects, the cell had been allocated – he refused to believe designed – with scant regard for human niceties. It was a cold, damp box, built of untreated granite and a rough grainy mortar which smelled of the sea. There was no latrine, except that most of the previous occupants – but not all – had used the end of the room which was slightly downhill. Matthew surmised that the cell was periodically sluiced and scrubbed, but as this had not been done recently, a telling stench hung in the air.

The warder, certainly, did not inspire hygiene. He was an overweight man in his late forties. His unwashed shirt hung to his knees and smelled of raw onions and stale beer.

Matthew's one relief from this was the small window which opened on to the street. By standing on the bench, he could glimpse the small terraced cottages running down to the quay. On the back of the wind were borne the distinctive scents of salted pilchards being pressed into barrels and the whiff of wet mud at low tide, and the tang of wet nets, ropes and baskets, drying in the damp morning air. People passed by. Fishermen and their boys, dressed in thick grey smocks. Young wives, clutching baskets of vegetables or fish, calling out to neighbours. And in amongst these, the merchants, businessmen and farmers, who made up the wealth of the borough.

He was still gazing out of the window when he heard the door open behind him.

'So, Trevanion, it seems Morgan was right.' Sir Anthony sounded brusque and ill tempered. He stood in the doorway with his hands on his hips and a look of weariness and disgust on his face. The events of the night, whatever they were, had obviously taken their toll.

Matthew got down from the bench.

'I swear—'

'I don't want your lies, Trevanion! What could you hold sacred, eh? Yesterday afternoon you came to Penzance and bought a length of cord in the market. I know because I have witnesses. A length of cord, and a lemon.' Sir Anthony stared at him humourlessly.

'A lemon,' he went on, 'which we found inserted into the mouth of Robert Tremaine, that is, the corpse of Robert Tremaine. Then there's a fisherman who saw you outside Pascoe's office. With your face like that, you're pretty distinctive, Trevanion.' The magistrate dropped his voice:

'This morning Edward Tonkin opened the office

as he normally does. He found Robert Tremaine trussed like a goose with his neck slashed open. A horrible mess, Trevanion. The poor man was so shocked he ran straight out to raise the alarm. It was only when he came back with help that he went into Pascoe's room.' Sir Anthony gave him a piercing look. 'Whoever killed Pascoe took their time. He'd been beaten and cut about the face. Also Carter reckons he'd been shot, though it's hard to say. The reason why it's hard to say is because someone had taken a sword and opened him up from throat to navel. I've just been to see the body.' His face told Matthew the effect it had had on him. 'Gutted like a pig. Look at you, Trevanion! You've cut your knuckles, you've got his pistol in your pocket!'

'I didn't do it!'

'And that's not all. On his desk lay an open Bible, and on the page someone had marked in blood Job nineteen, verse twenty-nine. Do you know it, Trevanion?'

Matthew made no response.

' "Be ye afraid of the sword: for wrath bringeth the punishments of the sword, that ye may know there is a judgment." What are you, man?'

'Listen to me!'

But Sir Anthony had already turned on his heel and left.

Towards lunchtime the warder brought him a piece of dry bread and a jug of brackish water. He ate slowly, mechanically. *Wrath bringeth the punishments of the sword.* He had to admit Sir Anthony had a strong case. If he didn't have good reason for killing Pascoe, who did? He was certainly capable of it. His head ached viciously. A sudden horror seized him. Perhaps he *had* killed him. He could see himself going through the motions, Pascoe's eyes bulging. He looked at his hands. He had scrubbed them in a stream on the way home, but when he put them to his nose the odour was unmistakable. What did it matter if he had his uncle's will? Or whether he was his father's son? What had the parson said? We are all children of Cain . . .

Later he thought of Lucy, alone at Trevanion. He would have liked to see her again, to tell her he was innocent, to be with her a while longer. At least with Pascoe dead, she could enjoy Trevanion in peace. The implication came to him suddenly. Events had turned out well for her, very well. Had Lucy read the deeds in Emily's desk? If she had, she would know, like him, that he was the rightful heir. And Pascoe? He was the one person who stood between Lucy and the inheritance.

Matthew sat down on the bench and sunk his head in his hands. Why had Lucy been so keen for him to go to Helston? And that look in her eyes, the hatred . . . He remembered the look in Emily's eyes. How stupid he had been. Mother and daughter, daughter and mother.

Matthew slept fitfully that night. He was awoken before daybreak by Carter with a kick in the ribs. He noticed that, even at this hour, Carter clenched a thin clay pipe – as yet unlit – between his teeth. Matthew shook his head. His chest and his side hurt violently. Breakfast was a chunk of yesterday's bread and a cup of the same foul, bitter water. Matthew swilled it round his mouth and spat it out. Half an hour later, as the sun slid through the thin bright mist, they saddled up: Carter, Simon Trelawne and a constable called Porkellis. Matthew rode next to Simon, his hands strapped behind his back.

It was a slow, uneventful journey. As the sun rose, the mist dissolved and gave way to a brilliant duck-egg sky. They made their way towards Camborne Churchtown, stopping every hour or so to let the horses drink. Launceston was two days away and Carter did not want to risk laming a horse. After the feverish events of the last few days, Matthew found the journey something of a relief. It gave him time to think, though to what end, he had no clear idea.

From St Erth they passed the smelting works that lined the Hayle valley, at Mellanear, Trelissick and Angarrack, and crossed Connor Downs to Camborne.

This was the heart of the mining district, the great parish of Gwennap, and the whole countryside was a swarming mass of industry. Everywhere the slim chimneys of the wheelhouses pointed skywards, or were under construction, and the knock and clang of the engines and the shouts of the working men arose from the valleys to meet them. Men, in bunches or long straggling lines, swarmed around the mineheads, like ants. Matthew could only guess at the hot dry air and the infernal darkness of their world, one hundred, two hundred fathoms below. Several times the small party had to halt before long trains of mules, seventy or eighty strong, trailing to and from the ports of the north coast, or heading down over the hills to the Channel. Under stannary law it was illegal to transport tin by night and in the dark months of winter and autumn this added to the congestion. Often two or three different mule-trains would converge at an intersection and then the drivers would fall to violent arguments, for the mules were stubborn and brutish creatures, hard to manoeuvre, and the drivers struggled to keep their schedules. The recent heavy rainfall had turned the trackways into ribbons of mire and slurry and it took them well over two hours to cover little more than four miles, and even this left the constables frayed and irritable.

Around them stood the great mines which would make this region famous: Dolcoath, Roskear, Carn Brea, Pednandrea, and to the south the great Basset mines, then past Killifreth, with its remote, sinister tower, Creegbrawse and Poldice.

Matthew remembered the bare windswept land-scape he had seen as a boy, and marvelled at the speed with which the fat lodes of tin and copper had spawned these growths of minehouse and smelting-works, dressingfloors and whim-engines. These monuments to human enterprise seemed to suck everything to them, like filings to magnets: strings of ragged low cottages and ugly knots of houses were coagulating round the tips and workings where previously plain gorseland and grassland had lain. Trees, never plentiful, had been cut for fuel and the land stripped naked, leaving it raw and disfigured. In return, from the bowels of the mines were spewed the offal, the unwanted waste of arsenic, zinc and malachite which leeched into the soil and soured the streams. If his uncle had discovered tin, or even better, copper, at Trewidden, or Boskedgean, this fate too lay in wait for their gentle farmlands. Matthew wondered at the excitement which inspired men to drive shafts deep into the earth, in the hope of wringing money from the loam and rock. Here in the crucible of mining, it was an almost tangible, almost sexual, thing, which buzzed and hummed in the air which was thick with metallic dust.

Eventually they left the region of the mines behind them and dropped down into the softer, curving lands above Truro. Stillness returned, punctuated only by the calls of gulls and cattle. The air was soft with the scent of damp leaves and fresh earth. Matthew thought of Rosmear and wondered whether he would see it again.

They arrived at Truro later than Carter intended, but in time for lunch, and drew up outside The Barrel, where Carter knew the landlord. He was not an unreasonable man and was happy for Matthew to eat with them. After the bread and water of the gaol, Matthew needed no prompting.

Carter was just downing a quart of ale when two men came in. They wore leather greatcoats and swords strapped to their waists. Carter recognised one of them and called out. The man was tall, with lank hair and a beak-like nose.

'How are you doing, Roskarren? I haven't seen you for a long time.'

The man grinned sheepishly and, ducking his head under a beam, came over. Carter ordered another drink. Nicholas Roskarren was a bailiff from Falmouth. He was also conveying a suspect to Launceston and, like most of the lawmen, he tended to stop at the same inns en route. Roskarren called his companion over, a younger man with smooth olive features, and more ale was ordered. Food was sent out to the bailiff left with their prisoner, though none for the prisoner, and more than an hour passed before the company decided to leave. Naturally they would travel together.

Matthew saw their prisoner as soon as he stepped outside.

Robert Henty was a large, heavy-boned man of about forty. Two hard grey eyes stared out from beneath a thatch of black matted hair. He slumped belligerently on his horse, head sunk between his shoulders. Matthew noticed he was missing two fingers on his left hand. He had learned that Henty, or Bob-eye Henty, as he was known, had been caught unloading eighty kegs of spirit at Restronguet. His comrades had panicked and made off in the dinghy, leaving Bob-eye stranded. Henty barely glanced at the new arrival.

'Sitting pretty, Bob?' called the smooth-faced bailiff who Matthew understood was called Benson. Robert Henty spat a piece of tobacco at him. It missed but landed on Benson's horse. Matthew watched the brown oily liquid trickle down the horse's flank. Benson swore crudely but did nothing. Bob-eye stared at him and grinned.

They set off, Carter and Roskarren sharing the lead, followed by Trelawne and Benson, each leading a prisoner's horse. In this way Matthew found himself next to Henty. The company, now eight strong, passed up from Truro, through more of the lush, rolling farmland, until, breasting a hill, they suddenly looked down on the fields of central Cornwall dropping away to Padstow, a vast quilt of browns and greens, crossed and scored by hedgerows and little squares of woodland. Over to their right lay the village of Mitchell and beyond that the road to Goss Moor.

'So what are you going to Launceston for?' The sound of Henty's voice startled Matthew.

'They say I murdered two men.'

Bob-eye let out an amused whistle: 'Only two? And did you?'

'No. I am innocent.' Matthew was aware how hollow those words sounded up here in the emptiness. 'I'm innocent,' he repeated.

Bob-eye chuckled. 'And so am I, my 'ansome, and make no mistehk.'

After this, as if a ritual had been satisfactorily completed, the conversation drifted on to more general topics, loosely connected with the practice of 'free trade' between Cornwall and France. It turned out they had a few experiences in common and swapped anecdotes amiably enough. Henty had never touched tin and was interested in the market. He had most to say about spirits and tobacco. Matthew noticed that as he talked, Henty kept casting an eye ahead of them, in an edgy, circumspect way, like a twitch. Presumably this was why he was called Bob-eye.

They approached Fraddon, a miserable village straggling along the highway. The sun's rays now fell weakly on their backs and Matthew reckoned it would be dusk within the hour. After Fraddon there was nothing until Bodmin. Carter had hoped to make Bodmin by nightfall, but the stop at Truro and the delays around Camborne had cost them time. An argument broke out among the men. Carter wanted to turn aside to St Columb. Trelawne and Roskarren were for pressing on.

A chill wind had sprung up from the west, and began to ruffle the horses' manes and make the gorse twitch. Carter struggled to cup the flame of his lucifer in his hand and cursed. Under the clear sky, the air was already cold and with nightfall would grow colder still. Matthew dug his chin deeper into his collar. What did it matter to him where they spent the night? Tomorrow he would be in Launceston. Bob-eye offered him a chew of tobacco. After a few minutes, Roskarren's argument prevailed. They would push on for Bodmin, and finish the last few miles in the dark if need be. The eight riders moved off. Goss Moor stretched out before them.

Goss Moor was a flat, almost featureless expanse of heathland, sunk with bogs and covered in gorse, heather and rough moorgrass, occasionally divided by a ditch or watercourse. In early summer, peat-cutters would dig out great swathes of the turf, turning it and stacking it to dry in the wind. But now their work had ceased until spring and the horsemen passed the derelict remains of that year's cutting: great coffin-shaped holes, filled with black gloomy water that cast no reflection.

Night set in, quicker than they had thought, and the world turned grey then black. Matthew could hear Carter and Roskarren talking ahead and saw the familiar flare of a match as Carter ignited his pipe, but gradually their conversation died and the company continued in silence. Henty also seemed reluctant to talk, as if he too were oppressed by the drabness of the place. They rode on, until all he could see were the shapes of the riders and the rim of the moorland against the vastness of the sky. He listened to the horses, snorting in the cold air, and the sound of their hooves on the rough highway, the odd jingle of a bridle, but even these sounds were soon swallowed in the moaning of the wind. Matthew felt his horse reluctantly obey the tug from the lead in front.

As the wind rattled and keened through the gorse, he remembered George Trevose sitting in The Lamb, glass in hand. He could almost imagine he heard the sound of a horse now, faint and far off.

Carter was yelling for them to keep up. Matthew's and Henty's horses were going slower than the bailiffs' and the party began to straggle. Roskarren rode back and gripped Henty's bridle. Porkellis did the same with Matthew's horse. 'Come on!' For the next mile or so, his horse was dragged and goaded into something approaching a fast walk. Henty swore loudly and began to curse Roskarren with some imagination. Now the going was tougher. Apart from the break at Truro, Matthew's arms had been tied behind his back all day, and they were cold and numb and painful. As they went on the pain grew more insistent in his shoulder and across his chest. Porkellis rode alongside, thrashing at the rump of his horse with his crop, and not caring if he clipped Matthew's legs.

'Leave the boy alone!' roared Henty. 'Leave 'im

alone, you bastard!' he repeated, louder this time, even though he was only a few feet away.

'Quiet back there!' shouted Carter.

'Quiet yourself!' answered Henty at the top of his voice. 'You can't treat us like this!'

'Shut your mouth, or I'll fetch you one myself!' ordered Roskarren.

Bob-eye fell silent and winked at Matthew. But as soon as Roskarren had returned to the front, Henty began again, if anything louder, cursing the bailiffs for all he was worth. He seemed to be deliberately provoking them, thought Matthew, though he failed to see why.

Then he heard it. Through the shrill moaning of the wind, the sound of a horse galloping wildly over the moorland. His blood froze. He listened again, the sound had gone, and all he could hear was the oak tree next to the road, shivering in the wind. He looked around him. The constables, the bailiffs, had their heads bent forwards and did not seem to have noticed anything. He tried to catch Henty's eye. There was the sound again. This time there was no mistaking it: hooves pounding over the rough ground. Behind them, no more than two furlongs away.

This time the other horsemen heard it as well. Porkellis muttered something to Trelawne and Trelawne called to Carter. Carter wheeled his horse round and came riding to the back. The riders were too far away to be identified, but everyone knew that a large posse of horsemen at this time of night only meant one thing.

Matthew looked across at Henty.

Bob-eye leaned back in his saddle and roared at the top of his voice: 'Here! Over here, boys!'

As if in answer, a voice came through the darkness: 'Hold! Hold there!'

Matthew looked over his shoulder: he could just make out a large body of men coming up the road. He guessed they must be twenty or thirty strong. Carter called his troop to halt and they drew their guns and waited.

'Who's there?' Carter cried out. 'Who's there?'

The riders came to a stop about forty feet away. Then a man called out:

'Is Bob-eye with you?'

'Over here, boys!' answered Henty. He let out a loud whoop.

'We are about the King's business—' started Roskarren.

'The King can kiss my arse!' yelled one of the horsemen. Several of his comrades broke into laughter, and shouted jokes and insults of their own.

'We've come for Bob-eye, an' there ain't one of you as can stop us!' shouted another.

Matthew considered the scene. The riders looked heavily armed. The constables wouldn't stand a chance.

'Now hold there.'

Carter's voice rose above the general hubbub. He sat heavily in his saddle, no more than five feet away from Matthew, one arm resting on the other. Carter seemed to have forgotten the horsemen and instead was looking Henty straight in the eye.

'You can ride free if you want, Bob, I'm not saying I can stop you, but from now on you'll be a hunted man. We'll have you sooner or later. Stay now and take what justice is coming to you. With luck they'll let you off with a fine.'

Henty spat on the ground: 'Go to hell.' He turned to Matthew:

'You coming, boy?'

Matthew had nothing to think about.

'If I stay here I hang for sure.'

He kicked his heels into his horse's flanks and the animal tugged at its lead. Matthew was about to call out, when he felt the lead go slack: Simon had untied the rope. Matthew's horse turned and walked slowly past Porkellis and across the empty space between the two groups. The riders had started to cheer: Henty was already there.

Then one of the horsemen rode up to Matthew and dragged his horse into the group and he was free. He looked back up the road. The bailiffs were still watching them. He heard Carter shout something irritably at Roskarren, and Roskarren shout something back, but still they did not move. Perhaps they would try to follow the horsemen when they left.

Matthew looked around him. The horsemen were one of the large gangs that took goods crosscountry. All of them carried muskets or naval pistols, and had powderbands slung over their shoulders. Presumably this was Bob-eye's gang.

'I won't forget this, Bob!' Carter called after them. 'I'll have you!'

One of the men next to Matthew levelled his musket almost casually at the bailiff. With a shock, Matthew realised the man was intending to fire, and that he could do nothing to stop him. He watched in horrible fascination as the man steadied himself against the buffets of the wind and took aim, his lips grinning with concentration. Carter was still calling to them. Then the musket jumped in the man's grip and gave a loud report. There was a shout from the other group. The constables were gathered round a figure on the ground, though who it was, he couldn't say. Closer to hand, some of the smugglers yelled in triumph, and Matthew thought they would all start firing. It was Bob-eye who restored order, and he rode up bellowing at the man who had pulled the trigger. Then he turned towards the officers and shouted:

'Is he hit?'

'Yes!' came the reply.

'Then get out of here and save yourselves!'

Two more of the smugglers fired, this time over their heads. The lawmen needed no further encouragement. Hauling Carter's body on to his horse, they retreated up the road as best they could.

A rider came up wielding a pair of boltcutters. He could not break Matthew's wristbands, but he sliced through the chains with little difficulty. Matthew flexed his arms painfully. Bob-eye, his hands also free, had taken command. They would be riding out soon, and Matthew worked desperately to restore some life to his limbs. Bob-eye reckoned that if Carter was wounded the officers would have to cross to St Columb, or carry on to Bodmin. Either way, the smugglers would have at least two hours' head start.

Then they were off. Henty left the highway and took them south, over the moor then into one of the deep valleys which drop down to St Austell. After a couple of miles they cut westwards across the hills, circling a cluster of mineworkings, blue and ghostly in the moonlight. The smugglers did not seem to care whether they were seen. Matthew guessed they would be a match for anything less than a squad of dragoons.

Once they had rounded St Austell they drove southwards again, the countryside softening and becoming easier. By this time Matthew felt exhausted. He had been sixteen hours in the saddle and the shackles had worn his wrists raw. He would have liked to stop, but had no choice but to keep up with the others. Then after an hour or so, the horsemen slowed and Matthew found himself descending into a sheer valley with a fishing village at the end of it. He turned to the man riding next to him and was told they were approaching Mevagissey.

Half an hour later they were enjoying a glass of rum in the warmth of a public house. Bob-eye came over and slapped him on the back.

'So,' he grinned, 'in the morning I'll have a smith cut your chains and you can be off. I know a boat who'll drop you at the Helford and you can make your own way home from there.'

Matthew thanked him. He had already forgotten about Carter. 'So did you know your men would rescue you?'

Henty winked at him: 'You know, I couldn't be sure, but once I heard the horses I knew it was either them or Peter the Devil.'

'Peter the Devil?'

The man next to him gave a loud laugh. 'It's nothing but an old wives' tale!'

'What is?'

'Peter the Devil.' The man turned back to the conversation he was having. Matthew tapped him on the shoulder:

'Tell me.'

The man seemed happy to share the joke.

'Men say he was curate of one of the churches on the moor in the time of King James. A man of exceptional height and strength, by all accounts, with jet black hair and eyes to match. Loved to ride and drink, even on the Sabbath, and a cruel master to boot. Some say Peter never grew old, but lived to be over a hundred, his hair as black as the day he was born. Said he was a practitioner of the black arts. Then one day he was found dead at the foot of his stairs, his face twisted into an expression of unimaginable horror.' The man grinned amiably. 'Men say that on wild nights when the wind is blowing, you can still hear him calling to his hounds and galloping over Goss Moor on his way to hell.'

Two days later Matthew watched from a fishingboat as the banks of the Helford slipped by. On all sides, richly forested hills rolled down to meet them – oaks, beeches, elms, sycamores – and creeks and inlets offered views of cottages in the nooks of hills and fleets of skiffs and luggers, tucked beneath the overhanging trees. The boat pushed slowly upstream, nudged by a sluggish wind, and the river sank deeper into the rich folds of the earth, until eventually they rounded a final spit of land and saw, nestling between three hills, the harbour of Gweek.

Matthew now had a choice. He could find a lugger bound for Newlyn, or make the journey overland on foot. Or he could abandon the whole enterprise and embark for Brittany with one of the merchants shipping tin from the blowing-house.

Perhaps in France he would forget the past. He smiled to himself wistfully. Emily was dead, and now Pascoe and Tremaine. And for what? The land of Trevanion, steeped in blood. That was all they would mine from Trevanion. The past. His inheritance.

He made enquiries at the inn. There was indeed a ship leaving on the morning tide – the *Rose* – bound for St Malo. He noticed that while he talked to her, the barmaid's eyes kept wandering to the ugly weal on his face. The scar would be with him until his dying day. Perhaps he would never forget the past, even if he wanted to. He had been hurt too much already.

That night he slept under the stars wrapped in his greatcoat. The next morning he woke while the sun was still a smudge in the east and looked down into the creek, where the *Rose* stood at her mooring. He stood looking at her for a minute, and then, slinging his greatcoat over his shoulder, he turned and headed over the hills towards Penzance and beyond that the land of his inheritance.

PART SIX

Chapter One

L UCY HAD BEEN GETTING READY for bed when a strange whispering sound disturbed her. Now she stood by the window in her nightgown, looking out. In the moonlight, the yard, barns and fields had assumed a white, hoary sheen. They looked strange, unreal. She touched the glass. It felt cold and leaning forward she pressed her forehead against the windowpane. She stared into the darkness, letting her mind roam over the miles of empty grassland and up into the moors beyond. A moth fluttered helplessly in the casement, its soft, feathery wings brushing against her arms. A draught crept around her ankles, and her skin tingled at the cold smoothness of the glass.

She was her own mistress now. Free of them all, of her mother, of Pascoe, free even of Matthew. She felt giddy with the sense of her potential. She ran her hand down over her breasts and stomach. Against her back the dying embers in the hearth cast warm orange tongues up and down her calves and thighs. She had never felt so powerful, so inebriated with her own self. Her breath formed little clouds of mist on the window, fine as tissue.

That afternoon Nathaniel Morgan had visited. She had misjudged him, even as they had misjudged her. Perhaps he would make a suitable mate. Perhaps, if need be, but not just yet. Her imaginings roamed further, to the gatherings and events at Truro, to the balls of the gentry, then out of Cornwall altogether, to Bath, Cheltenham, and the City. She realised with a shock that she was free of the past as well, free of her mother's past – what did it matter now? A world of possibilities opened up before her. She gazed out on to the barren landscape.

A hand clamped itself over her mouth. An arm, cold and hard, snapped round her waist. Before she could react, she was jerked backwards. She panicked and tried to struggle but found herself lifted bodily from the floor. Hot breath ran down the side of her neck.

'Hush! I didn't mean to startle you,' said the voice. A second later he had let his hand fall free of her mouth.

'Matthew!' She twisted angrily in his grip. Tears sprang from her eyes. 'Let go! Now!'

He did as she asked. She stood facing him, breathless and vulnerable. He raised a finger to wipe one of her tears. She slapped his hand away.

'What do you think you're doing! How did you get in?'

'One of the shutters in the drawing-room. You ought to be more careful.'

'And you ought to be in Launceston.'

He felt suddenly angry. 'Yes, I suppose that suited you nicely.'

'That's not what I meant!' She sounded hurt.

'I don't care what you meant! I found the documents, Lucy.'

'What documents?'

Lucy's eyes were wide with puzzlement, or maybe

fear. Her face, pure and unblemished in the moonlight, looked the very face of innocence.

'You know very well – the ones you hid, giving details of my uncle's will.'

'There isn't a will!'

He stepped closer to her. She pulled away but found herself backed against the cold windowpane. He held her jaw in his hand and stared into her eyes.

'You've never read them?'

'No. No.'

Then he bent his face close to hers. She tried to turn away but could not.

'You bastard! Do that again and I'll shout.'

'Would you really? If I did kill Pascoe, you'd be dead before the second word was out of your throat.' He gave her jaw a gentle squeeze. 'Don't forget that.' He released his grip. She was breathing heavily.

'Did you?' she asked.

'Did *you*? Who had most to gain from Pascoe's death, Lucy?'

'You can't be serious!'

'All people are capable of murder, Lucy.'

He looked at her, as if he were entranced by the logic of his words, as if he had stumbled upon a truth which had always eluded him.

'There is truly no crime worse than murder,' he continued. 'Take someone's life, and you deprive his friends, his family, his mother of that life too. No one has the right to do that. No one. Yet we do it, don't we, all the time? So easily, so quickly, for such transient, petty motives, which are gone tomorrow. But that life is gone forever.'

A moth was fluttering ineffectually against the

window. Without thinking, Matthew smeared it with his thumb over the cold glass.

'What do you want, Matthew?'

'Want? I came to see you.'

'You can't stay here,' she said quickly, then added as an afterthought: 'It's not safe.'

'Why not? This was my home!' he snapped, and then composed himself: 'No, I have no intention of staying here. I came for you.'

'But I don't want to go with you!'

Matthew grabbed her wrist and yanked her towards him.

'I don't care if you want to. You've got five minutes to get dressed or you leave like that.'

'And what if I refuse?'

'Then you will die, Lucy, don't you understand?' He drew her closer. 'Have you never wondered who did kill Pascoe and your mother? Whoever it was, won't stop there. You'll be next. Or me. And if I met the person at Sancreed, I can tell you, there's no escape. He'll slit your pretty little throat just like your mother's.'

Lucy burst into tears.

'How can I trust you?'

'You can't.' He smiled. 'No more than I trust you.'

They made their way over the fields. Matthew did not speak except to whisper instructions which he expected her to obey without question. Lucy did not dare argue. She had never seen Matthew like this. He was like a man possessed. He used his left hand to guide her, in his right he carried a pistol, cocked and loaded. Matthew refused to use the lane and kept to the middle of the large open fields. Often he would stop stock still and Lucy would see him straining his ears and eyes as if trying to detect the slightest hint of someone or something. Once they were startled by the sound of footfalls and Matthew threw her to the ground instinctively, spinning on his feet, his gun stretched in front like a lantern. It was a fox. Grim-faced, Matthew offered her a hand up. She refused. Even in the moonlight, she could see the beads of sweat standing on his forehead.

Because they kept to the fields they made slow progress, and it was at least an hour before Lucy smelled the sea air and could hear the sound of the waves breaking on the shingle.

'Where are you taking me?' she whispered.

'You'll see,' he said, then, thinking better of it, produced a large dirty handkerchief from his jacket. 'On second thoughts, you won't see, just yet.'

Ignoring her protests, he bound her eyes and led her forward. This made their going even slower, as often Lucy would trip and stumble, or Matthew would have to guide her round obstacles or over hedges. Lucy thought about screaming or shouting out, but there was something in Matthew's behaviour that made such thoughts seem unreal. She realised she was afraid, so very afraid, though whether of Matthew, or of the thing he listened for, she could not tell.

Now Lucy could feel rough shingle slipping and churning beneath her feet and her walking grew more laboured. She guessed they were at Porthmedn, then she slipped and pitched sideways and Matthew

291

hauled her to her feet. He half led, half dragged her
for the next thirty yards, until she felt the shingle
end abruptly. Now they were treading up a steep
winding path, muddy and slippery, and Lucy had
to step carefully, with one foot in front of the other.
When the path became steeper, she resorted to crawling on all fours, or Matthew lifted her bodily over
the worst parts. She cursed him from the depths of
her humiliation, but he ignored her, and said
nothing. Except for the large hand clutching hers like
a vice and relentlessly dragging her onwards, she
would not have known he was there. The handkerchief grew hot and sweaty. Matthew had bound it
tightly so that it dug into her face. They seemed to
be walking across a steep slope, perhaps a field. Then
the atmosphere changed and she guessed they were
in the shelter of a small wood. Twigs crackled under-
foot, and once Matthew held her still for what
seemed an eternity. She could hear a bird rustling
through the leaves. They walked on over grass and
turf, then down an uneven slope which made her
panic, then they were on to rocks. The sea was much
louder now and the wind seemed wet with brine.

'Not far now.'

Matthew's voice came as a surprise. They were
the first words she had heard for half an hour, but
he said nothing more and his hand tugged her forward. She was clambering over cliffs, she was sure
of it. The sea was beneath her to the left, and every
five or six seconds there came the familiar crash of
water on rock. She waved her left hand blindly.
Empty space. She wondered how secure her footing
was and whether Matthew really cared if she fell or

not. She imagined herself crawling along the edge of a cliff, a hundred feet above the rocks. She felt dizzy, sick and dizzy. What if he was going to push her off? They might never find her body. She imagined the black empty space around her and desperately tried to push the blind terror into the back of her mind. Just concentrate on the next step, the next handhold. He won't kill me. He can't kill me. Her free hand scrabbled over the smooth rock. Matthew's hand tightened its grip on her right forearm. That was her anchor-point, her one fixed point, as long as he held her she would be safe. Suddenly Matthew let go. She screamed, and swung her arms out on either side of her. Where was he?

'Jump!' he shouted from some way below.

Lucy did not move. Where was she? – presumably on some ledge or outcrop. Perhaps this was a trick, to send her stepping out into space.

'No,' she said quietly. 'I can't.'

'Jump,' he insisted, then with only a hint of humour: 'Trust me!'

'No.'

He was quiet for a moment: 'Take the cloth off.'

Lucy tore at the cloth. She was gasping for air as if she had been suffocated. She opened her eyes and had to clutch the rock to stop herself tumbling headlong.

She was standing on a lip of rock about two feet across. Behind her lay a broad, gently sloping flank of cliff, across which she guessed they had come. To her left was the sea, shifting sullenly in the moonlight. In front of her, about twelve feet down, Matthew stood in a small sandy inlet perhaps ten feet wide, curtained on either side by a sheer rock-face. He was looking up and grinning.

'Come on! Jump!'

She jumped. A split second later she was crouched breathless and winded in the sand, Matthew's arms around her.

'There you go.'

'Get off me!' She jerked herself from him. She saw now that the little beach on which they stood continued up underneath the overhanging cliff into a small cave. From this a faint auburn light emanated. She looked around her. On either side the cliffs had been worn smooth and featureless by the erosion of countless waves. They were virtually unscalable. The sole means of exit was provided by a crude rope ladder slung down from the cliff above. At the moment the tide was approaching its lowest ebb. At most other times, she judged the sea level would cover the small beach entirely, making it impossible even to reach the ladder, if it were still there.

Matthew took her hand and led her into the cave. The gradient rose sharply, and Lucy saw that the opening was deceptive: the cavern – for such it was – was in fact a good thirty feet long and at least ten feet high. It was carpeted throughout by the same fine yellow sand, and smelled powerfully of salt and stale seawater. Inside, on three upturned barrels placed around a fourth, George Trevose was seated, with Jacob Vean and Freddy Dunstan from the village. The three men did not seem surprised and hardly looked up from their game of cards. Behind them, large brandy-tubs, a half-anker big, were stacked to the roof.

Matthew smiled at the expression of disbelief on Lucy's face. 'Welcome to George's Cellar.'

George Trevose raised a glass to his lips: 'Welcome, welcome.'

'George is looking after you for a few days,' explained Matthew, 'until I can find a solution to our problems.'

'I'm staying here?' Lucy's voice was a mixture of bewilderment and horror.

'Whoever the killer is, you can't be protected outside. Besides,' he added, 'I'm a wanted man.'

'What if I want to leave?'

The three men glanced awkwardly at each other.

'You cannot,' Matthew told her. 'Not just yet.'

'This is outrageous!' Lucy exploded. 'It's against the law! George! Freddy!'

George Trevose put his glass back down deliberately.

'Murder is against the law,' he said gently but firmly, 'so is smuggling. I don't give a Spanish fig for the law, but I promise you, you'll come to no harm.'

Lucy stabbed a finger at Matthew.

'But this man's a murderer!'

George wiped his hand over his face.

'He's lost me my hundred pounds, that's for sure, but I'm not about to give up on him now. Hand him over to those bastards? Wouldn't be right. Besides,' he grinned, 'I've never cared for Pascoe anyway, always stirring up trouble. See, Freddy here's brought you a few home comforts.'

Lucy followed his gaze to a small mattress tucked into the corner of the cavern on an old wooden pallet. Next to it was a small clay stove.

'Best make yourself at home, my dear.'

Lucy cast a last despairing glance at Matthew. He was watching her impassively, almost distastefully.

'Trust me,' he said. 'Just trust me.'

Half an hour later, Matthew was gone, leaving Lucy in George's care. He had a lot to do before first light. George had told him the authorities assumed he had fled abroad, which was sensible enough. Even so, the slightest rumour he was back would bring the sheriff's men swarming over the area like locusts. He would have to be careful. George had given him three days to prove his innocence, or at least make some progress. After that he could not promise to keep Lucy. But, for the time being, she was safe.

And he was safe from her.

It was some time after midnight when Matthew entered Malaggan. The village was as silent as the grave. Hugging the sides of the buildings, he passed down the main street until he came to the silhouette of the church, rising out of the billowing mass of yew trees, and next to it, the square shape of the parsonage. Matthew tried first the front door, then the back. Both were locked. Standing to the rear of the house, he could see pale yellow light shining from a window on the first floor. That must be his mother's room. He found some loose pebbles from the garden path and threw them up. After a few moments, the tall figure of a man appeared at the window.

Richard let him in at the back with scarcely a word. He did not seem at all surprised. Matthew had been reluctant to take the parson into his confidence, but he had little choice. Besides, if his theory was right, he had nothing to fear from him.

'You must be careful,' Richard warned him. 'They know your mother's here. Trelawne will be keeping an eye on the parsonage.'

'Don't worry, I'll be gone by morning.'

The parson clasped him on the shoulder: 'Save your explanations for later. First of all, go and see your mother.'

Mary was still sick, but seemed to have recovered a little since he had last seen her. She was sleeping soundly and Matthew sat and watched her for ten minutes. Her forehead, when he touched it, was still warm, but it no longer burned with the same frightening heat as before.

When he descended, he found the parson nursing a brandy in the study. For the next half hour he told Richard as much as he judged desirable. He decided to make no mention of Lucy, or his abduction of her, at all.

'So what happens next?' The parson poured another brandy. 'It's only a matter of time before they catch you.'

'I know. I must move quickly. I will need your help.' Matthew studied his reaction carefully.

Richard only hesitated for a fraction of a second: 'You have it, as far as I can give it.'

'Good. There are two things I need. The first is the easier.' Matthew tapped his finger on the lip of his glass. 'I am beginning to see a way forward. I had thought Pascoe was behind things. And so he was, to a point. But he was obviously not responsible for his own death, even if he killed Emily.'

'What – you now think he was innocent?'

'I don't know. Plot and scheme, yes – that was Pascoe's way – but rip out throats with a skilly-knife? There's more to it than that. Whoever attacked me might have been in Pascoe's pay, but it certainly wasn't Pascoe, nor was it Tremaine.' A dark shadow passed over his face. 'Pascoe said something to me before he died. You will inherit the past, he said. Other people's lives. It was as if he knew something . . . more.' Matthew could see that this reference to the dead man made Richard uneasy. 'How about you? Don't you think I'm guilty too?'

The parson said nothing for a moment, then:

'I do not know. I have looked into your heart. There is a darkness there, a black thing. But look, I have said I will help you.'

'I am innocent, Richard.'

'No man is innocent, remember that. Not even I. Did you ask Pascoe what he meant by that?'

'No. I was too . . .' Matthew's voice trailed off. He appeared to be lost in thought, then he said suddenly: 'But if he did know something, maybe the secret lies in his papers.'

'Didn't you take them?'

'No. Why?'

'Because someone did. All his papers, all his files,

were gone. I spoke to Simon Trelawne. He said the place had been completely ransacked.'

Matthew cursed himself under his breath. He had meant to go through the papers before he left.

'When I spoke to Pascoe, he said he had copies stored somewhere else. Any ideas?'

'I could go into Penzance tomorrow and see if I can find anything out from his housekeeper. I owe her a visit. No, I can't go tomorrow – it will have to be the day after.'

Matthew could ill afford the day's delay, but he decided not to argue. He smiled: 'Good. That was the first thing.'

Richard looked him straight in the eye.

'Look, Matthew, I have said I'll help you. But only while I believe it serves the truth, do you understand? Truth – not convenience or your own well-being. There's a truth here waiting to come to light, I *think*. But I'll turn you in if I have to. Is that clear?'

'I wouldn't expect anything else.'

'Good. Now what's this second thing I can help you with?'

Matthew gazed into the hearth for a moment. He looked up.

'I want to dig up my uncle's body.'

Chapter Two

THE WIND MADE A GENTLE RUSTLING THROUGH the branches of the yew trees, but not sufficient to mask the soft thud of metal against soil. Matthew wiped his handkerchief across his forehead, and stood up. He had at least another three hours before anyone should be awake, but this did not stop him from feeling nervous, more nervous with each stroke of the shovel. He was two feet down now. At least another four foot to go. Then he must replace the earth. Provided, that was, he found nothing.

'Are you all right?' Richard whispered down to him. Matthew had only won his consent after a long discussion. Even so, the parson had refused to dig himself, and now he kept watch, hunched by the graveside in his cloak. But there was nothing else for it. He could still remember the encounter in the graveyard on the day of his uncle's burial. Sometimes in his dreams he was still there, staring at the figure across the slanted tombstones. After what his mother had said, his thoughts had grown so that he could no longer ignore them. Still, it was an unpleasant task.

'Yes,' he replied, 'just catching my breath. Don't forget I broke a rib a while ago.' The pain in his back was excruciating. 'Am I making too much noise?'

'You should be all right.'

'And, Richard? Keep a look-out for any ... any *thing*, do you understand?'

Matthew returned to his task. He planted the blade in the ground and jammed it down with his foot. The earth had not yet compacted and yielded easily. The tiring part was heaving it out of the pit. He decided to concentrate his efforts on one end of the grave. That way he would reach the coffin more quickly and could proceed from there. What if he did see his uncle that night? Or what if his mother had? He did not understand how it was possible – he had seen the body himself, seen it and held it.

He worked feverishly until he lost track of time in the endless dig-and-heave of the shovel and his back was soaked with sweat, cold and clinging. But when he paused he realised he was almost light-headed with fear. He looked out across the graveyard. There was something unnerving in the scene. Richard Morecombe was crouched a little way off, but either he was asleep or deep in thought, for he appeared quite stationary. The moon glittered on the diamond panes of the church windows. They reminded him of fish scales, sparkling as they are hauled in from the sea. The trees whispered and tossed their heads in the wind. He was four feet down now, maybe five, and it was becoming harder to fling the soil up.

In a fit of impatience he drove the shovel downwards, and felt its tip come up against something hard. Feelings of relief, and also of dread, came over him. Tugging at the damp soil he managed to clear away a patch, three or so inches across and eight inches deep. He pulled the shovel out and felt with his fingers. The wood was damp and ingrained with dirt. He scraped away more of the earth. It was the lid of his uncle's coffin. What was on the other side?

'Richard!' he hissed. There was no reply. He stood up and peered over to where the parson had been crouched. He was not there. Matthew scanned the churchyard: rows of gravestones stretched out in silent lines. There was no sign of the parson. 'Richard!' he hissed again. Something flickered in the corner of his eye, something grey, like the wings of a bat, but when he looked he could see nothing. Damn. Matthew glanced at the sky. It was still pitch black, but within an hour it would begin to lighten.

But when he looked into the pit at his feet, he felt an overwhelming reluctance to bend down and carry on – it would leave him exposed and vulnerable. He peered across the graveyard again. Where had Richard gone? Fighting off his fears, he forced himself back to the task at hand.

Now that he had a definite end in sight, his work became easier. He found he could scrape the soil off the lid quite quickly, and within a few minutes he was standing on top of the sturdy oak which John Mitchell had planed and crafted only a month before. For the first time, he wondered whether he was right to be doing this. But he had to know the truth. He felt around the edge of the lid. It had been secured with tacks, and would not be easy to lift off.

'How's it going?'

Richard's voice made him jump. The parson was standing at the lip of the hole, black against the sky.

'Where have you been?'

'A call of nature. Have you found it?'

'Yes. I'm just trying to open it. I thought something had happened to you,' he added, feeling suddenly foolish.

The parson gave a dry laugh, then said: 'I checked the clock. It's gone four. You'd better hurry.'

Matthew wedged his feet into either side of the hole, gripped the edges of the lid, and heaved. A sharp pain snapped across his back so that he gasped out, but the lid did not budge. He stood up, panting heavily.

'It's not right to disturb those whom God has lain to rest,' Richard observed.

'Not now,' he replied irritably. 'I'm almost there.' Matthew bent down again and repeated the same exercise, this time taking more care of his back, but with no more success. 'Damn! There must be some other way.'

'Have you tried this?' Richard leaned down and passed him an iron crowbar.

Matthew looked at him in amazement.

'If you insist on doing this, it's best you get it over and done with,' explained the parson awkwardly.

Matthew snatched the crowbar out of his hands and slotted it underneath the lip of the lid. Its tooth slipped on the wet wood, but on the second attempt, Matthew felt it gain purchase, and the top of the coffin began to ease up. He pumped the crowbar again. This time it bit deep, and the top came clean away. Matthew stooped down and raised the lid.

Underneath lay the body of John Trevanion. Matthew stared at it in silence. It was no more than he had expected, but even so he felt strangely disappointed. The body's skin was grey and dull in what little moonlight reached down into the bottom of the hole. Grey, dull, and starting to rot. There was no mistaking the smell of corruption which rose from the inside of the coffin.

'Are you satisfied?' asked Richard.

Matthew remained staring at the corpse. What did you know? he wondered. What did you see? John Trevanion said nothing. His features had collapsed into the final ghastly expression of death, and that was how they would remain. Matthew replaced the lid, but even then stayed staring down at the ground.

'Come on!' whispered Richard. 'We haven't got much time.'

Matthew looked up at him.

'I'm sorry. I had to know.'

Richard sighed to himself and stretched down a hand to pull Matthew out. Matthew saw that a second shovel lay on the grass.

'I can at least help you clean up the mess,' explained the parson. 'It's morning service in only a few hours.'

They put the last shovelful of soil back on to the mound just as the sun was creeping through the trees. Matthew looked around him. The church and graveyard seemed different now. Where before they had seemed possessed by some strange unearthly presence, now they were just stones, stones for the worship of God and the commemoration of the dead.

Then he heard voices, soft and indistinct, and the sound of footsteps. Richard must have heard them as well, for he had already crouched down and was motioning to Matthew. It was Freddy Dunstan and Jacob Vean. Matthew breathed a sigh of relief. They must be coming back from the Cellar. Luckily they were engrossed in their conversation, and they passed on into the village.

'I wonder what they're up to at this hour?' said Richard.

Matthew shrugged. Presumably Lucy was safe and sound. He wondered whether she was asleep, and if she was, what she was dreaming.

Richard shook him by the shoulder.

'Matthew, wake up! We need to finish.'

Although they had replaced the earth, it looked freshly turned and was bound to attract attention.

Richard went off and came back a few minutes later with a bucket of water. He tamped down the mound as best he could then splashed the water on top.

'There,' he exclaimed, straightening himself, 'that's better.'

'What about Penmarek?' Amos Penmarek was the sexton.

'He's not well himself. I doubt he'll be around for a couple of days.' Richard picked up his shovel and bucket. 'Come on. People will be up in a minute, Sabbath or no Sabbath.'

Matthew felt exhausted. It was only a day since he had woken in the field above Gweek.

'I need to be off,' he told Richard. 'Before anyone sees me.'

'What are you going to do?'

'Sleep. Then . . . I have some enquiries to make.' Matthew gave him a tired smile. 'And, Richard? Thank you.'

With that he left. But he did not go back to the

Cellar. He wanted to be by himself, at least for today. He would need all his strength for the night.

In the field over the hill stood a cattle barn. No one would go there on a Sunday. Matthew swung the door open and hauled himself into the loft. He lay gazing up into the old slate roof until he fell asleep.

At almost the same moment, Mary Vincent walked into the kitchen at Trevanion and saw the note Lucy had left her, propped on the table. Mary had learned to read her own name in Sunday School, but she had to wait for Beckie to come in before she knew more. It said:

Dear Mary,

When you read this I will be long gone. I have decided to go with Matthew to Brittany. We have friends there. Please do not tell anyone, and please do not worry. I am doing what is right. I shall return in a fortnight if all goes well.

Yours affectionately,

Lucy.

Chapter Three

IT WAS AN HOUR AFTER sunset before Matthew let himself out of the barn. He felt refreshed and suddenly optimistic. The night was mild and he would have enjoyed the walk in other circumstances. As it was, several people were still about and he had to keep to the fields. He had not eaten since the night before, and he decided to risk stopping at Rosmear.

There was still some bread in a jar in the kitchen, stale and its crust starting to go blue, which he ate, all except the worst bits, and some eggs in the barn. He looked around the cottage in the gloom. Someone – presumably Joseph or Nancy – had made an attempt to restore some order: the table and chairs had been set up and the smashed crockery swept into a heap. But if anything this only made the cottage more forlorn. A feeling of sadness came over him, sadness and sorrow, for his mother, for himself, for their life together. There was no going back, he knew. Even if he wanted to.

It took him only an hour to reach the small white cottage squatting on the hillside above Boskenna. He approached cautiously. No sound or light came from within. He knocked.

'Who's there?' The voice answered so quickly that his hand was still on the door.

'Matthew Trevanion.'

There came the sounds of a woman muttering and

moving about. Then the door clicked open and An Jenny stood squinting up at him. Her eyes glittered with amusement.

'I thought you'd come.'

Inside, the cottage was unlit except for a few red sparks in the hearth. He recognised the pungent smell of burned peat, but not the other more obscure aromas: spices, herbs, leaves and berries were festooned from the beams, and the air was impregnated with their heavy, woody odours. An Jenny scratched around and presently a flame appeared in an old lamp, casting huge yawning shadows into the recesses.

From what Matthew could see, An Jenny lived, worked, and slept in this one room. A misshapen straw mattress, covered with a blanket, was lumped in one corner. Facing it lay the hearth, with its pots and boiling pans overhead on struts. Next to this, a kettle stood on a brandis, and an iron and baker were propped against the fireplace. Running along the right-hand wall were a series of earthenware pots – buzzas, pancheons, pitchers – and above these large bundles of leaves and branches, hanging upside-down, and bunches of carrots, parsnips and radishes, and, on a small wooden shelf, pestles, mortars, mills and mixing bowls. On the left side of the room stood a large granite sink and dressing board. Long knives and other utensils glinted dully. While he was looking he saw Tiff, the great black cat, appear from underneath a stool by the fire. He hissed lazily. So this was the dwelling-place of the witch of Boskenna.

'So now you see how a witch lives,' said An Jenny,

uncannily echoing his thoughts. 'Many men would think twice before coming.'

'I had no choice.' He heard her give a shrill, coarse laugh.

'So you need my help. Man said you killed a man – two men and a lady to be precise.'

'Yes. I need to know the truth.'

'And you think I know something?'

'Don't you?'

An Jenny went over to the woodpile and began to build up the fire. 'You'd better sit down, and tell me about it.'

Matthew ran over the details sketchily. After she had finished with the fire, An Jenny sat on the stool opposite him. She seemed to find his tale quite entertaining, even amusing, and when he came to the exhumation of his uncle's corpse, she giggled like a girl.

'Was he warm and snug? I could have told 'ee, you were wasting your time.'

'I needed to know,' he said stubbornly.

'So you've come here.'

'Inherit the past, An Jenny. That's what a dead man said to me. I need to know. Something happened in the past – to my family, or the land – I can feel it.'

The old woman smacked her lips in thought.

'I know of nothing by hearsay,' she said at last. 'Though I've always thought something hung over that family. Always came to no good. And look at your poor father. That was a shame.'

The wind prowled outside the cottage. Tiff stirred and stretched himself.

'What about my father? He went away when I was young.'

An Jenny giggled. 'Went away? Is that what they told you?'

'No, of course not.' Matthew frowned. 'They always said "went away" when they meant "died". I suppose I've got used to the expression.'

'But you don't know what happened to him, do you?' Her eyes danced merrily.

He scowled. 'Yes. I mean, no. They always said he just went away. I have one or two memories, that's all. I can remember him telling me a story – about Captain Vincent – and me sitting on his knee. And I remember the man telling my mother he was dead. I was five years old.'

'And is that all? Can you remember what he looked like, for instance?'

'Tall? With fair hair?' Matthew shrugged. 'I don't know. I suppose any man seemed tall to me then.'

'Your father was a handsome man, Matthew. You're right – tall, fair, with pale blue eyes, the colour of the sky on a summer's day, and with what I call a ladies' smile – very popular with the ladies was your father.' Matthew shifted uncomfortably in his chair. 'But look at yourself. Do you see any similarity? Black hair, black eyes and no smile at all.'

He remembered Joshua Pascoe, leering up at him.

'He was my father, damn you!'

'Of course! Of course!' she answered quickly. 'Tell me, do you know how they found him?'

Matthew ground his teeth, so she continued:

'At the bottom of Penzer Point.'

'You mean he jumped?'

'Or was pushed.' The words fell softly from the old woman's mouth. She smiled mischievously. 'Have a care, Matthew. The past is full of surprises.'

'So he was murdered?'

'I don't know. I may look old, but I was a young girl then, quite sweet and lovely.' An Jenny paused in reflection. 'I am afraid my profession has taken its toll on me too. How old do you think I am?'

Matthew looked away uncomfortably. 'I wouldn't be able to judge, An Jenny. People say you've always been old.'

'I am forty-five, Matthew. That's all.'

Matthew stared at her in disbelief. It may have been just a trick of the light, but now, beneath her blotched and sallow skin, he thought he could detect the vestiges of her corroded youth.

'I was pretty too,' she went on, playing with a strand of white hair in her fingers. 'Pretty and desirable. Oh yes, by those same men who scorn me now.'

'What happened?'

An Jenny gave a shrill, metallic laugh.

'Some say I turned myself into a toad and the devil wouldn't turn me back.'

Matthew could not think of anything else to say, so he asked: 'Did you?'

'A toad?' A wild, crooked smile appeared on her face. 'Oh yes. Many times a toad. And often a hare. I would run!' She ran her fingers over the front of her dress. He was suddenly reminded of Marcy Towan, screaming at him.

'So you knew my father?' he said to distract her.

'Not well, boy. Not as well as I'd have liked,' she

added. 'I'd just come here then. When I was a girl I lived near Liskeard. They drove me away.'

'So who'd want to kill him?'

'Did I say anyone did?' she teased him.

'I need answers, not riddles! If this is all you can tell me, I'll be going.' He got up angrily.

'No! Don't do that.' An Jenny seemed suddenly nervous. 'Stay a while longer. I'll help you. I can show you the way back,' she explained. 'Into the past.'

He remained where he was. He had known coming here would be a mistake.

'I'll take you there,' she said quickly. 'Me and Tiff. You need to know, Matthew. Or else your past will kill you as well.'

She saw the indecision in his eyes, and suddenly laughed, as if in triumph.

'You don't want to leave, do you, because you know I'm right.'

Matthew sat down.

'Tell me.'

An Jenny tutted to herself. 'Not as easy as that, I'm afraid. It's going to take time. Now go and get some more peat for the fire.'

Matthew reluctantly did as he was told. When he returned, An Jenny was bent over her table pounding a mixture of dried roots and leaves. When he asked what she was doing she told him to be quiet and put a pan of water on to boil. As she ground the ingredients, she began to sing over them in the same seesawing, keening voice he remembered from his sickness. He waited for the water to boil.

At length, An Jenny was ready. From a clay pot,

she took out some dark green leaves, shrivelled, like nettles, and counted out two portions of seven leaves each. Then she shredded them and steeped them in two cups of boiling water. They gave off a bitter, earthy steam.

'Drink this,' she instructed, handing him one of the cups.

He sipped it warily.

'Quick!' she snapped. 'While it's hot.'

He took a mouthful. The liquid had a strong, pungent taste which reminded him of crushed ivy or tea-leaves. He wondered whether it was poisonous. Then he saw An Jenny had already drained her cup and was watching him impatiently. 'Hurry!' she was saying. 'Or you'll lose it!' Shutting his eyes, he tipped it down his throat and wiped his mouth. An Jenny was smiling at him warmly.

'What was that?' he asked.

'It will help you see things,' she told him.

'Things? What things?' But his voice came from a long way away and then she laughed at him, but not unkindly.

It must be late, he thought. He was already feeling thick-headed. He would need to sleep soon. He rubbed his eyes. Maybe the room seemed darker, or more blurred? He rubbed them again. No. He was just tired.

An Jenny took a handful of the ground powder and threw it onto the flames. The fire began to smoke, a thick grey smoke which stunk of peat and also something else, acrid and rooty. An Jenny gripped his hand – her skin was dry like paper – and drew him towards the hearth.

'Now we watch,' she said, and with that fell silent.

Matthew pulled up his chair. After the cold night, the gentle warmth of the fire was particularly welcoming. He stared into the billowing smoke and let himself relax. If this is what she wanted . . . After a while the smoke, which had been rising gently, began to settle and sink downwards. He watched it curl and slide across the floor towards him in thin chalky ribbons. The heat beat evenly against him. Lucy seemed far away now, he could barely imagine her. Next to him, he was aware of An Jenny's slow gentle breathing. Gradually, the smoke grew thicker, and rounder, until it seemed almost solid and the fumes mushroomed into forms which reminded him of rose-heads or hyacinths, fat, bulbous, before collapsing into a vapour of dust. The air also was warmer, and thicker, and redolent with half-familiar mustiness. Ivy, he thought, and recalled the dense black ivy which climbed over the oak trees behind the farm. When he was a boy he would clamber up, using the ivy for a ladder.

The smell faded. The smoke tumbled in rolls over the floor-matting. For a moment, he smelt a sharp tang, as of the sea. Matthew shook his head and looked around. He could not tell whether five minutes had passed or several hours. The lamp had guttered and gone out and the room seemed stuffy and close. He longed for clean fresh air. An Jenny was sitting on her stool, staring into the eddies of smoke spilling out of the fire. He watched them, as if he too were mesmerised, and sank deeper into his seat. He felt his eyelids closing. The air was warm and snug and smelled of tannin, yet it was no longer unpleasant, but familiar, secure. His mouth tasted as if it were full of earth. He closed his eyes.

He was a little boy again, alone in a long dark corridor. He was in Trevanion. He touched the dark green wallpaper. It was the same colour as the leaves An Jenny had put in his drink. Where was An Jenny? His small fingers pressed against the wall. It was hard and damp and emitted the same bitter earthy smell. A loud noise startled him. The grandfather clock at the end of the hall. The case was pitching with each swing of the pendulum. Right, left, right, left. Now there were voices. His mother and father talking in the parlour. They were arguing. He wanted to stop them. He had a terrible sense of fear. He must stop them. He ran down the corridor and into the room, but the room was empty, just as he had last seen it, only darker, larger. Then an old man stood in the doorway, his cranium pink and shiny except for a band of snow-white hair above each ear. He wore a dark bottle-green jacket and breeches, cut in an antique style, and white stockings. Matthew had seen him somewhere before. 'She's dead! Dead!' someone was wailing. Where were they? He looked up at the man. The old man seemed impossibly tall. 'Who are you?' asked Matthew. The man gazed sternly at him and opened his mouth, but instead of words there issued forth a thick inky smoke. The smoke spilled down and hung in a pall over the room. There seemed to be no end to it. It fell over Matthew like a blanket, fetid, damp. Then everything went black. Screaming. There was screaming, and he was choking. Something was around his neck. He heard another scream, louder, more insistent, and he realised he was the one screaming.

For a moment he could see nothing. Then he remembered he was back in the cottage. Dense, oily fumes were pouring out of the fire. They were choking him. He could still hear screaming and this confused him, then he realised it was An Jenny. The woman was rigid, eyes bulging, mouth open and shrieking. He heaved himself to his feet. His head was beating like a drum and he stumbled. Everything was so heavy. He had the taste of ivy in his mouth. He spat it out. He must sleep. His head spun and he thought he was going to fall, then he realised he was already on the ground. He looked up. The cauldron of water still hung above the fire. He rolled himself on to all fours. An Jenny was still screaming. Shut up. Shut up. He reached up with his hand. He couldn't reach, pushed with his legs, and the cauldron crashed on to the hearth, spraying water everywhere. The fire hissed and went out and plunged the room into total darkness. Screaming. She was still screaming. A high shrill scream that came in short, desperate gasps.

Matthew dragged himself upright and slapped her across the face as hard as he could. The old woman crumpled like a piece of paper. Grabbing her by the arm, he hauled her out of the chair and flinging the door open, threw her on to the ground outside. He sagged against the door-jamb, gulping air.

Face down in the dirt, An Jenny had started to sob. She sounded like a little child. Matthew let himself slide down the door-jamb and slumped on the ground, watching her. A cool breeze, fresh with the smell of the sea, blew over them.

His head began to clear. He felt sick and, leaning to one side, vomited on the ground as effortlessly as a dog. He needed water and found a pitcher of cold water by the door. He gulped it and splashed it over his face and neck.

A soft whimper, almost a sigh, reminded him of An Jenny. She had stopped crying and was lying motionless. A thin film of foam flecked the corners of her mouth. He poured a dose of water over her, and she stirred and opened her eyes.

'Water,' he told her. 'Drink some.' He helped her sit up and she took several small, cat-like sips. Then she too vomited.

Looking eastwards, Matthew could see the sky lightening. He would have to leave soon. He grabbed An Jenny by her collar, lugged her inside and dropped her on her mattress. The smoke had cleared now, but the same bitter scent hung in the air, and he knocked the shutters open and jammed them in place. An Jenny lay mumbling to herself. He wanted to be gone from here. He shook her awake and slapped her round the face and began to rub her hands. She opened her eyes and smiled at him.

'So you're still here, boy.'

'Are you all right?'

'I cannot help you.' Her expression became confused. 'There's something there. Something evil. It almost killed me.' Her breaths came in short shallow jerks as if she were being denied air. 'You saw it?'

Matthew felt embarrassed. He turned away as he answered her.

317

'I had a dream. What was in that drink you gave me?'

An Jenny smiled weakly. 'Never you mind. But you saw something?'

'I had a dream,' he repeated. He looked at her coldly. The excitement of the night had cooled in the damp grey dawn. She clutched at his hand, and he pulled away from her.

'Run home to Mother, eh?' said An Jenny darkly. 'Just like all the other boys. I felt you last night, Matthew. You were hungry then, you needed me, didn't you?' She looked sad.

'Can you help me?' he asked quietly, then added: 'I'm sorry.'

The old woman thought for a moment. 'Yes,' she replied, 'no doubt you are.'

'What did you see?'

'What did *you* see, Matthew? All I saw was blackness. I smelled him though.' An Jenny scratched her nose expressively and waited for him to answer.

'I saw an old man standing in Trevanion Hall, that was all.'

'Did he say anything?'

'No. He just stared at me.'

An Jenny looked at him seriously. 'A man, you say? No, the plant doesn't see people. It sees only good and evil. That was no man.'

'What was it, then?'

'A *bucca dhu*. One of the old ones.'

Matthew regarded her cynically. Yet there was no denying the feeling of fear which crept up his back.

She grinned. 'Look at your past, Matthew. The *buccas* don't live in the now, this is not their time.

Something has drawn him out of the past, that is where he has taken root. Seek it out. Dig it up.'

'I tried,' he said.

'Yes,' she comforted him. 'You tried, but you need to look elsewhere, or in a different way.'

'And when I do – if I do – find this thing?'

'Then you must destroy it. Or it will destroy you.'

'Is that it? How can I destroy the past?'

An Jenny was silent, her gaze seemed to be on something far away.

'I don't know,' she said. 'Perhaps all you can do is embrace it.'

When he got to the Cellar, George was nursing a bottle of brandy and waiting for him. Lucy lay asleep on the mattress. She had loosened her hair, and it splayed across the bedding like a tumble of black water.

'I hoped I'd catch you,' said George. 'Found anything?'

'I'm not sure.' Matthew slumped on to one of the barrels. 'I feel done in.'

'You certainly look it.' George poured him a shot of brandy. 'I thought you'd come back yesterday.'

'Got delayed.' Matthew sniffed at the brandy. Its fragrant bouquet smelled like a sickly, cloying perfume. He put the glass back on the table. 'Anything happened?'

George chuckled and jerked his thumb towards the mattress. 'She's been fussing and cursing. I couldn't leave Freddy alone with her, she'd been working at him, see?'

319

Matthew smiled grimly. Lucy could be very persuasive.

'I've got no choice,' he said. 'If we let her go, he'll kill her.'

George looked up from his brandy. 'So you say.'

'Believe me, I've met the man. Look what he did to my mother.'

'All the same, three days, Matthew. I can't risk more than that.'

'I know. You've been good, George.' Matthew clasped the man's forearm. George looked perplexed. It was not a gesture that came naturally from Matthew.

Matthew screwed up his eyes. 'I've got to lie down.' He got up and threw himself onto a heap of rushes in the corner of the cave and almost immediately was asleep.

George watched him while he finished off his brandy. Something was troubling Matthew, but what it was he couldn't say. He snuffed out the candle and yawned. Then, setting the bottle squarely in the centre of the barrel, he made his way out of the cave and off towards the village.

Chapter Four

W HEN HE AWOKE THE FIRST thing he saw was Lucy's figure, backlit against the mouth of the cave. She was looking out towards the sea and did not notice him as he stumbled onto his feet. He groaned. His chest was aching savagely, in fact his whole body ached and felt chilled and wretched. He shook his head and grimaced. Here in the cave, the events of the night before seemed no more than a phantasm, distorted and unreal, except for the aching in his chest and limbs.

'How long are you going to keep me here?' Lucy asked him suddenly.

'As long as it takes.'

'Freddy said they'll let me go tomorrow.'

'Freddy be damned! They'll keep you for as long as I say.' He lurched past her and out onto the little slip of beach left by the tide. His head exploded in a kaleidoscope of light. It was midday and a cruel brilliant sunlight bleached the horizon and splintered off the waters. Only in the shadow of the cliff did the water remain soft and green. He bent down painfully and dipped his head into the waters.

He was a sitting target. Lucy rushed out of the cave and pitched him into the sea. For a second Matthew's mind went blank. The water smacked the breath from his body. His eyes stung. He came up coughing, turned to stand up and, still floundering with the momentum of her push, lost his footing and tumbled backwards into the sea. He caught a glimpse of Lucy. She was laughing. Then the cliffs and sky disappeared under a flood of water. His limbs felt strangely leaden, as if still drugged. He flapped them numbly. Although he was tall, the beach shelved steeply, and he realised he was already out of his depth, yet it no longer seemed to matter. Abruptly, he stopped struggling and let his body relax, giving himself up to the water's embrace. Slowly peace returned. He was asleep again, and he thought he could hear, a long way off, the sound of singing. Although his chest still hurt, now the pain was no more than discomfort. He tried to breathe, but found he could not.

Suddenly a thin hand gripped his hair and shook him. He opened his eyes. It was Lucy. He was gazing up at her through the green waters. She looked concerned. Something must be wrong. He swam towards her, and suddenly felt an irresistible longing for air. The singing in his ears became the rushing of water, then she was dragging him up the beach and shouting at him.

They lay for a long time in the sand, tired and numbed.

'You didn't respond,' she told him. 'I thought you'd drowned.'

He looked out to sea. 'I must be sick.' An image came to him, of the smoke embracing him.

'So how long are you going to keep me here?' she asked petulantly.

'I said as long as it takes. It's not safe for you, don't you understand?'

'So you say.'

He turned towards her. He could not trust her, he knew that. But that very quality suddenly seemed strangely attractive, exotic. She pouted her lips. 'I want to go home, Matthew.'

'Don't we all?' The October sun, clear and hard though it was, had no warmth in it, and soon they would be chilled to the bone. He put his hand on her side, feeling her skin through the wet cotton. 'Come. We need to change.'

She picked up his hand: 'You're cold.'

She began to rub it between her fingers. Her hands were as soft and light as little birds. He studied the expression of concentration on her face, fascinated by the way she could manipulate him, almost at will. She looked him in the eye and lifted his hand to her mouth and began to kiss it. He could pull his hand away, he thought, and go back into the cave. But instead he leaned closer to her, wishing her to kiss his mouth. She did so, and entwined her thin, wet arms around his back. Her tongue met his. It tasted of the sea. She closed her eyes, and he wondered what she was thinking as she licked and sucked at his lips. A light breath of wind caught some wet strands of her hair and ruffled them against her forehead where they clung to her skin. He ran his hand over her dress and felt her body flex and arch inside the cloth.

Under the gaze of the hard white sun he laid her bare. Her soft white flesh gleamed like a pebble. He nuzzled into her hair and imagined dark tresses of seaweed swaying. He tasted her skin, warm and salty, lily-white. Her thin, sharp fingers plucked off his jacket and shirt. She lowered her head and softly, achingly, kissed and nibbled him.

She felt the great mass of his body move against her, hard, warm, a thing of flesh and blood. His face, lined and scarred, had taken on an expression almost of pain, and she felt a strange thrill of distaste and desire. She pulled him over onto her and his strong fingers kneaded and moulded her. Her body twisted and his breath licked her. She wanted to give herself to him so there was nothing left. Then, if he wanted, he could kill her. She gasped and clutched him between her palms, opening herself to him and forcing him into her, so that she felt him moving inside her and the sharp gravel of the beach against her spine. His hands gripped her, by the shoulders, by the waist, forcing her down and onto him until at last he possessed the softest part of her, and there was nothing left.

Afterwards they lay still on the beach and the waves lapped their feet.

They will always be here, she thought, when our passion is spent, when we are gone, they will still be here. Matthew rested his head on her shoulder, weak and dozing fitfully, only kept awake by the insistent chill of the air on their bodies. She let her fingers run through his hair. Has this resolved anything? she thought.

She felt him stir. Clutching their wet clothing around them, they got up and went inside. Neither spoke. Their passion had caught them unawares, betrayed them. In the cool shadow of the cave, they stood apart, awkward and shamed at their nakedness.

Chapter Five

'I'VE DRAWN A BLANK,' RICHARD told him at the door. 'His housekeeper had no idea if Pascoe kept copies or not. He'd got a safe at his house but his niece had already emptied it.'

It was evening and Matthew had just left George in the Cellar with Lucy.

'No matter.' He did not look unduly disappointed. 'I've been thinking – I'll tell you later. How's my mother?'

'Better,' judged the parson, but without any great confidence.

Once in the bedroom, Matthew saw what he meant. Mary was sleeping peacefully, and her temperature had gone. But her skin was ashen and her eyes sunk into their sockets.

'What's wrong with her?' whispered Matthew.

Richard took him to one side.

'I don't know. She just lies there. Doesn't open her eyes. Doesn't seem to hear us.'

To Matthew, she seemed thinner and frailer.

'Is she eating?'

The parson sighed and shook his head.

'Mrs Dunstan squeezes milk into her mouth from a cloth but I'm not sure she swallows any.'

Matthew walked back to the bed.

'Mother! Can you hear me?'

Mary Trevanion did not move.

Suddenly there was a knock at the door. The two men looked at each other.

'Who is it?'

'I don't know – I wasn't expecting anyone. Wait here.' Richard quickly left the room. Matthew stared at his mother. He could hear the parson shouting from the top of the stairs: 'Hello! Who's there?'

What if it was no ordinary visitor? he thought suddenly. What if it was the thing he had met on the road? The thing that had left his mother like this? He stayed by her bedside. She stirred and opened her eyes. 'Matthew,' she whispered. 'You've come back.'

At that moment, he heard the parson opening the door downstairs. There was the rattle of the door-chain.

'Hello? Who's there?'

He touched his mother's hand. It was smooth and cold.

'Yes.' He kissed her on the forehead. Then a voice came from the front door:

'Reverend Morecombe?'

He recognised it instantly: it was Carter, the bailiff. So he wasn't dead. Matthew froze. Then there was a second, softer voice:

'I hope we're not disturbing you, Richard?'

Nathaniel Morgan. What was he doing here?

Placing his mother's hand back on the cover, Matthew crossed quietly to the door and listened out. Richard was greeting his visitors on the doorstep.

Morgan coughed. 'Can we come in, Richard? It's damn cold out here.'

'Of course, make yourselves at home.' Richard sounded perfectly at ease. Matthew heard the two men rubbing their arms and stamping their feet as they stepped inside.

They went into the drawing room. Matthew tip-toed onto the landing just in time to see Richard close the door behind him. Damn. Presumably the parson had done this to let him escape, but Matthew would have rather heard what they were saying. He strained his ears. There was a sudden burst of laughter. Someone must have told a joke. Then the voices settled into the low and irregular tempo of conversation.

He was just about to creep down the stairs when the door swung open. Matthew stepped back quickly. Carter and Morgan were leaving already. Richard was patting them on the back and wishing them a safe journey. On the threshold, Carter turned to him, and said:

'If anyone else sees 'im, just let us know.'

Then they were gone and the door closed behind them. Richard waited until he could no longer hear their footsteps on the path outside, then he turned to where Matthew stood on the stairs.

'What was that all about?'

'It seems some farmer saw you yesterday. You must be more careful.'

'So what did they want?'

'They're going round all the houses telling people to keep an eye out for you. Nathaniel's off to Trevanion next to see Lucy.'

Matthew let that pass.

'So where did this farmer see me? What was I doing?'

'Apparently you were riding over to the north, up by Castle Chun.'

'That's ridiculous! I haven't been there for years.'

Richard shrugged. 'Well, that's what they said. It seems rumour is rife.'

'Hysteria more like. I wonder if they tell children stories about me yet? Matthew the Devil: I can just imagine it.' He laughed humourlessly.

'Don't mention that name in here! This is a house of God!' Richard looked suddenly angry. A vein, blue and swollen, beat on the side of his temple.

'I'm sorry. But it's farcical! I haven't even got a horse. What did Morgan want?'

'He said he's got a personal interest, Matthew.'

In Lucy you mean, he thought. He remembered her soft white flesh, wet with the sea.

'Richard, I've been thinking.' He chose his words carefully.

'Yes?' replied the parson absent-mindedly. 'Come into the parlour where it's warm.'

'Lucy as we know stands to inherit the estate.'

'She has inherited the estate,' corrected the minister. 'Brandy?'

'Would it make any difference if she was illegitimate?'

'Illegitimate? In what way?' Richard turned to him, two glasses in his hands.

'Well, that her mother and father were not married. Lucy told me, a long time ago. That's why she came back from London.'

Richard took a sip from his glass.

'Why bring this up now?'

'But if Lucy can't inherit, then who would?'

'You, of course,' the parson answered irritably. 'There's no one else. Do you really want Trevanion that badly?'

'That's not my point. If Lucy isn't the heir, the murderer won't know that. He'll still want to kill her, when all along he should be after me!'

Richard looked at him oddly.

'What makes you so sure these murders are to do with Trevanion at all?'

'An Jenny told me.'

'An Jenny? You consort with witches and demons!' Richard took a step backwards. 'In God's name!'

'I had a dream—'

'*Do not interpretations belong to God?* I cannot believe you, Matthew!'

'It's not like that! I wanted to find out the truth.'

Richard Morecombe glared at him.

'And do the promises of Christ mean so little to you? Truth and knowledge – what do I care for the truth of this world? There is only one truth and that is Christ. Does not all of scripture, all of life, show us that? Christ came, a man born of woman, to save us from the sins of the first man, Adam, and a woman. And what did they sin for? For false knowledge, false truth. And God saw them and they were naked before him and before each other and they were shamed at their nakedness.'

Matthew lowered his eyes.

'Yes,' he said quietly. 'You are right. Forgive me.'

'Do you really ask for forgiveness?'

'Yes. It was wrong of me. I sought truth. But I see now it was false.'

'Then your sins are forgiven.' The minister was quiet for a moment. 'You haven't taken your drink.'

Matthew was grateful for the distraction. The brandy was hot and fiery.

'Anyway,' asked Richard. 'What proof do you have, about Lucy I mean?'

'Parish records in Bristol apparently. That's how she found out.'

'Well, we could pursue this, but I don't see how it would establish your innocence. If anything it would give you a better motive for killing Emily, wouldn't it?' he asked pointedly.

'I suppose so. I hadn't thought of that.'

'Hadn't you? I'm not—'

'Wait a minute.' Matthew almost jumped in the air. 'Parish records! Of course! What records do you have here in Malaggan?'

'Nothing to do with Lucy, that's for—'

'Forget Lucy! Trevanion – that's what I mean! Forget what papers Pascoe had, surely the church must have something?'

'I don't know. Just the usual, I expect. Payment of tithes, baptisms, marriages and deaths.'

Matthew's eyes sparkled. 'Well, let's see them. Where are they kept?' Look in the past, An Jenny had said.

'In the vestry.'

Pausing only to grab a coat, Richard led Matthew into the churchyard. Nothing had changed from two nights before. The church tower loomed out of the darkness. Moonlight glittered off its windows. They entered through the south porch. The main body of the church opened out before them, its vaults and columns silent and cavernous, more silent, more cavernous, it seemed, than the night outside. Richard strode down the aisle to the vestry behind the pulpit. Inside, locked in a wooden closet, stood the volume of parish registers, leather-bound.

Richard pulled it down and held it up to the window. The pale blue moonlight was just strong enough. Matthew looked at the book. Baptisms, marriages and deaths. Inside would be recorded the names of John and Emily Trevanion.

'What do you want to see?' asked Richard.

'I'm not sure. Anything relating to Trevanion. Anything at all.'

'Anything relating to Trevanion.' The parson turned the pages slowly. 'Marriages, for instance?'

'Maybe, though I doubt it. John only married the once, didn't he?'

'As far as I know.' The parson ran his fingers down the entries. Malaggan was not a large parish, never more than three hundred and fifty souls, yet even so their matings, births and deaths had left many marks on the thick yellow pages. 'There's only one way to be sure, and that's to start at the present and work back.'

The first entry was for Emily. 'Emily Trevanion, buried Monday 29th September, 1749, God rest her soul.' Then came Philippa Odgers, then John. Matthew looked at the words. The parson had made the entries in a spare, simple style. There was nothing here he did not know already.

Richard worked his way methodically back through the book. All these he knew. Every birth, death, marriage, he had presided over them all.

'Here's your uncle's marriage.'

Matthew looked to where his finger pointed. It seemed more remote now than ever.

'How about my mother's marriage, would that be in here?'

'I'd have thought so. When was she married?'

Matthew shut his eyes. '1719, no, 18, I think.'

'Very well.' Richard turned towards the front of the book. Matthew watched him impatiently as he pored over the lists in silence. After several minutes the parson looked up.

'Are you sure it was 1718? They don't seem to be listed.'

'How about 1719?' Matthew tried to keep his voice casual. Is this what his father meant in his testimony? The minutes passed slowly.

'No,' said the parson at last. 'It's not there.'

'Let me look.' Matthew scanned the pages. The parson was right: Trevaskis, Treveath, but no Trevanion.

'Perhaps they were married in your mother's parish?' Richard suggested. 'It's not uncommon.'

'No. I was sure they married here.' He checked the entries for 1717 – no Henry Trevanion and Mary Samuels there either.

'I shouldn't worry if I were you. It'll be in some other parish register up the county, I'm sure.'

'You don't know yourself?'

'Me? No. Don't forget I've only been here five years. You know, I've often thought it strange that

John married so much later than his brother. Twenty-five years later. That's a long time.'

Perhaps Richard was right. Perhaps the wedding was recorded elsewhere. A thought struck him, and he turned the pages. 1721, March 1722, August, there! October 30th 1722. He read the words and reread them to make sure: 'October 30th, baptised Matthew Nicholas Trevanion, son of Henry and Mary Trevanion, nee Samuels, of Lower Rosmear.'

'What is it, found something?' asked Richard.

Matthew shook his head: 'No. Nothing important. What about my grandfather?'

'What was his name?'

Matthew remembered the inscription on the gravestone.

'Robert. Robert Trevanion.'

Richard took the register back and examined the frontispiece.

'I doubt it's here. This register only goes back to 1700. The old one's kept in the crypt.'

'Hmmm.' Matthew thought for a moment. 'What about deaths? Would my father be in here?'

'Almost certainly. When did he die?'

'In 1727.'

The pages turned. This time there was no delay.

'Here it is. "September twenty-third, 1727. Henry Trevanion, second son of Robert, of Rosmear, found dead this morning at foot of Penzer pt. Death by accident recorded." '

Death by accident.

'How old was my father, does it say?'

Richard shook his head. 'No. But his birth should be in here anyway.'

So it was. Under May 9th, 1700. ' "Henry Trevanion, third son of Robert Trevanion and Amanda." '

Matthew turned the words over in his head. Henry Trevanion. He looked at the parson.

'Third son? That can't be right! He only had one brother, John, and a sister, Rose, I think.'

'Well that's probably what they meant,' Richard suggested. 'See here, under the death it says second son.'

'Rose – when did she die?'

'I don't know.' Richard leafed through the pages. When he could not find the entry he retraced his steps and checked again. 'No,' he said at last. 'Not here. Must be before 1700. The first entry I have is second February 1700 – Thomas Draper, died of colic, aged sixty-three.' He thought for a moment. 'Isn't there a gravestone out by the south porch?'

Matthew tried to remember. 'I'd have to look.'

'Rose Trevanion?' The parson continued to himself. 'Yes, I think so. Died 1690 something, only a few months old.'

'That sounds like her. But that still makes Henry the second son. I suppose John Trevanion isn't in there either?'

'Only his death and marriage.'

'This earlier register – can we see it?'

'Of course. I'll have to lock up here first, though.'

But before they did that, Matthew checked through the rest of the book, just in case. The moonlight made reading difficult, and it was not long before his eyes were tired. There was little else. The Trevanions were no longer a numerous family. However, there were two other entries, under deaths, for

Robert and Amanda Trevanion, his wife. He recalled their inscriptions in the churchyard. He looked up, bleary-eyed.

'There's also the tithe records,' said Richard. 'But they seem to be in order, as much as they ever are, that is.' He carefully replaced the register and locked the closet.

'You know,' he said. 'I've just remembered. Joshua Pascoe asked to see these registers as well.'

'When was that?'

'About six, maybe seven months ago. Said he wanted to check on something or other, didn't say what.'

They walked back through the church, and out round the side of the building to where the crypt door was sunk in the wall. Richard twisted the key in the lock. The trees whistled slightly in the breeze.

'That's strange,' he said. 'The lock seems to be jammed.'

He pushed at the key, and the door swung open of its own accord. A black emptiness yawned before them, smelling of the damp and the earth. *Was that the smell in my dream?* Matthew thought. He stopped at the portal and let the parson enter by himself. There was the sound of scraping and shuffling. Something wooden was being moved. Then Richard reappeared at the door.

'Even stranger,' he said. 'The old register seems to have gone.'

Back at the parsonage they went over it once again. The old register had always been kept in the crypt.

The parson had last seen it – he thought for a while – when they laid out John Trevanion. Would anyone else, the churchwardens, for instance, have borrowed it? No. Not without his permission.

Matthew stood staring angrily at the portrait which hung over the fireplace. The inference was obvious. He turned to face the parson.

'If my father was the third son, and not the second, that means there was another son, another Trevanion. What records would there be about him?'

'None. Not unless he died or got married, and even then it would have to be in this parish.'

'And did he?'

'I have no idea. What makes you so sure this is important?'

'The fact the register's missing. It must be missing for a reason.'

'Must it? What if the register was taken for some other reason altogether?'

'No. There has to be a link. Must be. So there are no other records?'

'None whatsoever. Just think: if your uncle was still alive, and if he hadn't got married, what evidence would there be of him?'

'What if he died, this other brother?'

'Very likely. Rose did after all.'

They had found Rose's stone with the others, next to her mother and father.

'Do you remember what that stone said?' asked Matthew suddenly. 'The one for her parents, my grandparents? "Leaving behind her two small children to lament her untimely death." Two small children. That would be John and Henry. If there was a third brother, he must have been already dead, along with Rose.'

The parson crossed to the window.

'God rest their souls,' he said.

Chapter Six

MATTHEW LEFT THE PARSONAGE BEFORE dawn and made his way eastwards over the fields. By the time the sun rose, he was standing on the crest of the last hill before the sea. In front of him, Mount's Bay spread out like a sheet of beaten steel, glinting with mist and sunlight.

He knew it was a risk going into Mousehole, but he had no choice. With the register gone, there was only one person who could help him. The lane veered steeply downhill to his left, and disappeared into the huddle of small grey and white cottages which staggered up the hill from the sea. Because there was so little wind, most of the boats had stayed in today, and the harbour was a mass of masts and yardarms, flashing in the sun. The village would be busier than usual, he thought. He pulled his scarf around his chin and tugged his hat as low as it would go. Luckily it was still early and people were too concerned with starting their day to give him much notice.

Matthew kept to the backstreet. He had only passed the first few houses when a passageway opened up on his left and ran down behind a row of cottage yards. It appeared to be empty, so he took it. The passage bent a little to left and right, then ended abruptly in someone's backyard.

Matthew quickly crossed the open space and vaulted the wall opposite.

As he had guessed, the throughway continued on the other side and then he found himself in a lane running down from a piece of scraggy wasteland where some pigs were nosing and rooting around. He turned down to the right. It wouldn't be much farther. A woman was out scrubbing her step, and he marched swiftly past her, ignoring her call of 'Good morning'. The village was getting busier. A squall of gulls flew up from the harbour, grey and majestic. Matthew turned left down a steep alley and tripped over a small boy carrying a loaf of bread. Hurriedly he helped the boy to his feet. He seemed to be unhurt, but gave Matthew an odd look. Perhaps he's seen my scars, or perhaps it's strange for me to help him up? Pressing the loaf back into the boy's hands, he made off quickly, his boots echoing on the rough stone cobbles. I must relax. He slowed his walk. Two old ladies, shrouded in black shawls, were sitting on their steps darning what looked like a large bedsheet. They glanced up at him and he tipped his hat in reply. Where was it? Matthew had never visited Rachel Tregenza, but he had given Mary Vincent a lift in the cart once, years ago.

Up a small flight of stairs to his left stood a little terrace of seven cottages. This was it. They seemed more dilapidated than those set on the street, as if they had been forgotten and left to themselves, but he could see they were all still occupied: straw had been stuffed into broken windows, and household implements, jugs, pans, baskets, nets, leaned against their walls or were spread across the little dirt path which ran in front. Their paint had faded to a grey which seemed identical with the colour of mildew or the colour of white sheets that have been soiled with sweat.

Matthew looked at the houses in turn. He was sure it was one of these, but which one he could not say. He went to the first door, and was about to knock when he checked himself. No, it couldn't have been the first one or he would have remembered. The face of a young girl appeared at the window of the next cottage. He smiled at her, and moved on.

He strode purposefully to the third door and knocked. A woman in her thirties opened the door. Her hair was greasy and tied back in a bun. She was clutching a child to her hip.

'I'm looking for Rachel Tregenza,' he said.

She gave him an odd look, which reminded him of the boy with the loaf: 'Two doors down.'

He thanked her but she had shut the door already.

The green paint on Rachel Tregenza's door had faded to a faint olive and had started to peel. He knocked and the wood answered dully. He suddenly realised he had no idea whether Rachel lived on her own or with relatives. Too late for that now. She was the only person left. He waited. There was no answer. He knocked again, this time louder, and again. Although he was not hot, sweat was running down his back. He listened. Was that something?

The door was pulled open. An old lady stood in the doorway. Matthew knew at once she must be Rachel Tregenza. She wore a dress of coarse black material which had been worn and patched many times. Over this she had wrapped a black lace shawl of surprisingly good quality – presumably a gift. She stared up at him, blinking in the daylight. Her eyes were white and cloudy with cataracts.

'Rachel?' he said gently. 'I've come to see you.'

She listened carefully, nodding to his words, then her face lit up with a smile. She had no teeth.

'I've been hoping you'd come.' With no further explanation, she stepped backwards and beckoned to him. Matthew stooped beneath the lintel and entered.

A low passage led to the kitchen and scullery at the back. On his left a narrow stairway climbed to the top floor. On his right a door opened on the living-room, and it was in here that Rachel showed him. The shutters were drawn and apart from a few chinks in the slats, the room was sunk in darkness.

'Are you alone?' he asked tentatively.

Rachel stared up at him, her white eyes blinking.

'Have been for twenty years. Now sit yourself down, won't you?'

Matthew sat gingerly on one of the two armchairs. A film of dust lay over the seats, the furniture, and was thicker still on the window. The walls were mottled with blooms of mould. A turf reeked in the hearth.

'It gets so cold now,' Rachel explained. 'I do need a fire going all the time. Will you fancy a dish of tea? You'll like a dish of tea, won't you?' she repeated, mainly to herself.

Matthew thanked her and she scurried off to the kitchen, leaving him on his own. Had he been here before? He tried to remember. Perhaps when he was young, with his mother. From the kitchen he could hear Rachel bustling with the kettle and crockery. It was a wonder she lived by herself. She seemed almost blind. Kneeling down he built up the fire for her. It was not long before she returned with a tray which she placed neatly on the table next to him.

'I haven't seen you for a long time,' she told him cheerfully.

'No. It must have been years ago.'

Rachel poured the tea, and passed him a cup. He took it, and she sat down in the chair opposite him. Putting his tea on the floor, Matthew leaned over and waved his hand in front of her face. She screwed up her eyes a little, but the fixed smile on her mouth did not change.

'So, how are you keeping?' she asked him. 'Mary's told me all about you.'

'She has? What's she been saying?'

'What a big fine lad you are now. You do look well!'

Rachel said this with such conviction that Matthew wondered if she could, after all, see him. She put the cup to her face and sucked in a mouthful of tea through her gums. He sat and listened to her drink.

'I always told your mother you'd never settle,' she continued. 'Always a wild one.'

Matthew leaned forward and touched the old woman's hand.

'Rachel? I need your help. Can you help me?'

Rachel's head bobbed up and down. 'Why yes, my dear. What can an old woman like me do for you?'

'You know things, Rachel. Things no one else can remember. About Trevanion.'

'Ah yes, Trevanion.' Rachel smiled. 'It's been a while. I'd like to see it one more time, you know, before I die.' She fell silent, and let her head rest on her chest. Matthew was about to shake her by the hand, when her head tipped up and she said:

'You know I left when your father was still alive. That must have been a time ago.'

'Can you still remember those times, Rachel?'

'What?' Rachel looked affronted. 'Like it was yesterday, I can! Nothing else for me to do. Though, to tell the truth, sometimes I'm not sure whether I'm seventy-seven or seventy-eight next year. Five years after the Great Fire, the one in London, that's when I was born, but Lizzie, she reckons I'll be seventy-nine.' Rachel Tregenza cast her eyes to the ceiling and began to mutter to herself.

'Well, everyone knows you're the oldest person left alive,' said Matthew hastily. Rachel did not answer. He sipped the tea. It tasted peaty and brackish. 'Everyone knows you're the oldest person left,' he repeated, louder. Rachel jumped in her seat, her eyes wide.

'What? Yes, the oldest. Where was I?'

'I need to know something,' he reminded her. 'Something that happened when you were a girl.'

Rachel Tregenza sucked at her tea and blinked expectantly.

'It was about my grandfather. I need to know how many children he had.'

'How many children?' Rachel grinned foolishly: 'Why, that's easy. Two. Leastways two if you count Elizabeth.'

343

'Elizabeth?' Matthew was confused. 'That can't be right.'

'Ah, no, you probably wouldn't know Elizabeth. She died just five days old. Poor little thing. Mother said she were a sickly child, but as pretty as a rose in bloom. Your grandmother was bitterly upset.'

Another girl, dead in five days. He looked at her.

'Are you sure, Rachel?'

'Of course I'm sure,' she snapped. 'I wouldn't forget something like that, would I? There was Robert, then Elizabeth. Then Elizabeth died, and your grandmother didn't have no more after that. Barren as Sarah she was after that.'

Robert? Robert Trevanion? Rachel didn't know him after all. Suddenly everything made sense. Matthew coughed apologetically.

'Yes, of course. Only two, including Elizabeth. Now what about my father, Robert? What about his children?'

Rachel looked panicked.

'But don't you know, John?'

'Yes,' he replied. 'But since my mother's been gone, I've no one else to talk to.'

'Of course.' The look of anxiety left her. 'She was a fine woman, your mother, sweet as an angel. I left Trevanion after she died. Your father sent me away,' she added reproachfully. 'I wanted to stay, and look after you.'

Matthew leaned towards her.

'What was he like, my father?' and as he asked, he suddenly realised he already knew, at least in part: the old man he had seen in the dream, the same face stared out of a portrait in the hall at Trevanion, and underneath it the inscription: Robert Trevanion.

Rachel's face puckered as if she had sucked something sour.

'He was a hard man, Master John, God rest his soul. After your mother passed over, he was even worse. Course, there was only you and Henry left.' Tears welled up in her eyes, and her blotchy white knuckles tightened over the arms of her chair. 'Only seems like yesterday we buried her. I suppose it won't be long before they put me under.'

'What about my brother?' Matthew asked after a while.

'What? Henry?' Rachel gave him the same wild-eyed look.

'No. The other one. My other brother.'

'Oh.' Rachel sank back into her chair. 'Him. I haven't talked about him for fifty years.'

She went quiet again. Matthew watched dust slowly spiral in a chink of light.

'Tell me now,' he said gently.

'No, I mustn't, my dear. I promised your mother.'

'But everything's changed now.'

'I promised her,' Rachel said stubbornly. 'She was a fine woman.'

'You must tell.' He got up and held her by the shoulders. 'He's come back.'

Rachel suddenly looked afraid.

'No, that's not possible. They said he'd never come back.'

'He is back, Rachel, and four people have died.'

Rachel ran her tongue over her gums.

'It all happened so long ago. Thought I'd go to the grave before I saw his face again.'

'No.' Matthew laid his hand on her knee. 'Don't go to the grave without telling, Rachel, not if you want to rest in peace.'

Rachel seemed to be making up her mind.

'Well, perhaps your mother was wrong not to tell you. After all, you were his brother. You had a right to know.'

Matthew sat back in his chair, and took another sip of his tea, and Rachel Tregenza began her tale.

'A good year we'd had of it when you and your brother were born. Must have been ninety-three or -four, and the harvest came early. A glorious hot summer, and King William five years on the throne, yes. I spent the summer looking after your mother, for she was sick with you and the orchard was a mass of bloom. We would sit out there and tell each other tales. She was the best mistress I ever had. Even your father was happy. We had two dozen calves that year and I remember he sold the timber from Trewidden woods to a hooper in Newlyn, and your mother was carrying the two of you, but, of course, we didn't know it was twins then.

'I was only a slip of a girl myself. Twenty-two or maybe twenty-three.' She paused, counting to herself. 'No, twenty-two. I was engaged to Christopher Tregenza. He was your father's ploughman. Big strong man. We were married that August, and you were born just after.'

Rachel felt for her cup and took a long sip.

'Your mother had a terrible labour. Of course, she'd been sick all year, so it was no surprise. Two and a half days it lasted. And I never left her side once. She was screaming and crying, and your father was shouting for us to do something. So in the end we sent for Figgie Tyzack, from Sennen way. She was the best charmer there was. I remember her arriving on Bobby's horse, course we didn't have carts in those days, your father all tight-lipped and white as a sheet.

'Figgie Tyzack knew what it was straightaway.

' "Twins," she told us. "And fighting to get out."

'All through that night, me and Figgie stayed with your mother, and all the time groaning and weeping, till just after cock-crow, your mother grew tired – awful tired – and Figgie said she could feel a baby's head. Sure enough, out you both came one after the other, like peas squeezed from a pod.

'Of course, Penny Keast used to say that when you were born, the baby which came second was clutching the heel of the first, but that's nothing but a pack of lies. She wasn't even there, but she spread the story around until your father put a stop to her.

'But, to be true, that's where the trouble began.' Rachel bent towards Matthew. 'I suppose it was my fault, but I was so worried about your mother I clean forgot anything else. She was bleeding terribly and you and your brother were covered in blood. We thought we'd lose her for sure. But Figgie managed to stop the blood and by midday, she could sit up and hold you both. That's when your father came to see her.

' "Which one's the oldest?" he asked. The first thing he said. And you know I'd been so concerned for your mother, I'd just wrapped you both in sheets and put you in the cot. I didn't know what to say, for there was nothing to choose between you. Your father was furious, and he'd have beaten me for sure only your mother begged him not to.

' "Well," he said at length. "Better make the best of a bad job," and he reached into the cot and pulled out one of the babes. "Yes," he said. "This one will do," and he made me fetch a piece of red wool and tied it round your ankle, and that was you, John, the eldest.'

The eldest.

'So what happened next?'

'The winter was terrible that year, and came in early, and your mother was terrible sick, right through till February. Rained for forty days and forty nights it did, just like in Noah's day. Rained and rained. Then the cattle got sick and out of all those calves, there were only four which lived to see the spring. Then if that wasn't bad enough, your father lost his boat in March.'

'Boat?'

'First trip of the year. Your father had a boat he'd send to Brittany and back. Lost every man on board except for Peter Trevose. He was ship's mate. Had a boy called George not long after, and two little girls. So anyway that was a disaster all round. Then in April, the rest of the cows got the rot. Terrible. Almost thirty went in less than a month. They burned them over in the Seven Acre Field.

'Your father was never the same after that, as if it had taken the best of his strength and broken it. Yet all the while, you and your brother were getting bigger and stronger. His only joy, he said. I remember how you enjoyed being up on my knee.' Rachel smiled sweetly.

'And what of my brother?'

'What? Tobias?' Her smile faded.

So that was his name. Tobias Trevanion.

'Identical twins, you were, no one could tell you apart, except me and your mother. Yet inside I've never known two babes so different. Why, he would cry and scream for pap all day and night. Your poor mother could hardly cope. A greedy spiteful little devil, he was! And we were worried for you, because he left nothing but the scrapings. So in the end your father sent for Molly Vincent to wetnurse him. And what a temper! He'd roar like Tregagle, why, he was only a year when your father gave him the strap. And after that he was even saucier! He'd chase the cats and clip their tails with his pocket-knife!'

'Was he always like that?'

'Right from the first. Wasn't long before people began to talk. A changeling, they called him, and so he was. Always roaring and raging.'

'So what was I like?'

'Now you weren't no angel, John, don't think you were. You'd chase the cats and all. I remember once you spilled the cream over the pantry floor. But you were a good boy at heart, and you loved your mam and your nanny. No. Tobias wasn't like you.

'And all the while you were growing, the farm was falling to rack and ruin. The cows stopped giving milk the next year. Spent all day eating, yet by the evening their udders were as dry as an old maid's paps.

'We had Figgie Tyzack over again. Tried everything. Even bled them, but all to no good. "The cattle's been overlooked," she told your father. "Cursed by the little ones." "Lies and nonsense!" your father shouted, and drove her off the land. But she was right. Whatever your father turned his hand to, went bad.

'Then your father would lock himself in his room for days and do nothing. Drinking, I suppose. If it wasn't for Mortimer – he was your father's steward – I think the farm would have failed already, not that he got any thanks for it. Maybe your father took Figgie Tyzack's words more to heart than we thought, who knows?

'I remember that summer they were slow bringing the wheat in. Mortimer was all for doing it straightaway, but we hadn't the men free, and your father wouldn't hire more, so they left the wheat standing. Then the rains came and it was flattened in the fields. That was cruel. And it wasn't just Mortimer he blamed. Your poor mother as well, rest her soul.'

Rachel licked her gums uncomfortably.

'I remember one afternoon he came in from the fields and caught us laughing. Why, he grabbed her by the hair until there were tears in her eyes. And when she pleaded with him, he swore and . . .' Rachel paused ' . . . called her a whore, he did, and a deceiver, a deceitful lying whore! And with that he just threw her down and stormed out. "Do not blame him, Rachel," she says to me afterwards. "But, mistress," said I, "how can he treat you like that? What about your father, what would he do if he knew?" But she just wept all the more. She told me she'd received a letter saying her father was mortal sick with the palsy. Of course my mistress wanted to see him, but Master Robert wouldn't let her. And seven days later there was a second letter saying he was dead.'

Rachel's eyelids fluttered. Then she wiped her mouth and said:

'Of course, the master was a changed man after her father passed away. A model husband. I remember catching them once in an . . . embrace which should be kept for the bedchamber.' Rachel's white eye winked. 'And instead of cursing me, he laughed. Laughed! "Myself and Master Trevanion have resolved our differences," she told me later, with the happiest smile. "With the inheritance of my father's estate, our problems are over."

'Shortly after this we found your mother was pregnant again and in the autumn she had a little girl called Rose. A real little cherub she was, wonderful blue eyes. You were four years old by then and your mother was thrilled with her. She'd always wanted a girl.

'Even Toby was smitten. Strange in one so wicked, but he was forever bringing her bunches of flowers, and singing to her, and chattering away like a sparrow. And you didn't care for her one way or the other. But you were as good as gold.'

Rachel's face took on a waxy grin. Matthew looked at the shutters and tried to guess what time it was beyond them, but found he could not. After a while Rachel stopped smiling and became quite solemn. She looked straight at Matthew and said:

'Of course, I didn't know what would happen, did I? No one could, but afterwards I blamed myself. It was shortly after Rose was born. You and your brother were helping me in the kitchen with the bread. I say you were helping, but of course you were playing really. You were cutting little figures and shapes out of the dough, or some such foolery. Then you, it was you, rolled the dough into balls and made two little dolls. They looked just the same.

' "This one's John and this one's Toby," you said, as if you thought it was very funny. Of course, Toby disagreed. "No," he said. "This one's Toby and this one's John." And the two of you fell to arguing and pushing until I lost my patience and gave you both a good bang on the head. It was silly really.

'Then you said, "But which one is Toby and which one is John?" all serious like. And without thinking I said: "I don't know. You both look the same to me, just like the day you were born." "Then how do you know who's the elder?" asked Toby. "Your father knew," I answered. I did that because if ever I said "Ask your father" everyone knew that was the end of it, but not Toby, he was as sharp as a razor.

' "But you said my father wasn't there when we were born," he said. "He came in directly afterwards," I replied, but it was no good. The little devil had guessed the truth. "Then I could be the elder and John the younger," he said. "I suppose so," I had to admit. "But you're not. John is the elder and you came next." But he wouldn't listen. "Why should John get everything?" he asked. "And I get nothing?"

'After that he was more wicked than ever, so your father had to beat him almost every day, and still he wouldn't behave. Always naughty, and fighting!

Your mother was worried sick: you were getting cuts and bites, hellish bite-marks, from the brat. So in the end we kept you separated. You'd stay with your mam, and Mortimer Tonkin would take Toby out on the rounds.'

'So what happened?'

'Well,' Rachel nodded gravely. 'Things couldn't go on. In spite of what your mother said, they didn't get no better. The farm was bleeding away. The men were leaving and going to the mines. And your father became awful queer. He'd stay in his study all day with his brandy and his dice. "I keep throwing bad, Rachel," I remember him saying. "I keep throwing bad." And whenever anything went wrong, he would curse the men. Mortimer should have left, but he was loyal, see?

'Then we discovered your father was seeing Figgie Tyzack. "The farm is cursed," she was telling him, "cursed by the devil," but she couldn't cure it for all that, and your father fretted all the more.

'One day during Advent, your mother tried to comfort him and he struck her so hard that she fell against the fireplace and broke her nose.'

Rachel shook her head.

'Your mother was sick till Christmas. But I think the real hurt wasn't in her face, but in her heart. She'd lie in bed with Rose and cry and wouldn't get up. He had deceived her, see, and that's what hurt most. That Christmas was wretched. Your father sat in his chair and scowled the whole day, and your poor mother by his side, her face as pale as a water-lily. All through January and February it seemed that a terrible storm-cloud hung over us.

'Then one day in spring it happened. I'll never forget. Your mother had left Rose in the orchard while she was in the kitchen. Rose loved the orchard. You could leave her there for hours, giggling and chirping away. But this morning when your mother came back, the cradle was empty.

'I didn't know what to do – at first none of us believed she was gone. Your mother was screaming and crying her name. And I was crying as well and hugging your mother. We called the men in from the fields, but they hadn't seen anything. Jackie Maddern reckoned the gypsies must've taken her and went riding off to catch them. Everyone else – even you, Master John – began to search the farm and your father was cursing and yelling and running round like a madman.'

Rachel paused for a moment as if she could still hear the sound of voices, and running feet, the panic on her mistress's face.

'It wasn't too long before they found her. Poor little thing. Wrapped in her swaddling clothes behind a bale of hay in the barn. As dead as dead can be.'

'How did she die?'

'We were never sure. Smothered, some said, or choked. Or maybe her little soul just up and left. I undressed the body myself and there were no marks on her, none at all. But she was dead all right. "Who could have done this?" your father was asking. I'd never seen him in such a rage. Your mother was crying and he just pushed her aside. "Who's done this to me?" he kept saying, and he began to look at the farmhands. "Was it you? Was it you?"

'Then someone remarked how your brother Toby

had also disappeared. In all the panic over Rose no one thought to check where Toby was. This was too much for your mother and she fainted right in front of me, and we had to carry her in. But the truth was even worse than that. They found Toby all right, alive and well. And do you know where? Up in the hayloft – above where they found poor Rose.'

'He killed her?'

'Well, we never rightly knew. He never said he did, and there was no proof. In fact he didn't speak at all when we found him. Just stared ahead with this queer look in his eye. I can still recall that look. And when he heard your mother had fainted, he gave a queer little grin.

'That was too much for your father. He called Toby a changeling, a child of the devil, and said he'd killed Rose. Then he grabbed him by the hair and he'd have shaken the life out of him if the men hadn't stopped him. But still Toby didn't say anything.

'We were in a terrible confusion. Then the next thing we know, your father locks your brother in the barn and calls for his horse. "Don't talk to him until I get back!" he says and rides off as if the devil were after him.

'He was gone maybe two hours. And when he returned, we saw he had someone with him. It was the Reverend Jago, from Madron.'

Rachel licked her gums.

'Now the Reverend Jago was a remarkable man. You don't get parsons like him nowadays. A man of great knowledge. Men said no sooner was a crime committed in Madron but the parson knew who'd done it. Jackie had seen him pick a thief out of a crowd, and the fellow had kneeled down and confessed on the spot. With spirits it was the same. There wasn't a ghost in Madron who didn't obey the parson's summons. People said that when he went riding, he didn't take a groom. He just struck the ground with his whip and a demon groom would spring up and serve him. Now, I never saw that myself,' Rachel conceded, 'but he didn't come with no groom that day neither.'

Matthew nodded his head. Even fifty years on the exploits of Reverend Jago were common lore.

' "My son's been possessed by the devil," said your father, just like that. "He's brought a judgement on us all."

' "I see," replied the Reverend Jago. "Bring him to me."

'I remember watching from the parlour, as they led Toby out, with his head held sort of stiff. Then the Reverend Jago kneeled down and took Toby's jaw and peered into his eyes.

'I learned from Jackie what happened next, because he was close enough to hear. Apparently the parson began to ask your brother about our Lord and the teachings of the church.

'Your brother wouldn't answer to start with, but the parson pressed him. Then suddenly Toby opened his mouth and let forth a torrent of abuse and blasphemy. Like a foul sewer of filth, said Jackie, such thoughts and wickedness. His sweet little face!

'It made a terrible impression on all who heard him. I remember Jackie years later saying he could recall every word of it, so foul it was, and everyone was asking themselves, where could he have learned such filthy lies?

'The Reverend Jago was shocked. He sprang away from the boy. "Some devil is at work here!" he said to your father, and a terrible dread came over us. And Toby stood there and began to laugh at them all, and curse them, and mock them. One of the women – Annie Tonkin, I think – ran out of the yard screaming and Mortimer had to go and comfort her.

'Of course,' Rachel explained, 'that was a long time ago, when the devil's works were everywhere. There were witches in every village then – Zennor had whole families of witches – and we went in mortal fear. As scripture says, the devil, as a roaring lion, walketh about, seeking whom he may devour. And there the devil had devoured little Toby right in our midst. The men wanted to take him to the courts immediately. Then he'd have burned for sure, I'd say. But the parson would have none of it. It was his work to save souls, he said, not condemn them, and no one dared argue, not even your father. But something had to be done, that was certain: the boy was a monster.

'So the Reverend Jago asked them to hold Toby quite still in the middle of the yard. At first no one would go near him, but in the end he persuaded Jackie and Billy, on the guarantee of their immortal souls, none the less. Then he began to speak words over the boy, and pray and such things, a beautiful voice, he had. This went on for maybe half an hour or more, but all the while Toby didn't say a thing, but just stared ahead, until the parson looks up and, "Yes," he says, "there is a spirit, who won't be banished hence," and we thought of the legion of devils our Lord had driven out in the land of the Gadarenes. "But," said the parson, "maybe I can chain him yet." And he paced round the yard in a most earnest manner, until he turns to your father and says: "Is there an old well, a disused well, hereabouts?" No, said your father. "Then what about pigeon-holes?" he says. "Or any place that's good and tight?" Your father looked puzzled, but he showed him the pigeon-holes all the same. "They'll do just fine!" said the parson, and he ordered mortar and bricks to be brought up.

'No one knew what to expect. Then, when all was ready, the Reverend cracked his whip over his head and called on the spirit to come out of the boy. Like a crack of thunder it was. Then, "Out! Out!" he shouts and drives the spirit into the pigeon-holes, snapping his whip and making an awful racket, so the spirit didn't have a chance. "Quick!" he cries. "Seal him in good and proper!" And they stopped up the holes with brick and mortar. Then the parson spoke prayers over the wall, and bade the spirit rest till Judgement Day.'

'You actually saw the spirit go into the pigeon-holes?' asked Matthew.

'No. But the parson saw him, and no mistake. "Keep those holes sealed," he said, "and that'll be the end of it." '

'Where were the pigeon-holes?'

'By the gate. You won't remember. Your father built a shed against that wall not long after.'

Matthew said nothing. He wondered whether the parson really thought he was driving the spirit into the holes. Or was he merely saving the boy from a lynching?

'So what happened to Tobias?'

'Well, now he was marked as a changeling, and a murderer too, some said. Your father swore he'd never let him under his roof again. You see, the estate had been cursed for so long. So the next day, your father takes him to Penzance where they're loading pilchards for the West Indies. Now your father had a cousin, in Jamaica, I think, who'd gone out years ago with the Fleet. So your father packed him off on a boat for Kingston with a letter for his cousin, and that was that. I suppose he thought it was the best he could do. And so did we all. I mean, what if the little devil got hold of you, John? He couldn't be trusted, see?

' "Never let him return," wrote your father, "for he is no longer my son." Whether your father sent money with him, I don't know, but he never came back. Of course, your mam was bitterly upset. To lose a daughter, and then her son!

'She swore me to secrecy, but in fact no one would talk about it anyway, not even among ourselves. We were all too afraid, or ashamed.

'I think they said Rose died of the spring ague, which was awful bad that year. What they said about Toby is anyone's guess. But maybe Figgie Tyzack was right. For once Toby was gone, things got better almost straightaway! That summer was one of the best we had. The crops came in and the cattle were as fat as Pharaoh's. And your father sold off your mother's land. I remember Mortimer said he was a fool and was betraying your mother's family, and things like that, for the Hamblyns had a lot of land in Gwennap, and she was too upset to care. But sell it he did, and as I said, things got better for a time, not that it made them any happier. Two years later your mother had little Harry, and in three years she was dead.'

Rachel Tregenza fell silent. Matthew found himself back in the grey-lit room with its musty furniture and dingy walls. And now, out of this tale, Tobias Trevanion had returned, like an unlaid ghost to claim what, but for a young maid's carelessness, might have been his.

'I always knew you'd visit,' Rachel said suddenly. 'Mary said you'd forgotten me, but I said no, not Master Johnnie.' She beamed at him. 'Was my story any help?'

'Yes,' he said. 'I'll have to go now, Rachel.'

'So soon?' she looked hurt. 'I'd hoped you'd stay for dinner. I can make a pie. Just like you always had!'

'No,' he said, gently but firmly. 'I have things to do.'

'Busy on the farm, I suppose,' she said. 'That's my Johnnie!' She paused abruptly, as if trying to hear a voice coming from a long way off. 'Didn't Mary say you'd been ill? Something about a funeral?'

'No. Don't worry, Rachel. Look, here I am.' Matthew kissed her on the forehead. She smiled and looked relieved.

'Good,' she said, 'I couldn't bear to think of anything happening to you.'

It was some minutes before Matthew left. The next

morning when her daughter came to bring her food as usual, she found Rachel Tregenza still sitting on her chair in the front room. It had been some while since she had stopped breathing.

Matthew made his way up the valley to the north of the village. If Rachel was right, it explained everything. Except one thing.

Beyond the hill a huge church tower soared over a cluster of cottages. This was the village of Paul.

It took several minutes before he found the grave. At the head of the mound stood a sheet of slate, freshly carved, which read:

> Here lies Marcy Poldeen
> Beloved sister, wife, and friend
> Born January 4th 1720
> Died November 24th 1748
> May the Lord have mercy on her soul

Matthew read the inscription several times. What was interesting was not what it said, but that someone had paid to have a stone erected. Marcy was supposed to have been penniless and desperate. He saw a man with a bucket and shovel eyeing him suspiciously from across the graveyard. Matthew walked over.

'Are you the sexton?'

The man nodded and answered in Cornish. Matthew understood him well enough. 'I'm looking for the stonemason,' he asked, 'who made the gravestone over there.'

The sexton scratched at his face. His cheeks were

a mass of poxmarks, red and ugly. Then he stabbed a finger towards the row of cottages below the churchyard.

Now he listened, Matthew could hear the ring and tap of a chisel on stone. The mason was busy at an elaborate engraving when Matthew disturbed him.

'The stone for Marcy Poldeen – was it you who made it?'

'It was.' The mason laid down his hammer. 'Only finished a month ago.'

A month.

The man squinted up at him. 'Why are you asking?'

'She was a friend of mine.' The mason said nothing, so he continued: 'We were due to marry.'

This seemed to mean something, for the mason's features took on a respectful air.

'They say she was with child when they found her,' he said.

'Yes,' said Matthew. 'Could you tell me who paid for her stone?'

'You don't know?'

'I've been away,' Matthew explained. 'In Jamaica.'

The man nodded.

Then he told him.

PART SEVEN

Chapter One

MATTHEW WENT ROUND THE SIDE of the parsonage – he was not sure whether Mrs Dunstan had left yet – and peered through the window. The kitchen was quiet: the fire in the grate had been bedded down and the pans hung from their hooks. Richard must have dined early. He put his nose to the glass. A whiff of fish and vegetables twisted his stomach into a knot: he had eaten nothing all day. For a moment, he gave way to his feelings of weariness. All he wanted now was an end to this. And when all was done, a homecoming.

And it would be soon, very soon.

He tapped on the windowpane. A few seconds later Richard came through. He seemed tense. As soon as he saw Matthew, he visibly relaxed.

'I was hoping it was you. How did it go?'

'I have found the enemy.' Matthew rubbed his hands together. 'I'm starving, Richard!'

'I'll get you something in a minute. Tell me all about it,' Richard said heartily.

'No. First, how is my mother?'

'A little better, but only a little.'

Richard was pleased to see him, and clutching his arm led Matthew through to the parlour. A log fire crackled in the hearth and the scent of burned pine mingled with the heavier aroma of tobacco.

'Mrs Dunstan left early tonight?'

'I gave her the afternoon off. Take a seat. Here.' Richard gestured to an armchair facing the fire, its back to the door. 'So you've found something?'

'Yes. The register – it was in there all—'

'Don't get up, Trevanion. We've been expecting you.'

Matthew recognised the voice immediately. Richard was looking past him, towards the doorway. He seemed nervous, but not at all surprised. Of course – the pipe-smoke – he should have known.

Michael Carter struck a lucifer and coaxed his pipe back into life.

'It's funny. You thought I was dead, and I thought you'd gone to France.'

Matthew could see he was not alone. Behind him Nathaniel Morgan had descended the stairs and now stood in the doorway in an heroic posture. Matthew ignored them both.

'I'd have thought a kiss would be more appropriate, Richard.'

'You betrayed *me*, Matthew,' the parson replied somewhat stiffly. 'Last night Nathaniel called to see Lucy, as he said. When he called again this morning and she was still out, he became suspicious, until eventually Mary told him the truth, as she thought. It seems she left a note saying she'd gone with you to France. Lies, Matthew, lies!'

'Richard, I can explain—'

'Save it for the jury!' interrupted Carter. 'I'm sure they'll be fascinated.'

Matthew went to get up. Before he was out of the seat Carter had a pistol trained on him. For a large man he was surprisingly quick.

'Another move and I won't bother bringing you back to Penzance.' Carter sounded like a coachman talking to an unruly passenger.

'Gentlemen, there'll be no violence in this house!' Richard lay a restraining hand on Matthew's shoulder. 'If you're innocent, it may be for the best,' he added, though without conviction.

Then Nathaniel Morgan walked up and punched him in the stomach as hard as he could.

He spent the night in Penzance gaol. When he awoke he asked the warder whether they would move him that day. The warder shrugged and threw a piece of bread on to the floor. The flagstones had not been cleaned since Matthew's last visit, so he left the bread where it was. He had been expecting Sir Anthony to visit, but by midday no one had come.

It was just as well. He could afford to be patient. He recalled the frustration on Nathaniel's face. Morgan had so wanted him to make a last desperate bid for freedom. He ran his fingers over his cheek. The scar had re-opened, but it had been worth it.

The warder brought a thin dirty soup for his meal and another chunk of bread. Matthew caught it before it landed.

The warder grinned at him unkindly. 'They found the lady,' he said on the way out and scratched himself under the arm. 'Turned up at the parson's house early this morning.'

It seemed she had been blindfolded and left at the edge of the village. Lucy claimed she had no idea where she had been held. Matthew was the only person she could identify.

He smiled spitefully to himself. Presumably George had agreed things with her. And with Matthew arrested, why shouldn't he? He sat on the bench in his cell and broke his bread into small pieces. The soup reminded him of laundry slops.

The afternoon passed slowly. Even the street outside seemed quieter and more subdued than usual. Eventually he judged by the dirty grey of the clouds that it must be approaching four o'clock. He stirred himself and banged on the door until the warder jammed his face up against the grille.

'Stop that or I'll fetch you a thrashing!' His words were accompanied by a fine mist of spittle and Matthew was glad he had stood well back.

'Send for Sir Anthony Bevis,' he told him. 'I wish to make a confession.'

Chapter Two

'You HAVE THE DEVIL'S LUCK, it seems, Trevanion.' Sir Anthony greeted him angrily from the doorway. Night was falling, and the cell was dark and murky. Matthew looked up from the bench.

'I didn't ask you here to pay me compliments. Time is vital.' Matthew leaped to his feet as if suddenly galvanised by his own words. 'Do you have a clerk, papers, ready?'

'That can be arranged.'

'Sir, I would not have asked for you, were it not a matter of some urgency! Someone's life depends on it.'

'Whose life is that?' The magistrate sounded disinterested, sceptical.

'Lucy Trevanion.'

Sir Anthony coughed in outright disbelief.

'Good God, man! From my own understanding, you are the very root of the evils that have befallen the poor lady! How could you possibly help her, except by confessing your sins speedily and have done with it?'

'Sins? Crimes or sins? There is a difference.' Matthew gazed at him intently. 'Sir, I accept my lot, that is all. What if I were to tell you there was another man, still loose, who this night will kill her?'

'I'd say I didn't believe you,' Sir Anthony replied, but there was something in Matthew's voice that made him hesitate. Matthew stepped forward, his face animated by a strangely compelling and nervous excitement.

'Think of it. She herself said I had accomplices. They will kill her, I promise you!'

'Do you expect a pardon for this? Is that it?' Sir Anthony was delighted he had found his enemy's motivation.

Matthew stopped and stared at the ground.

'No. If I am condemned, I am condemned. But I don't want Lucy's death on my conscience.' His words came in a rush. 'I have dreams.'

Sir Anthony weighed up the situation for a moment. Then he too felt his blood quicken. He clicked his tongue.

'Very well. I shall indulge you.'

'Thank you. Please, there isn't much time ... Could you send for Mr Tonkin?'

'What? Pascoe's old clerk?' Sir Anthony stared at him in amazement. 'Great God! You murdered the man's employer!'

'Pascoe was the Trevanion solicitor – so is Tonkin. If I'm going to make a confession, I want it done properly. Besides, I didn't kill Pascoe!'

Sir Anthony pursed his lips as if he were chewing on a lime.

'We can at least ask him,' Matthew suggested. 'If he refuses, I'll do without.'

'Hmmm. And you claim Miss Trevanion is in danger tonight?'

'Yes!' He paused. 'I'd wager my life on it.'

Sir Anthony banged on the door for the warder.

'Rickard, send for Mr Tonkin, of Pascoe's. Tell him

it's urgent. I'll be in The Four Kings until you get back.' He turned to Matthew. 'This had better be worth it, Trevanion!'

Matthew managed a smile.

'It will be, Sir Anthony. I promise.'

Edward Tonkin came quickly, as Matthew was sure he would.

The clerk had not changed since they last met, except that now he wore a suit which was no longer faded and patched at the elbows. He regarded Matthew with a strange mixture of fascination and distaste. They shook hands.

'I gather you require my pr . . . professional assistance?' Tonkin was evidently nervous.

'Yes.' Matthew sat down carefully. 'I wish to make a full statement of the crimes that have been committed. Would you draw it up for me?'

'What sort of statement?'

'As I said, full and complete. Ah, Sir Anthony!' The JP appeared scowling in the doorway. 'I was just explaining things to Mr Tonkin.'

Edward Tonkin smiled ingratiatingly and awkwardly.

'Sir Anthony! A pleasure to see you here.'

'Hardly,' the JP remarked brusquely. 'Can we get started, do you think? Miss Trevanion's life might be in danger.' He stressed the word 'might'. 'Well, Mr Tonkin?'

Tonkin hesitated, then wrinkled his face. 'B . . . Begging your pardon, Sir, but I will need some light, and a d. . . . desk of some sorts if I am to pr . . . proceed.'

'Good God, man, pull yourself together!' Sir Anthony grumbled to himself, then called to the warder. But Rickard had no means of light available.

'This is no good!' said Matthew impatiently. 'We're wasting time.'

'Then why the hell didn't you call me sooner!' snapped the JP. 'Rickard! Go and fetch Carter. Tell him to bring this man to my house, now! He can make his confession there.'

Edward Tonkin smiled weakly and went to press Sir Anthony's hand, but the Justice of the Peace was already marching out of the cell.

So far, so good, thought Matthew. Because he wasn't lying, at least not entirely.

Lucy would die tonight.

Chapter Three

As Lucy walked into the courtyard, she surveyed the tumble-down barns and manorhouse from a fresh perspective.

It was strange she would never see Matthew again. Nor Emily, nor John, nor Pascoe. She felt neither bitterness, nor passion, only numbness. It was better that way. That way she did not have to examine her thoughts too closely.

Just then Mary Vincent ran down the steps and wrapped her in her arms.

'Lucy! Lucy! Am I glad to see you.' Her face shone with happiness.

'Yes.' She smiled awkwardly, and kissed Mary on the forehead. 'Reverend Morecombe brought me back.'

'My lord, Lucy, I thought you were dead, or gone over the Channel, or I don't know what. Josey! Luke! Beckie! She's back!'

Before she knew it, Lucy found herself hugged and kissed by Rebecca, and her hand shaken by Josey and Luke. Then Mary sat her down in the kitchen, brewed her a cup of the best tea, and made her tell her story again and again until in the end Lucy believed it herself

'Do you know what will happen to him?' asked Mary suddenly.

'I don't know.' Lucy carefully smoothed down the pleats of her skirt. 'He'll probably hang, I suppose.'

At this the room fell quiet.

'Strange,' said Josey after a while. Then: 'I must be getting back to work. Good to see you safe and sound, Miss Lucy.'

He laid an embarrassed hand on her shoulder, then was gone, with Luke and Joey, and Lucy was left with the women. Will the ghost of Matthew Trevanion always haunt us? she wondered, and resented him all the more.

She looked at Mary. 'We've got work to do.'

When evening fell, Lucy stared out at the sun splashed red across the sky and let herself relax for the first time. It was hers now. Hers alone. She smiled, and if her smile was tinged with sadness, it did not show.

The sound of a horse in the court below surprised her. Looking down she could distinguish a man alighting, clad in a large black cloak. So, she would not dine alone tonight, after all. It was Nathaniel Morgan.

Beyond the manor, beyond the fields and the ditches and the farmsteads, rose the raw, naked hills of Penwith. And up among these wastelands, where the dark of evening massed in the dips and runnels of the earth, something darker than the surrounding hills began to stir and a cold wind bowled down over the shallow pasturelands to the sea.

Chapter Four

A T THIS SAME TIME, FIVE or so miles to the east, Matthew was entering Sir Anthony's dining-room. With him were Tonkin, Carter and Sir Anthony himself. Carter had insisted on the strictest security and two further guards waited in the hall. The dining-room was a blaze of light. In the corner, the grandfather clock rang six o'clock and Sir Anthony clapped his hands together impatiently.

'Well, Trevanion, you've got what you wanted – at considerable inconvenience to us all, I might add.'

'I only hope we're not too late,' Matthew replied simply. 'Let me make my statement and you'll have your man.'

'But can't you tell us his name now?'

'No. I've done that before and no one believed me. This time I'm going to prove his guilt beyond any doubt.' Matthew leaned his hands on the table. 'Now if you can leave, I'll start straightaway.'

'Leave?' Sir Anthony stared at him. 'Impossible! Preposterous! What do you think, Carter?'

'I need to consult my solicitor,' Matthew insisted. 'In private.'

Tonkin glanced nervously at his host.

'Sir, my client has a p . . . point.'

'I don't give a damn what point he's got!'

'This man here shouldn't be left alone with

anyone,' interrupted Carter. 'I wouldn't trust him farther than I could spit.'

'Well?' asked Sir Anthony. 'Can we proceed?'

Matthew remained silent. The others looked at him expectantly.

Abruptly he stood up.

'Take me back to the cell.'

'What on earth?'

'Will you at least let me talk to my solicitor in my cell?' he asked.

'Sir . . .' began Tonkin.

Sir Anthony gave a gasp of exasperation.

'Carter, surely if we lock the doors and keep guards in the hall he can't go anywhere?'

Carter looked ill contented.

'Carter?' snapped Sir Anthony.

'I suppose so, Sir Anthony.'

'It would certainly be far more preferable,' added Tonkin quickly.

The clock chimed the quarter hour.

Once they were alone, they sat in silence while Tonkin shuffled papers and arranged them in orderly piles. He glanced at Matthew but avoided his gaze.

'So,' said Matthew impatiently. 'You are ready?'

Tonkin wet his lips and nodded.

'Good.' Matthew rubbed his hands together.

'I want to give a complete statement of the events surrounding the deaths of my aunt and Mr Pascoe, and also my uncle, John Trevanion.' At this Tonkin raised his eyebrows. 'But this is not a confession of my guilt,' Matthew went on quickly. 'No. The guilty person is someone else. I want to make this statement

now before his next move. He will kill again, or
perhaps he will claim to be the rightful heir. But if I
wait till then, no one will believe me.'

Tonkin coughed politely. 'I'm afraid I do not
understand.'

'That's because you don't understand the killer,
Mr Tonkin.' Matthew paused until he was sure he
had the solicitor's attention: 'John Trevanion had
another brother, Tobias.'

Edward Tonkin blinked at him.

'No one knows about him but me, and I only
found out by chance.'

'And you say he's responsible for these murders?'
asked the solicitor. 'Why on earth?'

'Revenge.'

'Ahh,' Tonkin paused. 'The purest and noblest
motive of them all.'

With that Matthew gave him a brief account of
recent events. However, he took care to avoid all
mention of Rachel Tregenza.

'This is certainly most ... remarkable,' Tonkin
observed as he finished. He stared at the blank sheets
of paper in front of him. 'But what actual proof do
you have? I'd have thought there was nobody left
who could remember.'

'There isn't, not now. But about six months ago,
my uncle told me he had a lost brother, and out of
curiosity I went to the church and looked in the
register, and there it was.'

'And this record is still there?'

'No. It disappeared, but I have a copy I can
produce.'

Tonkin looked impressed.

'Do you think this confession will save you?'

'It might save Lucy.' Matthew smiled. 'It will be my revenge on Tobias.'

'Quite, quite.' The solicitor swallowed nervously.

Matthew flexed his wrists so his handcuffs rattled. 'What is it, man? We haven't got much time!'

'Sir.' Tonkin blinked nervously. 'I cannot advise you to do this.'

'Lucy's life is at risk!'

'But can't you see!' Tonkin's words came in a rush. 'This whole tale is, well . . . poppycock, a fabrication! A long-lost brother returns from the Americas – to wreak vengeance on people he's never even met. Ludicrous, sir! Ludicrous! No jury could take you seriously.'

Matthew answered slowly and deliberately.

'It may well hang me, Mr Tonkin, but that is the truth. Pick up your pen.'

Tonkin struggled to keep his voice to a whisper.

'Sir, you cannot,' he hissed. 'I will be a laughing-stock.'

'I have no choice.'

'No! You have a choice.' Tonkin seemed quite frenzied. 'You can escape! Go to France, the Americas – why not go to the West Indies yourself?'

Matthew paused for a moment.

'I gave that up a long time ago. Come on, this is idle speculation.'

Tonkin dipped his quill in the ink jar. Suddenly he dropped it on the table. A thin trickle of ink ran across the wood.

'There is something I must tell you!' he blurted out.

'What, now?'

'Your uncle's will.'

Matthew spoke carefully. 'He never made one.'

'No! He did!'

Matthew tried to look surprised.

'And you were the main beneficiary,' Tonkin continued. 'Pascoe suppressed it, pretended your uncle changed his mind.'

'But why would he do that?'

'I can guess.' Tonkin looked guilty. 'Do you remember Lady Trevaillance? When she died, she left ten thousand pounds, to her two grandnieces, and she asked Pascoe to be the trustee. Just over a year ago, Pascoe was offered the chance of investing in a venture being floated on the Exchange. It was speculative, as ventures are, but almost guaranteed success – it was about to win a contract for the Far East, we were told. To cut the story short, Pascoe laid out a considerable amount of his own money, and when he was offered more, he used Lady Trevaillance's bequest to boot. After all, he had her best interests at heart. I also pledged what savings I had,' he added stiffly.

'Is there a point to this?' interjected Matthew. It was almost half past the hour.

'Can't you see?' asked Tonkin, his lips white. 'The whole enterprise was nothing but a ruse! At first we suspected nothing, but when our letters went unanswered, Pascoe sent an agent to the City. It transpired that this contract was quite illusory. It had, in fact, been awarded to a rival enterprise, and the directors of our company had squandered the capital in their attempts to curry favour – or, as I suspect, had embezzled it from the first. Pascoe was ruined. Almost eight thousand pounds in debt!'

'So you made a bad investment. What's that to me?'

'But don't you see? If we hadn't suppressed your uncle's will perhaps none of this would have happened? I knew we were wrong, but Pascoe insisted.' Tonkin's face was taut, like a mask. 'I couldn't let you go to the gallows without telling you. That's why I came. It's been on my mind since Pascoe died.' He reached into his jacket pocket. 'Perhaps you could escape after all.' He placed the dull metal object carefully on the table. It was a pistol.

Matthew stared at it in disbelief.

'You're suggesting I take it?'

'Quickly, before we are disturbed!' Tonkin's eyes flickered towards the door.

Matthew picked up the gun. It was a small, neat affair, with a cherrywood stock.

He smiled.

'Very well, Mr Tonkin. If you insist.'

Five minutes later, Carter was surprised to hear a knock on the dining-room door. He had expected them to be busy for at least another hour. He opened the door and was even more surprised.

Matthew had his left arm tight round Edward Tonkin's neck, so tight that the solicitor was almost hoisted off the ground. In his right hand, Matthew held a small, intricately patterned pistol. Its barrel was jammed hard into the solicitor's mouth. Behind his glasses, Edward Tonkin's eyes bulged horribly.

His face was a livid grey, and from his throat came a dreadful whimpering noise.

'Back!' Matthew told him. 'Back! And your boys. All of you!'

'Don't be stupid, Trevanion.'

'Get back, now!' Matthew repeated. He spoke calmly but his eyes were dancing and feverish.

Slowly Carter and the two guards stepped backwards.

'Go on, back! Keep your hands in front.' Matthew edged Tonkin forward, forcing the gun farther into his mouth until the man squealed in agony. He could not afford to make a mistake.

'Come on, Trevanion.'

'Shut it, Carter!' The bailiffs had backed against the far wall, but he could see they were looking for a chance to come at him. 'Stay where you are!' he ordered. 'Now, sit.' They did not move. 'Sit! On the floor, now!' His voice was shrill in his ears. Their eyes met and he squeezed Tonkin's neck even tighter. The bailiffs sat down.

Good. Edward was beginning to gag on the barrel. Matthew let him for a moment to prove his point, then slackened his grip, but only slightly, and half lifted, half dragged him backwards over the fifteen foot of floor which separated them from the front door.

'Right. Now, I want you all to stay very still. He won't get hurt.'

'You won't make it,' said Carter. Matthew ignored him.

'Tonkin,' he hissed. 'Open the door.'

The solicitor was so panicked that his fingers slid

helplessly over the brass handle. Matthew swore. He kept his eyes riveted on the bailiffs. How much longer could he keep this going?

'Come on!'

Tonkin's hand grasped the handle and turned.

'It's locked,' he said.

'The key! Where's the key?' Matthew demanded.

'You won't make it,' repeated Carter. 'None of us have the key, do we, boys?'

Matthew thought desperately. There was no way back. He wondered whether he could break down the door before Carter and his men reached him. Don't be stupid, he told himself. The key must be somewhere. His eyes fell on a pretty walnut desk next to the door. When he left with the Reverend Morecombe the time before, the drawer had been open. Sir Anthony had let them out himself. He inched his way over, and told Tonkin what to do. The man was sweating like a pig. Sure enough, there in the middle drawer was a large brass key with a red and gold sash. A few seconds later, and Matthew felt the front door ease open.

The three bailiffs watched him sullenly.

'Because of Tonkin here, I'll be going slowly,' he told them. 'If you follow, I'll have to take my chances, and he dies. Understand?'

Carter made no reply. Matthew reckoned he'd have a minute at best. Where did Tonkin say he'd left his horse? Matthew jabbed the pistol up against the solicitor's palate. Letting go with his left arm, he reached down and quickly locked the door from the outside. That should give him a chance. He pulled the gun out of Tonkin's mouth. The man stood there gasping. In the heat of the moment, the barrel had cut his top lip, and he began to mop the blood.

'No time for that!' whispered Matthew. 'Run!'

Tonkin had to be shaken as if half-asleep and the two of them ran down the street. They separated at the first corner. Carter would be forcing the door by now. Matthew left Tonkin looking bemused and ran on, his feet slapping on the wet cobbles. He skidded round the next corner and collided with a woman lugging a huge basket of pilchards on her back. He sent her sprawling and cursing after him, her precious fish slithering and flashing over the cobbles. He took the next alley, then across a wider space, through a gang of workmen wandering back from a drinking house. He clutched at the chains hanging from his wrists, but the men were tired and merry and he was past them before they had noticed. He was light-headed and went slipping and stumbling into the next street. Carter would be out by now. Now he cut up to his right. There was The King's Head, and, outside, four horses were tethered. Which one was Tonkin's? Snatching the reins, he flung himself on to the first horse in the line.

'Oi!' A man standing opposite, talking to two passers-by, let out a great roar. 'What are you doing?'

Glancing across, Matthew kicked savagely at the horse's flanks. The man was running towards him.

'Come here!'

The horse stumbled into a walk. Matthew shook the reins and yelled at the horse. As the man came close, Matthew raised his boot. He had a fleeting vision of the man's sideburns, his angry mouth, and his coarse, pocked face, then he sent him sprawling sideways. The man's acquaintances were also running, but now the horse broke into an irregular canter, its hooves ringing on the empty streets. Matthew heard them call once, twice, for him to stop, then he was gone, up through the street, then into the next, keeping always to the left, away from Sir Anthony's residence, until he hit the road to Newlyn. He rounded a large cart, laden with barrels, its driver cursing crudely in Cornish, then along the lane until it fell into a dip. Matthew slowed the horse, and steered it over a ditch into a steeply climbing paddock. Up through this, until he came to a gate, then up again, moving westwards and northwards by turns, until he had gone at least a mile. He turned and looked back.

The country fell away into a roll of small hills, then down to Penzance, Newlyn, and the sea. In the thick, murky night, he could make out the occasional dark smudge of trees, and the charcoal lines of hedges, but nothing else. A strong wind was already blowing from the north, cold and blustery. He strained his ears. He could hear nothing but the wind and the breathing of his horse.

Matthew reached into his pocket and pulled out Tonkin's pistol. Then his finger closed on the trigger and squeezed. Just as he had thought.

When he loaded the pistol, Tonkin had not used any gunpowder.

Chapter Five

'I DON'T BELIEVE IT!' LUCY glared angrily at the two bailiffs.

'I'm sorry, ma'am,' said Carter woodenly. 'It was Sir Anthony himself who sanctioned it. None of us thought he had a gun.'

'Incompetence! Blind incompetence!' Nathaniel Morgan shoved back his chair. 'This fellow Tonkin – what happened to him?'

'Penmarris found him in Cripplestreet, clubbed over the head. Trevanion could be anywhere by now.'

'So what are you doing to recapture him? This man is dangerous!'

'I've sent word to the customs officers to keep an eye on the ports—'

'If they did that there wouldn't be a cup of tea in Mousehole!'

'It's the best we can do, sir,' explained Carter, with an effort to remain polite. 'Tomorrow at first light, we'll alert the boroughs up the county. He won't get far.'

Nathaniel Morgan drained his glass and looked sceptical. Lucy laid a reassuring hand on his arm.

'What I don't understand,' she said, 'is why he was let out in the first place.'

'He insisted your life was in danger.'

'Danger?' Lucy glanced at Nathaniel. 'Did he say what sort?'

Carter shook his head dismissively: 'If you ask me, it was a ruse from the start. But Sir Anthony thought there might be something in it, which is why we're here.'

'Presumably Sir Anthony didn't know I'd be with Miss Trevanion tonight,' said Morgan.

'Even so, I'm most grateful,' Lucy told him quickly. 'I won't feel safe until he's caught. Please, make yourselves at home. There's meat in the kitchen and we can find you something to drink. Tomorrow I'll decide what I'm going to do.'

Nathaniel nodded sullenly and reached for the bottle of claret. He had hoped to have Lucy alone tonight. Their conversation had shown signs of promise. But he could be patient.

'Gentlemen,' he announced, with mock seriousness. 'Let us drink to the health of the mistress of Trevanion. And her immortal beauty.'

'The mistress of Trevanion!'

Lucy blushed, but not unhappily.

Nathaniel put his lips to his glass. It would be a long night yet.

Outside, Matthew waited. After the bailiffs arrived, he made a circuit of the house, then took up his position in the hay barn – the same barn where the body of Rose Trevanion was found all those years ago. The yard, the outbuildings, the manorhouse – everything looked the same as it always had, and Matthew was seized with a moment's doubt: what if he was wrong? What if he didn't come? Yet in his heart he knew that Tobias Trevanion, if he existed at all, would come that night. But it would be late, when the moon was past its zenith, and the people inside were asleep or their senses dulled. He wrapped his coat around him and rested his head against a bale of hay. There was a dry scratching behind him. Barn rats. Somewhere an owl hooted. Light glimmered through chinks in the shutters, and he could just make out the indistinct sound of voices. He felt vaguely envious. At least it was warm here. He let his mind relax, and was aware of a familiar numbness stealing over his limbs. Across the yard a breeze began to blow in little gusts. His eyelids blinked, slowly and reluctantly, so that when he opened them he could not tell whether a few seconds or a few minutes had passed. Angrily he chewed his lip and pinched the tips of his fingers. Was he out there, he wondered, really out there? The owl called again. A cloud blew in front of the moon and the grey silvery light yawed and disappeared, pitching the yard into blackness.

He opened his eyes. The yard was awash with the frosty glow of the moon. He stared at the scene for perhaps half a minute, before he realised he had been asleep. How long? He shook his head dumbly, and stared at the manorhouse again, straining his eyes in an effort to see the invisible. Why had he woken? Had anything happened? The yard and the buildings gave no answer.

Lucy heard it first. From her bed it came as no more than the soft noise a pine branch makes when it is bent beyond breaking-point. She lay in the darkness, not moving, scarcely breathing. The house was silent, save for the scratchings of a mouse beneath the floor and the creak of roof-timbers. The wind must have got up. She was beginning to think she had heard nothing.

There it was again. From somewhere downstairs, she was sure of it. Perhaps it was Carter or Penmarris, looking for a drink of water. At two o'clock they had checked the doors and shutters and turned in for the night, the bailiffs on the floor of the dining-room, Nathaniel in the room next to hers. Yet there was something about the noise, its very gentleness, that disturbed her.

Wrapping a thin dressing-gown around her, Lucy got up and tiptoed to the bedroom door. Carefully taking its weight, she eased it ajar. A cool draught of air brushed against her face. Downstairs the clock was ticking. Then the noise again, this time the definite noise of wood scraping against stone.

Last time Matthew had broken in he had not made a sound. She paused for only a second before shouting down the stairwell.

'Carter! Penmarris! Get up! He's here. Matthew's here! Get up! Carter!'

Her words seemed to die as soon as they left her mouth. There was no answer, not even an echo from the walls. A sudden panic gripped her. What if she were the only one awake? He could be with her before anyone even stirred. She flung Nathaniel's door open. In the darkness she could dimly make out his face blinking up at her from his pillow. He had obviously been asleep.

'What is it, my dear?'

'Quick! Get up!' she hissed. 'I think Matthew's trying to break in.'

Nathaniel's eyes bulged open. He was out of bed and buckling his sword over his nightshirt before he said:

'Get under my bed. He won't find you there.'

She looked at him apprehensively.

'Where are you going?'

'Are the others awake?'

'I shouted but they didn't reply.'

Pushing her back into the room, Nathaniel edged his way on to the landing. He held his pistol out in front as if it were a lantern. He could see nothing. There was a crash of wrenching timbers from somewhere below.

'Carter! Penmarris!' he yelled. Then there was the sound of a door – what else could it be – being battered or knocked into. A gun went off. Then another. The report was dull, muffled. Then someone was screaming. A high, hideous scream. Nathaniel stood rooted to the spot. The cold night draught wound up the stairs and clutched at his thighs.

'Nathaniel! What is it?' Lucy called out from behind.

'Shut up! I don't know!' What should he do now? The house was silent again except for the sound of a man sobbing in pain. Someone swore. He thought it was Carter but he couldn't be sure.

'Who's there?' he called out. Nothing. The wind howled on the roof outside. A timber creaked. He peered into the abyss of the stairwell. Was that a footstep? The darkness began to play tricks with his eyes, concentrating into patches of pitch blackness, then dissolving again. He thought he saw a dark mass, indistinct, condense momentarily at the foot of the stairs, but when he looked more closely it had gone.

Nathaniel realised that for the first time in his life he felt real terror. Not fear, no, he had felt fear many times, but never terror, huge, monstrous, vast as the ocean. He realised he dare not go back to his room, for then the enemy would come up the stairs to him. Yet he dare not, could not, descend. He stood on the landing in blackness as if he had been there for all eternity.

What was Matthew playing at? Where was he? The man was a fiend! The screaming had ceased now, although, very softly, he thought he could hear a low, weak whimpering in its place. Then a door opened.

'Who's there?' he called again.

'Morgan? Is that you?' It was Carter, somewhere below. At the door of the dining-room, he guessed. Nathaniel wondered if Carter was afraid. Carter's disembodied voice came to him like a lifeline to a drowning man.

'Yes.' His voice was scarcely more than a whisper. 'I'm here. What's happened?'

'Penmarris has been shot. In the stomach.'

'Is he bad?' Nathaniel tried to sound as level-headed as possible.

'Yes.'

'Where is he?' Meaning Matthew.

'I don't know. I fired at him. Don't know if I got him.'

'So what do we do? Can you come up to me?'

Nathaniel hoped he did not sound as desperate as he felt.

'No,' came the reply. 'I can't leave Penmarris. And there's no light, dammit! This house is as dark as the Pit. Miss Trevanion – is she with you?'

'Yes.'

'Good.'

'So what do we do?'

'Sshh!' Carter seemed distracted, as if he had suddenly heard something. Nathaniel strained his ears. Suddenly there was a muffled thud, like a sack of flour being dropped on the floor, then silence.

'Carter! Are you all right?'

There was no answer. Nathaniel Morgan almost began to cry. He wanted to be home. He wanted to drop his pistol and run out of the house. He wanted to live. If only there was some light!

'Trevanion! Are you there?' Perhaps he heard the merest rub of cloth against cloth. 'Listen to me! We don't have to fight. We can talk.'

'Lucy – where is she?' The voice rose out of the stairwell.

'Here in the bedroom.'

'Give – her – to – me.' The voice was cold and heavy. The voice sounded like wet soil on slate. It suddenly occurred to Nathaniel that he was being offered the chance to save himself by betraying Lucy. He felt scared. Scared of his own desperate terror. He almost trembled with a strange, fearful joy. He would live! Let the girl take her chances!

A huge hand, cold and hard as stone closed over his face and jerked him bodily from the floor. Nathaniel had not known about the small servant's

staircase at the end of the landing. He tried to scream
or shake himself free or struggle but found himself
pinned tight. Light! Light! Arms flapping like a
child's, he swung wildly with the pistol and fired.

'Thank you,' said the voice in his ear, and a foul
stench came with it so he struggled for breath. Then
the blade entered him. Unbelievably cold and hard,
it moved regardless of bones and flesh. Nathaniel
Morgan had a fleeting vision of white cabbage
butterflies fluttering over a meadow of cowslips and
dandelions in July. He was a little boy again. Then
his soul was cut clear of his body and he felt no
more.

Matthew crossed the courtyard at a run. He was still
dizzy from sleep. He shook his head angrily. The
sound of gunfire was unmistakable. He ran round
the building. The house was shuttered and silent
now. He suddenly thought that nothing had happened, he had dreamed everything. Then he saw it.
One of the shutters at the rear of the kitchen, looking
on to the orchard, had been prised open and hung
from its hinges. He put his head to the opening.
Somewhere inside, a man was in pain. He smelled
cooked lamb and gravy. Clenching one of his pistols
between his teeth, he grabbed the window-frame
and hauled himself in. I'm too late, he thought. Too
late. He sank into a crouch. Because of the shuttering
the interior was impenetrably dark.

Bending double he crept through the hallway. He
sensed the dining-room door open to his right and
flung himself to one side. There was no need. No
attack came. Inside someone, a man, was breathing

with horrible difficulty. He didn't go in. Tobias wasn't there. Where would he have gone? He had a sudden feeling that Tobias was right behind him. He spun round. His pistol met with empty space. Damn! Then a floorboard creaked above his head. Of course. Lucy was upstairs. Matthew felt his heart pounding. Which way should he try? The main stairs or the servant's staircase round the back?

He thought for a moment. If Nathaniel was still alive, he would be up there. He wouldn't know about the servant's stairs. Matthew retreated through the kitchen to where the oak panelling opened into a narrow staircase, no more than two feet wide, which ran up the far end of the house. In the small enclosed passageway, a familiar whiff came to him, bitter and stale. It was the odour he had smelled in An Jenny's cottage.

He reached the landing. He remembered its length and breadth from his childhood. Perhaps Tobias had played the same games? Now he could see only the faintest outline of the corridor ahead. Slowly he moved forward.

There was a heavy thump from one of the rooms up on his left. Lucy's room! He clenched the pistol and was about to jump forward when he heard the door behind it open ever so quietly and a pale white figure slipped out. Lucy! She'd been in the guest room. Ugly thoughts swarmed over his mind, but he pushed them away. She was tiptoeing towards him. From inside her room there came another thud, the sound of someone blundering about in the dark. Matthew pressed himself against the wall. She obviously couldn't see him. In a minute she would be level with him. He waited. Come on! The door of her bedroom swung open abruptly. He saw Lucy freeze on the landing. She was no more than six feet away.

'Come here, my child.' The voice was thick, guttural, enormously potent. It filled the whole corridor.

Lucy gave out a little gasp.

'There is ... no point in prolonging ... the ... agony,' continued the voice. 'Everyone ... is dead.'

From where he was crouched, he could see that Lucy visibly relaxed. It was as if she were mesmerised by the voice. Her death was inevitable, she knew that now.

Tobias was moving down the corridor towards them. Another minute and it would be finished. Matthew sprang forward and grabbed the neck of her nightgown. Lucy screamed and he jerked her roughly back.

'Don't! Don't!' he shouted into the dark void of the corridor.

The sound of low, heavy breathing – the sound he had heard that night in the woods – came from fifteen, maybe twenty feet away.

Lucy shrieked hysterically, scratched and clawed at his face. He threw her on to the floor. He could not take his eyes off the corridor for a second.

'Lucy! It's me. Get up!' he hissed. Still nothing in the corridor except the breathing. Matthew's eyes jumped right and left, trying to find some hint, some clue. Lucy was crouched on the floor. She had stopped screaming and was trembling violently. So was he.

'Matthew . . . Trevanion.' The words were almost an indictment. 'I never knew your father, boy.'

'Don't move!' Matthew shouted. 'I've two pistols. Quick,' he whispered to Lucy, 'get down the servant's stairs, wait for me in the kitchen.' She hesitated for a moment, then he saw her pale white shape retreat down the corridor. He stared towards where he judged Tobias Trevanion stood. The breathing had stopped.

'Don't move!' he ordered. 'I can see you.'

Then he heard a plank creak. The main stairs!

Matthew hesitated for a second – no more – between running after Lucy or pursuing Tobias down the stairs. Either way, his enemy might reach her first. Trusting to luck, he ran forward and plunged into the abyss of the stairwell.

Tobias heard him coming, as he knew he would. Matthew launched himself from the platform where the stairwell turned halfway down. The blackness rushed up to meet him. Below, Tobias swung his sword up in an arc and the edge of his blade clipped Matthew's heel as he leaped overhead and landed heavily in the hallway. Matthew realised the sword had been aimed at his abdomen in the split second before Tobias was on top of him. Matthew pitched to one side and fired. There was a loud bang and the tang of burned gunpowder. He heard Tobias stumble and he sprung backwards down the hallway towards the parlour.

'Matthew! Is that you?' Lucy's voice floated out of the darkness.

'Quick! He's right behind me! I'm in the parlour.' Then she was with him. He clutched her to him and had a fleeting sensation of the softness of her stomach through the nightgown, but he trained his gaze on the doorway into the hall.

'Fair try,' came the voice. 'You almost grazed me, boy.'

Matthew stared at the door. He had one pistol left, Tonkin's lightweight pistol. He wondered if it would stop Tobias if he charged. He doubted it.

'Can you get light?' he hissed.

Lucy slipped away and he heard her scrabbling with a tin further back in the parlour. Where was Tobias? He could see nothing. Then there was a soft flash, as she struck a lucifer, and the pale light of a candle began to flicker, and sent vast shadows lurching and swaying across the room. He looked towards the doorway. The light stopped short of the threshold. He glanced at Lucy. Her skin seemed unnaturally white. Her hair hung flat, plastered to her skull. Their eyes met briefly, then she turned away.

'Tobias, are you there?'

Out of the blackness, Tobias Trevanion emerged in the frame of the doorway.

Matthew stared at him in disbelief. He was staring into the face of John Trevanion – the face he had seen in the graveyard those weeks before – the same broad head, the same heavy jaw, and the mouth cut in granite, except that a lifetime in the tropics had left his skin the colour of burnished walnut. Lucy made a sound of surprise. The face broke into a smile.

'Does my appearance trouble you, my child? It

troubled my brother, the poor wretch. This physiognomy is proof and title to my inheritance.'

The voice moved slowly and menacingly over the syllables like a wind traversing the face of the deep. The accent, English and yet unidentifiably exotic, coated the edges of his speech like molasses.

'Your inheritance?' said Matthew. 'What have you inherited here?'

Tobias Trevanion laughed, slowly and humourlessly. He stepped into the room. In his right hand he held a broad sabre, and he fingered its cutting edge with his left hand.

'What more would I want? My work is almost done.'

Matthew looked at him. He was truly a giant of a man, then so had been John Trevanion. But Tobias seemed larger somehow, as if he was swollen by the enormity of his deeds, and his expression, his manner, were different from those of his brother. It was as if John had indeed arisen from the grave, but it was no longer John's spirit that possessed his body, but something else, monstrous, evil. Underneath his thick canvas coat, Tobias' neck and shoulders were bunched and knotted like a bull's.

'So,' said Matthew, 'all this for vengeance.'

'And why not? It is the purest and noblest motive.'

'But Trevanion was never yours. John was the elder.'

'Paah!' Tobias' lips curled in distaste. 'My whole life has been based on that falsehood.' His eyes glittered coldly. 'Have you ever contemplated what is a falsehood, boy? It is that which is not. Plato taught me that. That which is not. Yet for the last fifty years my life has been dictated by this ... thing which is not. Can you comprehend that? Can you? I had to, boy. I have gazed into the depths of this falsehood until I saw the truth it contained.'

Tobias paced slowly across the room. In the candlelight, his blade was black with Nathaniel Morgan's blood.

'Stop it, please!' Lucy was pressed against the far end of the parlour wall. Tobias turned and looked at her affectionately.

'Do I distress you? Let me apologise. Soon this blade will gorge itself on your sweet flesh.' His lips pouted into the form of a kiss.

'Don't make another move!' shouted Matthew.

'Or else you'll do what, boy? One bullet won't stop me.' Not taking his eyes off Matthew he continued to pace up and down the breadth of the room.

'The things I have seen,' he mused. 'Skies as blue as lapis lazuli, seas of the brightest turquoise, beaches the pure colour of bones, yet never in all those years could I see what was mine.'

'You are wrong,' said Matthew simply.

'Wrong? Me wrong?' Tobias laughed at this contradiction in terms. 'I lost my home, my mother, when I was four years old. I lived on the scraps of another man's table while my brother supped at my mother's breast!

'Do you think I could forget the wrong done to me? Do you think I could forgive?' Something seemed to catch his eye. 'Here,' he said, 'that tapestry behind you, do you know who it represents?'

Matthew glanced at it.

'Esau and Jacob.'

'Esau and Jacob.' Tobias smiled 'Very good. I remember when I was a boy of fifteen, it was raining one Sunday and I sat on the veranda and read that tale for the first time in my uncle's Bible. Esau and Jacob. I read it and my eyes were opened.' Tobias repeated from memory: ' "Two nations are in thy womb, and the one shall be stronger than the other; and the elder shall serve the younger." I recalled when we were babes, our nurse would balance us on her knee. Esau and Jacob, Rachel called us. And when I remembered that tapestry, I understood her.

'Do you know the story, boy? Esau and Jacob were twins. Esau was the first-born, and as Jacob came out of the womb, his hand clutched Esau's heel. Esau grew strong and tall – a great hunter. But Jacob stayed in the tents with his mother and was her favourite.

'And do you know, when Isaac lay dying and wished to bless his sons, Jacob tricked Esau and stole his birthright? Isaac was old and blind, so Jacob dressed in his brother's garments, and placed goatskin on his arms. So Isaac was deceived, and gave Jacob the blessing he meant for Esau. I read the words of that blessing which Jacob stole until I knew them by heart:

' "Let people serve thee, and nations bow down to thee: be lord over thy brethren, and let thy mother's sons bow down to thee: cursed be everyone that curseth thee, and blessed be everyone that blesseth thee." '

The room rang with Tobias' words. The entwined figures on the tapestry strained but did not move.

'That was what I lost, boy. But when Esau discovered he had been betrayed, his father did not leave him empty-handed. Do you know what Isaac gave him?

' "Of thy sword shalt thou live, and shalt serve thy brother; and it shall come to pass when thou shalt have the dominion, that thou shalt break his yoke from off thy neck." '

Tobias grinned proudly. 'And I have broken that yoke.'

'But I talked to Rachel. She said she did not know which of you was the elder.'

'She lies!' Tobias roared. 'Esau and Jacob she called us, she knew! And so did my mother, but *he* turned her against me. I saw it all, how John had dressed himself in my skin and stolen my birthright. He tricked us all.'

'So you killed him.'

' "Of thy sword shalt you live." I knew one day I would reclaim what was mine. I treasured those words, night and day I treasured them until I knew them and they were mine.' A smile ran across his face, his eyes half-lidded at the sweetness of the memory.

'But these things you speak of happened fifty years ago.'

'Does that make them less wrong? I was patient in my knowledge, boy, and the words came only in the fullness of time. For years I toiled and brooded on my injuries, and the rich soil of Jamaica bore me sweet, succulent fruit, on which I feasted, until at last my appetite was quenched and I felt the spirit move within me and call me home. And surely it was a good thing? For the usurper had had his way with my land, and taken it unto himself, and now I would take it from him, and visit ruin on him and despoil him of it piece by piece. How he wept when I told him.'

'You killed them all, didn't you?'

'Every one of them. And before I killed, I told them of the abhorrent falsehood of their lives. You two are the last. After that I can sleep.'

'And what of Rose? Why did you kill her, Tobias? Your own little sister.'

Tobias stopped abruptly.

'What could you know of her? She was the sweetest child. Like a bluebell, so pretty and dainty.'

'So why did you kill her?'

Tobias let out a laugh, so hard and bitter.

'Do you still not understand? I loved Rosie more than life itself. She was an angel, an angel. But John was his mother's darling. Right from the first she favoured him, but when she had Rosie all that changed. Rosie was more precious to her than either of us. Now, I will tell you a secret: it is always in the fairest apples that the worm lies. So it was with John. The apple of his mother's eye, he was, yet inside rotten to the core. And do you know what happened? No, you don't. I saw it all.

'Mother had left Rose in the orchard, and I saw John take her and carry her into the barn. I saw, because I'd been playing in the hayloft and fallen asleep in the hay. Something awakened me, the creak of a door, maybe, or an infant sigh. But I awoke and looked down, and there on the threshing-floor, my brother John had done my sister Rose to death. He had held his hand over her face until she breathed no more. I watched him place her body on the floor.'

'John murdered her?'

'In all truth, boy. I climbed down from the loft and held her in my arms. She was so warm and soft. I kissed her on the cheek, and whispered in her ear. I did not understand.'

'Didn't they find you with the body?'

'No. After a while I heard people coming and hid. I watched them bear her body to the house, and there was my mother screaming and John ran and clung to her skirts, and she picked him up and hugged him in a way she never did with me. And I realised then the falsehood of this world. Whatever I did, whatever John did, he would be my mother's little darling. And Rosie would be buried. They were all so proud and stupid. I hated them all!' Tobias lifted up his sword as if to strike the air, then he assumed a look of calmness, and continued:

'Do you know, in the history, Jacob flees from his homeland for his sins, until he returns to beg forgiveness of his brother. Yet in my story, I was the one who was banished. It was I who lived my life in penance for my brother's sins.

'Men say that on the night before he met Esau, Jacob wrestled with God Himself by the banks of the river Jabbok. All night long they wrestled, and neither could throw the other. Often have I thought of that. Two naked men in the dead of night, wrestling, holding each other close, straining yet unmoving, each listening, feeling for the other's weakness and finding none. Often I pictured the black light of the moon on the silver sweat of their bodies. Perhaps

Jacob was wrestling with himself. Perhaps he was wrestling with his past. To strive that hard, and no harder, how sensitive must have been the hand of his opponent – have you thought of that? – how magnanimous, how merciful. I have watched wrestlers competing on the hot sands of Montego and in the lagoons of Trinidad and whenever the match endured, I thought of that contest, that night-long contest. How beautiful it must have been!

'It should have been like that when I met my brother, for are we not as perfectly matched? So I thought, I dreamed. Inside, John was as soft and rotten as a milking-girl. I held him close and kissed him once on the lips and in that instant I felt his neck snap.'

He looked at Lucy. Spittle was dribbling down his chin. 'Your mother was a game one, girl. She begged me to spare her. Begged me.'

Lucy's face was frozen. Her lips exposed her sharp white teeth in an expression of horrible fascination, but they made no sound. Her fingers plucked at the thin fabric of her nightgown. Matthew realised he felt strangely weak and enervated, weaker than he had ever been. It was as if Tobias' tale had been leeching their wills, draining them of their vitality, while their enemy seemed stronger now and more confident. Was this what it was like for the others, he wondered.

'Stop it!' he shouted, but his voice was thin as a boy's.

'Yes, I shall stop soon. When I have spitted and gutted you.'

'You forget. I have told other people.'

'I forget nothing. My mind is like the ocean. And who would they believe? Even your lady is not yours, why I'd wager that she—'

'No!' shouted Matthew. He could feel Lucy cringing behind him.

'—will go with any man who pays her the price of a new dress. You'd better pray I kill you while your boy is still alive, girl, for then I'll be quick and clean. But if you're the last, I'll—'

Matthew stepped towards him.

'Come on, boy, closer now,' Tobias urged him.

Matthew steadied his pistol and levelled it at Tobias' chest. Tobias was walking backwards and forwards across the room, his thumb running up and down the lip of the blade. Matthew's aim trailed after him. If he shot now he might well miss, they both knew that. Then the game would be up. Tobias caught the look in his eye.

'Go on, boy! Shoot me! Lay my poor soul to rest.' Tobias was goading him, daring him, willing him to pull the trigger. 'Stop me if you can. Put me to sleep with my ancestors. Here. On my native soil.' His voice had become excited, restless like the waves on a beach, as if he were aroused by the possibility of his own annihilation. His eyes glinted in the candlelight. The light wavered. Tobias' eyes glinted all the more.

'Lucy!' Matthew shouted. 'The candle! The light is going out.'

'Time's almost done, boy.'

Matthew grabbed Lucy by the forearm.

'Come on!' He began to drag her towards Tobias. Lucy screamed and slapped her hands against him.

The candle sent huge swinging shadows dancing across the walls. Tobias smiled.

'Get back!' shouted Matthew. 'Get back!' He pulled Lucy towards the doorway.

Tobias did not move. He drew himself up to his full height and waited.

'Out of the way!'

'You'll have to shoot me, boy.'

Matthew was only fifteen feet away now. Twelve. Ten. Lucy had stopped struggling. He would have to shoot and be done with it, or else he'd be too close. Suddenly Tobias withdrew towards the staircase. Matthew pointed the pistol after him. He let go of Lucy and she darted past and began to work feverishly at the bolts securing the front door. He heard the heavy iron pins sliding back. Tobias was watching from the shadows. He was smiling gently. The lower bolt was drawn. Lucy was twisting at the key. Often the old lock jammed and had to be teased open, but tonight the key turned smoothly and evenly and the door swung free on its hinges. Icy wind came tumbling into the hallway, and snuffed out the candle. The hall was plunged into a second's blackness, then the soft light of the moon streamed in. Still Tobias did not move. Matthew stepped backwards towards the door. One step at a time. Eyes never leaving Tobias. Matthew wished he would say something, anything. Then he heard Lucy scream.

From the open doorway came a voice:

'Quiet, woman, or I'll do you now!'

Matthew knew who it was. He turned cautiously, resting his back to the wall. There, wrapped in a cape, his face a white mask of terror, stood Edward

Tonkin. In his hand was a pistol of matching design to the one Matthew carried.

'Edward! What a pleasant surprise,' Matthew greeted him.

Lucy retreated back into the hallway. She stood staring pathetically at Tonkin in fear and disbelief. She hugged herself through her nightgown.

Tobias emerged from the shadows: 'Put down your pistol, boy. I think you are a dead man. Come, I will not hurt you.' He sounded almost avuncular.

'You said there'd be no killing for me,' said Tonkin peevishly.

'You don't need to soil your hands,' Tobias answered. 'Let me.'

Matthew still clutched the pistol but he felt suddenly powerless, as if he were no more than an onlooker at his own execution.

'Wait!' said Tonkin. 'Will it look convincing if we kill them here?'

Tobias chuckled.

'Does it matter? As far as they're concerned, he's already guilty. And the irony,' he turned towards Matthew, 'the irony is, we needed you free.'

'That's what I gambled on.'

Lucy looked at him in bewilderment. 'You mean you knew he would come here, to me, if you escaped?'

'I've been their accomplice right from the start,' said Matthew. 'Isn't that right, Tobias?'

'Yes, my boy. You did well. Without you to take the guilt for our deeds, none of this would have happened.'

'And I'd have gone to the gallows for something I didn't do.'

'You're a Trevanion, you're guilty enough,' said Tobias. 'It's in your blood. And now you'll die for it in any case.'

'But I don't understand,' said Lucy.

Tonkin looked nervously at Matthew. His gun was shaking in his hand. Matthew remembered the expression on his face in Sir Anthony's house.

'It's all right, Edward,' he said quickly. 'I know why.'

'You do?'

'Forget that,' said Tobias. 'Cover him!' He took a step forward.

Matthew pressed himself against the wall, trying to keep them both in view. Which one? He guessed Tobias would attack first, but Tonkin had a wild look in his eye.

'Hold it!' shouted Matthew. 'Kill me now, and you'll lose everything.'

Tobias laughed. 'I've got what I want,' he said.

'No! No you haven't. I've got the will!'

Tobias hesitated for a second: 'Edward?'

'It's possible. You know it wasn't there when we looked. But that doesn't matter. No one's read it, and you're the only claimant left.'

'No you're not!' Matthew spoke quickly. 'I left instructions with a friend. If I don't return, he'll lay the will before the courts tomorrow.'

'What does this mean, Edward?'

Tonkin licked his lips nervously.

'Because he survived his uncle, then that means the manor will become part of his estate.'

'And I also have a will,' said Matthew. 'If I die, my estate will pass to my mother. And if she dies, her sister will inherit everything.'

'Is this true?' Tobias asked Edward as if he held him personally responsible. The prospect of an endless chain of wills stretched before him into eternity.

'It's certainly possible.'

'Then you'll die anyway!' Tobias roared. 'I'll not be brooked.'

'No! There is a way,' said Matthew. 'I could write a new will. You could still inherit. But there's a price.'

'The devil always has his price.'

'Let her go.' Matthew looked Tobias straight in the eye.

'No. She's his brood. She must die.'

'No, she's not, she's no blood relation.'

'So how would you rewrite your will?'

'Tonkin will tell you. I could date it a month or two ago. I could actually leave the estate to you, in your name.'

Tobias' lips parted sensuously.

'In my name, eh? Could he do that, Tonkin?'

'You don't need her,' said Matthew.

'She's seen us!' said Tonkin. 'She knows!'

'Quiet!' snapped Tobias. 'What do you know, girl?'

Lucy shrank from his gaze.

'I don't know anything.'

He laughed at that. 'The sweet little innocent! Tonkin was an innocent as well, weren't you, Tonkin?'

'No,' said Edward. 'Not here.'

'But I know,' said Matthew. 'That's why I knew you'd help me escape.'

'Shut up!' shouted Tonkin. 'Shut up!'

'What's that, what do you know?' asked Lucy.

'I should have guessed when I saw your initials in the table at the drinking house. You followed Emily, didn't you?'

'She deserved what she got. They all did,' Tonkin said quietly.

'The will, Tonkin! The will!' Tobias reminded him.

'Will you let her go?' asked Matthew.

Tobias seemed to consider for a moment, then curled his lips into a grin.

'I reckon you're lying, boy. And anyway, you misjudge me. I did this for revenge. That was all.'

'The purest, noblest motive,' interrupted Matthew. 'I remember Tonkin used the same phrase. You poisoned his mind.'

'No. He'd already looked into the abyss,' said Tobias. 'After what my brother did.'

'Yes. Sweet Marcy. That was a shame,' said Matthew.

'Shut up!' screamed Tonkin.

'And all this for revenge?' said Matthew. 'There must have been a better way.'

'You don't understand, do you?' said Tonkin. 'You don't understand at all.'

Matthew twisted back to Tobias. He was inching towards him.

'Don't worry!' Tonkin called out. 'He's got my gun. It isn't loaded.'

Tobias smiled. 'All this time? You're good, boy.'

Lucy screamed.

'Now,' said Tobias. 'Kill her.'

Matthew heard a sharp intake of breath. Tonkin

was aiming. Matthew spun round and shot him through the chest. A look of surprise appeared on Tonkin's face and he tumbled slowly backwards. Lucy gave a short cry and ran into the courtyard. Tobias was charging from behind. Matthew attempted the unpredictable and instead of rising, rolled to the right. Tobias' sword passed clean through his left shoulder. Matthew did not notice this immediately. All he felt was a hard knock to his collar-bone. Then Tobias twisted the blade and he screamed in agony. Tobias had him spiked like an insect. The man leaned over him, his huge mass blotting out what light there was. He was fighting John again, in the field at Rosmear. Desperately he levered his right leg up and against Tobias' chest and held him there. Tobias strained down. At the last moment, Matthew saw a thin, curved gutting knife in his right hand, the kind the fishermen used. He punched his leg out as hard as he could. Tobias was forced back a foot or so. It was far enough, and the knife bit on empty space. They braced against each other, grunting like pigs. Thick drops of blood fell on Matthew's face, stinging his eyes. So he had grazed Tobias after all. This sudden proof of his enemy's mortality inspired him. With a final push he sent Tobias toppling backwards. Tobias landed heavily against the far wall of the hallway. The heavy-eyed paintings of his ancestors gazed down. Matthew rolled over. His breath came in thick pants.

Suddenly he heard footsteps. Lucy had come back. He looked up, wiping the blood from his eyes. She was clutching a pitchfork. She must have run to the barn. He stumbled to his feet and snatched it out of her hands. From the other side of the thin iron teeth, Tobias looked back at him. He grinned painfully as he got to his feet. Matthew could see he was going to charge.

'Wait,' he said. 'This is not the way. There is another way. A better way.'

He let the pitchfork drop to the ground and held out his empty hands in front of him.

'Are you mad?' asked Lucy but he brushed her aside. Tobias stopped and smiled and placed his own sword carefully on the floor.

'You are right,' he said.

'Then come,' said Matthew, and stepping over the body of Edward Tonkin, he led the way into the courtyard. Tobias followed. He did not notice Lucy standing in the shadows. Nor did he glance at Tonkin.

Matthew looked at her.

'Leave us,' he said.

She stared at him in confusion.

'It's all right,' he said gently. 'This is how it should be.'

Tobias rubbed his palms against his thighs.

'All my life I've wanted this,' he said. 'Your father was a disappointment to me, boy.'

'Your father?' asked Lucy.

But Matthew made no response. He and Tobias walked out of the courtyard and disappeared into the enfolding darkness.

There in the fields overlooking Trevanion, by the light of the moon, Matthew and Tobias embraced each other. And as their flesh met and their arms entwined, their faces contorted into expressions which were neither those of pain nor joy. And so they fought and held each other for the length of the night, until the sun sent its first pale wash over the sky.

Chapter Six

IT WAS AN HOUR OR so after dawn when Lucy saw
Matthew walk back into the yard. He was limping.
She ran to meet him and they embraced on the steps.
He winced and she looked at him.

'I'm all right,' he said.

'And Tobias, what of him?'

'He's at peace now.'

'What happened?' she asked, but he did not seem
to hear and walked slowly past her into the house.
Everything seemed more normal than he had
expected. The place where Edward Tonkin had lain
was now empty. Perhaps there was a red smudge on
the threshold, but it could have been mud.

'The others?' he asked her.

'Trelawne's been here already. He took the bodies
away. They're all dead, except for Carter. He's lost
half an ear and been cut to the bone, but he'll live.'

'Can I see him?'

'He's sleeping. But don't worry –' she looked at
him – 'he heard almost everything. He told Trelawne
this morning. I'm expecting a visit from Sir Anthony
later.'

'And Morgan?'

Lucy lowered her gaze.

Matthew sighed. It all seemed so irrelevant now.
He stood in the hall, looking at the faces of his
ancestors. He felt tired. He put his hand to his

shoulder. His shirt was soaked with blood. He leaned against the door-jamb. Lucy put her arm round him, but he made no move.

'I didn't think I'd see you again.'

At that moment, Matthew felt his legs give way. It happened very slowly. He slid down the wall, and looked up at her.

'I'll be all right. Just get me something to drink.'

'Are you sure?'

He shook his head. 'On second thoughts, get me to bed. I need to sleep.'

Between them, Lucy, Mary and Josey carried Matthew up the stairs and set him on the mattress in Lucy's room. He lay there while Mary fussed over him and cleaned and bandaged his shoulder. Lucy watched anxiously. He had lost a lot of blood.

'He will be all right?' she kept asking Mary.

Mary patted the blankets over his chest. 'Nothing a bit of rest won't cure. You should stay here, until you're better,' she told him.

'What – and have you wait on me?' He smiled at her. 'I want to talk, Lucy.'

'Later,' said Lucy. 'Not now. When you've slept.' She stood there watching him long after Mary had gone out, but by then he had drifted into sleep.

He was still sleeping while Sir Anthony Bevis rode into Malaggan where the bodies of Edward Tonkin, Joseph Penmarris and Nathaniel Morgan were laid out in the church crypt. He did not stay for long.

'I don't understand,' he told Carter later.

Carter sat up in bed and lit his pipe.

'Neither do I,' he replied. 'But it happened. Matthew Trevanion is as innocent as a babe.'

'I still don't understand,' Lucy said to Matthew that afternoon. 'Edward Tonkin. He talked of revenge with such passion. What were we to him?'

Matthew closed his eyes, and pushed his head back into the pillow.

'I felt sorry for him,' he said. 'Our family did him great wrong.'

'But how? I've never even heard of the man.'

'His father was steward to my grandfather, Robert Trevanion. After Robert died, he became steward to John. If not for Mortimer Tonkin, John wouldn't have had an estate to inherit. But as soon as he turned twenty-one, he dismissed him and drove him off his farm. He shouldn't have done that. He had no right. But John had influence, and nothing came of it. It broke Edward's father, he was an old man.'

'Farm? Which farm?'

'Rosmear. John took it from Mortimer to give it to my father. My home.' He considered the irony of the situation. 'But that wasn't all. No. Maybe Edward could have forgiven that. But we owe him much more than that. Marcy Towan – Poldeen, I should say – was his sister.'

'But what did she have to do with us?'

'When Richard Poldeen died, Marcy took to working in The Pelican in Mousehole. Maybe she earned some extra money from the customers, I don't know. She wouldn't be the first.' An odd expression passed across Lucy's face. 'But be that as it may, that doesn't change what happened. John raped her,

Lucy. Raped her and beat her. When I first saw her, the bruises on her face were his bruises. The child in her womb was his child.'

Lucy looked at him in horror.

'It can't be true.'

'It is true. I don't know why. Perhaps everything Tobias said about him was true. It seems John always blamed Mortimer for the demise of the estate. He was obsessed with finding some way of restoring our fortunes, Lucy. Think of the mining. Even with Mortimer dead, he wouldn't leave the family alone.'

'But Tonkin worked for Pascoe!'

'Who do you think got him the job? My uncle. He couldn't leave them alone. Don't you think he liked seeing Edward scraping and bowing?'

'But if all that is true . . .' She wanted to say something, but realised there were not words for how she felt at the moment.

'Yes,' he said.

There was a long pause.

'You thought I was guilty,' he said at length.

'You gave me little choice.'

Matthew remembered the day when she and Emily stepped out of the coach at Trevanion. That was the past now. He wondered if it could still reach forward into the present.

'I remember how it used to be with us,' he said. 'Do you?'

She said nothing and walked across the room to the window. His gaze followed her.

'Do you ever think of those days?' he asked.

She seemed to be playing with the beads of her bracelet.

'Lucy?'

'It was all so long ago,' she replied. 'Too long ago.'

'It could still be like that.'

She waited a long time before answering. Her face glistened with soft autumn sunlight. She could be crying, but he could not tell.

'No.' She kept her face to the glass. 'It could never be like that.'

'Why not?' He breathed painfully. 'You loved me once. Last night, when I came for you, didn't you love me then?'

She paused.

'I've been thinking about what you said last night, about the will – was Tobias right? Were you lying? You said it to save me, didn't you?'

He looked at her through half-lidded eyes.

'Yes,' he said. 'I was lying.'

'Thank you. I'll never forget what you did.' She looked sad. Relieved and sad. 'I did love you once, Matthew, before all this. But last night, when he came for me, I really thought it was you. I thought you were the killer. I have my own life to lead now.'

Now that she was mistress of Trevanion, she meant. He thought of his uncle's will, signed and sealed and wrapped safely in the hiding-place at Rosmear.

'We could try,' he said.

'We've tried enough,' she said. 'We've both tried living with the past, in the past. It will never work. Everything has changed.'

'I love you,' he said. But she did not reply, and went to leave the room.

'I love you,' he repeated, this time more insistently.

On the threshold which led on to the landing, she turned towards him. Tears were streaming down her face. She looked for a moment as if she was going to speak, then she ran out of the door.

Matthew waited a few minutes then swung himself off the bed and went out. He felt stiff and tired, but nothing worth staying in bed for. Quietly he trod down the stairs and into the hall. The hall was empty, save for the old familiar paintings and the grandfather clock in the corner. It was half past three. There, on his right, by the foot of the stairs, hung the portrait of Robert Trevanion. Matthew remembered it now. The familiar hard black eyes stared back at him, the chin clenched tight, part grin, part grimace.

Robert Trevanion had worn a tight-fitting suit of bottle green when he had posed for his portrait. He was standing behind a table on which could be seen a Bible, various tomes of classical authors – Virgil's Georgics, Horace, Livy, and Pliny's treatise on agriculture – and a map of Cornwall, depicting towns and churches. Behind him on his left, a mantelpiece bore a small vignette of Jesus on the Cross and a bracket clock. Pheasants and a musket hung from its side. On his right, an open window looked out on to a recognisably local view, only slightly idealised, of rolling pasturage and the squat village of Malaggan.

The perfect squire, thought Matthew. He studied the hard, black eyes, but they gave nothing away. He looked again at the picture. There was something Tonkin had said, just before he died – You don't understand, do you? You don't understand at all. The words irritated him. He had thought he understood everything.

My mind is like the ocean, Tobias had said. I have stared into the abyss. Yet what had he really seen? Nothing. Time is an abyss into which everything must fall. Nothing ever comes back. He thought of them all: John, Tobias, Rose, Henry, Emily. Who could say what was their truth? We imagine what we will, but the past exists no longer and we are left with the present, the wretched here-and-now. Out of these scraps we construct what we want, and everything else is lies. Perhaps it did not matter what the truth was, for how can something be true which no longer exists? Yet for the people concerned – for Tobias, for Edward – the past did matter. It mattered more than the present.

He turned to go, then something in the picture caught his eye, and he remembered John Trevanion looking up from a map a long time ago.

That map was the same as the one in the picture. He was sure of it. He looked at it more closely. It was not easy as the map lay obliquely across the table, and the paint had yellowed with age, but the outline was clear enough. As well as the main towns of Cornwall, the artist had shown other places as well: Trevanion, Rosmear, and the other farms held by the estate, but there were more names, names he didn't recognise, the names of farms in mid-Cornwall. Of course, he realised in a rush, Amanda's inheritance. Robert had sold her land to repay his debts. Matthew suddenly understood.

It was obvious.

He went upstairs, back to Lucy's room. The key was still on top of her wardrobe. He reached up on tiptoe and pulled it down. He remembered puzzling over it with Lucy. But the answer was simple: it was not Emily's key. There was only one person tall enough to put it there. He took the key, and decided to try the most obvious place first. After all, John Trevanion had never meant there to be anything difficult about it. He had never expected to die that Sunday evening.

The room next door was his uncle's old bedroom, and underneath the four poster bed, his uncle's old chest. It was already open, and inside, at the bottom, was an old iron-bound case which had been left untouched. Matthew tried the key in the lock. It turned smoothly and the lid lifted open. Inside was a roll of papers, mainly in Pascoe's spidery scrawl, and a thick bundle of title deeds. He flicked through them quickly, but he already guessed their content. When Robert Trevanion had sold his wife's inheritance, he had been in need of money, but not desperate need. He had not sold the mineral rights. He recalled the conversation he had had with Jonathan Hocking. When Robert died, there was little or no mining in the area of his wife's lands, and the rights had been forgotten. But now the parish of Gwennap was potentially the richest source of copper in the world. If these rights were brought before a court, the heir to Trevanion could be unimaginably rich. Matthew read Pascoe's notes. This was why the solicitor thought the estate so valuable.

He folded the papers carefully and placed them back in the box.

There was still one more thing to do. He went downstairs. His shoulder was aching savagely. He would rest soon, but not yet.

'Lucy?' He called for her, but there was no answer. The manor seemed strangely deserted. Out in the lane, a group of young boys were peering into the courtyard. They must have heard about the murders. The whole countryside would be agog.

He rode slowly into the village. He met several people on the way, and they stopped and called to him, but he made no effort to reply. Let them think what they will.

Richard Morecombe was waiting for him at the parsonage.

'I knew you'd come,' he said. He looked tired. Their eyes met briefly. 'I'm sorry.'

'I've come to see my mother. How is she?'

'Better. Much better I'm glad to say.'

Matthew walked past the parson and ascended the stairs. His mother was sitting up in bed, drinking a cup of tea.

'Matthew! Thank God you're all right. Richard told me the news.'

He went over to her and kissed her gently on the cheek, but when he lifted his head, she saw with a shock the coldness in his eyes.

'Why didn't you tell me?'

'What?' she replied, but without conviction.

'Don't lie. The truth. The truth about my father.'

'How did you—'

'Tobias. He knew. I'd already guessed as much. But I want to hear you say it.'

Mary turned away.

'It's true. John was your father, Matthew.'

So, the estate was rightfully his, whichever way he looked at it.

'Why?' he asked, then: 'No, don't tell me, I can guess. Besides, I have too many ghosts already.'

Twenty-two years ago, Henry Trevanion had hit the ground at the foot of the cliff. He got up to leave.

'Matthew?' she called after him. 'You must understand, I—'

But he was already gone.

He found Richard Morecombe in the parlour. A brisk fire popped and fizzed in the hearth.

'Drink?' he asked. 'Brandy? Port?'

'Brandy,' Matthew answered.

He waited while the parson poured them each a glass. They drank in silence. Outside the sun was sinking behind the yew trees. It would be dark soon.

'Sir Anthony came round earlier,' said Richard eventually. 'He wanted to know where he'd find the body of Tobias Trevanion.'

Matthew stared into his glass.

'He won't,' he said. 'He's gone.'

Richard waited for Matthew to say more, but Matthew continued to stare into the bottom of his glass.

'Gone? How do you mean, gone?'

'They're all gone,' said Matthew. He reached down beside his chair and Richard noticed he had brought an old canvas bag with him. Out of the bag, Matthew produced an old leather-bound book.

'I think this is yours,' he said.

Richard took it. 'The missing register.'

'Yes.' Matthew waited, then went on: 'Turn to the year of Rose's death, 1699.'

The parson turned to the back of the book.

' "March thirteenth, 1699," ' Matthew recited from memory. ' "Buried Rose Marie Trevanion, died of the ague, aged six months." ' The parson's head nodded.

'Now read the entry which follows it.'

Richard looked at him, then read: ' "March fifteenth, 1699, buried Tobias Samuel Trevanion, son of Robert and Amanda, died of the ague, aged four years and six months." What does this mean, Matthew?'

Matthew stared into the flames. 'According to the register, Tobias died fifty years ago. I'm sure the parson agreed it was for the best.' He looked up from the fire. 'Who will ever know? I no longer do.'

He stretched himself painfully and leaned back in his chair. 'So much passion, so much hatred,' he thought out loud. 'It corrupted each one of us. Changed us. Tobias said something to me. He said he understood the truth and the truth had consumed him.' He gave the parson an unreadable look. 'Is there any hope for us at all?'

Richard thought for a long time. Outside they could hear footsteps on the gravel path. Richard got up to answer the door and turned to Matthew:

'There is only one hope, Matthew. And that is God's love. That alone can redeem us and make us better than we are.'

'And we are nothing without it.'

'Nothing.'

He left Matthew sitting by the fire. Matthew heard him walk down the corridor to the front door, and the door open. No words were spoken and he heard the parson returning with his visitor. He put his drink down and looked towards the doorway.

Lucy looked back at him. She was very pale.

Then she smiled, and he knew there was hope after all.

ONE CROWDED HOUR

Stewart Ross

'*Watch, Tom Verney.*
Watch, or the world will bite you.
Tom vain Verney.'

When a blind beggar woman on the London road gives this advice to the handsome, eighteen-year-old Tom Verney, the confident student lawyer fails to listen. To his considerable cost . . .

The year is 1622. London and the corrupt, sophisticated court of King James are no places for the naive and unwary. Based at decaying Clement's Inn, all too soon the impressionable Tom is studying the law, breaking it and finding favour and consorting with those who make it – including the wily king. Politically and emotionally way out of his depth, he wrestles to square his heart with his conscience. Meanwhile a plot is being hatched. A plot that will draw Tom down a desperate path of peril, folly, lust and revenge – towards his one crowded hour of glory . . .

A thrilling and sensitively written first novel – evocative, amusing, tender and always exciting.

☐	One Crowded Hour	Stewart Ross	£5.99
☐	Lady of Hay	Barbara Erksine	£5.99
☐	Kingdom of Shadows	Barbara Erksine	£5.99
☐	Too Deep for Tears	Kathryn Lynn Davis	£5.99
☐	Shaman	Noah Gordon	£5.99
☐	Physician	Noah Gordon	£5.99
☐	Lukan	Domini Highsmith	£5.99

Warner Books now offers an exciting range of quality titles by both established and new authors which can be ordered from the following address:

Little, Brown and Company (UK),
P.O. Box 11,
Falmouth,
Cornwall TR10 9EN.

Alternatively you may fax your order to the above address. Fax No. 01326 317444.

Payments can be made as follows: cheque, postal order (payable to Little, Brown and Company) or by credit cards, Visa/Access. Do not send cash or currency. UK customers and B.F.P.O. please allow £1.00 for postage and packing for the first book, plus 50p for the second book, plus 30p for each additional book up to a maximum charge of £3.00 (7 books plus).

Overseas customers including Ireland, please allow £2.00 for the first book plus £1.00 for the second book, plus 50p for each additional book.

NAME (Block Letters) ....

....

ADDRESS ....

....

....

☐ I enclose my remittance for ....

☐ I wish to pay by Access/Visa Card

Number ☐☐☐☐☐☐☐☐☐☐☐☐☐☐☐☐☐☐

Card Expiry Date ☐☐☐☐